CH

D1052724

THE BIG CROWD

BOOKS BY KEVIN BAKER

The Big Crowd
Strivers Row
Paradise Alley
Dreamland
Sometimes You See It Coming

NONFICTION

America, The Story of Us

GRAPHIC NOVEL

Luna Park, with Danijel Zezelj

THE BIG CROWD

Kevin Baker

HOUGHTON MIFFLIN HARCOURT

Boston | New York

2013

For information about permission to reproduce selections from this book,
write to Permissions, Houghton Mifflin Harcourt Publishing Company,
215 Park Avenue South, New York, New York 10003.

www.hmhbooks.com

Library of Congress Cataloging-in-Publication Data
Baker, Kevin, date.
The big crowd / Kevin Baker.
pages cm
ISBN 978-0-618-85990-0
I. Title.
PS3552.A43143B54 2013   813'.54—dc23   2013010177

Book design by Patrick Barry

Printed in the United States of America
DOC 10 9 8 7 6 5 4 3 2 1

TO PAM AND MARK, WITH LOVE,
AND MANY THANKS FOR ALL THEIR KINDNESS,

and

TO DENNIS HOLT (1935–2012),
WHO WAS COURAGEOUS WHEN IT MATTERED MOST,

and

AS ALWAYS, TO ELLEN, FOR EVERYTHING

THE BIG CROWD

1

New York, 1939
Big man.

He saw him for the first time looking up from the ship's hold. *His brother.* Filling up almost the entire hatchway of the *Saint George,* a tall man in a good gray coat and matching fedora. Broad-shouldered and big-chested, standing wide-legged against the Manhattan skyline, smiling and confident as he bellowed out his name.

"Tom O'Kane! Seaman Thomas O'Kane!"

His eyes blinked and watered in the darkness. Blurred now after his five days in the hold, the fourteen before that zigzagging their way all over the North Atlantic, trying to give the slip to the U-boats. It was a month after the *Athenia* went down, just sixty miles past Rockall, and they were crazy with worry for the submarines. Any available hands scanning the rough gray waves of the Atlantic all day long, trying to spot the telltale periscope.

A madman's task — and what would they have done if they *did* see one? A single freighter, ten thousand tons, out on the ocean alone in those days before the convoys. *Say a Hail Mary, and kiss your ass goodbye.* Keeping radio silence, trying to run outside the usual sea lanes, maneuvering this way and that like a staggered pig, trying to fool the torpedoes. Running with their lights off at night, the men sweating in their hammocks. Listening to the engines rumble, each silently asking himself did they have to make so goddamned much noise.

He loved every minute of it. His first big adventure, not five months out of Trinity. Setting forth from Lismirrane with the *spalpeens,* off to reap and bind the oats, and take in the harvest for the Cotswolds farmers. The lot of them walking thirty miles to Kilfree, just to catch the train for the coast. The poorest men in all Bohola: wiry and earth-hardened, bent in obeisance to the ground, from so many years of pushing some other man's dirt about. Their traveling clothes already half in tatters, patched coats and threadbare shirts, boot soles flapping on the road. Carrying all the belongings they would need wrapped in a neckerchief or a flour sack. Lowly even compared to the sailor's duffel he had made so sure to buy used from the gombeen-man in Dublin, knowing he would be traveling with them.

All his life he had seen them come and go. Men too poor to own any noticeable land of their own, and too proud to work the fields of their neighbors. Gone for the harvest at the end of each summer, to work the fields of Somerset and Devon, Gloucestershire and Hereford. Back with the first frost, thinner and browner than ever, to lie with the wife and sow another mouth they couldn't feed, then off again in spring for the planting.

He'd always wondered what it was like, where they went and how they lived. Thinking of them years later when he heard something that a remorseless killer his brother sent to the chair liked to say, a man called Dasher Abbandando, who journeyed to cities all over America to murder other men for money.

"Hey, Dasher, where you been?"

"On adventures."

"Hey, Dasher, where'd you get all the cash?"

"More adventures."

They had no cash, these men of his village, had spent their whole lives laboring for the smell of a pound. They walked half the distance to Kilfree that first night, then made camp on the side of the road. He feared at first they did it for his sake. It had been many years since he'd walked fifteen miles in a day and never in shoes, wobbling openly from the blisters by the time they stopped. But no, he was relieved to see, they laid their burdens down by a familiar copse, the stumps and the circle of charred earth from old fires there like a faerie ring. He realized this was part of the adventure, too — camping out on the road like tinkers, and the wind rustling in the trees over their heads, telling themselves for a night that they were free men.

The talk and laughter around the fire seemed constrained at first, in the presence of the schoolmaster's son. He was frantic to make sure it wasn't, giving out with the two whole bottles of the White Bush his old man had made sure to slip into his duffel for just this purpose, fixing him with his hard look: "This is for making friends, not for you. Nobody likes a drunken man."

He passed them both around liberally that night, though he had intended to save one for the boat. They wondered at its smoothness, their own small flasks filled with the raw poteen made out in the bogs behind the school, all they had ever had in their lives: "Ah, you can *feel* how that goes down!"

And as the night went on their reserve fell away, sharing their food around the fire. The talk gayer and the voices rising, men at the start of journey. Telling stories and singing the old songs, "Travelling Doctor's Shop" and "Kilkelly," and assuring him of the high regard they had for his father, a Cork man they couldn't see fitting at first, until he married Pat-Peggy's daughter and built his own house right among them, and helped out each year with the *mehil*. Talk he didn't want, and was embarrassed by, but was pleased to hear anyway in the soft October night, so much the way he had always pictured it.

The next day they made the train at Kilfree—a wooden toy of a train, he understood later, laboring like the devil up and down the low hills. Taking six hours to get them to the coast, where they caught the boat for Liverpool. A ragged excitement running through the travelers even there, so soon after the *Athenia*—*Do ya think we'll be torpedoed, then? Ah, no, never, the Jerries want us on their side. "Us," is it? You think we matter to them more than a flea on a pig's backside?*—all of it spoken with the confidence unique to those absolutely ignorant of a situation.

There were lifeboat drills, and on deck a soldier in full gear, with bayonet and washbasin helmet, much to the sniggering delight of the *spalpeens*. Grim gray destroyers knifing through the seas off both sides, signal flags bristling in the stiff wind—a startling change to the ageless world he had just left. He walked the deck the whole time, taking it all in, delighted to find that he kept his stomach even on the choppy crossing. Then they were over, the men from home chirping their goodbyes as they went to catch their train to the south. Whistling as they went, cheerful about the war, sure they would get a good wage with all the English lads off to play soldier boy.

It was easy enough for him to get a ship for much the same reason, the tramps all desperate for hands. Hired on without so much as a question about his experience, though he knew he must have looked as out of place as a bishop in a brothel. He was indeed the worst sailor alive, something Charlie twitted him about ever after. He set his hand at most everything, like the rest of their ragbag crew, and was good at none of it. The work more exhausting than he could have possibly imagined. Stoking the boilers for a watch, proud to be doing it because he knew that Charlie had once done the same all the way from New York down to Rio de Janeiro and back — his father reading his letter about it to them all, over the kitchen table.

"A crew like that, it's no wonder you missed the torpedoes," Charlie liked to tease him later. "The Jerries couldn't tell which way you'd steer the thing."

When they made New York Harbor, the captain half dead on the bridge from work and worry, he fairly danced about the deck to take it all in. The Frenchman's statue, sure, with its green arm held aloft halfway between a salute and a traffic cop's challenge. But more than that the mountains of skyscrapers around the Battery, and the madness of the harbor: tugboats and fireboats, freighters and garbage scows. Rail barges over from Hoboken and the fishing trawlers making for the Fulton Market, and the passenger ferries from Staten Island, and sleek, swift sailboats, and rich men's yachts, sailed up from Long Island Sound or down the Hudson. Each of them as proud as an admiral's flagship. A dozen collisions barely avoided every minute, as each blasted away with its horns and whistles and random, triumphant ejaculations of water shot high in the air.

All his life he would marvel on it. A whole city of people — the biggest city in the world — saying over and over, *Here we are, here we are, here we are,* in all their grand gaudiness, and their arrogance and self-obsession, and their wonderful audacity.

That was all he saw of it, then, before they were herded belowdecks. The captain rightly afraid he'd have no crew at all to sail back through the torpedoes once they got their pay and hit dry land.

Tom hadn't counted on that. Sure that he'd be able to steal off once he reached New York, even if it meant jumping into the harbor. Finding himself stuck instead deep in the hull of the *Saint George,* with its thick stink of bilge water and diesel fumes, machine oil and human excrement. The rats running over their feet in the daytime and their faces at night. The captain keeping constant guard at the hatchway, himself or the first mate with a shotgun, promising to blow off the head of the first man who tried to come up. The rope ladders pulled up in any case, no way to rush him even if they wanted to call his bluff.

No one knew he was there. There'd been no time to wire off a cable to Charlie, they had left Liverpool so quickly to catch the tide and sneak out past the U-boats. There was no one in the world who knew where he was, no way to get word out to his brother, and he realized in his maudlin self-pity that if they sailed back with him still in the hold, and got torpedoed somewhere out along the broad Atlantic, he would die without a soul to know what happened to him.

It was the longshoremen who saved him. Swinging down into the hold like some lost tribe. Hooks slung over their shoulders, stripped bare to the waist despite the cooling days.

He had wondered, before leaving Liverpool, what there could possibly be left to ship out from England. All the last odds and ends of Empire: Frozen trout and salmon. Clotted cream, and single-malt whiskey, and fine-tailored tweed suits, and even a set of grandfather clocks. And underneath it all the gold. He and the shipmates spent a good deal of time staring at *that,* once they discovered it. Shipped in bars too long and heavy to possibly steal or hide, stamped with the imprimatur of the Bank of England, and His Majesty's government, and packed in long, thick crates like coffins. The body of England, come to rest in America.

They moved it all, with astonishing alacrity. Using only a hook, a net, a rope and pulley. Communicating solely through a few knowing grunts and gestures, a symphony of leverage and brawn. Faces burnished and cryptic as Indians, eyes glinting at the work at hand. Saying nothing to them. Men held at gunpoint in the hold of a ship no concern of theirs, nothing they had not seen before, as he would come to learn.

He tried to talk to them, asking them to call Charlie, attempting to slip them a note with his name and last known address on it. One of them at last pausing in mid-haul of a grandfather clock, an item so ludicrously fragile and vulnerable in the iron hold of the boat — replying in a voice so low Tom didn't realize he was even talking to him at first.

"Charlie-O? Judge O'Kane? Yeah, all right, he's a jake guy."

The precious slip of paper with Charlie's telephone number and address disappearing into one giant hooked hand, the wicked point nearly scraping Tom's chest. Summoned, he appeared at the hatchway not two hours later, calling out his name.

"Tom! Tom O'Kane!"

The next thing he knew he was being hauled up out of the hold, Charlie's own thick hand grabbing onto his collar. Yanked up on the deck like a gasping mackerel, eyes blinking in the unaccustomed light of the Port of New York. Charlie propelling him down the deck, dismissing the protests of the outraged captain and his shotgun with a wave of his hand: "Call the League of Nations, if ya don't like it!"

Then they were hustling down the pier that seemed to be a mile long, its glass sheds looking to him as high and ornate as cathedrals. Redolent with all the smells of the world—ripe bananas and oranges, cocoa and coffee beans, exotic spices and hard metal.

At the end of the pier sat a line of idling trucks, stretching as far as he could see. A streetcar careened around the corner like a runaway team, barely missing them, Charlie jerking Tom's shoulder back with one hand. More trains twanged and rattled along the elevated line above their heads. The City a blur of motion before him, infinitely bigger, and busier, and faster than even Liverpool had seemed in his few hours there. He hung back involuntarily from this dynamo.

Charlie plucked him up again, literally hauling him into the City like one more errant crate. The black Plymouth sedan sidling up to the curb like a barracuda. The chauffeur a huge, looming man in a blue suit. Charlie introducing him as Neddy Moran, as he crushed Tom's hand in his own first, wishing him well in America before ushering him into the car that looked as if it might hold the whole of Bohola.

"They're all waitin' for ya, Michael an' Jack," Charlie was telling him, referring to the brothers, who were already over in Ameri-kay too, and had been gone so long he barely knew them any more than Charlie. "An' my boy Jimmy, who you have to meet, he's nearly your age now!"

Then they were being driven through the streets of New York, Tom in the back seat with Charlie—Charlie his brother, who he had never met before this day—beside him. Old enough to be his father, with the hair gone silver around the temples, making him look all the more distinguished. Charlie the judge, in his fine coat and clothes, with his own court clerk to do the driving. It seemed funny to him then, and they laughed about it all the way up to Mrs. Maguire's boardinghouse on West 103rd Street where everyone was waiting, and for many nights afterward, laughed about it all, unable to help themselves.

Not having to say a word, each of them knowing what the other was laughing about, Tommy and Charlie, off to have adventures in America.

2

Mexico City, 1953

Turning and turning and turning, the plane began its descent, diving down between the snowcapped volcanoes at a dizzying angle. Tom's eardrums popping under the pressure, his hands clenched around the armrests. Staring out the window at the endless expanse of green parks, and churches, and gracious white buildings that suddenly materialized beneath them.

Charlie's city now.

He spotted the car, and the slender, solitary figure waiting beside it, before they touched down. By the time they disembarked she was waiting at the bottom of the stairs with the car—a blue, new-model Rolls, as sleek and curved as she was, pulled up on the tarmac beside her like a heeling dog. Waiting for him with her dirty-blond hair tied back and the same wistful smile he remembered. His brother's wife.

"Hello, Tom," she said as he came down the stairs, her arms wrapped around herself. Opening up only when he got to her, to pull herself up on him then and plant a quick kiss on his cheek and a hand on his shoulder. Just like that. As if there had never been more, casual and intimate at the same time. The familiar touch and the smell of her jolting him like an electrical shock.

How long had it been? Almost three years . . .

"Hello, Slim," he said, fighting it, only squeezing her arm in return. Fighting it, fighting it already as he looked at her. Poured now into, of all things, a skin-tight, black matador's costume with lavish gold embroidery. Like some child's dress-up outfit, though, it made her seem all the smaller and more vulnerable, and he wanted to grab her up right there, and press her to him.

"I didn't know it was Halloween," he said instead.

"I have a lesson with Chu Chu in half an hour."

"So you're still doin' *that?*"

"You should meet him." She turned to saunter back to the car. "He's really an artist, you know."

"Oh? Up north we call it an abattoir."

"Have you ever seen a bullfight, Tom? We'll have to go while you're in town," she said brightly, refusing to rise to the bait.

"No, thank you. I saw enough men cut to pieces in Italy."

"Don't mention it to Charlie when you see him, will you? He's already crazy about it."

"The Rolls Chu Chu's?" he asked, barely able to get that ridiculous boy's name through his teeth.

"No," she said without elaboration, her voice brittle as a pane of glass. "Last month he was on about my water-skiing instructor. The month before that it was some cliff diver. He's never stops being suspicious now."

"He has reason to be."

She looked down, arms clutched tightly around herself again, and to his surprise he saw her lips trembling, all the defiance slipping away.

"Jesus, Tom, will you give me a break already? You've been here two minutes, and you want to pin the scarlet letter on me."

"Sorry," he said, and he was, more than he could say, and nearly overwhelmed by the desire to take her in his arms again. "It was more my own self I was chastising."

"Is it that bad? What you read at home about . . . us?" she asked, facing him again, the wetness visible on her cheeks now, so that he had all he could do to keep from pulling out his handkerchief to wipe it away.

"No, not really."

"You never could lie, Tom. That's why you shouldn't go into politics," she said, half smiling now, lowering her sunglasses, and he realized that he had not yet seen her eyes.

They were eyes you could fall into. Eyes to draw you across a room full of important and powerful people. Inviting and challenging at the same time, with more than a hint of mischief in them when she was happy. They were colored a startling green, with flecks of gray in the iris, something he knew from staring into them for a long time. She had a small, perfectly straight nose, a wide, generous mouth, and what *Life* magazine called an aristocrat's cheek-bones — a direct and sensuous face, beautiful in many different lights and from many different angles, a photographer's dream.

"Did you really play the bull with him, Slim?"

She laughed out loud at that. The sound high and clear as a chime, surprising him in its uninhibited mirth. Just like that she was the Slim he remembered again, fearless and delighted.

"Oh, God. It was my Spanish literature class. They couldn't understand how a woman could be learning to bullfight. They kept talking about it, sure I couldn't understand enough to know what they were saying. I couldn't stand it anymore, so I invited all of them out to watch a lesson. Once we got there, it was just an impulse. I picked up a pair of the horns they train the apprentices with, and then I put them on my head and charged Chu Chu with them, just like I was the bull."

She put a hand over her face and shook her head, the grin seeping through, the green eyes shining.

"I couldn't help myself. I know I shouldn't have, but Jesus, Tommy, you should've seen their stupid round faces staring at me. I knew then it was a mistake, it was nothing they could ever understand. Screwing the bullfighter, they could understand, but never the rest of it. So I charged at Chu Chu, and he waved the cape over me, made a perfect *veronica,* and for some reason it just made me laugh: Chu Chu standing there so serious and elegant, and me with the bull's horns on, and all their fat, stupid faces staring at us. You see the absurdity in it, don't you, Tom?"

"Yes—"

"I started laughing, and then he started laughing, and then we were shaking with it, we couldn't stop ourselves. And I looked over at all those grand ladies with all their airs, their mouths hanging open in shock for once without anything to say, the magpies. And I knew then that I'd made everything worse than ever."

They were both laughing then, too, in spite of themselves.

"A week later a photographer shows up, and I let him take some snaps with me facing a real bull. Thinking then at least they'd see I was serious — that *Charlie* would see I was serious. The next thing I know it's in *Look,* and all my relatives and my mother's friends are calling me up long-distance, asking me in that very genteel, very southern ladies' way they have, if I haven't lost my mind."

She sighed, shaking her head. The sadness washing over her all at once the way it used to do, too, the way he remembered it, and if she had taken a step closer, he would have grabbed her to him.

"Oh, I'm a scandal, Tom, I know. I can't seem to help myself anymore."

"You're not that, either."

"Let's be friends again," she told him, offering her hand. "I know you're here to help. God knows he could use it, after everything he's been through. After everything I've put him through. Friends?"

"Like brother and sister," he said, holding her hand in both of his, giving her what he hoped was a reassuring squeeze.

"Do you think you can help him, Tom? Like you wrote?" she asked, her voice sincere. "It's just so goddamned sad, the way he sits around that hotel all day. None of it's really been the same since, well, *you know* . . ."

"Yes, I know," he said softly.

Remembering when he'd talked to her last, two years before, once Charlie had made it back to Mexico City on President Alemán's personal plane. Slim's voice crackling and frantic over the long-distance line: "He collapsed at the airport, and now he's locked himself in the library! He won't come out; he won't eat anything. What the hell went on up there?"

What had happened? But that was what he was here to find out . . .

"I think I can help him," he told her, trying to sound official and reassuring. "But he's got to help himself. He's got to tell me all of it. No more trying to shield Neddy Moran, or any of his other friends."

"Ah, you know how he is with friends, Tom." She shook her head once, and he tried not to notice how the light struck her hair as the chauffeur, a short, muscular, smiling man with the map of the Maya upon his face, came back from the terminal with his bags and they got into the Rolls. She shook her head again.

"He and his goddamned friends."

It was the biggest thing that ever happened. He didn't understand that until later—didn't understand it even in those hours when Charlie wasn't on the stand, and he'd had all he could take of the sweaty, overstuffed hearing room in the federal courthouse. Stepping out across Foley Square, he could see for himself how deserted it was, no more than a few stray pedestrians, mostly unwashed, or wobbly, or exceedingly interested in pigeons, wandering by.

He walked a few blocks toward the river, then uptown, but it was the same. The sidewalks vacant, buses and subways half filled at best. The streets emptied out as if it were one of those science-fiction scenarios that were so popular now, after the Russians dropped the A-bomb on the City. Those solid citizens he did see were knotted up in front of the display windows in department stores, and television repair shops, watching the images raptly even if they couldn't hear a word of what was being said. More still gathered around TV sets in bars and diners, barbershops and beauty parlors, offices and hotel lobbies. The marquees of the movie theatres even offering it up as a public service, as well as an enticement: FREE TO PUBLIC KEFAUVER SENATE COMMITTEE TV HEARINGS. The major department stores rearranging their hours, posting clever if puzzled notices all over the City papers:

LADIES
we know that Costello,
O'Kane et al were fascinating
BUT
you must look pretty for Easter
SO
Bonwit Teller will be open
tonight till 7:00.

He should have seen it coming, through all the months that the committee took to work its way up through one city after another: Los Angeles and Las Vegas, New Orleans and Chicago, Detroit and Philadelphia. Drawing closer and closer, like some out-of-town show en route to Broadway. Exposing, everywhere it went, the inner workings of their civilization. All the dirty deals and the sordid friendships, the festering stew pot of politics that everyone knew was there all along but still couldn't look away from. The same material, really, they had been reading in their newspapers every day. But now with a difference: *those damned pictures on the tube.*

What he had always loved about his city was how he could look up from the top of a double-decker bus, or through the back window of a cab, and glimpse the rows and rows of bookcases in one line of apartments after another. Now all he could see was more television sets, their antennae like a bramble wood atop each apartment building. It was worse when he walked home through Bay Ridge at night, the spectral blue glow still emanating from the windows of each and every one of the semidetached houses, all of them showing the same thing — the words no longer necessary.

Just those damned hands. Clenching and unclenching, fiddling and crumpling up endless balls of paper. Hands that might as well have been around his brother's neck.

"It's not just here, Tommy, it's everywhere," his law partner and Charlie's old friend, Natie Cohen, telling him back at their office downtown. Bleary-eyed behind his big, round glasses, wearily holding up a stack of out-of-town newspapers from Hotalings. The copies of *Collier's* and *Life* with their twelve-page spreads.

"It's the same all over the goddamned country. Twenty million people! Nobody can eat, nobody's on the street, they can't take their eyes off it! It's like they're trying him in public, Tom. It's supposed to be a hearing, but it's like he's already tried and convicted on their goddamned TV sets!"

During those days they felt like drowned men, all of them who loved Charlie. Floating on the tide from one disaster to another. Watching helplessly as Charlie let himself get drawn into furious scuffles with Rudy Halley, the chief counsel of the committee. Bickering with the blustery, balding little Republican senator from New Hampshire, losing his temper and making wild accusations.

Charlie was still getting over the flu, but the cameras lovingly captured every movement. Patting his forehead repeatedly under the glaring TV lights with a precisely folded white square of a handkerchief. Looking as if he was sweating under questioning. Having to enter and leave each session passing the next gangster or gambler, the next mob boss or crooked union secretary on his way to the stand. The audience in the tightly packed room crowding in behind him, their faces clearly registering disbelief at the answers the witnesses gave.

"Do you see them?" Cohen railed, tie askew, shirt sticking limply to his belly by the end of a day in front of the television. "They're like a cheering section, telling the audience at home what to think. They're like a goddamned Greek chorus! What he *says* doesn't matter anymore. It's what the audience *sees!*"

Worst of all were the hands. *Frank Costello, "the Prime Minister of the Underworld."* His lawyer wouldn't give permission to focus on his face, so instead the cameras turned his hands into an epic. Costello continually folding little pieces of paper over and over again, fumbling with cigarettes and lighter. His avuncular, big-nosed, character actor's face unseen. Just those guilty hands— and the scrape of his raspy voice becoming more maudlin and evasive with every question.

"I just don't remember."

"I just don't even remember that conversation."

"I wouldn't know. I never went into details."

"Well, I can't remember everything."

"I am begging for you to treat me as a human being!"

By then both he and Natie were begging Charlie to bring in an attorney. His brother still refusing, insisting that it wouldn't look right to have one more mouthpiece at the witness table, raising objections and whispering in his ear.

"I can't have some lawyer there, telling me to take the Fifth like I'm some kind of goddamned communist!" he insisted. "I have to let people see that I have nothing to hide."

"Let *me* do it. I'm your brother, Charlie—"

"But I was the mayor, Tom. I was in charge. Besides, how would it *look*—"

"Right now, Charlie," Natie said, cutting him off, "you *look* guilty."

He wouldn't listen to them. Instead he stuck it out almost to the end. Tom had to give him credit for that much. Fighting back the flu. Coming in each new day of the hearings looking starched and pressed, in the best suits he had. Sparring with Halley and the righteous, sparrow-breasted Republican senator over everything, his eyes frosty and alert, refuting every accusation they made.

They put him through it. His interrogators poring over every peccadillo, every last detail of his administration. *"No administration on earth could look good if you went over it like that!"* Natie Cohen complained bitterly.

The deceptively soft-spoken, bespectacled lawyer hauling up before the cameras a seemingly endless parade of bookies and crooked cops, grifters and fixers, racetrack owners and strong-arm men. All the dirty underwash of the City government. Charlie demanding to have his say, confronting every charge — until, that is, they went all the way back to before his days in City Hall. To before the war, and the Little Man Who Would Not Stop Talking. The little man who went out the window . . .

Only after that had he folded up and let them put him on President Alemán's private plane back to Mexico. Slim's voice crackling over the long-distance line: *What the hell happened up there?*

And he had to admit, to this day, he still did not know.

𝕭

New York, 1953

"He went out the window. That much we know for sure. He did go out the goddamned window," Hogan repeated, rolling his chair back from the desk and slapping the file down. Five inches thick, at least, with the photographs spilling out, recording the same scene Tom had looked at live, a dozen years before.

Abe Reles. AKA Kid Twist. AKA *the Little Man Who Would Not Stop Talking.*

He lay stretched out on his back in the pictures, shirt split open to his waist. Those grotesque tattoos visible on his bared arms. His left arm flung up over his head, right one pointing down, as if making some last, secret sign.

That was a lie, too, he knew. All the lies upon lies, and here they were hoping they would add up to one big truth in the end.

"They let the doctor turn him over, pull out his jacket and his shirt before the photographer got one goddamned shot," Hogan recited, his stern, thin mouth widening, one eyebrow hiked skeptically.

"Beside him are the bed sheets, and the insulated wire he was supposed to have used to climb out of a sixth-floor window. *Tied-up bed sheets, for chrissakes.* They posed *them,* too. Took the picture with them propped up against a windowsill. *They posed the goddamn bed sheets!* And for what? To show us what the sheets might have looked like coming out the window?"

"Nobody was thinkin' very clearly that morning, Boss."

He could still remember how Charlie's face looked when he had stopped by the Brooklyn DA's office on his way to law school that day. Firm-jawed and unruffled, trying to make a show of it for the men — but with every bit of color drained away.

"Nine feet of sheets, tied to four feet of wire — to navigate a drop of forty-two feet," Hogan told him, though by now the numbers were engraved on his brain, along with every other fact of the case. Including the one he had concealed.

"The FBI lab boys say the whole contraption wouldn't have held more than a hundred ten pounds. *One hundred and ten pounds.* When Reles, who knew more about ropes and knots than a goddamned Boy Scout, weighed one seventy. He could've told the moment he set foot on the ledge it wouldn't hold him."

"That's right."

"But laying a finger aside of his nose, out the window he goes!"

Hogan flung himself back into the chair. The pinstriped Brooks Brothers suit jacket tucked away in the closet by now, three-point handkerchief still neatly folded in the breast pocket. The rest of him as meticulous as ever. Starched shirt still held at the wrists by cufflinks, stickpin stuck straight as a rail under a tightly knotted silk tie. A whiff of bay rum from his neck and his face shaved as carefully as a chorine's leg.

In a moment he was up again, brainstorming over the case the way he liked to do late at night. Fiddling with his pipe, something else he had taught Tom. *"Always get yourself a good prop. It helps in court when you can't figure out what the hell you're going to say next."* Going over the evidence again and again, gnawing at every contradiction like a dog with an old shoe.

"None of it makes any sense. That theory the Old Man came up with, God bless him? 'He was doing it for a laugh, a prank.' Jesus jumped-up Christ. His wife says he was walking in his sleep. The men on duty said he was trying to escape — with two dollars and thirty-five cents in his pocket, and half of Brooklyn thinking they'd be set for life if they dropped a nickel on him!"

"He was sick. The TB."

"And that was his greatest joy in life. You saw the testimony. Going around, showing everyone each time he coughed up another mouthful of blood. Saving it all in a glass he kept by the window. The man was a human spittoon, Tom. But like so many of us, he was precious in his own eyes."

"I know it, Boss."

It was after the Kefauver hearings that he decided to go work for the district attorney's office. *The spectacle of his brother exposed before the TV cameras, melting under the light. Dabbing away at his forehead with that handkerchief, the dark splotches growing on his shirt . . .*

Natie Cohen was incredulous when he told him. No more so than Hogan's current assistant DAs. They told one another behind his back — sometimes to his face — that he was a red, a spy, a plant just trying to get information for his brother. Hogan as suspicious as any of them, at the start.

"What, did you run out of government agencies to sue, Mr. O'Kane?" he asked at his interview, leafing through a folder. He was a slight man, thickening a little around the midriff as he pushed fifty, with a once impish face grown a little priggish around the mouth. Hairline just beginning to recede, exposing a faint skirmishers' line of liver spots. "The feds, the state, the City. The Board of Ed. Met Life —"

"I didn't realize they were part of the government. Yet."

Hogan didn't look up.

"Funny! You sued on behalf of Jewish war refugees. For the rights of a subversive alien operative during wartime —"

"He was a German hotel waiter."

"— to keep the City from banning a book on Thomas Paine. To integrate Stuyvesant Town, to integrate Levittown, to integrate the major leagues —"

"Is that my FBI dossier you have there?"

"No," Hogan said, slapping it shut and looking up at him then. "It's our own. And that's only about the half of it. Don't think we don't know about all that funny business on the docks. Shipping out bazookas to the Haganah so they could use them against this country's closest wartime ally."

"Just trying to even the odds a little."

Hogan gave a little snort. "Actually, I don't give a good goddamn about your liberal hobbyhorses. I only want to make it clear that the DA's office is not the place for you to right the ills of the world. We're here to catch criminals and enforce the law. Do you understand that?"

"I do."

"I'm also not interested in salvaging your brother's good name. What I want to do is to break the waterfront rackets, once and for all. I want to make a case, and I want to follow that case no matter where it leads. Is that clear?"

"That's all I want."

"What you want doesn't matter. What matters here is what I want, and I want to make a case. I think you might be useful for that. I think you just might get all sorts of people who won't talk to us to talk to you."

"I think so, too."

"The cops, the rats. Maybe Frank Bals and Jack McGrath. Maybe Neddy Moran, up in Sing Sing. Maybe even your brother."

"Him, too."

Hogan's eyes challenging, aggressive across the desk from him. Tom let him stare.

"No doubt you're sure he's innocent, and you want to prove that," he said.

"No doubt."

"I can't sway you from that, I know — not yet at least — and I don't care. But I don't want you lifting a finger on his behalf if it means endangering anything to do with this case. You got that?"

"I do."

"All right. I trust you to be as good as your word. You know I'm sticking my neck out on this, but that's my concern, not yours."

He tossed the folder he'd been reading from onto the desk in front of Tom — then pulled two more, much fatter ones from the briefcase on the floor next to his chair.

"Here's what we have on you, in case you're interested. And here's your brother."

He looked down now at his brother's file, flipping aimlessly for the thousandth time through the clippings, the photographs, the police interrogations. The grand jury minutes. The articles from the tabloids with their headlines half an inch thick. The drawn-in lines and arrows in white chalk, showing

Reles's room on the sixth floor of the Half Moon, and where he had landed on the roof of the hotel's kitchen, forty-two feet below. The *Daily News* headline, in gleeful block type, six inches high: THIS BIRD COULD SING BUT HE COULDN'T FLY!

"It's rotten, Tom. It's rotten now, and it was rotten then. Abe Reles, the greatest mob witness of all time. The man who put away Murder, Inc. He sent seven men to the chair and made eighty-five capital cases in less than two years — and who knows but he wouldn't have made two, three dozen more."

"The man who would've sent up Albert Anastasia," Tom finished, "and brought justice for Peter Panto."

That gently smiling boy, not yet thirty. Bringing twelve hundred longshoremen to their feet down at the Star Hall. Speaking of justice, and rights, and America there on the waterfront, as if it were a movie. His smiling face, under that silly little black hat. The thin moustache he was so vain about, which Tom used to joke made him look like a gigolo.

Then they were pulling the remains out of the lime pit, on the little man's say-so. Brown bones and a skull sticking out of the gelatinous earth, while he retched behind the chicken house.

"Charlie wanted that, too, Boss. I know he did."

"I know you think he did, Tom."

"I know. I was there."

Remembering the barely contained panic in his brother's office that morning the little man went out the window. Uniforms and detectives running up and down the halls, the phones jumping off the hook. Everyone trying to keep it from leaking before they could figure out what the hell to say to the press. Frank Bals wringing his hands, his wide, red face melting like an old woman's at a funeral.

"I swear to God, Charlie, I don't know how the hell it coulda happened. I stopped in just before midnight, an' everything was in order. They had orders to call me at once if anything — *anything* — went wrong!"

"He was being kept under protective custody."

Hogan was counting the facts off his fingers, the way Tom had watched him do many times before a grand jury. Cherishing the hours they had to work together, especially at night like this, just the two of them. Learning something every time.

He had found the whole experience nearly unbearable at first. The offices up on Hogan's eighth-floor fiefdom of the Criminal Courts Building more like a library, or the Harvard Yard. Swarms of Ivy League law grads to match the acres of red and gold broadloom on the floor. Nobody speaking above a murmur. Hogan insisting on opening everyone's mail, issuing statements to the press in pretentious Victorian paragraphs. Displaying the huge plaque on his desk that read COURTESY IS THE GOLDEN KEY THAT OPENS EVERY DOOR.

Yet they had come to an unspoken understanding after their initial, mutual suspicion. Tossing back and forth the Latin aphorisms that both of them loved, two self-made Micks showing off. Tom having to admire how much more efficiently and orderly Hogan ran the DA's office than his brother had back in Brooklyn. This was not a place where things would go missing. Things like a witness.

"Twenty-four-hour police protection. An entire hotel suite — a whole god-damned wing, for chrissakes! — locked off behind an iron door. Eighteen cops on guard, working in shifts of six, twenty-four hours at a time. Three other witnesses in there with him, fearing for their lives. The iron door bolted and locked from the inside. Nobody gets in without the guards getting a good look at him first through the peephole."

"That's right."

"Detectives supervising every single thing prepared for him down in the kitchen. More uniforms strolling the lobby, and the boardwalk outside. His testimony scheduled each day with no advance warning, no one told when he was coming or going. Taking him back and forth to court in a goddamned armored car, so no one can cut him off, stage an accident."

"And instead he goes out the window."

"Instead he goes out the window."

Hogan sighed and stood up, lacing the fingers of both hands behind his head while he walked around the room. He went back to the file and pulled out the autopsy report — Tom flinching involuntarily, and hoping he hadn't noticed.

"The autopsy said there was no sign of a struggle. Not a mark on the man — all trauma consistent with death by a fall from high places. No sign he'd been shot, or stabbed, or tapped on his pointy little head before they chucked him out. Nothing on the toxicology report. No one poisoned him or drugged him. Nothing at all —"

"Except the alcohol."

"Except the alcohol. And not much of that. Only about the equivalent of a shot, the medical examiner said."

"But it was in his stomach."

"But it was still in his stomach. Too soon to be absorbed by the brain, where it might do any harm. And how did it get there? There wasn't a bottle in the whole damned suite."

"No."

"And how did he drink it? The guards swore they walked up and down the hall every ten minutes, checking on all the sleeping little squealers. So we're supposed to believe that — sometime between seven in the morning and seven ten — Abe Reles jumps up out of bed, dresses in his best testifying clothes, ties his bed sheets to a length of wire, ties the whole contraption to his radiator, takes a pop for good luck, and makes the bottle disappear. Then off he goes to join the Flying Wallendas."

He dropped the autopsy report back onto the desk, Tom's eyes flicking over at it.

"And that's all," Tom said softly.

"That's all."

Not quite all. Tom thinking of the little slip of paper he had found tucked away in the autopsy report. Just a loose slip, not even paper-clipped to anything, its one line written in Dr. Robillard's hand. *Enough to hang a man, seen in the wrong light . . .*

"It's the greatest locked-door mystery in the history of the world. And it's twelve years old." Frank Hogan sighed, sitting back down.

"At least we got to the bottom of some of it," Tom said softly.

"I know we did, Tom. And it was because of the work you did."

"I was just doing my sworn duty."

"I know you did, and I appreciate your work, Tom. That's why I want you to go down there and talk to him. That, and to show there's no hard feelings."

"He knows that, Boss."

"I want to make sure he does. Honest to God, Tom, it's nothing to do with the mayor's race, or my ambitions. Tell you the truth, I'm just as glad not to have the job," Hogan told him, leaning forward to impress him with his sincerity, though Tom knew this was a lie, too. Wondering, *Does anyone ever tell anything but lies to anyone else? Even those they love most in the world — especially those they love most?*

"I have no need to be mayor. I'd be just as happy to stay here till the day I die, putting the bad guys away. It's nothing personal."

"I know, Boss."

Tom the only one in the office able to get away with calling him "Boss." Unwilling, even after he'd come to respect him, to give in to the airs of some Connecticut Mick like all the other, younger assistant DAs, worshipfully calling him Mr. Hogan. Going so far as to order the same lunch Hogan had Ida bring in every day from Schrafft's, half the office gulping down a chicken salad sandwich and a cup of coffee.

It was another thing that separated them from Tom. He wasn't just out of law school but already in his mid-thirties, a veteran, and not inclined to worship anybody anymore. Instead he insisted on using "Boss" with all its sarcastic, *Amos 'n Andy* connotations — his little way of keeping his independence.

"That's why I want *you* to go down there. You know the case better than anyone. And with you he'll know he's getting a fair shake."

"He'll appreciate that. I appreciate it — I appreciate your trust," he stammered.

Even if I've already betrayed it.

"Good, Tommy." Hogan squeezed his shoulder across the desk. "Because you know, it's a risk for you, too, if you ever want to get elected to so much as the school board. You go down there and exonerate him, it'll be seen as a big whitewash. If it goes the other way — there's plenty of fellas who'll never vote for the man who sent away his own brother."

"I know it. It's not about that," Tom told him. "I *want* to do it. I want to find out the truth."

"Ah, well, the *truth,* is it?" Hogan smiled slightly, leaning back in his chair. "Let's just hope we have a *case.* Because your brother's the linchpin to the whole thing. If he can tell us *anything,* maybe we can clear his name in the bargain. If he can't —"

"Then the waterfront stays buttoned up. Billy McCormack rides again. And Peter Panto might as well have stayed in his grave."

The flash of that smile, his kind eyes under the silly black hat. Reles, the little man who wouldn't stop talking, describing his death so matter-of-factly while he bit into the tuna salad sandwich Charlie had sent out for.

"Mendy said he hated having to put that boy away. Said he fought like a real man. He knew he made a mistake when they brought him up to that house and he tried to fight his way out. Woulda made it, too, if Mendy hadn't a mugged him."

The little bits of tuna sticking to his stubbled face, mulched into white gobs in his open mouth. Until Tom had wanted to pick up the closest chair and smash his damned head in.

"Yeah, he almost made it outta there." He gulped another lump of sandwich, smirked up at their faces. Flashing them his horrible, imp's grin. "Almost."

"Did you see he was back?"

"Yes."

Hogan opened the two-page spread of the *Daily News* before him to the booming caption: MR. BIG IN TOWN TO APPEAR BEFORE WATERFRONT COMMISSION. Looking as hale and hearty as ever despite his nearly seventy years, wearing a splendid new vicuña overcoat and a Stetson fedora. Chest thrust forward, head flung back with his usual combative grin.

> "Big Bill" McCormack, the alleged "Mr. Big" of the waterfront, leads his family into the sanctuary of Saint Francis of Assisi upon their arrival at Penn Station from the Greenbrier resort in West Virginia. McCormack, a Knight of Malta and of the Grand Cross, and a Grand Knight of the Holy Sepulchre, makes a point of always taking his family to pray immediately on their return to the city, to thank the Almighty for their safe journey and abundant blessings . . .

"Look at him, the grand knight of the double cross!" groused Hogan. "You know, the *Daily News* has started calling him 'the Little Man's Port Authority'? I wonder what press agent dreamed that up for him."

"They always do run some sweetheart piece on him when the heat's on," Tom agreed, scrutinizing the picture.

Behind McCormack in the picture, filing dutifully into Saint Francis's, were his wife and daughter. Then the son, Bill Junior bringing up the rear. His face as always the very image of his father's, but lacking the older man's ebullience. It was as though they switched places, Tom thought, the younger man always looking more somber, aged — even troubled.

"It's a simple cash deal. He lets the *Daily News* trucks take their newsprint off the docks for free. Every other paper has to pay. All hail the power of the free press!" Hogan told Tom. He pointed to McCormack's liveried chauffeur and bodyguard barely visible at the edge of the picture: "See that one? I happen to know he shot three men up in Providence. Maybe they're saying a novena for them."

"You know McCormack's a daily communicant?"

"Mmm. With the emphasis on the last syllable."

Hogan slapped the photo with the back of his hand.

"How many years have we been after him now! And nothing, even after the other papers finally picked up that he was Mr. Big. Hell, I remember when we were trying to get him back in 1937. He simply wouldn't see the investigators. Told them, 'Mr. McCormack doesn't care to discuss his affairs'!"

"And he got away with it?"

"Sure. He's got a hand in every game in town. Sand and gravel. Mixed concrete, dredging the Sound. Real estate, his own bus line now. The biggest chain of filling stations in the state!"

"And the dock unions."

"The key to the whole City. If they don't work, nothing runs. Not to mention it's ten, even twenty thousand votes he can deliver, every time, through King Joe Ryan and his longshoremen. He's got a hand in the pocket of every businessman and every politician in this town. Little wonder we couldn't lay a glove on him —"

"Until now."

"Until now. The governor's commission will finally make him testify, at least. But that won't be enough to take him down . . ."

"Unless?"

"Unless we can find out exactly why and how it was that McCormack put Abe Reles out that window, and Peter Panto in the ground. Which is why we need to know everything that your brother knows."

They were silent for a moment, Hogan's last words hanging awkward between them.

"Tell me, Tommy," Hogan said, trying to break the tension. "Tell me, when was it that you *knew* it was all bad?"

"When I saw the key," Tom told him, his voice distant. "I guess I knew the moment I saw that key. It just took me twelve years to figure it out."

He could still see it clearly, after all this time. Just weeks before the war. Charlie standing on the kitchen roof at the Half Moon, looking out at the ocean, with all the seabirds whirling and diving against the steel-gray sky.

He rode out to Coney Island with them. Neddy Moran driving as always, a hulking figure up front with Captain Bals. Tom in the back seat with Charlie, eavesdropping as his brother worked the radio car phone, fielding the calls from one frantic cop and assistant DA after another. Listening more than talking, Tom impressed as always by his brother's ability to know just what to ask, trying to string together some coherent story of what happened. His hands trembling ever so slightly as he lit up a cigarette.

He turned his face to the window, watching the broad, lovely, tree-lined boulevard of Ocean Parkway glide by. The siren off. Neddy stopping for the lights, not wanting to raise even the ghost of a commotion. Tom watching the neighborhood come awake as they passed through it: Orthodox Jews in their yarmulkes and broad hats and black wool coats, striding down the stairs of their nice brick houses to work in their shops or the Diamond District or to spend the day in the rapture of a musty synagogue somewhere, still trying to ferret out what the hell the Almighty was talking about after five thousand years. Kissing goodbye their plump, pretty wives in babushkas with a baby on their hip, striding off to their cars or the subway, and who would ever have believed it back in Lismirrane: a whole city full of Jews, living as well as the English people.

The City made up of worlds within worlds. The idea never ceased to enthrall him. He still stumbled into entire neighborhoods that he never knew existed before—communities a man might live his whole life in New York and never even suspect. The neighborhood of good, God-fearing Jews—and Brownsville, the neighborhood of bad Jews who shot and garroted men in the darkness, and dumped their bodies in the far, lonely reaches of the City. The world of the good Italians, and the world of the bad Italians, and the good colored and the bad colored, and the good and the bad bohunks, and Arabs, and Polacks, and the Chinee, and the Irish in all their possible guises, good and bad. The worlds intermingled, pressed right up against one another, house against house, wall against wall, and all of them going about their business every morning like none of those other worlds next door had anything in the least to do with themselves.

They took the boulevard all the way down to Surf Avenue, then followed it out to Twenty-Ninth Street and the Half Moon Hotel. When they turned, Charlie set down the radio phone and said the only words he spoke to his brother the entire ride: "You know, we had a perfect case of murder in the first degree against Anastasia."

"Sure. Yeah, I knew that, Charlie," he replied, perplexed and oddly touched at the same time.

"I just want you to know that. When you hear what people will say."

"I know that, Charlie. Who cares what they say? You'll nail him yet."

His brother gave a half nod in the back of the car, an expression of what looked like gratitude on his face.

"We were *close*. We were that close. Before all . . . *this.* "

He stopped talking as abruptly as he had begun, and turned his face to look out the window. Coney Island quiet and desolate in the mid-November morning light. All the fabulous amusements shut up for the season, the crescent moons of Luna Park no longer spinning, and the trellised glass palace of Steeplechase still and unlit behind the grinning idiot's face and slogan: STEEPLE-CHASE FUNNY PLACE. The whole cacophony of the penny arcades and the shooting galleries and the funhouses locked away behind their metal shutters. Only the bathhouses still open, and Nathan's Famous, with a little knot of garbage men and subway conductors and other workingmen in their uniforms standing outside, having their morning coffee and maybe a cruller or a hot dog before they started on the day's same, monotonous tasks.

The Half Moon was another ten blocks down the beach, snug on the boardwalk. Sixteen stately stories high, and crowned with a gold dome that had begun to peel. Standing out above the apartment houses and the two-family homes and the summer bungalows that sheltered under it like peasant huts against a castle. When they got out of the car, Tom could see the gaggle of cops and hotel employees already clustered around something on top of the kitchen roof, two stories in the air. Just above them a faded mural advertising DIME A DANCE for some long-padlocked clip joint.

Charlie saw them up there, too, and swore aloud.

"Goddammit, do they think it's a *wake?* Invite all the neighbors in, and the priest to boot!"

They strode in through the lobby, in its faded, Moorish palace splendor. The décor a leftover from the twenties, an age as long ago now as the Middle Ages. The soft leather chairs and the divans torn and stained, the tiled arches dingy and cracked. They walked past locked and darkened doors advertising the Fabulous Isabella Dining Room, and the Galleon Grille, and the Grand Ballroom, Home of the Half Moon Radio Orchestra, which was where they met Jack McGrath just coming down the steps.

"He's upstairs, Charlie, on the roof of the kitchen extension," McGrath told him.

"I know, Jack. I saw the mob scene when we came in."

"'Where the vultures are gathered, there you will find the body,'" McGrath said, twisting his mouth in disgust.

The rest of them smiling like idiots anyway. Visibly relieved to see him, their own backs straightening. *The Old Man is here, surely everything will be all right now.* Still rigid as a parade-ground sergeant at sixty years of age, body broad and burly as a bear's. His captain's uniform brimming with department commendations, starched as stiff as a British field marshal's.

Tom had already heard the stories a hundred times. *Jack McGrath, the greatest policeman ever to walk a beat. Who single-handedly drove all the child molesters out of Brooklyn, like Saint Patrick driving the snakes out of Ireland.*

"The doctor's on his way—"

"*What?*" Charlie's face ruddy. "No doctor's seen him yet? Jesus, Jack, are ya sure he's even *dead?*"

"He ain't breathin'. And he ain't movin'." The Old Man brushed a hand dismissively through the air. "That's evidence enough for me."

Out on the roof of the kitchen was a wall of men in blue uniforms and over-coats. Tom noticed the police photographer among them, camera the size of an accordion hanging from his neck. But he wasn't snapping anything, not with that mob of men all around the body. Charlie swore again, his brow look-ing red enough to blow off the top of his head.

"Jesus *Christ,* Jack, half the police brass in New York must be up here!"

"Word's breakin', Charlie," the Old Man warned, putting a hand on his shoulder. "The birds from the press will be here anytime now. You better get upstairs to see the men before they find 'em."

"All right, Jack. Just gimme a minute here."

The Old Man had the uniforms push the crowd from the body, and when he saw him lying there, Tom's first thought was that he looked like everyone else — like a hundred other pictures of the dead he'd seen in his brother's of-fice. It was the first and only time he ever felt sorry for the man.

He was lying with the left side of his face on the graveled roof, one arm out-stretched, one leg tucked up beneath him as if he were still trying to get some-where. His tongue lolling out over thick, meaty lips, blood smeared beneath his nose and his gray suit pants split down the middle.

Abe Reles. Killer of at least sixty men. The man who brought down Murder, Inc.

"Just like any other shmuck," one of the cops said with a snicker.

A civilian knelt down next to the body and put the end of a stethoscope next to his chest. Next he gently lifted Reles's head from the ground, bits of gravel dropping from the pockmarked side of his face.

"Yep, he's gone," he said casually, standing up. The Old Man was on him at once.

"Who the hell are *you?*" he demanded, grabbing the man by the lapels of his coat, Tom half expecting him to backhand the doctor like he would some sex pervert. "Who are you an' who sent ya?"

"Dr. Max Silberman, Coney Island Hospital," the doctor managed to get out in a shaky voice. "The hotel uses me when they have a problem —"

"Jack, that's enough!" Charlie barked, stepping in between them. "Thank you for your services, Doctor, that'll be fine now."

"Don't you say a word to anyone else!" the Old Man snapped, grabbing the doctor again by his coat as he started to walk away. "*No one,* you hear me?"

"Jack! Go on upstairs with the men," Charlie told him. "I'll be along shortly."

McGrath did as he was told without another word, his rough, pitted face glaring once more at the doctor before he left. Soon after, Dr. Robillard, the assistant medical examiner, came up, along with the hotel manager, who pushed forward a pale, elderly gentleman with a white brush moustache, who had been the first to spot the body.

"And who are you, sir?" Charlie asked, pumping his hand as if he were at a campaign stop.

"G. Dennis Holt, chief clerk of the draft board. I opened up the office, seven sharp—same as I always do—and I saw him laying there," he said, his voice shaking. "I didn't half believe my eyes, sir—"

"Who did you tell about it?"

"Just the desk manager. I called downstairs—"

"Good work, man. An officer will take your full statement."

Charlie moved away from the scene then, and only later did Tom realize that he had barely looked at it. Dr. Robillard knelt down, turned the body over, and went methodically to work. Gently ripping open Reles's jacket and shirt, the buttons popping away. Turning down the sleeves to reveal his enigmatic tattoos: the words TRUE LOVE and MOTHER around a weird, naked dwarf of a woman on his right forearm. On the left arm, the one flung over his head, there was a heart with two women's heads attached to it.

Next he laid a bright white handkerchief out on the roof gravel and began emptying the dead man's pockets. Dictating everything he found, every move to his assistant leaning over his shoulder and jotting it all down in shorthand on a wide stenographer's pad.

"No gunshot or knife wounds visible.

"No visible signs of trauma to the head, or beating marks to the body.

"Victim's coat is turned up on the left side, a gray checkered cap in the left trouser pocket.

"Victim's trousers are split down the middle seam for approximately ten inches, as are the underdrawers."

There was another snicker from one of the cops.

"On the victim's person are: one Waltham pocket watch, with chain. Two dollars and thirty-five cents in one-dollar bills, and change. One key—"

"Hey, Doc, all right I take a picture now?" the police photographer spoke up, his legs bending up and down in place. "It's gettin' cold out here."

The quiet conversations around the roof came to a stop, Dr. Robillard looking up sharply at the photographer through his bifocals.

"You mean you didn't take a picture already? Before you let me turn the body over?"

"The Old Man told me not to!" the photographer protested. "Said he'd have my nuts if I shot anything before he gave me the okay."

"My God, what's going on around here —"

"Just get on with it!" Charlie snapped, stepping back into the scrum around the body. "We all can see where he ended up, can't we? Makes no difference now."

Charlie wandered back out to the edge of the roof, while the doctor continued with his inventory of the dead and the quiet conversations rose up around them again. That was when Tom, looking down at the medical examiner's bright white handkerchief, noticed the room key, and the dark blue letters etched on it: 623.

The key that was the first clue, though he didn't realize it then.

Why the room key of a man who was being held under twenty-four-hour guard, and checked every ten minutes, was found in his own pocket. Why it was still there after he had supposedly tried to flee for his life . . .

. These were things that he would not think to ask about for many years yet. Mostly because he had eyes only for his brother — watching him as he walked to the edge of the roof, and looked out at the flat ocean and the seabirds cavorting against a gray sky. Until a uniformed officer came down and told Charlie that Captain McGrath thought he'd better see the men, and Charlie nodded and went upstairs.

Mexico City, 1953

They drove into the city along a gleaming white highway, the Rolls hiccoughing apologetically over each new section of fresh concrete. There was a billboard overhead every mile or so, proclaiming the Miguel Alemán Expressway in Spanish and English, and beside the road, crude wooden shacks that looked as if they'd been pieced together with tin and plasterboard. The highway full of old-model American makes and little *peso* cabs, all of them racing and passing fitfully, pulling up within inches of one another yet seeming never to collide. Horns blaring as soon as they started up again, as if they were somehow attached to the wheel mechanism.

When they reached the city, they turned into the wide, graceful boulevard of the Paseo de la Reforma. Traffic slowing to a crawl when they reached the Centro, the shrieks of traffic-cop whistles as continuous as the horns now. There were cranes, and construction holes everywhere, steamrollers and cement mixers grinding away. They could hear the solid *chunk* of the air hammers, and the smell of cooking asphalt penetrated even through the closed windows of the Rolls. Each construction site fenced around by boards pasted with incredibly busy red or yellow or orange posters promoting movie stars, wrestling matches, boxing matches, bullfights, and brands of beer.

Every building he could see, it seemed, was being built up or torn down, under signs proclaiming the new Miguel Alemán this or that. The air thin and crisp in his lungs when he rolled down the window. There was a scent of grilling meat and chilis, rotting vegetable matter, and wild herbs — marjoram, thyme, even peppermint. The ash trees bent graciously high overhead, their tops blue in the afternoon sunlight, and there were stands full of dried and fresh flowers lining the curb.

Slim sat smoking with the window open now, dunking her ash every few seconds, eyes hidden again behind her Polaroids, a strand of hair blowing loose.

"Isn't it great what they're doing?" she asked flatly. "Tearing out everything with even a hint of beauty left in it. All to build these wonderful international buildings."

"Is that what they are?"

"Yes. *International* — as in, no place at all."

Tom nodded, but he kept watching, unable to turn his eyes from the spectacle of destruction. The bulldozers crawling along the ground like tanks he remembered back in Italy.

"Charlie loves it, of course. It's just like in New York."

"But you don't?"

"The Centro used to be filled with students — all these beautiful young people, in love with something, or someone. Now it's a place you go if you want to see about a disease."

"The price of progress?"

She leaned forward to say something in Spanish to the driver, her body angling athletically, exciting him even with that little movement.

"Beneficio is going to take you to Charlie's hotel after he drops me off for my lesson," she told him.

"*Charlie's* hotel? You aren't living together anymore?" he blurted out, watching her face fall.

"He didn't tell you . . .?"

"No, he never did. Ah hell, Slim."

"I'm sorry." She sighed. "Poor Charlie." She looked at him directly, lowering the sunglasses on her nose. "Poor, poor, Charlie. Because you're not really here to help him at all. Are you, Tom?"

Catching him by surprise, the way she always did.

"I am, Slim. I swear to God," he said helplessly.

"Because that's what men from the DA's office do, isn't it? Fly all over the world, just trying to help people. You're here to bring him back to New York—"

"No, Slim, really—"

"—to make him testify. Maybe even indict him. Your own brother. Is that the price of progress, too, Tom?"

He took a breath of the crisp, intoxicating air.

"I only want the truth, Slim. That's all. I know he's holding back something, but if I can get the truth from him, I can help him. Get him back his good name. And yes, let him come home, if he wants."

She looked at him for a moment longer, then pushed the dark glasses up and turned back to the open window, blowing trails of smoke out of her nostrils and laughing mirthlessly.

"The truth is all you want, Tom? Good luck! With Charlie you never get *just* the truth. I'd have thought you knew that by now."

They passed jumbled rows of buildings, new apartment blocks next to Victorian and even colonial mansions. Most of the latter sitting obscenely in various states of evisceration, with their fronts ripped open and the tattered inner rooms exposed.

Next to the road was a broad swath of soft-packed earth, the people stomping it softly down as they walked. He thought that much of the midday crowd looked as varied and familiar as any moving through Times Square. Men in Brooks Brothers suits and women in elegant, black and white dresses, lounging at outdoor cafés. Laborers in overalls, teenagers in white T-shirts and blue jeans, little boys in shorts and knee socks. Vendors in paper hats, selling roasted corn ears and chunks of jicama sprinkled with lemon. Men in dark glasses and ill-fitting sharkskin suits, trying to look like gangsters and failing, selling obviously fake, glass baubles and fool's gold.

But walking slowly alongside them all, always with them but not yet of them, was something different: little phalanxes of campesinos, in white shirts and trousers and dresses, obviously just arrived in the city. Men with straw hats and actual sombreros bobbing off their backs, women with their hair beaded and braided, their faces a deep weathered red. They hauled their babies against their chests and their possessions in bright serapes tied over their shoulders.

Like what it must have been seeing the famine Irish walk into New York, a hundred years ago? he wondered. *Yes, Charlie would like that . . .*

The Rolls swung about a traffic circle, under a golden angel holding up a laurel wreath, then passed through a neighborhood of still more grand, decaying buildings with mansard roofs, and then past a golf course — pulling up finally by the side of an enormous, perfectly rounded arena.

"Where are we? Yankee Stadium?"

"I'd really like you to see this," Slim said, taking off the Polaroids again, her eyes pleading now as the chauffeur sprang out to open the door for her. When Tom got out he could see the sculptures of bulls and horsemen with lances festooned along the stadium walls. She let them in through a small side door, and then they were walking under the stands, their footsteps echoing along the pavement in the emptiness, an overripe odor that he couldn't quite place filling his nostrils.

"I just want you to see it," she repeated, taking him by the hand. "So you know I'm not crazy."

"Ah, Jesus, Slim!"

But her palm was smooth and small in his own, just as he remembered it, and he let her lead him out from under the stands and through a high wooden gate into a rectangular side ring. A tall man was standing there, holding a sword.

She called to him in Spanish, and he came over to them, each stride a performance. He was wearing the same tight, black-and-gold-embroidered suit that she was, complete with the matador's hat. He doffed it when he reached them, and Tom saw that his jet-black hair was slicked down tight as shellac. Deep brown, soulful eyes eating Slim up from head to foot.

"How about that, this one's got the Mickey Mouse ears to boot."

"Tom," she said, shooting him a warning frown, "I want you to meet Chu Chu, my teacher," and the matador bowed sharply from the waist, tucking the little black hat and his cape under his arm in one elaborate motion.

"I never met a Chu Chu," he said. "The opportunities are limited in Brooklyn. Better in Chattanooga."

She gave him another look. The matador's eyes were uncertain, but he picked up the general meaning well enough, his mouth turning up in a tight little smile.

"Pardon me, señor," he said, "my English is not very good. Just what Señora O'Kane taught me."

"I bet."

Chu Chu's eyes flickered again at his tone, and then Slim was between them, a hand on the Mexican's chest, guiding him back into the ring.

"*Por favor.* Nothing *macho*. I just want Tom to see this." She glanced back at him. "To see I'm not crazy."

"O-kay," Chu Chu said, taking her slender, elegant wrists in one hand, his face brightening. "I got a *toro* for you. Just right." He looked back deliberately at Tom. "Not so big. And very old."

"Perfect, Chu Chu, I trust you," she said quickly, still walking him away, Tom feeling his palms itch as he watched him hold her arm.

"We do . . . just a few *tandas* today. A few *veronicas* with the muleta, then we make a *faena*—beautiful ending. Pretend, of course." He pulled her closer, glancing over at Tom, then back at her, the cold smile spreading wider. "For your friend. We don't want to frighten him with the blood, I think."

"Come again, Chu Chu?"

But Chu Chu ignored him and tossed her the sword, which she gripped around the blade. Tom could see to his relief that it was made out of wood.

"*Estoque simulado,*" Chu Chu said, turning again and smiling with his teeth back at Tom while he made a stabbing motion from the waist. "The false sword. When the bull is done, then we use the *estoque verdad.* The real sword."

He handed Slim a red cape, which she snapped open as easily as another woman might handle a fan. Tom grabbed her elbow, hard.

"Jesus, Slim, you're not really going to do this?"

When she faced him, though, her stare was level, her hands sure on the cape and the sword. Chu Chu looked at both of them, then gave a little shrug and walked a few feet away.

"Don't worry about me, Tom. I know what I'm doing."

"I wish you did," he said, but she persuaded him to go sit in the couple of rows of bleachers that lined the ring while Chu Chu went to get the bull.

It was warm in the stands, despite the crisp air, and he could feel the dust from the ring in his throat. He recognized the overripe smell now — it was the scent of old blood, and meat, like walking into a butcher's shop, and he would never be able to tolerate it again. She turned to him only once, before she went ahead, calling back across the ring.

"But what if he doesn't want to go, Tom?"

"What?"

"What if he doesn't want to go to New York?" she said, then turned sharply back to her purpose.

He watched her small figure in the center of the ring as she held the cape and the wooden sword loosely by her waist. Then Chu Chu rolled back the gate of the pen, calling something to her in Spanish, and she nodded and the bull came out.

Even he could see right away that it *was* old and slow, but still immense, and dangerous by its size alone. Its broad black chest looked twice the width of her, and it moved across the sand with casual menace, as if it might do anything, without any warning. He realized he had never been this close to a large animal, had felt this primal sense of fear only once before in his life, outside of the war.

Slim snapped the red cape, and the bull came right to her, lowering its horns. Tom found himself on his feet. She slid smoothly, effortlessly around it, though — the animal charging through the cape, looking bewildered, while above the gate Chu Chu the matador clapped his hands and yelled, *"Olé!"*

It made another pass, then another, still looking as deadly as ever to Tom, its long, pointed horns glimmering in the afternoon sunlight. She dodged it every time, to his astonishment, moving her body sinuously closer and closer to it, until the bull was brushing her legs. Growing more maddened but also weaker and slower with each pass. Its eyes looking sunken and dazed, white foam bubbling up over its snout while Chu Chu kept shouting *Olé!* and she turned about and about, this graceful wraith of a woman, snapping the cape before it, one hand holding the sword poised high above its shoulders, like a preying insect, he thought, or some statue of an avenging angel, holding up a laurel to the heavens.

5

Mexico City, 1953

The first thing he thought when he saw his brother was how much he looked like any other tourist. Asleep out on the little roof garden of his hotel. Wearing loafers with no socks, a pair of gray slacks, and a blue, button-down shirt, with his pipe and his book on the arm of his deck chair. All that was missing was a white dollop of sunscreen on his nose.

The garden had a sign proclaiming it "El Ranchito," though it was no more than a square of red tiles, with a dozen chairs and beach umbrellas and a service bar manned by a tall, dour, moustachioed man in a crimson tuxedo. Across the roof sat a pair of middle-aged American women in flowered two-piece suits, eyeing his brother covetously while they sipped daiquiris through a straw.

"Hello, Charlie."

His face looked redder than Tom had ever seen it, redder than anything attributable to the sun, an unhealthy, glowing shade. His jowls sagging like wattles when he brought his big head up. He blinked as he tried to focus, unsure of where he was or who was speaking to him for a long moment, and Tom thought, *You got old, Charlie.*

"There you are," Charlie said when he recognized Tom. He promptly held his arms out before him, one wrist crossed over the other, smiling with his mouth alone. "Come to put the cuffs on and drag me back home?"

"It's good to see you, Charlie."

"No? You sure?" he asked, more than a hint of hostility lurking in his professionally friendly politician's voice. Then he pulled himself up to shake his brother's hand.

"Christ, but it's good to see you, too, Tom."

His head craned a little to one side—face pulled back into the regal profile that Tom remembered from the campaign posters. His own face, only much improved upon—wider and nobler, with its deep brows and high forehead and its slightly hooked, hawk nose, a wave of dark hair rapidly silvering now.

The face of a district attorney from the movies, he had always thought—and he knew he wasn't alone.

"Slim didn't come up with ya, did she, Tom?" he asked plaintively.

"No, she said she'll meet us for dinner later. Jesus, Charlie, why didn't ya tell me?"

The noble face seemed to recede into his jowls.

"She's gone off on her tears before. She'll be back. Anyway, she never cared for the hotel much, Tom. You know how she is."

"Yes, Charlie."

"She was raised with certain comforts. But it suits my needs just fine. When you're brung up in Bohola, you know, any old hotel penthouse will do."

"Sure, Charlie."

Charlie packed up his pipe and his book, and a towel from the deck chair.

"Whattaya readin'?" Tom asked him, and Charlie held up a biography of Daniel Boone.

"I'm feelin' more an' more of an affinity to the great woodsman these days. D'ya know, when he got fed up an' couldn't take it anymore, he went an' left the good old USA himself?"

"No."

"Yep. Went across the Mississippi into Missouri, which was part of Spain back then. They made him a judge. Well, a prophet is not without honor . . ."

They walked back over the tiled terrace, past the service bar and a forest of vents and chimneys that marked the limits of El Ranchito. Charlie bowed ceremoniously to the women from the States across the roof, setting off a series of fluttering noises that included no comprehensible words.

"Ladies."

They blushed and cooed at him. Women in huge sunglasses, with kerchiefs tied over their high hair. Bathing suit bottoms pulled up tightly over the navels of their fish-white torsos, tanning oil glistening on legs that were beginning to blue around the ankles with varicose veins. Fresh divorceés, perhaps. He could picture them arranging their deck chairs, waiting for his brother to come out each afternoon.

"Besides, I couldn't move now, not after all those papers in the States writin' about my 'swank penthouse.' But she should have better," Charlie chattered, leading him to one of two little blockhouses built on either end of the hotel roof, a structure Tom had mistaken at first for some sort of utility shack.

He had seen the hotel before Slim's driver let him off downstairs. From the postcards Charlie sent, scribbling, *"Now you can see what all my ill-gotten millions got me!"* on the back — taunting the feds and the IRS men, but also preparing him, he realized. The Prince Hotel was a brand-new, dreary seven-story rectangle of concrete layers, catering to the budget tourist. Charlie's penthouse was built to look like some authentic, adobe hideaway, but inside — with its sky-blue ceiling and its beige walls, and carpet, and curtains — it could have been an economy suite in any hotel in the world.

"Welcome to my little corner of Mexico!" he proclaimed, ushering Tom in. "The City of New York, by contrast, is three hundred and nineteen square miles — and not a single place where I can lay my head!"

"Ah, Charlie —"

"Oh, I'm very grateful to have what I have, Tommy," Charlie said, cutting him off. "You know, President Alemán and some of his friends, they offered to put a mansion at my disposal, here or in Acapulco. But I knew that'd get the rumors crankin' again. I told 'em I wanted only what I could afford myself, no better an' no worse."

The sitting room was maybe twelve feet by twelve feet, barely big enough to fit a lamp, a table-and-chair set, a bookcase, a chest of drawers, and a kelly-green couch with a coffee table in front of it. The bedroom only a little bigger, with a double bed, another couch and chest of drawers, a writing desk, and of course another bookcase. This one full of works on Mexican history and literature, as well as the usual Shakespeare, and Addison and Steele, his favorite writers. *What would Charlie be without his books?*

Hanging in the narrow passageway between the rooms like a pair of thrones were two framed magazine covers. On the left was Charlie's portrait on the cover of *Time,* from five years earlier. Looking twenty years younger, his face smiling and confident, with the hint of a prosperous double chin. Behind him, a busy, tangled caricature of the City, with planes and boats and cars crowding the skyscrapers, the subways burrowing underground like worms. The caption with his proud quote: "New York's Mayor O'Kane: 'The Big City is the work of man.'"

Hanging next to it was Slim on the cover of *Life,* from two years later, in a black and white Eisenstaedt photo taken from the waist up. Her face warm and luminous, like a gentle admonishment to the pure male hubris of Charlie's cover. Wearing a pearl necklace and earrings and an immaculate cocktail dress, smiling easily beneath a Stetson some visiting Texas mayors had insisted on placing on her head: "New York's First Lady Entertains the Nation."

How short a time it's been, he thought, *and how splendid they were.* The ex-cop and the fashion model, the Irish immigrant and the society girl . . .

"The place looks nice, Charlie," was what he said. "As long as you're comfortable with it."

"Just a hundred sixty a month for the whole kit an' kaboodle — try findin' *that* in a Manhattan hotel! Here, christen it with me, Tommy. Sit down, and let me get you a drop of the creature."

He pulled a bottle of Black Bush from out of the bottom drawer of the chest and fussed about like a maiden aunt, making their drinks.

"I got you a room on the seventh floor, just down the stairs," he said as he came over to hand Tom his glass and sit next to him on the ugly green couch.

"Yes, I know, Charlie. That's fine, thanks."

"I hope it's all right, let me know if it isn't. They have rooms here for as little as twenty-five pesos a night, that's about two ninety American. I didn't know what Hogan would spring for on an assistant DA expense account these days."

"I'm fine, Charlie. And you know it was Frank wanted me to come down here — it was he who suggested it."

"I *bet* he did." The redness in his face boiling over in sudden anger. "That's just what he'd do. Put you an' me both in the soup. If you don't haul me back in leg irons, it's pure nepotism. And if you do, who'd ever vote for a man who put away his own brother?"

"It's not like that, Charlie. Frank said the same thing —"

"The hell it ain't! Jesus, Tommy, how could you fall for it? Whatever possessed you to go work for a man like that in the first place?" Charlie's voice a plaintive whine now. "Frank bloody Hogan, with his high moral tone and his rich Republican friends! And against your own brother!" His face red as a cooked lobster's.

"Nobody's *against* you, Charlie," Tom said quickly, trying not to let his alarm show.

"Ah, forgive me, Tommy, but you don't know what it's like having to live down here, knowing every man's hand is turned against you in your own city!"

He got up from the couch and began to walk about the little room, declaiming with a sweep of his free arm, the ice jiggling furiously in his glass.

"All those *b'hoys* in the press writing about how I'm gettin' a million dollars sent to me by secret wire transfer!" He gestured dramatically about the drab little room. "Does this look like a million dollars to you, Tommy?"

"No, Charlie."

"Blackening your name at every turn! Turning everybody you know, everybody who's heard of you against you! Even you, Tommy! *Even you!*"

Tom rose slowly to his feet.

"That isn't true, Charlie," he said evenly, trying to hide his confusion.

It seemed to him as if his brother was putting on some kind of performance. But looking at him closely, he saw that his eyes looked dull and fearful. *An old man's eyes.*

"You're kiddin' yourself," Charlie snarled, his mouth twisted. "He's just tryin' to knock you off now so you won't run against him down the road. Get the whole brace of O'Kanes with one shot!"

"You know that isn't so, Charlie."

Tom went over to his brother on the couch, putting a hand on his arm.

"The truth of it is, Charlie, I want to get this done so we can clear your name, once and for all. So you can come home again. Don't you think Slim would like that?'"

The fearful, confused eyes seemed to focus again, a smile forcing its way to his lips. He patted Tom's hand.

"I'm sorry, Tommy," he said, sitting down on the couch again, and putting his whiskey up on the table, all but untouched. "It's just you don't know what it's like! All those goddamned headlines about the wire transfer: A MILLION BUCKS FOR O'KANE! Then, once they realized it was a routine embassy transaction, just a one-paragraph correction, buried on page nine a week later!"

"You can't let that eat you up, Charlie."

Charlie grunted and took a deep swig from his glass.

"But then it's not your good name they're taking, is it, boy-o? It's not you who's bein' buried alive down here."

"That's why I'm here, Charlie."

"Well, it took you long enough, didn't it?" he snapped. "Three years! Jesus, Tommy, you didn't even come down after those goddamned Kefauver hearings! No, then *nobody* wanted to come visit!"

"Charlie—you know how much work I've had to do, on my own, just to straighten out your tax case," he told him, keeping his temper. "You know who I'm working for now, and the delicate nature of that work."

"I know," Charlie said grudgingly, looking down like a scolded boy.

"You know I can't be seen hopping down here every few weeks to consult with you like I'm your private counsel."

"You're right, you're right, Tommy."

He made a visible effort to regain himself, sitting up straight on the couch, taking another gulp of the whiskey in his hand.

"Listen to me, just an old man, getting so black. I'm glad you're here, Tommy, I really am. So is Slim, you should've heard her talking about it."

"That right?" Tom swallowed, thinking of the other thing he needed to tell his brother. That would have to wait.

"I appreciate everything you're doin' for me, Tommy. Really, I do. That reporter you got down here from *Collier's* did a fair enough job. Much fairer than those wire-service vultures I had to have thrown out of the embassy, that's for sure! That quote he got from the prosecutor? 'Charlie O'Kane may be a sinner or a saint. All I know is, I've never been able to prove he took a dollar!'"

He slid open the drawer of the coffee table. On the table's surface, Tom saw, was a green map of Ireland under glass, adorned with shamrocks and leprechauns and the names of the "First Families of Erin." Charlie pulled out a large floppy magazine, with a bright, illustrated over.

"I could've done without the cover art. Here I finally get a caricature done by a great artist, Covarrubias himself, and look at it!"

"I know, Charlie. It was on all the newsstands for a week."

"Oh, I bet the boys got a laugh out of that. Look at me! With a sombrero, and a Mexican blanket over me shoulder, and a big single tear falling from one eye! Like I have anything to be sad about. And there in the background, d'ya see that? Slim runnin' off with a matador! Boy, it's one thing to kick a man when he's down, but to throw in his woman, too!"

He got up, walked across the room and held the magazine up against the wall, next to the triumphant covers already there.

"How d'ya think it would look, Tommy?"

"Charlie, what the hell?" Tom could only say, taken aback all over again.

"I was considerin' having it framed, Tom. You know, so the next time some big investigative reporter comes down here, I can show him I'm laughin' in the face of my misfortune. Who would've thought I'd ever rate a caricature by the great Covarrubias?"

"Why torture yourself, Charlie?"

Charlie stepped away from the wall, and it was as if all the air came out of him, his shoulders visibly hunching. Sitting back down, he thumbed manically through the magazine — its close, thick print already badly smeared, as if someone had paged through it many times before.

"Because I know what they're thinkin', that's why. Did you see what else he wrote here? 'The questions everyone in New York wants to know about: Why don't he come home an' clear his name? How much of a pile did he stash away? What sort of deal is he up to in Mexico? Why is his wife runnin' around on him?'"

When Charlie looked up again Tom saw that his eyes were glistening now, hands rattling the copy of *Collier's*.

"Jesus, Tommy, can you imagine writin' that about a man? As if he's a dog, not a human being. As if he ain't got feelings — as if he's a criminal on the run."

"I know it, Charlie."

"Why did she leave me, Tommy?"

"I don't know, Charlie," he said, hoping that was true.

"Did you see that picture they ran of her in here, with that goddamned Chu Chu? You know I should've nipped that foolishness in the bud!"

"You know how Slim is, Charlie. You know how that would've gone."

Charlie smiled unexpectedly, then ran a hand across his eyes and swallowed the rest of his drink. He poured himself another, then waved the bottle at Tom, who shook his head.

"She does have her ways, that one. Headstrong as a young horse. Not broken in the way Ma made sure we was — the way she made sure I'd go off an' try to become a priest. Ten whacks with the sally rod every day, drivin' me closer to God."

"I've got those scars, too, Charlie. And she always wondered why her children went so far the hell away."

The both of them were laughing then, Charlie lifting up to rub his backside in remembrance.

"Oh, she could go up in the air, our ma! She loved to tell her stories, though. Do ya remember the one she used to tell about *her* ma — how she caught the leprechaun up in the Ox Mountains? Did she tell ya that story, too, Tommy?"

"Oh, yes, it was her favorite."

"Up in the mountains havin' a picnic near Foxford, an' she grabbed up the plump little fella right there, when he walked out bold as cock robin. She used to tell us that story under the eaves at night. How she fetched him up an' told him, 'Tell us where your gold's hid!' And how he squirmed, an' tried to put her off an' get away, until finally he cried out, 'Look, Foxford is on fire!' And when she looked away for just a moment, he was gone."

"She did, Charlie."

"Ah, I got the little man, too, Tommy. Trouble was, he never knew when to *stop* talkin'."

"How's that, Charlie?"

"Never mind, Tommy, I'm just ramblin'. Not used to having any of the creature. You're wise to take it easy! You have to be careful up here, you know.

We're seven thousand feet above sea level; a man's head can get turned very quick that high up."

"That's good to know, Charlie."

"Oh, we'll have some fine times. I can't wait to show you the city. It's a helluva place, Tom, a helluva country. Younger than ours in many ways, even though it's older, if ya know what I mean—"

"Can't wait to see it, Charlie."

He was suddenly all glib patter, the tourist guide again. Talking about Mexico City the same way Tom remembered him talking about New York, the night he'd arrived—

"I'll have to take you up to Chapultepec, Tommy. That's where the emperor Maximilian and the Mad Carlota had their palace. An' Los Niños Héroes, and the San Patricios—did you ever hear about the San Patricios, Tommy?"

"Only the usual, Charlie," he said, shrugging, wondering why his brother was bringing it up. *A dark story, usually told in soft and bitter tones, late at night. If it was told at all.*

"They were a bunch of deserters from the U.S. Army, durin' the Mexican War. New immigrants, most of 'em—didn't know where their loyalties should lie. They went over to the Mexican side because their Protestant officers treated 'em like beasts of the field, or for the sake of the church, or because of their love of social justice, I dunno. They fought like madmen, because they knew they'd be executed if they were captured—best artillery battalion in the whole Mexican army!

"A bunch of them were captured anyway. They sentenced thirty of them to hang and put 'em on wagons where they could see the last battle of the war. They tied their hands, an' put nooses around their necks, and told them 'em once our flag went up over Chapultepec, they'd be hanged. All day, they had to stand out there in the sun, an' watch the marines an' the army storm the fort. Then down goes the Mexican flag, up goes the Stars an' Stripes. An' you know what they did, those men?"

"What's that?"

"They cheered."

"Why was that?"

"Damned if I know. Whether it was because they were sick of standin' out in the hot sun all day, or some residual love of their new, old country, the glorious United States of America? Or was it because they just wanted to give a big fuck-you to their executioners? But they cheered, an' then they whipped up the horses, an' they hung them all."

"Jesus. Nice story."

"Mmm," Charlie said, sipping his whiskey slowly again, and looking Tom in the eye now. The grin wavering on his face as he spoke: "All of which is to say, it can be a hard thing, sometimes — knowin' where your real loyalties lie. A hard thing, and a dangerous thing —"

"Charlie." Tom cut him off, smiling as reassuringly as he could manage. "You have nothing to worry about. It's like I wrote you: I just want to find out what happened, once an' for all. That's all!"

"That's all, is it?"

Charlie turned away to pour himself some more whiskey, then looked back at Tom and squeezed his knee, his eyes brimming.

"Well, you know, that's an interesting thing, the tricks memory can play," he said, giving another small, bitter chuckle. "It's like how back home, every now an' then somebody would say, 'D'ya remember old O'Sheehan, who played the fiddle and had the big ears?'"

Tom shrugged.

"And everyone would join in: 'Do we remember O'Sheehan!'" his brother continued. "And it was just like yesterday, with O'Sheehan and his fiddle there big as life, an' you couldn't figure how the years had passed. But none of us *really* remembered old O'Sheehan. And yet we knew he must've played the fiddle an' had big ears, and what *more* d'ya need to know?"

⑥

New York City, 1953
He waited on the stoop of the neat little house in Bensonhurst as the spring afternoon turned into evening. Gauging how much smaller it was compared with every other home on the block. A modest two stories, with a single-car garage, a narrower front porch. Its smallness ameliorated, up to a point, by

how conscientiously it had been kept up over the years, the carefully painted trim, and the rosebushes planted by the front steps. The small front lawn groomed to a half inch of carpeted green perfection. But the house itself still small and inconspicuous, tucked back far from the street as if it were trying to hide between its neighbors.

He caught a glimpse of movement in the windows behind the porch but ignored it, intent on the figure he saw striding down the sidewalk with the aggressive pace of a policeman.

"Officer Roberts," Tom said, getting up from the wooden stoop where he knew he had barely been visible — a gift for concealment he had learned on an Italian hillside during the war. The man stopped at the head of the short flagstone path that led through the meticulous lawn, saying nothing.

"Nice home you have here," Tom said, approaching him. "Nice neighborhood, too. Clean streets, good schools. No crime to speak of."

"It's all right," the cop said, and shrugged. "A lotta I-ties, but it's okay."

"And what a good job you've done keeping it up, too — as if you planned to live here all the rest of your days. It's good to see a man with a healthy respect for his property."

The man stood where he was, a roll of clothes and a small brown bag balanced on one hip. His body stiffening, but too wary of Tom's unexplained appearance to do anything more.

"Whattaya you, from Home an' fucking Gardens?" he said.

"Tom O'Kane, Manhattan DA's office."

He flipped his credentials at the cop, who remained silent for a long few seconds.

"This is Brooklyn, Mr. O'Kane," he said at last, and Tom thought for a moment he might try to barrel his way past him and into the house. But he stayed where he was.

"Do you want me to subpoena you then, Officer? All I'm lookin' for is to have a little chat, about events that happened a long time ago."

"I seen you," Roberts said, the suspicious eyes narrowing to hyphens. He was a big man, with a big head and a broad chest, just starting to go a little soft in the gut, and Tom could see why he'd been picked for the guard detail. He must have made an intimidating figure at the time, with his hard, rutted face and quick, suspicious eyes.

How like Charlie — to see the outer display of the man and not pick up on the weakness within.

"I seen your picture in the paper. You're that lawyer, O.K. Charlie's brother," the cop continued. "Always on the picket line. Always tryna get the coloreds into Stuy Town, or Levittown."

"What I believe in is every man getting a fair shot, based on his character," Tom said slowly, grinding the back of his molars to hold on to his temper. "That's what I can offer you right now."

The man's eyes opened wider, and then he shrugged, shoulders falling as if a yoke had just been dropped around his neck.

"Sure. We can talk out here," he said, gesturing toward the steps. They sat next to each other, Tom close enough now to notice his drinker's nose, burnished red and deeply veined.

"Your brother was a right guy. He dealt with me fair an' square, at least."

"Oh? How's that?"

"He coulda let me bounce," Roberts said, squeezing his lower lip contemplatively between his fingers. "That's what Commissioner Valentine wanted to do, the son of a bitch. Make me take that last walk to his desk, to beg for my job. That's what he used to do, ya know — make you come in an' beg, just so's he could tell you that you were a disgrace to the uniform, an' fire your ass anyway. But your brother saw to it that I just got busted down from detective to patrolman, so I could keep my pension."

"But how's that a square deal?"

"Huh?"

Tom clicked open his briefcase and pulled out the sheath of testimony from the inquest twelve years earlier, watching Roberts's face freeze in alarm. He let him dangle, pretending to consult the pages before him, though he knew them by heart.

It was only when he'd started with Hogan that he realized he had never seen the transcripts from the inquest. It took place in the weeks right after Pearl Harbor, when he was already on the way to basic training in Alabama. Charlie off to the provost marshal's office, with just Neddy Moran left to mind the store.

When he found the transcripts, he read through them night after night up in the office. Beginning with the testimony from the guards: the three detectives and two uniforms on duty that night in the "Rats Suite," as the newspapers called it. Two more patrolmen stationed downstairs along the boardwalk. Tom reading everything they had to say, checking all of their testimony against one another's. Until he found what he was looking for.

"You testified that you took turns patrollin' the corridor of the witnesses' suite at the Half Moon. All of you did," Tom told the cop. "And all the witnesses slept with their doors open. So that every ten minutes you or one of the other officers could take a walk down there an' make sure that all the little squealers were snug in their beds."

"That's right," Roberts said, the words sounding as if they had been pulled out of him with pincers.

"You also testified that you were the last man to make the rounds. You swore—*under oath,* Officer Roberts—that Abe Reles was asleep in his bed when you checked at seven that morning, and that he was gone by seven ten, when you made your next walk around. That's how they settled on what time he went out the window."

"Is it?"

Roberts turned to spit into his rosebushes, his face a mask in the deepening dusk.

"Yes, it is. You and the other men guarding the witnesses testified that Reles must have been feigning sleep. That he must've jumped up once you went by at seven. Flung on his clothes, wrapped an insulation wire and a couple of rolled-up bed sheets around a radiator, an' then gone out the window—all *before* you got back at seven ten."

"Then that's what musta happened."

"Horseshit."

Officer Roberts moved his face very close to Tom's.

"Are you callin' me a liar?" he said, trying to sound as hard and intimidating as he could. But there was a hollowness in his voice that matched everything else about the man.

"Worse. I'm callin' you a perjurer, Officer Roberts. And an accessory to murder."

The Old Man telling Charlie to hurry and get upstairs to talk to the cops.
All of them left there together, up in the Rats Suite, while he and Charlie stood
gawking over Reles's body down on the kitchen roof.

Roberts started to stand up, but Tom simply stared at him until he sat all the way back down. He ran a hand through his oiled hair, making nervous little whistling sounds with his lips.

"All of you — every cop who was up in the Rats Suite — testified to the same thing. The *exact* same thing. You saw him sleeping at seven; by seven ten he was dead on the roof," Tom continued. "But you know it's nonsense. 'All the witnesses had to have their doors open' — but somehow you didn't hear Reles gettin' up, putting on his Sunday best, rollin' up the sheets, an' tyin' a wire around the leg of a metal radiator. Never mind goin' out the window."

"He liked to keep the radio on. Said it helped him sleep."

"No doubt closin' and locking his door helped him sleep, too," Tom said.

He pulled the room key out of his pocket then, brandishing it in front of Officer Roberts's face. *Number 623.*

It had still been there when he started going through the boxes and boxes of evidence files a few months before. In a small manila folder, along with everything else he'd watched the medical examiner pull out of Abe Reles's pockets and lay so neatly on his handkerchief. There on the kitchen roof of the Half Moon Hotel, while his brother paced about, watching the gulls wheeling and careening through a steel-gray sky.

The key to Reles's own room. In his own pocket.

"If all the squealers had to leave their doors open, why did they have the keys to their rooms?"

"Well, you know. When they had family visits. Or with their lawyers —"

"Stop yer lyin', Officer Roberts. Stop it right now, an' maybe I'll help keep you out of prison."

"*Prison?* The hell with that!"

The cop standing up again, furious and surprised. But his eyes darted up to the screened-in porch, Tom noticed. He caught another glimpse of a dark form moving behind the porch window. Officer Roberts sat back down.

"When the hotel deskman called up, to report that Abe Reles was lyin' out on the roof, that was the first you'd heard about it. *Wasn't* it, Officer Roberts?"

"That's not so! I'd already spotted him an' was on my way down —"

"Yes, that's what Detective McCready told the deskman. No wonder he'd made detective, a man who could think on his feet like that. But it wasn't true. *Was* it?"

"If that's what he testified, then it must be true," Roberts said, holding fast to the last shred of his defiance.

"Dennis Holt, the draft-board man, got in at seven on the dot and spotted the body. *It was already there.* I was there when Holt told the Old Man an' my brother just that. So how is it that *you* didn't find out until seven ten?"

"I don' know," Roberts muttered, "but that's how it was."

"It doesn't add up. How could Reles already be dead, down below, at seven . . . when you say he was in bed at seven? Then you say you were already on your way down by the time you got the phone call from the desk. That doesn't work, either. Give the old draft-board coot a couple minutes to call down to the desk, a couple minutes more for the deskman to call up. That don't get us to seven ten, Officer. So how could it be that you'd already discovered the body . . . *when it wasn't even time for your next turn around the hall yet?*"

"I don't know. *I don't know!*" His raised voice reverberated in the quiet neighborhood. The old nightmare swimming up at him out of nowhere, this pleasant spring evening, on the porch of his very own house. "They musta got the time mixed up," he said, lowering his voice. Trying to banish the nightmare.

"Let's say they did." Tom took a deep breath, drawing the light spring air into his lungs. Officer Roberts's rosebushes looking fine. The yards all up and down the block sprouting buds and blossoms. It was the one trouble with this town — the springs didn't last long enough, he thought. Dissolving from dismal, soaking winter into summer, almost without pause.

He made himself wait another long moment, then hit Officer Roberts with the sixty-four-dollar question: "So then . . . *why are you so damned grateful?*"

"What?" Roberts frowning, peering at him through the dusk to try to figure out what he was driving at.

"Let's say it all happened exactly as you claim, Officer Roberts. *Then why the hell are you so grateful to my brother?* You did everything by the book—an' you get busted down from detective to patrolman, just because some piece of filth decides to go out the window."

He understood it now—saw the trap. Looking out at his perfect, green lawn. The neighbors strolling home from the subway. Wondering, maybe, if he'd ever see such a pleasant evening again. Tom playing out his line, letting him take all the time he needed to surrender.

"He *was* filth, too," Roberts said at last. "Abe Fucking Reles. You ever hear what he an' pals did to that poor girl singer? That little shit with his glass full of blood. Always pullin' somethin'. Always doin' some wise-ass shit. You turned away from your meal for a minute, he'd dump so much pepper in it you'd be coughin' the rest of the night. You fell asleep, he'd tie your shoelaces to the radiator, or give you a hotfoot. A real live wire, huh? When he got bored enough, he'd wad up a big bunch of toilet paper, soak it in the sink. Then he'd call you in an' throw it in your face. I wanted to throw him out the goddamned window myself. A piece of shit like that, livin' in a hotel with a view of the Atlantic Ocean, when real people were starving!"

"He had it coming?"

Roberts stared at him for a long moment, his teeth showing, face stretched with contempt.

"That little shit? Just to watch him eat was disgusting—spittin' his food all over the place. He didn't care. He liked it. After a while he stopped showerin' most days, until he stunk up the whole suite. Playin' that goddamned radio all night. He'd get drunk, an' start screamin' at everyone. Even if you weren't on duty, he'd call you up at home. Three in the mornin'—ask if you were bangin' the wife, an' then he'd laugh an' laugh. Puts himself into *my* home, with *my* wife in *my* bed—"

"Wait a minute. You said he'd get drunk?"

"Yeah. They let him have a bottle, time to time."

"So where was it when the investigators went up to the suite?"

Roberts gave a heavy sigh. "One of the fellas threw it down the incinerator. Thought it wouldn't look good. An' you can put me up under oath an' ask who it was, but I still won't tell you because I honest-to-God don't remember. All I know is that it wasn't me. Satisfied?"

"And a phone? They could use the *phone?* Witnesses being held in protective custody could use the phone without askin' anyone's permission?"

"That was the rule, we didn't make it up. We was just told to keep 'em happy—"

"Jesus."

There was a short silence between them, Tom looking back at the house. He had a vision, then, of another time when Officer Roberts came home from duty. The woman on the porch not standing in the shadows but greeting him out on the front stoop, with a kiss for him and maybe a bottle of beer. The both of them imagining when the lawn would be littered with a bicycle, a baseball glove, maybe a kiddie pool—instead of becoming the immaculate, middle-aged homeowners' lawn it was today.

He looked down at what Roberts was carrying.

"What's in the bag?"

"Huh?"

"What's in the bag?"

He turned it over to Tom, looking a little sheepish. "Peanuts," he said.

"That's right, you're not even a regular patrolman anymore. Are ya? Peanuts to feed the squirrels. You're a *sparrow* cop."

"Prospect Park," Roberts said grudgingly.

"Where there's no chance for any grease from all the dear little creatures of the brush. No payoffs from the squirrels an' the pigeons, so grateful for your protection. Sure, every now an' then you get to put on the jodhpurs, if you're lucky, an' ride the horsies around. But that's about it for a sparrow cop, isn't it?"

"Yeah. So what?" Roberts grunted.

"So back to my original line of inquiry, Officer Roberts. Which is . . . *Why?* Why are you so *grateful* at bein' busted down from lieutenant an' given the worst assignment in the City? Where there's not so much as a single whorehouse, or a crap game to shake down?"

"Hey, I never *touched* whore money—"

"You're a shining example to the force! But my question stands. *What makes you so damned grateful?"*

Roberts just stared at him, eyes glowering in the near darkness.

"I meant what I said before," Tom continued. "This *is* a nice home, Officer. But it's the smallest one on the block. The smallest one for five blocks."

"So?"

"So you've been here for almost twenty years. Payments made to the bank like clockwork. Fifty-eight dollars an' six cents, every month. Well, not quite like clockwork. Sometimes the check comes in a few days late. Even a week—"

"You been checkin' up on me?" His face creased in fury, his drinker's nose glowing red.

"The wife still takes on a little extra work sometimes around holiday season," Tom went on. "When they're hirin' extra cashiers up at May's, or Gimbels—"

The cop's fists curling up now, Tom watching the bag of peanuts fall and open on the porch steps.

"You leave her the hell out of this! I have to sit there an' listen to some goddamned, nigger-loving lawyer talk about my wife—"

"Peace, Officer Roberts! What I'm sayin' is . . . you're clean as a whistle," Tom said, his voice smooth and hushed now. "Not a dollar to be had on your daily rounds of the trees and the petunias. No secret bank accounts, no new cars. One small house that you're holdin' on to for dear life. For a Brooklyn policeman, Officer Roberts, you live like a goddamned monk."

"So? *So?*" His voice confused now, hands still clenching and unclenching. "You gonna nail me for bein' too *honest?*"

"So what was it that happened in the Rats Suite, Officer Roberts? I'll tell you honestly, I thought what I was gonna find was that one of you—maybe all of you—were livin' the high life with the money you took—"

"You can go to hell!"

"But there *is* no money. Not so much as a trace of money, anywhere. Which means you weren't paid off to throw the little man out the window. Not you, or any of the others. No need to clam up—I already checked all their records and their little houses. Seven little policemen, and all of 'em workin' some beat in a park, or out in Indian country. Seven police officers more grateful to be makin' an honest living you never seen in all your life."

Roberts subsided again into his porch, carefully picking up the spilled peanuts, saying nothing.

"So tell me, Officer Roberts. Tell me what makes you so grateful to my brother. Tell me now, before I get one of the others to tell me—and I *will* get them—and you find yourself far away from this nice little house, and the understanding woman you married, watching us there from the porch. Tell me now, before this all comes back, an' your I-talian neighbors get to see you in the papers every day, bein' marched in handcuffs out of the courtroom."

The cop stood up again, and this time Tom stood with him. Roberts at least a head taller than he was and twice as wide, and Tom knew that even with the extra years and the extra pounds, the cop could take him apart. His eyes looked wild, and for a moment Tom thought he was really going to hit him, and he was trying to figure out what he should do then. But instead the cop's head turned toward his perfect lawn—away from the shadow of his wife.

"We fell asleep," he said softly.

"What?"

"We fell asleep."

"*All* of you?"

"Sure. Why not? There was five extra rooms in the suite. Plenty of beds. You had an iron door across the entrance, for chrissakes! Nobody was gettin' through that without a bazooka, an' besides, you had the uniforms downstairs. The rats were all too scared even to pull the shades up. They wasn't goin' nowheres."

"Mother of God. The guards asleep at the tomb."

"Huh? Anyway, it was a twenty-four-hour shift," Robert said plaintively. "You don't know what it's like, bein' on twenty-four hours straight with that pig Reles and those other three bums. It wears a man out. I took it 'cause you got forty-eight hours off between each shift, an' 'cause I thought I'd get in good with the Old Man, but—"

"What did you say?"

"I thought I'd get in good with the Old Man, he was askin' for volunteers—"

"My brother didn't pick you? You weren't on the DA's special squad, under Captain Frank Bals?"

A spark lit in Tom's brain. Thinking, *This might be just the break we need*—but careful not to get ahead of himself.

"Sure I was, but it was the Old Man who picked the guards," Roberts confirmed.

McGrath hurrying his brother upstairs to talk to the cops, before the press could get to them.

"Was Inspector McGrath the first man up to the suite?"

"Huh?"

"The morning Reles died. Was the Old Man the first man from outside to come up to the Rats Suite?"

"Uh, sure, yeah," the cop stammered, shaking his head. "We called Captain Bals at home. But the Old Man was there in no time."

"Was he the one who put you all in a room in the suite together? You *and* the three surviving witnesses you were guarding?"

Tom coming up into the suite after all the business downstairs on the roof was done. Coming in after his brother and Jack McGrath, surprised and puzzled for reasons he couldn't quite articulate at the time, to see them all there.

The seven cops from the detail and the three surviving squealers. All of them in the same room together. Sitting up very straight in chairs and on the edges of beds, like schoolboys on their best behavior. The Old Man suggesting questions to Bals and his investigators, directing the photographer to take this or that picture . . .

"Sure, yeah, hell. It was him." Roberts thrust both hands into his pockets, shifting his weight on his feet uneasily. "How's he doin' these days? I hear it's cancer."

"He's dying," Tom told him.

"Aw, geez, I'm sorry to hear that —"

"So am I. But it was him that had you all in there together?"

"Yeah, look, I don' wanna get him in any trouble, you know? It was him what saved our asses as much as your brother did."

"Another right guy."

"Look, all he said was, 'I'd hate to see seven good men lose their careers over a piece of filth like that. You boys better stay in here an' get your story straight, right now.'"

"So you did."

"Hey, it was the right thing to do. I'd just hope I would do the same, if it was my ass on the line —"

"So the truth was, you were all dead asleep."

"I couldn't say for sure about the others, save for Detective Malone. We usually shared the same room, number six twenty-eight. It had two single beds."

"You were both asleep there. With the door closed."

"Yeah, until the phone rang. An' then all hell broke loose. And you know, it *seemed* like everybody was asleep, all right. When we heard that phone ring, everybody come scramblin' outta those rooms like it was a Chinese fire drill, pullin' their pants on—"

He gave a dry little chuckle thinking about it, and Tom fixed him with a look until he was still.

"So when was the last time you really saw Abe Reles alive?"

The cop shrugged again, twitching a little, almost smiling in his embarrassment. By now there was a silhouette of a woman standing plainly in the light from the porch window, making no effort to conceal herself.

"I dunno. Maybe three, four that morning? I got up for somethin' an' went into the kitchen, an' there he was. He liked to stay up all hours, listenin' to that goddamned radio."

"D'you remember what he was listenin' to?"

"Yeah, some show from that crazy doctor's station, down in Mexico. You know it?"

"You mean Dr. Brinkley, the goat-glands doctor?"

"Yeah, that's the one! He was listenin' to some announcer talk about goat glands, an' he told me as soon as he finished sendin' his old friends to the chair an' got outta the Half Moon, he was gonna go down to Mexico an' get some a those goat glands put in him. He told me he was gonna do that, an' then he was gonna go fuck every girl he saw, includin' all our wives."

"He was a charmer, our Mr. Reles. And that was it?"

"Yeah. Then I went back to my room."

"And shut the door, an' went back to sleep?"

"Yeah."

"And Reles went back to his room. And shut his door—the one he had the key to."

The cop clutched his elbows, looking wistfully at the silhouette in the window. *The woman who has waited too long. Who still has to work the Christmas shifts in the department stores to make the mortgage every month, and has never seen those kids' toys out on the fine lawn, and never will.*

55

"Yeah. Hey, they said to keep 'em happy."

"An' that's all you know. You didn't hear another thing?"

The cop shrugged, half grinned again, looking toward his house once more for sustenance. Tom wondering idly if it was the woman, or the whiskey, or merely the safe harbor of his little home that he was picturing.

"Not a thing. Truth is? Between how tired I was, an' the two doors, an' Abe's radio . . . you coulda thrown Al Capone, Frank Costello, an' Adolf A. Hitler out that window, an' I never woulda known the difference."

7

Mexico City, 1953

They took a taxi to the Hotel del Prado for dinner. Charlie, still a little tipsy, he could see, talking quickly to the driver in Spanish, the man smiling and nodding patiently.

"I told him to drive around a little, let you see some of the city. We still have plenty of time!" he informed Tom expansively.

They plunged into the rivers of ceaseless, bumper-to-bumper traffic, veering and accelerating past the peso cabs, and the squealing yellow streetcars. The buses with their heaps of religious figurines and paper flowers behind the wheel, and the ads hand-painted on the doors. The pace much like that of New York, maybe even faster: hordes of office workers, men and women going out or going home, scrambling across each intersection. Men in uniform — chauffeurs, doormen, and soldiers — standing outside of dark, shabby little bars. Not talking to one another, just standing there sweating next to whores trying to fix their stockings and taking their time about it.

Tom was sure that Charlie was aware of what he was showing him, a city so much like his own, or maybe his own fifty years before — full of color and life, with countless little shops and street scenes. A people in a hurry to get somewhere.

"Maximilian himself built this broad avenue here," Charlie told him, gesturing at the wide expanse of the Paseo de la Reforma. "Built it straight from the National Palace here all the way up to Chapultepec, so he could keep tabs on the wife, up in their palace." Charlie grinned weakly at him. "Not a bad idea, if you ask me. Wish I'd done the same!"

They circled past still more construction sites, most of these, too, with the name Alemán on them. In the darkness, the bright posters looked faded, while atop the new, tall buildings the neon signs blazed to life, flogging liquor and beer, insurance companies, newspapers. Charlie pointed out one squat, brutal structure of mostly concrete with little slits for windows, occupying the better part of a city block.

"The new American embassy building," he said, shaking his head. "Look at those windows — it's like a castle! They're back to the old ways, just tryin' to intimidate and overwhelm. Well, it won't work anymore!"

Their driver grinned back at them over the seat, as he had been doing almost constantly since they'd left the hotel, the gold gleaming in his teeth.

"The Americans I drive always want to know what Mr. O'Kane is doing," he said in his earnest English. "I tell them he is best ambassador we ever have from U.S.!"

"D'ya know this guy, Charlie?" Tom teased him.

"I ride with him a lot. Now, José, stop! My brother here'll think you're my new publicity agent." Charlie blushed, though he was obviously pleased.

They pulled up in front of the Del Prado. There was a whole new cluster of street vendors on the sidewalk outside — men selling sugared peanuts and fake-alligator bags, and an organ grinder playing and singing something plaintive. By the hotel entrance, slender young women in dyed blond hair, black dresses, and white gloves smoked cigarettes and pretended to be oblivious.

They pushed their way out of the cab and into the crowd. As Charlie was paying the driver, a small boy in a tattered blue shirt planted himself in front of them, waving long, narrow sheets of paper covered with numbers under their noses, shouting over and over, *"La lotería! La lotería!"* Instantly, more vendors seemed to swarm around them. Someone selling sweet potatoes and hot roasted corn, from a cart with a mournful steam whistle attached. Another man selling balloons, another what looked to be cut sections of honeycomb.

"Nacional! Forty thousand pesos — forty thousand for tomorrow!" chanted the little boy with the lottery strips.

"C'mon now, that's no way to sell 'em," Charlie said jovially, digging a handful of change out of a pocket and pulling out one of the sheets, handing it to Tom while the hotel doormen roughly and casually pushed away the other hawkers.

"The national lottery," he explained. "Everybody's crazy for it. You remember, I wanted to start a lottery when I was mayor? Take the money out of the hands of all those policy boys and put it in the public coffers. But the old blue-noses wouldn't let me, and then they wanted to put me in jail for what the bookies were doin'—*Dario!*"

Inside the hotel the maitre d' threw his arms around Charlie, exclaiming, "Mr. Embajador, we love you!" before seating them at the best table in front of the orchestra. The room heavy in gold and silver, chairs and booths upholstered in dark leather, with long tapered candles and bowls full of roses on every table. The men in tuxes and tails, the women exclusively in long white and black gowns, their necks and wrists laden with still more gleaming metal. Charlie in white tie, too, wearing at least half of his countless decorations from the war, Tom saw, despite his embarrassment. All the medals he had secretly memorized, and could still recite by heart: the Legion of Honor and the Legion of Merit, the Aztec Eagle and the Pan-American Collar—shiny stars and suns and hearts from all over Europe and the Americas, and even a long ceremonial chain from somewhere, which he used to tease his brother about unmercifully.

Slim joined them at the table, with her hair up and wearing a strapless red Balenciaga gown and a small, gold pendant that hung down between the top of her breasts. Her entrance drew a long collective murmur from around the room, and the ruffle of a dozen ladies' fans. She posed for a moment by her chair, taking a long look.

"Why, they're wearing even more hardware than you are tonight, Charlie," she said, leaning in to kiss him on the cheek.

"Hello, Slim. It's good to see you," he said, his voice barely a croak. But she had already moved on.

"Hello again, Tom," she said. Barely sliding her face along his, her cheek fragrant with a light perfume, lips grazing his ear.

"I begged him not to wear the necklace," Tom joked, pointing to the ceremonial chain around Charlie's neck, and Slim smiled.

"Oh, don't worry. I'm the spectacle here. That's why I decided to wear this. I thought I might as well show my true colors —"

"You shouldn't be talkin' like that, Slim," Charlie told her. "You know everybody loves you."

"They think I'm a whore. But they still love *you*, Charlie."

"Ah, now, Slim —"

A line of tuxedoed men were already making their way over to the table, shaking his hand and embracing him, chatting animatedly in Spanish while their wives stayed back at their tables, peering in their direction. The orchestra struck up as slow a cha-cha as was humanly possible, and when Slim looked at him imploringly, Tom took her out onto the half-filled dance floor.

"Damn, Tom, I can see you haven't been wasting any time at nightclubs," she said, laughing, as he stumbled over his feet and hers.

"Sorry."

"That's all right. You never could dance," she said softly, leaning in close. "It's one of the things about you I always found endearing."

"Who's all that?" he asked her, trying to distract himself from the feel of her against him.

"Charlie's friends? They call them 'the Big Crowd.' The Alemanistas — sort of a combination of café society and Tammany Hall. There would be more, but right now half of them are lamming it in Europe, along with our glorious ex-*presidente*."

"They seem to like Charlie, all right."

"What's not to like? He's the most charming man *I* ever met. Plus they're convinced he must have some money somewhere."

"Are they?" he asked, alarmed. "What makes 'em think that?"

"Because *they* do, silly. Stashed away in Cuba, or Spain. It happens with every new president, though it really got out of control this time around. They're saying they took eight hundred million dollars. But when the heat dies down they'll all come back, buy themselves a new hacienda or a yacht."

"So they think Charlie must've done the same."

"Sure. Doesn't everybody?"

"But you know that's not true," Tom said, the bile rising in him at the thought. "The IRS has been through everything. So were Rudy Halley and the Kefauver Committee. He must be the most investigated man in America, and none of 'em found a thing! Hell, Slim, *you* know all he's got is his mayor's pension."

"I know that better than anyone," she said in a low voice, and slipped her arms around his neck. She was all he could look at then. Her body as slender and supple as ever, her shoulders brown from the sun. Her face still so beautiful and inviting.

"God, I missed you, Tom," she said. "I missed your indignation. I missed how much you care."

"That's just what he needs—more rumors, more innuendo. We have to *help* him, Slim," Tom said. But he knew they were just words now. All he was aware of was how her breasts grazed against his chest, the trace of perfume that made him want to put his cheek against hers again, and kiss her mouth in front of everyone.

"Does he look like he needs any help?" she asked, nodding toward him at the table.

It was true, he looked better than Tom had seen him since he'd arrived. Ebullient now as he always was on the stump, pumping hands and slapping backs. Laughing heartily, his face a more natural color.

He pulled her arms gently down from around his neck. "Slim—"

"Oh, Tom, I'm already a spectacle," she said, trying to smile at him. "Did you know the first week I was here, I was trying to tell El Presidente Lammistero that I liked riding horses. It came out, *'Me gusta montar caballeros'*—I like to ride men. It was all downhill from there—"

"Slim!" he said, admonishing, and she pulled back, seeing that she was embarrassing him.

"Oh, don't worry about me," she told him lightly, letting him lead her off the floor and back to their table. "It's him you have look out for."

Looking at Charlie surrounded by the Big Crowd, Tom thought for an instant that he could be looking at their father, the schoolmaster. *Sitting at the kitchen table of a Saturday night, when he sent to town for the Dublin papers, and read them by the kerosene lamp to any of the neighbors who happened to come by. Patiently explaining what something meant when they asked. His soft, reedy voice effortlessly filling the house. Looking out over his spectacles and his pipe when he wanted to have a little fun with an item, usually to tease their mother . . .*

Charlie now just as self-assured. Rambling away on one topic or another. His voice—a politician's voice—deeper and richer, and more blustery than their father's, switching effortlessly from English to Spanish and back again. Regaling the men standing around their table with the old stories, from when he was mayor.

"—a Mrs. Throckmorton Updike asked me if she might plant forsythia along the traffic islands on Park Avenue. And she was a nice old lady, so I gave her permission, which was my fatal mistake. Next thing I know, the Parks Department is wantin' to know, am I aware the forsythia blooms just one month a year? An' next it's some precinct captain wantin' to know why there's no forsythia planted in *Democratic* neighborhoods, an' then it's the botanists askin' didn't I know there's dust an' car exhaust on Park Avenue, an' terr-ible vibrations from the subway . . ."

Tom noticed to his disgust that his brother's voice had slipped into a brogue. The men clustered around the table laughed and smiled dutifully—though he saw that they pointedly paid no attention to Slim, who ignored them in turn.

"But it was all worthwhile. A month later I get the nicest note from Mrs. Throckmorton Updike, sayin' she would even consider votin' for me the next time, assumin' there wasn't a qualified Republican in the race!"

The men laughed on cue, and shook his hand, and except for a pair of nearly identical well-dressed men in their forties, circulated away. Charlie went right on.

"You know, I've been reading a lot about Daniel Boone recently, and my old friend Cortés," he said, taking a big swig from the glass of red wine before him, the waiter instantly refilling it. "A man could be great then. There was rhythm, there was movement in those days."

"*Which* days? They were three hundred years apart," Slim remarked, but Charlie paid her no mind, though he reached out to grip her wrist. Tom noticed the familiar gold cufflinks with his initials on them—the ones that inspired some of the columnists to start calling him *O.K. Charlie*.

The two men who remained listened attentively. They had thinning hair, thin moustaches, and the steady stare of hyenas, Tom thought. Charlie introduced them as two of the Pasquel brothers, and asked how President Alemán was.

"More to the point, *where* is President Alemán?" Slim interjected.

"Now, now, I won't have a man condemned before he's given his day in court," Charlie said, chastising her. "I know what that's like. What did that fella in the *Collier's* write about me, Tom? 'The mayor of New York can make a hundred thousand a week in kickbacks from building and supply contractors alone, if he likes.'"

"Something like that."

"'And Mr. O'Kane's administration built a billion and a half dollars in housing, and hospitals, and schools, and roads, without a breath of scandal!' *Without a breath of it!*"

The Pasquels nodded politely in acknowledgment of his honesty and made their excuses. Charlie leapt up to pump their hands and thump their backs. Tom was certain he could see the faint bulge of a gun through each of their dinner jackets. Slim took the opportunity to move to the other side of the table.

"Those two fellas have a hand in everything," Charlie said confidentially to him. "You know they run the Mexican League—"

"Sure, they're big stuff. I remember when they signed Danny Gardella off the Giants," Tom said, rapidly getting fed up.

"Jorge, the older one?" Charlie continued as if he hadn't heard a word. "He's Presidente Calles's son-in-law. He owns ships, cattle, has a big car business, even his own publishing company—"

"They say he killed a man, too, with that cute little gun he keeps in his tux," Slim said softly, smiling brightly at them.

"I'm trying to buy into an auto dealership with a friend down here. I figure all I need is about twelve thousand a year, American. Maybe just nine thousand. Of course, if I really wanted to play my cards right, with the people I know in the Big Crowd I could make a hundred grand a year—just for starters!"

Slim looked away, staring off over the dance floor. Her bare back was magnificent in the low light, taut and sleekly muscled, and Tom remembered how it used to feel when he held her.

"— if I wanted to show them up north it was money I could make, I could make it. But they'd just assume I'd stolen it, like always —"

His brother's babble of words felt unbearable.

"I know, Charlie," Tom said, cutting him off. "You wrote me about it —"

"Sure, I wrote you! But it's not the same thing for you to see it, to meet the people down here, an' see how it is for yourself —"

"Charlie!" Slim said sharply, without looking back, and Tom watched as his brother's face crumpled, then tried to recompose itself.

"Well, let's get back to that some other time. You know, you never did tell me how it is back home," Charlie said haltingly.

"You know how it is —"

"Oh, I see the kind of things they write about me. That *Collier's* fella? 'O'Kane was an almost great man. You might say he was fifty percent genius, and fifty percent jerk.'"

"They write plenty of good things, too —"

"Sure! How's this one? 'He was a true tragedy. A great man, but there was a hole in him somewhere'! C'mon, Tommy — d'ya see a hole?" He pulled at his white dinner jacket, and then the shirt underneath, popping a couple of his shirt studs. Two waiters scrambled immediately under the table to retrieve them.

"How could ya do it, Tommy?" he asked, his mood changing rapidly to despair, then to righteous anger: "Jesus, Tommy, how could ya let 'em do that to me?"

Charlie finished the wine in his glass with a flourish, and Tom realized that he had never seen his brother drunk before. Tom tried to wave the waiters away, but they had already brought another bottle. One of them quietly placed Charlie's sprung studs in his hands.

"You have to be careful with this stuff up here," Charlie said again as he brought the glass to his lips. "Remember, we're seven thousand feet above sea level! It goes to your head."

"Yes, Charlie."

"If it's good for the world to crush a man, let the world do it," he said resignedly, slurring his words.

"Charlie, there's millions who love you —"

"You know I think sometimes about how it was when I was still on the magistrate's bench, back in Brooklyn. You were there when I was still a magistrate, Tom."

"I remember."

"Those were the happiest days of my life. I remember Claire sayin' it at the time, God rest her soul. 'This is where you belong, Charles,' she said. 'You've found your own level. Now be content with it, an' do some good.' Why did I ever not listen to that woman!"

"Please God, Charlie, no more stories about the magistrate's court," Slim said from across the table, turning back to them and snubbing her cigarette out savagely.

"Decidin' all those neighborhood quarrels between the little people. You remember how it was. There was 'the defender,' an' 'the complainer,' and 'the bailer.' I can still remember a couple of neighbors, Meyerowitz an' Klein, feudin' over a tree. The tree that grows in Brooklyn — only what they were arguin' over was the little bird that lived in the tree, an' soiled the wet wash in Mrs. Meyerowitz's yard!"

"I remember it, Charlie."

"And that old fraud on the bench — what was his name? George Folwell! You know, the one who spoke fake Italian? One session, the translator was out, so Judge Folwell decided to do the job himself. He comes out with a big long spiel of it, an' the defender looks at Folwell an' says, 'Sorry, judge, I no unnerstan' so good the English.' Oh, I thought the whole damned court was about to die laughin'!"

Tom tried laughing with him, but the next moment his brother's face had gone sour again.

"That's where I shoulda stayed, Tommy. Keepin' the peace between the people of Brooklyn —"

"You did a lot more than that, Charlie."

"— all the little people, who think I'm the thief of all the world!"

"Are we discussing leprechauns again?" Slim asked.

"They don't, Charlie," Tom tried to tell him, but his brother was past hearing him.

" 'I see before me the Gladiator lie,' " he recited, rocking back in his chair.

"He leans upon his hand — his manly brow
Consents to death, but conquers agony,
: . . The arena swims around him — he is gone
. . . Butcher'd to make a Roman holiday'!"

"Jesus, Charlie, will you give it a rest?" Slim asked, but he only stared at her out of unsteady, drunken eyes.

"Don't you think I've wanted to say that to *you* a few times?" he shot back — then recited again: " 'Masters with no authority in their house/Their women out playing night and day — ' "

"Which book is that from, Charlie? *One Hundred Narrative Poems About Unfaithful Wives?*' " she said, fuming, her voice rising enough to attract stares from some of the grand *donas* about the room. "What's it do for anything, all this feeling sorry for yourself?"

"Runnin' around here with everything in pants," Charlie said, pretending to ignore her, turning to appeal to Tom. "Did you see that picture in the magazine of that rancher fella, Gandarias, helpin' her strap on her gaucho chaps? How close he was standin' behind her?"

"Charlie, so help me God —"

"Jesus, Tommy, I ask you: what did *that* look like to you?"

"Honest to God, Charlie, I thought he looked old enough to be her father."

Stopping dead on his own faux pas, while Slim put her hand over her mouth but burst out anyway into uncontrollable laughter, drawing further stares from the wealthy Mexican women all around the room. Charlie's sunken eyes sliding from one to the other of them, still not comprehending. Looking as dazed and exhausted as the bull Tom had watched her fight that afternoon.

"I think you've had enough now, Charlie."

"Ah, listen to him, my own little brother! No, no, Tommy, I'm not drunk. Have you ever seen me drunk?"

"No, Charlie. Not until tonight."

"You know who taught me not to get drunk? Ed Dunphy the waiter, that's who! Back before the Great War, when I was workin' as a hod carrier. I had an education of sorts, but I didn't have any manners. So every Saturday night that summer, after I got my wages for the week, I'd have the barber give me a trim, an' shave, and a shampoo, and an iodine treatment. And then I'd put on me one navy blue suit an' my best white shirt and my only tie, an' my eighty-five-cent straw hat. And I'd go down to see Dunphy, where he worked at Healy's famous restaurant, on West Sixty-Sixth Street."

"So you told me, Charlie."

"He was quite a man, Ed Dunphy. By then he owned two apartment houses, bought just with what he saved up waitin' tables. He'd sit me down an' teach me everything. How to read the menu, and how to eat the salad, an' use the silver oyster fork."

Tom tried to get the bill but the maitre d', still smiling broadly, waved him off. Instead he helped pull out Charlie's chair for him and lead him to the door.

"Looks like the floor show's over, folks!" Slim said as she followed, waving openly to the women seated around the room, who glowered back at her.

"He told me never to be a showoff. He told me he could tell a showoff by how he talked to the hatcheck girl, an' he said he'd rather see his own daughters in a convent than goin' around with a showoff. He told me, 'I like nice people, rich or poor, who take one cocktail and order properly, an' up they get an' go away. The kind that always says, 'Thank you, waiter.' That makes me feel good.' He taught me all that, an' when he was through, he said, 'I've done all I can for you here. When you have a steady job, get married to a nice girl an' stay home with her. Places like this give a lad bad habits.' "

Dario, the maitre d', halted them with a cautionary hand at the door, pausing to take the rescued studs from Tom's hand. Then gently, lovingly, he reinserted them and closed his brother's shirt again.

"He was a gentleman, was Ed Dunphy—just like you, Dario!" Charlie called after the maitre d' as they carted him on out. Dario only giving a small bow and dispatching the doorman to flag down a cab for them. Slim walked past them out onto the sidewalk to have a cigarette, Charlie barely seeming to notice.

"Ah, me, Ed Dunphy! I was such a greenhorn in those days! I remember how *you* were Tommy, when you first come over—before you knew what the score was?"

"Sure."

"When you were tryin' to work your way through law school at night, and I got you the job on the Camarda docks in Red Hook?"

"I remember."

"First job you had in America, workin' as a checker—"

"First day out, I saw a man lift a whole side of ham," Tom said, and sighed. "Just picked it right off the hook and walked away with it, and I reported it. Next day, they fired me."

"You can't go by the book, Tommy. We had a rule book back when I was walkin' a beat, too. If we'd gone by that, the whole City of New York woulda been left defenseless."

Charlie stood wavering by the door, waiting for his cab, not unhappily. A light rain was falling now, a cooling air blowing gently into the entrance of the Del Prado. Tom could see Slim pacing under the awning in her red dress, drawing impatiently at her cigarette.

"Then you took up with the union. That was some trouble! You didn't know it, but oh, those b'hoys wanted to throw you right in the river!"

"*Did* they now, Charlie?" Tom asked, struck by that remark but unable to say just why. Thinking that his brother might be right—the thin air making it hard for him to concentrate, after only the half glass of wine he had imbibed.

"Do you remember that meeting down at Saint Stephen's hall? When you gave your first speech?"

"Don't remind me, Charlie! I worked on that speech for two whole weeks," Tom said, shaking his head ruefully. "The priests down there helped me write it all out in Italian. I memorized all the pronunciations, the accents . . ."

Going over and over it in his room up at Mrs. Maguire's boardinghouse. Studying every gesture in front of the mirror as if he were O'Connell himself, out to talk before a monster rally.

"It was a full house, too," Tom continued. "All those longshoremen. And I did read it *beau*-tifully, if I say so myself. And then I said—in Italian!—'Freedom of speech has come at last to the waterfront, where now a man may speak without fear!' Oh, you should've seen it, Charlie!"

"I wish I did. I wish I did!"

"And then, when I was all done, I hear a voice from the back of the room. 'Mister,' it says in English—"

A voice like a hoe being raked over gravel. As serious as death.

67

"'Mister,' the voice says, 'why you mean anybody can go up there an' speak?' And I say, 'That's right, man. That's what we're here for.' And the voice asks again, 'You mean anyone can just go up there an' speak right now?' And I says, 'Put away your fears! Come forward now, an' tell us your name!'"

"And up comes Tony Anastasio!" his brother chortled. "Tough Tony, brother of Albert Anastasia, the Lord High Executioner himself!"

"Oh, but you shoulda seen 'em scatter! 'My name is Anthony Anastasio,' he says, in that bear growl a his, an' ten seconds later there wasn't another soul left in Saint Stephen's hall."

They were both laughing hard now, laughing as they had not done together since years before in Charlie's office, recounting the follies of other men.

The cab came at last, and the doorman helped Tom cart his brother out to it. Pushing him gently into the middle of the back seat, Slim getting in after him, and Tom going around the other side so he'd be propped up between them. The boy in the tattered blue shirt running up, Tom saw — too late. Waving the *lotería* strips at them again, the lists of numbers flashing by the window.

Charlie still talking as they pulled away from the curb. Mumbling now, and almost out, but Tom realizing nonetheless that he was listening to both a defense and a confession.

"So isn't it possible," Charlie said, slurring his words, "isn't it possible your big brother didn't know what the hell he was doin' either?" before he passed out in his seat.

Brooklyn, 1939
All that fall, from the Brooklyn Bridge down to Twentieth Street, the crowds were growing steadily in the little parish churches and the union halls. He brought them out with his speeches, a man with kindly eyes and the lilt of Southern Italy still on his tongue. Speaking to them quickly and forcefully

about unbelievable things — about their rights, and America, and how they were free men.

Nobody had ever seen anything like it. No one could remember anyone challenging the Camardas on their own docks, with all their goons and their *shlammers*. The squat, swarthy enforcers, with dead eyes and new coats. Strutting the docks all day with their hands shoved deep in their pockets, their lengths of lead pipe wrapped in newspapers. Walking right through the men when they came down to the wharves, like wolves culling sheep.

Then Panto started holding his meetings all over Red Hook and the Heights. He looked too thin and too tall to be a longshoreman, but he was wiry and deceptively strong. Not yet thirty years old. A kindly smile under that silly little moustache and the silly little gigolo's hat he wore, hook slung over his sleeveless undershirt. For the rallies, he took care to dress up in his one good suit and tie, the hat slung over his eyes at a rakish angle. In the movies, he would have been cast as the bad guy, the mafioso, or the false lover. In person there was something touchingly genteel about him, something careful and dignified, the air of an impoverished provincial *signore*.

They loved him in the musty local halls, where there hadn't been a union meeting for ten years, twenty years, or maybe never. In the little parish churches built by congregations of long-vanished Protestants. The walls painted the color of the Mediterranean now, filled with statues of the Virgin, and the favorite saints of Sicily and Calabria, Castellammare and Altomonte. The men shouting his name from the moment he walked up to the front of the hall, or to the altar, standing on chairs and pews just to get a look at him. To hear him tell them the same thing, every time.

"We are strong. We are many. All we have to do is stand up and fight."

From the Mother Local over on Eleventh Avenue came King Joe Ryan himself, president-for-life of the International, to try to reason with them. But the men shouted him down, ran him back to Chelsea in his two-hundred-dollar suit with his diamond stickpin. King Joe crying out, "People are going to get hurt!" in his pipsqueak brogue, as they surged in around him, his bodyguard of ex-cons kicking and punching furiously to get him clear.

"Starting with *you!*" the longshoremen shouted at him, pelting him with apples and rolled-up newspapers as he ran the gauntlet out the front door.

Even Camarda and the worst of his *shlammers* fell back when Panto led them down Columbia Street to the Mooremack Line on Pier 15. Striding like men again, with him at their head in his silly black hat, smiling that kindly, diffident *signore*'s grin. The goons jeered and cursed him, but Tom could see they were fascinated by the man, too, their eyes following his every word and movement.

"What they can't crush, they want to follow," Father Carey, the priest from Saint Francis Xavier's, told Tom. "That's the way of this world, where men live entombed in fear and ignorance."

They lay for him anywhere they might get him alone, in the alleys down by the slips, and outside every saloon and greasy spoon. But Panto didn't go out drinking, he didn't go into the saloon save to talk to the men. He had a girl, took her out to the big movie palaces and the nice restaurants up in Park Slope, always very public places with lots of people around.

Down on the docks, the men wouldn't let him go anywhere alone. Everywhere he walked there was a crowd around him, carrying their longshoremen's hooks and their own lengths of pipe, warding Camarda's goons off. A phalanx of men surrounding him, the only sign he was even with them that hat, bobbing up and down above the rest.

In their frustration, the *shlammers* cut out victims anywhere they could. Waiting to get them drunk, and isolated, and away from the rest. Men bloodying one another with fists, and sticks, and other primitive weapons, breaking one another's heads along the ancient, cobblestone streets of the waterfront. Tom saw men he knew and like pull down one of Camarda's goons and stretch his leg out over the curb, while two more men took turns jumping up and down on it until it shattered. He would never forget the sound of breaking bone, the shrill squeal the man made, held down helpless over the curb while they shattered his leg, writhing in his fine coat like a cockroach on its back.

Yet somehow it did not frighten or repel him. Despite himself, he welcomed the chance to fight something. Coming back proudly to Mrs. Maguire's with his first broken nose a few days later. Charlie expressing alarm while he snapped it back into place with one quick turn of his hands.

"You should be careful," Charlie told him, referring to more than the street brawls, Tom understood. "Nothin's ever what it seems down there on the docks."

"Seems clear enough to me."

"Is it? I hear you're runnin' with a lot of reds."

"Who told you that?"

"Friends of mine. They say you're off with that communist lawyer, Longhi—"

"There's more priests than Communists down by the waterfront these days," Tom said, snorting.

"The waterfront's a world to itself, Tommy," his brother warned him. "You think you can see it plain enough. But there's always somethin' else goin' on— somethin' you *don't* see. I know. The first beat I ever walked was down in Red Hook, an' they would've had to fish me out of the bay, if it hadn't been for the Old Man. You got to watch yourself down there."

"You should be down there now, Charlie."

"Where's the center of it, Tommy? Where's the fight?"

"Pier Fifteen."

"The Mooremack Lines, that's Billy McCormack's pier. He'll get it straightened out."

The first time he had ever heard that name from his brother. Even down on the docks, no one spoke it much, save in low voices and while looking over their shoulders.

"We don't see Mr. William bloody McCormack down on Pier Fifteen very much, Charlie. Instead, we got the Camardas. You want to work, you have to play ball with those fellas," he said, growing heated.

"But that's the way of it everywhere, Tommy. You want to get on, you have to play ball."

"Do ya know what they do to the men down there, Charlie? They squeeze 'em every way they can—squeeze 'em till there's no more left to get. They give up half their wages just to be in the shape-up. Men like that—strong men, proud men. Having to stand out on the dockside and see if they're good enough to be *allowed* to work.

"They make 'em take out loans from the Camardas' shylocks, whether they need one or not, an' they make 'em give their nickels to the Camardas' policy bankers, whether they want to play policy or not. They even make 'em get their hair cut by the Camarda barbers, an' buy their grapes from the Camarda fruit dealers, whether they're gonna make their wine that year or not. And every couple weeks the Camardas send one of their torpedoes around to make 'em buy a ticket to another of their charity rackets. Another banquet for King Joe Ryan!"

"I know what you're sayin', Tommy," his brother commiserated. "But give Bill McCormack a chance. He's a businessman, he wants things to run smooth—"

"They got fourteen thousand men down there, Charlie! Fourteen thousand, from Owl's Head to Greenpoint," he snapped, exasperated. "Jesus God, it's the biggest racket in the world! Squeezing out blood money penny by penny, from the poorest sons of bitches in the City!"

"Just make sure it's not your blood they squeeze, boy-o."

Tom berated himself that it wasn't. He wasn't much use to them, he knew, still thin as a rake handle. After getting himself fired from the checker's job he tried working the holds, quitting after a week and before he killed somebody, such as himself. It was the hardest work he had ever done, made reaping and thrashing the oat sheaves back in Bohola seem like a Sunday outing.

He managed to catch on as a recording secretary with Panto's Rank-and-File Committee. Helping the priests help the men where he could. Working the docks with the committee in the day, then off to study the law or work on his brother's campaign for Brooklyn DA at night. Falling asleep on the long subway ride home after midnight to Mrs. Maguire's on West 103rd, and again the moment he set his head to the pillow.

He had never felt so tired, but also so exhilarated. It was as if every one of his senses was piqued to a point he had never experienced before. He loved being on the docks in the early morning, as the sun was coming up. The gray and white skyscrapers emerging through the dirty yellow half-light at the water. The great bridges, and the rising bustle of the harbor, coming to life like some grand orchestra tuning up around him. The battered freighters, the rusty-black hulls rising out of the water, fat little tugs pushing and worrying them into place at the dock.

He loved the smell of the City around him—a very different smell from the early mornings he had known in Bohola, or Dublin, or back at his boarding-house in Manhattan. The brine and the diesel, and even the stinkwash of the garbage slicks lolling around the moorings. The coal smoke, and the incinerators from the tenements by the waterfront, the gasoline of the dockside generators, the choking richness of thousands of pounds of raw sugar, or tea, or coffee being poured down the chutes.

Then there were the men. Walking down to the docks in their shabby, loose clothes, pants legs maybe tied with cheap twine, so they wouldn't get caught in anything. Tattered checker jackets worn against the growing cold, or fraying leather coats worn down to the consistency of sandpaper. Soft caps that could be easily folded and stuck into pockets, sandwiches or a couple of doughnuts wrapped in wax paper, if they were lucky. Standing for hours in the shape-up while the hiring bosses decided who they would and would not deign to choose for the day. Picking out the ones favored by the Camardas by the not-so-secret tokens they wore, the little toothpicks or the union buttons, or the cigarette tucked behind an ear.

As the weeks went on, he could see the change come over them, the pride growing visibly in their every movement. The men standing straighter, no longer in the defensive half crouch of whipped dogs. Yelling out at the hiring bosses when they tried to ghost-cut a ship, the top gangs insisting on staying together. He came to know them as he worked the tiny Rank-and-File head-quarters on Remsen Street, their friendship steadily widening his existence. They took him home with them, feeding him, introducing him to their families, to their mothers, who all wanted to put some meat on his bones.

Such food! Like nothing he had ever tasted before. Heaping Italian suppers, brimming with garlic and peppers, homemade tomato sauces, deep troughs of lasagna. Hand-rolled spaghetti and linguine, made in the kitchen that morning. Washed down with homemade grappa, or the tart wine stomped in the tenement basement, wine with a bite in it, bitter as vinegar. He loved it all.

It was not just the Italians, either, but the Bohemians and the Poles and the Swedes, every possible people under the sun. Mixed on the waterfront, all of them, working shoulder to shoulder like some labor song of solidarity. All save the coloreds — the one exception to the international brotherhood of the long-shoremen's union. Kept to their own dingy little local hall, at the far end of the Hook. Neglected even by the Camardas in their rackets, making so little they weren't worth the trouble. Allowed on the white man's waterfront only when there was some particularly odious cargo to be unpacked, usually bananas, which came crawling with tarantulas bigger than your hand.

"That's not right," Panto conceded to him one evening when Tom was over for supper at the home of his fiancée, Alice, a sweet young woman with large black eyes and long hair, and the lovely, full breasts that all the Italian girls seemed to have.

"They're men, too; they deserve dignity. We take care a that. We gonna take care of everything, so they can never divide us again."

There was a rare hesitation in his voice, eyes sincere but dropping down to where he played with the linguine on his plate, twirling and untwirling it with his fork.

"What is it?"

"Only . . ."

"Only what?"

"Only maybe not right away —"

"Jesus, Peter, how long do they have to wait —"

"I don' mean that. I don' mean put 'em off forever an' ever," Panto said patiently, making Tom blush for mistaking him. This *good* man. "I mean we got to win somethin' *now*. Or it's gonna be too late."

"Win *something?*"

"We got to get it, Tom," he said, bringing his hands close together, as if narrowing in on something, eyes struggling to convey exactly what he meant. "Because the men won't last out there much longer. Too many outta work, not enough coal to get through the winter. We gotta get somethin', then go on from there."

"You don't mean giving in?"

Instantly ashamed of himself again, but confused, wanting to know what he meant. Missing it, he knew later. Missing what he was really saying.

"No, no." Panto shook his head again, almost sorrowful at being misunderstood. His face looking heavy-eyed, and lined well beyond his twenty-eight years. "We don't give in. Never. But we got to win *somethin'*. I been hearing from a few people — never mind for now. Reasonable people. Maybe we can make them listen."

"He's smart, your boy." Charlie had nodded approvingly when Tom told him about their conversation. "Sure, Tommy, it's shameful how they treat the coloreds down there. It's shameful how they treat everybody. But he's right. He's got to win something *now*, if he's going to hold on till we can get in to help him."

He wanted to argue, even then. Wanted to ask, *How can you be neutral in this?* But he listened, for it was Charlie who had opened up this dizzying new world to him. Back when he had first arrived at Mrs. Maguire's, just a few weeks before, spouting all his big Dublin university talk about the superiority of Irish culture, and letters, and everything else. They had laughed in his face, Charlie, and Michael and Jack, his other older brothers, who were working now one as a fireman, the other a policeman.

Wait'll you see this town, they had told him, and done their best to show him, each in his own way. They tutored him on his manners, on how to buy a suit and eat in a good restaurant. Taking him to the museums, and to the Polo Grounds, and Carnegie Hall, and the top of the Empire State, and all the other great and grand buildings.

It made him feel ashamed of his own ignorance, to have come from such a small, backward corner of the world and not know it — not just Bohola and Lismirrane, but even Dublin, and the whole of Ireland. He'd been amazed to learn that his brother had a Jew law partner, knew colored men and Puerto Ricans from East Harlem — even invited them over to break bread with him, in the attached house he had bought out in Bay Ridge. The place three times the size of the home they had all lived in back in Bohola, and remarkably quiet and neat by contrast. A place of shadows and low lights — the way that Claire, the wife, liked it. A constant presence in the background, her face already nearly rigid as a mask by then. Confined to the wheelchair, Neddy Moran or Jimmy always standing over her, looking to see if there was anything she needed.

Jimmy, the adopted son, in his last year at Fordham by then, and a natural rival at first. The two of them feeling each other out warily across the dinner table, but soon enough fast friends, the boy's natural enthusiasm and good-heartedness shining through. It was a place where he always felt at home, going over for Sunday dinner, or maybe a Saturday-night crack with Charlie and the brothers.

It was, too, that same fall that Charlie ran for Brooklyn DA. Opening up to Tom yet another world where men vied for power. The campaign wildly exciting, the nights filled up with torchlight rallies, and long cars careening around quiet Brooklyn streets. Neddy Moran at the wheel, and Charlie's law partner, Natie Cohen, or maybe the Old Man always at his brother's side.

"It is an education," his brother liked to tell him. Watching him, Tom knew, to see what he was picking up.

He remembered one evening out in a tiny *lansmen*'s hall in Brownsville, before a crowd of Jewish tailors, butchers, and pushcart vendors. He never liked going out to that part of the world. It always seemed dark and shabby, and infinitely old, somehow, though he knew there was scarcely a building standing that had been there forty years. The side streets lined with monotonous three- and four-story brick apartment houses, or slumping wooden row houses, even old farmhouses rotting slowly into empty lots littered with bottles and discarded gravestones from some upturned local cemetery. The streetlights smashed and stripped cars abandoned along the curb. Above, the elevated trains roared like a waking nightmare through the dark. Even on Pitkin Avenue, the bustling shopping district, many of the stores looked dilapidated and stuffed willy-nilly with cheap goods, as if the vendors' pushcarts had just been shoved inside, Yiddish writing scribbled in chalk above the entrance.

In the little hall on Stone Street, the crowd was already agitated before Charlie said a word, maddened by news of the latest atrocities from Poland. He had just started in denouncing the Nazis when a workingman in baggy canvas pants and a cap tugged low over his brow pushed his way to the front of the crowd, shaking a muscled arm at him.

"Never mind the goddamned Nazis. Whattaya gonna do about the Coughlin thugs, right here in Brooklyn?" he yelled out, bringing the house down. The men stamping their feet in the murky yellow light, drowning out his brother's speech, while Tom and Natie looked about apprehensively.

"*What's* your question now?" Charlie asked from the platform, holding out an ear and looking slightly stunned.

"You know damned well who! The Christian Mobilizers!" the angry man sneered. "They come right into our synagogues with their baseball bats! Why don't you get your Bishop Molloy to do something about it?"

A yell of affirmation resounded through the little hall, the spontaneous cry from the throats of half a thousand garment cutters, and warehousemen, and pickle sellers. Charlie waiting until it died down before he would answer.

76

"If I come out of my house, and a gang of no-good hoodlums descends upon me, and beats me on my stoop, do I go runnin' to the *bishop's* for justice?" he asked evenly, the slowly rising heat in his voice enfolding and carrying away their own anger. The crowd noise dying down as they hung on his words now, unsure of what he would say.

"Never mind the bishop! I go to the police. *I go to the law!* And I tell you this: when I am the district attorney of Brooklyn, *the law will do an honest day's work,*" he told them, waving his fist right back at the crowd. "No man will be able to attack another, no man will desecrate a sacred house of worship, without paying the full penalty of the law!"

The hall reduced instantly to pandemonium, the workingmen stamping, and clapping, and whistling now in approval. Even the angry man who had just been shouting at him nodding his head in grudging assent.

"Boy, you were quick on your feet with that one," Tom told his brother admiringly in the car afterward. But Charlie had just shrugged, while Natie grinned up in the front seat.

"Oh, we knew that was comin'."

"What? How?"

"We planted it."

"That was *your* man there?"

"Natie had heard that sort of thing was goin' around. So we made sure to drag it out in the open, where we could kill it."

Charlie turned to him, smiling a little smugly in the faint light from the dashboard. "Don't ya see it, Tom? Whoever was spreadin' that kind of talk wanted to set me against the bishop. If I said he wasn't responsible, I'd lose every Jewish vote in the borough. And if I said I would go talk to him, I'd lose every Catholic vote."

"So you really did hear the question."

"If you wait—if you seem bamboozled by the question like that—they let their guard down," he said matter-of-factly. "They wait to hear you hang yourself, rather than try an' shout you down."

"It's all a sleight of hand, then," Tom had said, marveling, feeling let down somehow.

"Let me ask you this, Tom: Would it've been better to tell 'em that the bishop's a lovely Catholic gentleman, but that those b'hoys from the Christian

Front don't answer to him? Or even to the pope for that matter? To advise 'em to arm themselves, an' go do battle in the streets?"

Charlie shook his head, still smiling in the shifting light of the street lamps as they passed.

"No, that's not what they want to hear. I tell 'em that we'll take care of it — *which we will, I promise you that.* That's what they really want to know: that they're not in Poland. That they live in a place where the law of the jungle has been abolished. They want us to take care of it, an' so we will. *That's* the art of politics, Tom. Tell 'em only as much truth as they want to hear."

The City was not a pleasant place just then. It seemed like an aquarium world, a place of unsuspected depths and terrors, seen always in the half-light from under the elevated lines. Not nearly as rich as it would be after the war. Still grimy, and hard starved by the Depression even though it was recovering, the pace picking up, the crowds visibly growing on the trains to work in the morning. *Like a man who's nearly died, back up and walking around . . .*

And yet there was such a step to it. He liked nothing better, in the few hours he had to himself, than to sail out into it. Riding high on the double-decker buses, or swinging up on the trolleys, or simply walking off in almost any direction, to see what he could find. The City seeming to expand infinitely around him, as if some Hollywood set crew was building more and more of it every day. Moving through whole neighborhoods he'd never seen before and never would again.

Worlds within worlds, gears within gears, spinning on forever.

It fired him in his work. Made it feel all the more wrong to him that anyone should have to slave and bend the knee in such a place. Charlie smiled at his chasing windmills, but he was sure that they were gaining.

By the end of October he could feel the quickening. The crowds in the churches bigger and louder than ever. The men making fires from old wooden cartons in the trash cans, faces glowing in the dark. Everybody aware that their agitations had to come to a head. Everybody ready for something to happen. Peter Panto telling them all, his eyes shining: *"They are nothing to us, if we are together."*

* * *

He was with Panto when he almost walked into it down on President Street. He and Protter, one of the lefty lawyers they had volunteering for them, had spotted him out alone and insisted on going with him, or who knew what would have happened.

They turned the corner, and right there was Emil Camarda, with Albert Anastasia and six of his boys. All of a sudden they were very close, cutting off any chance of retreat, hands jammed into the pockets of their fine coats. He could smell their sour, acid breath, they were so near, could feel their visceral menace, their animal physicality, as he would never feel anything else, until that bull Slim brought into the practice ring in Mexico. Thinking, *My God, they're going to try to kill us right here ...*

"You wanted to speak to me," Panto told their boss, his voice hard and un-flustered.

Tom glanced at the goon closest to him, who was Anastasia himself. He looked short but solid as a lead safe, his muscled arms and chest bulging at his overcoat. Impeccably dressed, a white carnation in his buttonhole, his hands jammed into both his pockets, clutching God only knew what. His plump, dark face was closely shaved, a high wave of brilliantined hair pushing up his hat. Eyes unblinking and expressionless, fixing on Tom like a predatory bird's.

"That's right," Camarda said, blowing cigar smoke in their faces, staring out at them through slitted eyes encircled in flesh. But there was an uncertainty in his voice that even Tom could pick up. Something was wrong — something he hadn't counted on. He turned his gaze speculatively on each of them, still giving no indication to his *shlammers.*

"I'm not gonna say nothin' in front of your henchmen," Panto told him coolly. Camarda made a small gesture then, and Anastasia's eyes blinked, the raptor's stare broken. He nodded, and on that signal he and the rest of the goons skulked away, like wild dogs cheated out of a carcass.

They went up to have coffee with Camarda in his office then, a long room in the old sugar company building. Where they could sit and see half the harbor, and the enormous grain elevators off Red Hook, and the Statue of Liberty, and act just like they were civilized human beings. Drinking the incredibly dark, bitter coffee the Italians drank in tiny little cups, Panto and Camarda dickering perfunctorily across the table. Tom and Protter listening for the slightest pressure on the old floorboards outside, their eyes darting continually between Panto and the door.

"I like you, Pete," Camarda told him, the pig eyes trying to open as widely and sincerely as they could. "I think you're a very fine fellow. A lotta people think you're a very fine fellow; you got guts to come down here an' talk to me like this."

"You like me? That's nice."

Panto smiling that sweet, kindly smile that made him look like a kid.

"Don't be a wise guy, be smart." Camarda frowned. "What I wanna know is what you want, smart guy. You wanna be a hiring boss? A local president? It's all yours."

"It's not what I want. It's what the men out there want. *They* choose, with a real election."

"Then how d'ya keep control over anything?" Camarda said, sounding genuinely baffled.

"I don't want anybody to control it," Panto told him, rising now with that stately, Old World dignity of his and putting on his hat. "Not you, not me. I want to break it up."

"You know, some of the boys don't like some of the things you're doin'," Camarda told him, his face looking flushed and infuriated. "Maybe it's better you don't do them no more. You know what I'm sayin'?"

Panto nodded and smiled, that strange, kindly smile again. They started to go, Tom the last one out, when Emil Camarda buttonholed him with his eyes.

"You're Charlie O'Kane's brother, ain't you?" he asked, grunting when Tom nodded his head, as if he had satisfied himself about something. "Tell your brother I hope he wins."

"No, you don't," Tom told him, mustering every last bit of courage within him.

Then they were back out on the street, walking as fast as they could away from the water. Pete's hand shaking a little as he pulled out a cigarette, the first sign of fear Tom had ever witnessed in the man.

"Jesus, what the hell're you thinkin', goin' out to meet with a man like that alone?" Protter said as they hurried away.

"He invited me, man-to-man. I didn't think he'd do nothin' in daylight," Panto admitted, then gave a short, rueful laugh. "Guess I was wrong."

"It's no joke. He could've killed you right there," Tom said soberly. "That's what he had in mind."

"I know," Panto said, blowing out a long train of smoke as they walked on. "I thought I had a guarantee, that's all."

"From who?"

"Don't worry," he told them, though the smile turned grim on his face. "I'll never trust the bastard again."

"The scripture instructs us to be gentle as doves and as wise as serpents," Father Carey said when Tom told him about it, out early one morning while they were waiting for the shape-up, warming their hands around an open trash fire. "But he hasn't got that in him. It's a powerful disadvantage when all you have to work with are snakes."

They were near the far end of the waterfront, by Buttermilk Channel, where the wind wiped away even the steady hum of the City behind them. The only noise the jangling of the lines and the water slapping against the hulls in the dark.

He'd grown to like the little priest with the impish, Bing Crosby smile. Wearing an old gray sweater everywhere and walking with his head down. Telling Tom of his vocation in the idle moments.

"It wasn't any great light from above. I was playing ball uptown, across from the Palisades, and I looked over at those tremendous rocks, and the sand beneath them. I'd learned a little about geology in school, and I knew that with time, all those high rocks would be ground down into sand, too, and in that moment I understood it — the whole long skein of time, and how little we mean in it. And I thought, I'll be gone, too, and if I'm only going to live a little time, I'd better make the most of it."

Running his labor school out of the basement of Saint Xavier's, up on Sixteenth Street in Manhattan. Talking about raising up a whole generation of union men, like his father had before him, trying to organize the streetcar conductors. But both of them knowing it all came down to one man on the docks.

"It's blasphemy to say it, but sometimes I think this must be what it felt like when He walked among us."

"And you know how *that* worked out," Tom told the priest, summoning his last ounce of atheism, though he knew exactly how he felt.

"But that's just it. I don't know how we'd replace him. We're not the apostles here, and I don't know that the men are ready. That's why you can't ever let him go anywhere alone again."

"We won't, Father," Tom promised, and then the dawn was upon them, and they watched as the men began to emerge one by one along the gray desolation of the docks, in their shabby, tied pants and boots and patched checker jackets, waiting to see if they might be allowed to work on that day. Dwarfed by every other thing around them—the great, rusting black ships, and the grain and sugar elevators, the mountains of sand and gravel, the apartment houses, and farther off the skyscrapers, and the statue in the harbor.

"Look at them there," Father Carey said softly. "They're human beings—men—and yet they're the only element that keeps it all going. It's a machine, don't you see?"

"Come again?"

"How everything works down here," he told him. "We like to think it's the way of the world, but in fact it's something manmade—an enormous, terrible machine. Everything about how these men live is part of the machine—the way the hiring is organized, the loan-sharking, the numbers games. A perfect, capitalist machine, all of it designed to squeeze every last drop of blood and sweat from these men, and give it over to the politicians, and the crooked union bosses, and the owners."

"Talk like that could get you in trouble, Father," Tom said, grinning.

"Ah, but it's a good thing, for if it's just a machine—just a manmade thing—then men can change it. Just as all those big ships, and those elevators, and those great buildings are nothing without men to give them meaning. It's simple enough. All we must do is get it across to them that they are part of the Body of Christ, and that their work is a sacred vocation, and it must be honored."

"Is that all, Father?"

"And that's your sermon for today," Father Carey said, grinning back at Tom—half daft with their cause, the way they all were in those days, all of them on the docks. "But whatever you do, don't let anything happen to Panto!"

They redoubled their efforts to have men with him wherever he went after that. Tom trying to make it his business to know where he was every minute he was down on the docks. Yet just days later he was with him and his fiancée in his boardinghouse room on North Elliott Place when Panto told him he'd arranged another meeting, one that could change everything.

"You can't trust them! You can't trust anyone!" Tom implored him. "Why can't you see that?"

"The men can't fill their bellies with my words," was all he said in response, confidentially, his voice dropping as if it were a secret. "The Camardas cut off their work, soon they have to give in. Then—*pfft!*—we got nothing. All the air goes out. It's like what that McCormack said—if they don't like it, they can eat cobblestones."

"McCormack? When the hell were you talkin' to him? Listen, just wait until after Charlie's elected—"

Panto cut him off. "Your brother's right—we have to choose what victory we can. That's why I'm going. Don't worry, I'll only meet with them if I get the guarantee I want."

"That's what you said the last time—"

"Don't worry. This is different." Speaking now to Alice, his beautiful and dark-eyed girl, listening with a look of despair on her face. "I only go if I trust it. But it's nothing to take some risk for the men. They take their risks for me every day."

"Don't do this," Tom told him. "They will kill you, sure as we're standin' here. You saw them—"

Circling them in the street like a pack of dogs. Their animal desire to hurt someone, smash something almost tangible. If they can't crush you, they will follow. If they can't follow, they will crush you . . .

"Don't worry," Panto said.

But three days after that, when he was getting ready for his date with Alice, the candy store down on the corner sent word up to his rooming house that he had a phone call. He bounded downstairs, meeting her on the stoop, and she said that he seemed relieved, even happy, "as if a rock had been lifted from his chest." He was dressed in his good suit, the one he always wore for her, and he told her to call the police if he wasn't back by ten the next morning.

A car came for him, "a long car," she'd said, a shiny new sedan, with three men already inside it — that was all she saw — and he put on his fedora and climbed inside. And then he was gone.

9

Mexico City, 1953

Charlie sat slumped between them, his great head lolling on his chest, eyes flickering open, then closing again as the taxi took them back to the Prince. They rode in silence, Tom noticing out the window the number of campesino women now asleep in the doorways of some of the nice new buildings, or on the steps of the old churches, their babies still grasped to their chests. Clumps of wet newspaper and cornhusks choked the gutters, though he didn't remember it raining. The air had turned much colder, as if they had switched from one season to another, going from day to night.

At the Prince the doorman, a huge Indian in a long military coat had to help them get Charlie out. Taking him in the elevator and then up a short, rickety staircase to the tiny fake-adobe penthouse. Holding his brother so gently around the chest as he helped him in and out of the elevator, then carrying him up the stairs almost single-handedly, like an exhausted child after a long drive, before they laid him down on the bed in that beige apartment. His aged face sagging, the chain of valor drooping to one side as he began to snore. The big Indian waiting at the door to make sure he was all right but adamantly refusing any tip.

"Don't worry, señor, the *embajador* has been through this before," he told them gravely. "He is always fine in the morning."

"How much has he been through it?" Tom asked. But the doorman just waved him away, bowing back toward the roof stairs.

"He will be fine!"

"They really do love him, you know," Slim said when she came back out to join him in El Ranchito. Moving across the rooftop in the strapless Balenciaga with her effortless, model's grace.

"Not just the Big Crowd — everybody."

"He always had the common touch," Tom said, only half sarcastically.

"You should've seen it when we'd drive into some dusty little town, out in the middle of nowhere. Charlie would sit up front with the chauffeur, waving to everybody like he was riding up Fifth Avenue on Saint Patty's Day. And they would bring out a brass band and throw confetti. Real confetti — as if they'd been saving it up for years."

"That's nice."

She walked over to the edge of the deserted roof garden, near where he sat, in the deck chair Charlie had been sleeping in that afternoon. The whiskey and water he'd made for himself downstairs resting on the same arm where his brother's book on Daniel Boone had been. Listening to the city below, the bursts of mariachi music that swelled up, then cut off abruptly as someone opened and closed the doors of a tourist joint. The sounds and smells different from New York, more like those he remembered from his rural childhood. He could hear the stirrings of chickens and the cooings of doves, disturbed in their rooftop hutches. The pungent odor of poinsettias, the crowing of some addled cock floating up to him.

"We went everywhere, all over the country. It was fun, too — for a while. Sometimes I think we might've made it if we could've just kept moving."

She lit another cigarette, tipping the ashes out into the city, and held her arms around herself against the growing cold.

"If it was too far to drive we took this little two-motor plane. *That* scared the hell out of me. It felt like flying on a lawn mower with wings. But you should have seen how diligent he was about it. Rushing into his study when we got back to write a full report to the State Department. Notes on the freshwater shortages in the Yucatán or the sewage system in Acapulco. The disparity in agrarian incomes in Sonora! All carefully printed out and bound in little blue notebooks. God knows where they ended up."

"Why didn't you tell me it was this bad?"

"How could I? How could I possibly write that to you? You needed to see it for yourself."

"I know. I wouldn't have believed it. Does he always drink like that?"

"No, not usually. I'll give him that. He's more nervous with you around, I think."

"Me? Why is that?" Tom frowned.

"I don't know, exactly. He doesn't quite trust you, I think —"

"But why —"

"— but then I don't think he quite trusts anybody anymore," she said, looking back at him, her hair down now and floating in the light breeze that came with the night, partly hiding her face. *The face of a thousand golden mornings, moving on to the West. Of endless cattle land, and empires of wheat, and orchards, and* Mayflower *ancestors. The face of old money.* Or at least as they had always dreamed it.

"Or maybe it's more that he's ... *ashamed,* I guess. He thinks he let you down — thinks he let everybody down. The whole damned City of New York."

"That's a lot of people to let down."

"You wouldn't know this, Tom, but there's nothing worse than being disappointed in yourself."

"Don't be so sure."

He got up and went to talk to her by the parapet wall, and she watched him coming coolly, the strands of blond hair still floating over her cheek.

"Doesn't he know I just want to help him? The reason I'm down here is to see him vindicated — to drag the whole truth out of him whether he knows it or not."

"That's what's so sweet about you, Tom. You always think there's a whole truth somewhere, just dying to be dragged out into the light."

"This isn't philosophy, Slim. It's my brother's life," he snapped at her. "They made him the fall guy. Other men, crooked men, who steal and cheat and kill as easily as they eat breakfast in the morning and say their prayers at night. They stuck him with their dirty crimes, and it's *they* who need to be pulled out into the light, once and for all."

"And how likely do you think that is, Tom?" she asked, her face slightly flushed from the wine, or the rising heat in her words, he wasn't sure. "How likely do you think it is that the men who got away with this are going to be caught out *now?*"

"These days, empires rise and fall on the testimony of one man. I've seen it happen, Slim."

"And brave Tommy O'Kane, counsel for the dispossessed, is going to bring them all down! Just a couple of speeches like that one, a couple of withering cross-examinations in a courtroom, and they'll surrender. Is that what you're going to do, Tom? Bring them all down? The men who run the greatest city in the world? Or are you just going to get *him* all tangled up again, get him living in another dream?"

"I have to do something, Slim," he said, almost pleading with her now, just inches from her face as she leaned over the roof parapet, scornfully flicking away the butt of her cigarette. "I can't just let it go. He's my brother. I can't just let him go on like I saw him tonight."

He was very close to her now, in the near darkness, their only light a half-moon and a torch in a cage flickering on the other side of El Ranchito. Over the roof, though, half the City was spread out before them, a giddying stretch of construction cranes, and darkened parks, and pretty white churches, with rows of little blue, and red, and yellow and white lights strung between them. It was not the overwhelming, bonfire illumination of Manhattan at night but fine and delicate as Christmas tree lights.

He looked back at her face, twisted in unhappiness.

"Jesus, how do you think it was for me, Tommy? You didn't want to know anything about it, but this is what it's like every night, with Mrs. Throckmorton Updike, and Dunphy the waiter, and all the goddamned *little* people! And you blame me for leaving him!"

"I don't blame you for anything, Slim. I blame myself for not being stronger—"

"Christ, *stop* it, Tom! Stop taking all the blame. You and your causes. First the Jews, then the Puerto Ricans, then the Negroes—and now Charlie O'Kane! You didn't do anything wrong. All you did was for once in your life reach out for something you really wanted."

"Didn't *they?* Isn't that the justification they all use?" he sputtered. "All the gangsters, and the businessmen, and the Mr. Bigs? They reached for something they wanted—"

"But here's the difference, Tom. You reached out for something that wanted you back."

He took her face in both his hands and kissed her then. He kissed her for a long time, just as he had been longing to do since the moment he got off the plane. Then she kissed him back and he stroked her cheeks with the back of his fingers. She put her arms around his neck the way she had on the dance floor, and he kissed her again, his mouth lingering on hers, his hands on her hips. They stood there just holding each other for a minute, then another and another. Her head bowed against his chest, her slender body shivering a little in his arms.

"Goddamn, how did I ever spend three years away from you, Tom?" she asked. "Goddamn, but I missed you."

"You did because you're my brother's wife," he said, pulling himself away, although he felt the loss of her body against him as a bottomless ache. Stalking back toward the chairs, furious at himself.

"We did because it's not right, that's why."

"How can you say that?" she asked from the edge of the roof, her eyes moist now, her face looking grave and hurt and alluring as ever. "How can you say that after—"

"It's a *betrayal*, is what it is."

"I would have left him anyway, Tom. I *am* leaving him, no matter what. Stop fooling yourself about that, the way you're doing about everything else now. Stop it before you end up like him—"

"What's that supposed to mean?"

"You know what it's supposed to mean. You wrote me you were engaged, Tom. And now you stand there and talk to me about betrayal."

She sighed and walked over toward him, pulling another cigarette out of her purse where she'd left it on the table. He slumped back into the deck chair.

"She's a wonderful girl, Ellie," he said numbly. "She doesn't deserve this. She doesn't deserve me."

"There you go again. The martyr."

She came over and sat on the arm of the chair—the chair where his brother had been sitting, just that afternoon, reading a book. She ran a hand through his hair, and he let her. Her hand moved down, tenderly, along the side of his face, and he wished she would do it forever.

"You should've seen him, Slim," he said quietly. "You should have seen what he was like."

"You mean, before me?"

"I mean back when I first knew him. When I was fresh off the boat, and he was still on the magistrate's court in Brooklyn. Oh, but Jesus, you shoulda seen the man he was then."

It had been even more impressive than Charlie in the hatchway — sitting up over the courtroom in his black judge's robe. A gavel in his hand, a look on his face that was serious but not unamused. Calmly directing everything that went on: the fulminations of the attorneys; the whole rummaging buzz and disorder of the worn little court, continually filling up and emptying with the defendants' families, speaking in all manner of tongues to one another, bringing entire, pungent meals along to get through the long day . . .

"And he sitting up there like God His Own Self," Tom remembered. "Presiding over it all, bringing order out of the chaos. He really did look out for those people."

"I don't doubt it."

"The court used to be full of 'fixers,' you know. That's what they called themselves, but they never fixed a traffic ticket. They were just a bunch of grifters who used their connections with the clubhouse to hang around and buttonhole these poor, ignorant people. Tell 'em they could get to the judge, get the case continued till a more lenient man was on the bench. These people didn't know any better. They'd pocket five, ten dollars from the defendant's gray-haired old mother.

"Charlie wouldn't stand for that. He tossed them out like Jesus heavin' the moneychangers outta the temple. He had 'em thrown in jail for contempt, till they stopped coming around. Oh, how the clubhouse boys howled, but Charlie didn't care!

"I remember, he wouldn't put a picket in jail for love or money — not even when they struck the *Brooklyn Eagle*. The paper was *payin'* the cops to haul 'em in, you see, figurin' at twenty-five dollars a head for bail they could break the union. That's how things used to work all the time.

"But Charlie wouldn't do it. When each striker was brought up, he'd ask him, 'D'ye have a stick of furniture at home?' An' when they answered yes, he brought the gavel down — *bang!* 'Bail secured on the basis of household furnishings!' No other politician in the borough would stand up against the *Eagle*, but Charlie didn't care. This was a man. Oh, but you shoulda seen him, Slim!"

"I saw enough."

She leaned back on the arm of the chair, still running a hand absently through his hair. A real sadness in her voice, he thought.

"I know what he was like; you don't have to tell me," she said. "Did I ever tell you about the night we met?"

"He did. But not you."

"It was at this gala at Grand Central, some benefit or another. I was coming off my rotten first marriage — my *first* rotten marriage — and I needed to make some money, and a friend got me back into modeling. They cleared out the whole station for it, and set up spotlights. I walked out across the floor on a pathway of light, wearing this white Dior gown. And all the most beautiful and powerful people in the City — some of the most beautiful and powerful people in the world — were up on the balcony over us, watching and applauding."

He could picture the scene, as he had after Charlie's telling, years before. A single spotlight following her along the floor of the great station. The stars twinkling in the zodiac painted along the blue, domed ceiling. The light following her across the vast room, drawing every eye.

"Afterward, they invited some of us to come up to a private room. Some secret apartment I never even knew existed there, an old robber baron's hidden lair. It was decorated like a medieval castle hall, or someone's idea of one. The lights were very low, and I remember I went in and said out loud to my friend, 'It looks like a speakeasy in here!'

"And then I hear this deep, beautiful voice just behind me.

'Young lady,' it said, 'you are both too young and too well bred to know what a speakeasy was like!' And I turned around and there he was: the mayor of New York."

"And did you love him, Slim? Did you ever love him?"

"Sure I did. I remember when he took me to see *South Pacific,* and Ezio Pinza sang 'Some Enchanted Evening.' Charlie sang it to me on the way home. Believe me, Ezio Pinza had nothing on Charlie. He was the real item. I thought, this is the first true man I've ever known, and I don't care how much older he is, I love him, and anything's possible."

"I know he thought the same."

"But here we are, in El Ranchito."

She leaned down and kissed him then. He kissed her back and pulled her to him. All of it coming back to him in a muddle, the taste of her, the feel of her lips, and her waist in his hands. They stayed there for a long time, lying out in

the deck chair, necking and holding each other. Slim lying over him, uncon-
cerned about her fine red gown, stretching her long legs down over his. He
held her, and kissed her, and moved his hands over her until he had no sense
of anything else, no sense anymore of where he was, or what he was doing, or
how anyone else might be concerned.

"You have to take it easy at this elevation—it goes to your head," she whispered to him, her breath warm on his face.

"Slim—"

"Yes?"

"Slim, don't you see, we have to help him? It's not just him, either. It's for
everything else that's at stake here."

She stood up abruptly, smoothing her gown, looking down at him with an
expression of anger and regret.

"I'm in love with you, Tom," she said, before she walked away across the
roof. "It doesn't matter to me what I was to him. I don't give a damn about
your marriage, or mine. What I care about is us. But I'm not a bad person. If
you just want to help him, I'll do whatever you want. Just don't tell me I have
to save the goddamned world."

"Slim—"

He watched her go but didn't try to stop her. Instead he sat out where he
was on the roof, listening to the distant sounds of the traffic and the stray tunes
of the mariachi bands somewhere off in the distance, and thought about his
brother in a fancy hotel ballroom.

New York City, 1953

Ellie had been there from the start, helping him to work through all the files of
the grand jury presentations and the special investigator's findings. She was
one of the new assistant DAs, in the same class as his. One of only a handful of
women lawyers in the office, and the only one who didn't look as though she

had come direct from the Seven Sisters. She had olive skin, hair and eyes dark as a plum, and she wore bright red or black dresses that seemed a little too sharp, popped a little too much for anything like a courtroom.

She didn't appear to care, continually adding some little adornment—a silver pendant, a bracelet, long earrings—that made her stand out all the more. One of her hips was slightly higher than the other, just enough to put a sway in her walk that men couldn't help but notice. She didn't possess the sharp-chinned hauteur of the other women ADAs, padding along Mr. Hogan's deep-pile carpeting with their designer skirt sets and their daddies' money. What she did have was a pair of laughing eyes, and full breasts, and that sway in her walk, an easy sensuality that had every man in the office looking after her.

Three months into the job, they had been pawing through the files for almost ten hours straight when Tom finally called a break. Looking at her face, he knew she was ready and willing to continue, but he made her stop as much for his own weariness as for hers.

"Don't you know? We have to work twice as hard," she said later, taunting him, the small, roguish smile that made him love her playing around the ends of her lips. "Don't you ever notice the hours the other women put in? Or the colored lawyers? We're still here when everyone else has gone. But then of course you don't notice much. You're a man."

He took her out to the Schrafft's on Maiden Lane. At lunch the place was packed with the secretaries and the stenos from the courthouses around Foley Square, but now, an hour before closing, it was all but deserted. A teenage girl came staggering by under a wide tray, offering them an array of pickles and relishes and a basket of small, warmed walnut muffins. Tom picked one up and held it contemplatively in his hands.

"Don't worry, it won't bite," Ellie said, laughing, and drawing out a cigarette. "I don't suppose you get in here much, do you?"

"Well, it is sort of a ladies' tearoom," he ventured.

"Sure. That's why I love it. I like to come here after work sometimes, and watch the old dears drinking gin from their teacups at the counter," she said, blowing the smoke out through her nose, the little pirate's grin still playing about her mouth. "Sometimes I drink it with them. Though tonight, I think I'll have a manhattan."

"We still have work to do, y'know," he warned.

"Oh, don't worry. I have some speed in my desk back at the office," she said, and smiled again when he looked startled for a moment. He bit into the little walnut muffin, which was delicious, and studied the menu for a moment to hide his embarrassment.

"So what'll it be? Cup of coffee and a chicken salad sandwich?" he asked, trying to rally, and to his relief she burst into a genuine, full-throated laugh.

"My God, if I never smell those two things again it will be too soon!" she said, referring to Mr. Hogan's invariable lunchtime order from Schrafft's, imitated ad nauseam around the office.

A gaunt and ancient woman, dressed in a black skirt and blouse with a spotless white apron and cap, came over to take their order. Ellie greeted her by name.

"Hello there, Katie. They've got you on the lobster shift, too? How're the feet holding up?"

"They're murderin' me," the waitress said in a brogue thicker than anything Tom had heard back in County Mayo, much less the States. "If I lose the fight, I want you to indict 'em for homicide, dearie. This here a new boyfriend, or just some informer?"

"We like to call them witnesses, Katie."

"If it helps your conscience, dear. So he's a love interest, then?"

"I'm not sure. What do you think, Katie? Does he have husband potential, do you think?"

She looked him over dourly.

"Skinny as a hoe pole. And Irish as Paddy's pig's lawyer. Careful, y'know, they drink."

"Tom O'Kane," he said, extending a hand to Katie, who continued to scrutinize him carefully through glasses that looked as if they had originally been cut for a telescope. "Late of Bohola. And sober as a judge, I swear it. I work with Miss Abramowitz."

Katie tisked. "Worse an' worse," she said, while Ellie beamed across the booth at him. "Y'll not have a bit a fun with this one."

Ellie ordered a turkey club with her manhattan, and he felt obliged now to have a coffee with his hamburger. Watching Katie shuffle off, stockings thickly bunched over blue swaths of varicose veins, he saw that she was by no means the oldest waitress in the establishment.

"My God, it looks like the Ancient Order of Hibernians' Ladies' Auxiliary Retirement Home in here."

"I should've warned you. It's best not to order something hot," she said. "But they do have some stories."

"So you really do drink gin with them at the counter."

"Sometimes. It's fun. And they know everything that goes on, feds to the magistrate's court."

"Is that what you talk about, too, when the rest of us are gone? The ladies of the office, I mean, and Franklin and Lawrence?"

"No," she said, stubbing out her cigarette, her large, violet eyes staring frankly at him. "Mostly we talk about you."

"Me?" he said, genuinely surprised, though when he heard it he found that he wanted to laugh for some reason. "What could there possibly be to talk about concernin' me?"

"What you're doing here. What you must've had on Hogan to get hired." Her smile teasing around the edges of her mouth again.

"All I'm here for is what you see me doing," he told her, the weight of it descending on him again. "Just trying to make this case."

"Because you think it will clear your brother's name."

"It will," he said, his eyes challenging her across the table. She looked right back, drawing out another cigarette and lighting it.

"What if it doesn't?"

"It will. You'll see. But I'll tell you the same thing I told Mr. Hogan. I won't bend a hair of the truth to do it. I won't have to," he said just as confidently.

Thinking, even as he did, of that note tucked inside the autopsy report. The one that had slid out of the file so easily, unnoticed over all these years, just like the key that Reles had to his own room. Clearly written in the hand of Dr. Robillard, the medical examiner: *Withhold information by order of DA.*

The DA—meaning Charlie. This one clue he had never shown to anyone, not even Hogan. *And now not her.* Beginning each relationship with a lie. *Unless it wasn't a lie. Unless he could prove there was a perfectly good explanation for it, which there surely was. Though the question remained: Why would Charlie order the medical examiner not to release an autopsy report to the press?*

"Really?" Ellie said, looking unimpressed. "Because I wouldn't trust you within ten feet of this case."

"You don't think he's innocent?"

"I think *you* think he's innocent." She paused, as if stopping herself from saying something more.

"I have a sister," she said instead. "And I know that if she'd done something—anything—I'd destroy every piece of evidence I could get my hands on. Even if it meant going to jail myself."

"She must be a wonderful sister."

"She is."

"You know she would never do anything that bad. She would never do anything truly bad at all. You know that as surely as you know anything in the world."

"I do."

"Well, so do I."

They looked at each other for a long moment, the smoke from her cigarette dangling in the air.

"I know Charlie's faults," he said at last. "I know what he's like. He trusts people too much, and he lets things slide. He always will, and he always has. He's sloppy around the details, and sometimes he doesn't like to look a thing in the face. But I know he would never do anything like . . . like *this.*"

Katie brought them their meals, all business this time, and hustled off as soon as the food was on the table, picking up on the charged silence between them.

"Well," Ellie said, and smiled again. "That's how I feel about my sister."

He smiled back at her. "I know you do."

"There's one more thing I'd like to ask you."

"Fire away."

"Did you really run guns to the Haganah?"

She grinned as she asked it, and he had to laugh again.

"I plead the Fifth, Counselor. But let me say that I do have knowledge of certain suspicious containers that made their way from the Chelsea docks to Haifa."

"I can't wait to introduce you to my parents. They'll adore you."

"Am I going to meet your parents, then?" he said, and was pleased to see that she blushed faintly. "I'm sure they're as fine as your sister."

"They are. They're the best people I know."

"They live in the City?"

"Ever since they came over as kids. Down on Orchard Street, where I was born, too. They're up in East Tremont now — or at least they will be until Robert bloody Moses gets to tearing down their block."

"Ah, the great man."

Her face turned serious, and angry — an anger he liked, too.

"What he's doing up there is obscene."

"I know it. But good luck stopping him. I know I tried to often enough, back when Charlie was mayor."

"But *how?* How can a whole neighborhood be wiped out for a highway? On the say-so of one man?"

"But you're fighting it?"

"My mom is. I help when I have time. Which isn't often."

"What's Mr. Hogan got you on? I mean besides my brother?"

"Oh, the Jelke case, mostly," she said, looking down to toy with her drink.

"The margarine playboy?"

"Go ahead and laugh. He thought it needed a woman's touch."

"And does it?"

She picked up her cigarette, then put it down, waving the smoke away impatiently.

"Mostly it's just sad. This poor little girl from the Lower East Side, trying to pretend she's part of café society. While he sells her to his rich friends at the Stork Club, just for some kicks."

"Jesus — excuse me — that does sound sad."

"Don't worry," she said, and chuckled. "It's not my Jesus. How about you?"

"The point-shaving stuff. Pretty sad, too. Buncha kids, first in their families ever to get to college, going in with gamblers to shave points off a basketball game for a few bucks. Throwin' away their lives for fifty bucks a game."

"Are they going to jail?" she asked somberly.

"Some of them, if we have anything to say about it." He sighed. "And they'll lose their scholarships, an' be expelled. All so we can uphold the integrity of basketball tournaments in Madison Square Garden."

"Does it make you wish you hadn't signed up?" she asked.

"Sometimes. That's what you get when you work for the state. Even when it's right, the law's like one of your Mr. Moses's steam shovels. It cuts through anything that gets in its way."

"What made you decide to stay?"

"It was Hogan himself."

"Me, too. I thought he was purest corn at first. With that great big plaque on his desk for the press: COURTESY IS THE GOLDEN KEY THAT OPENS EVERY DOOR. "

"Yes! But then he gave us all that talk—"

" 'Courtesy is an appreciation that this is a public office, and the public is entitled to be served,' " she recited by heart, as he knew probably every assistant DA in the office could. " 'Not as a matter of grace or condescension, but because of a man's or woman's basic human worth. You have to know what a shattering experience it is to come into this office, either as a victim of a crime or a defendant.' "

"I liked it when I heard it, and the more I thought about it, the more I liked it," he said quietly. "He really does run this office for the people. And he runs it better than my brother ever did in Brooklyn."

They were both quiet again then, looking at each other—the silence no longer awkward but anticipatory.

"So . . ." she said slowly, that smile working its way out around her mouth. "I think I'm beginning to understand why you ran guns to Israel."

"Do you? I'm still not sure," he said, smiling himself. "I guess I just got tired of all the big men, and the big countries, deciding for everyone, and nobody else havin' a fighting chance. Especially after I met some of the people from the camps Charlie got into the country, when he was at the War Refugee Board. For people to go through that, an' still not have a home—"

He remembered their bodies like wraiths, all the ones Charlie had first gathered in Italy and seen to it they were brought over. Forced to rush them right from the piers over to Hoboken, then up to Oswego, by order of the State Department. Watching them go, in the Red Cross overcoats, and the suits and dresses that hung off them like old clothes off a scarecrow. Reduced to this, looking as sallow and underfed as Bowery bums, and he had expressed his shock to Charlie when he looked over their papers.

"And all of them shopkeepers and housewives back in Vienna and Prague.

Even musicians and artists. Reduced to bums," he'd said — adding hastily, *"Not that it would've mattered if they were* bums."

"But that's what was done to them. That reduction of all they were, and all they'd worked their whole lives to be," Charlie had said softly. "And we fought to save them from it, which is why we owe them now."

"I'm beginning to see why you think so much of him," Ellie said, serious now.

"Right from the start, when I came off the boat not knowin' what the hell I was talkin' about, he opened my eyes. Protected me whenever he could," he said earnestly. "He showed me how to get something done in the world, when I was all talk. If he's in a little trouble now, it's the least I can do to help him."

She leaned over the table and kissed him. Just a quick peck, on one cheek. The brush of her lips, and the mixed smell of the manhattan, cigarette smoke, and the trace of her perfume suddenly against his face.

"What was that for?" He tried to laugh, embarrassed and thrilled and surprised at the same time.

"For explaining your brother to me. For talking to me like I'm a fellow adult instead of a little girl. For being what you are, Tom."

Katie came up on them as quietly as a Fifth Avenue bus wheezing into a stop.

"Ah, Jesus, a sober prosecutor! Yours'll be a fightin' household," she said, leaving the check. "You won't have a moment's peace!"

"Katie, we have all the peace we need sooner or later," she said, grinning at Tom as she snatched the check away from. "My treat. Just as it has been all evening. Race you back to the office."

They put in another two hours just for form's sake, and because it needed to be done, and out of fealty to Mr. Frank Hogan, gone home at a normal hour for once but with his office door still yawning accusingly open at them. When they had gotten through the thirtieth or thirty-first box of files on the day, he took it out of her hands, put it to the side, and kissed her full on the mouth, putting his hands along the side of her face and gently pulling her to him. She kissed him back, the two of them standing there in his office together for a long time, her head resting against his chest.

They took a taxi up to the quietest bar he knew, in the West Village, one where there was no television or jukebox, or — even rarer in the Village — no drunken writer or artist pontificating. They ordered beers, and talked for hours, telling each other about themselves, and their families, and everything they wanted, and everything they intended to do in this life. The place wasn't very far from where she lived, in a basement apartment on Charles Street, and he walked her home and was about to try for another long kiss beneath her stoop when she unlocked her door and took his hand.

"Ellie —"

"Like I said, I'm a grown woman," she told him, looking him in the eyes. "I'm not drunk, and I'm old enough to know what I'm doing."

He hesitated for a moment more, until she kissed him again.

"At this rate, you never would've gotten those guns to Haifa."

She pulled him inside, into her kitchen. They kissed again there, for a long time, as she ran her hands all over the muscles of his back and shoulders. Then she undid the clasp on her skirt and pulled the zipper down, letting it pool around her feet. He could see the lace of her slip, blue in what moonlight filtered down to them, and then she was leaning down to slip off her shoes as well, pulling him back from the windows.

"Let's spare the neighbors a performance of *Wonderful Town*," she said, grinning again, and he thought then that it was a grin he would like to see every day.

They kissed more, moving back through the tiny living room and into her bedroom as he took over undressing her, delighted with each new part of her he uncovered, her full breasts and her bottom, the hips he had watched swing through the office for so many days, the lovely whiteness of her skin. She pulled him into bed, on top of her, and she grinned then, too, shocking him a little when she whispered, "I've been thinking about this." And then later, when he rejoined her in the blissful confusion of a strange bed, and a strange apartment, and the gloss of a few drinks, she whispered to him, "Such a good man." To which he could only think, *Another lie.*

11

Mexico City, 1953

Tom didn't realize he had nodded off in the deck chair until he came awake in the last hour of the night. He thought for some reason that he must be back on the docks in the early morning, but the air was full of the scent of chilis and peppermint and poinsettia, and not the diesel fuel and brine and coal smoke that laid so heavy on the tongue.

He stretched himself, stiff in the impression of the deck chair — then started when he saw his brother by the edge of the roof. He was standing in the same place where Slim had been, staring out at the city in the same way. To Tom's surprise, he looked none the worse for wear. His silver hair carefully combed back. Dressed much as he was when Tom had seen him the day before, in a light-blue, short-sleeve sports shirt and a pair of navy blue pants with no socks. *Another day at El Ranchito.*

"'Mother of pleasures and ocean of souls/ ... Fair flower of cities, the West's glory bold,'" Charlie recited before turning to face Tom.

"It's the coming place, now that Europe's blown itself up again. Give 'em another twenty, thirty years — maybe less! — and Mexico City will put New York to shame. This is the hemisphere of the future, and it's perfectly located, right smack-dab in the middle. There's no port, of course, but air is the thing now anyway. Besides, a port never brought anything but misery to a city."

"Well, at least we'll still be in the hemisphere of the future," Tom said, walking stiffly over to stand next to him.

"Can you imagine what those first Spanish conquistadors must've thought when they saw it?" he asked — and studying his face closely, Tom thought he didn't look bad at all, eyes a little bloodshot but genuinely engrossed with what he was saying — as always.

"You mean, before they set about slaughterin' the population?" he asked.

"The whole city, built on islands, an' floating gardens. Outside each house, a banner made entirely from the bright feathers of exotic birds, lighter than air. And a pot in which they would burn colored salts. Layers and layers of floating colors, everywhere. The Spanish must've thought they stumbled into heaven."

"Heaven, or a death camp. With bodies an' skull crammed into every available nook an' cranny," Tom said. "And the temples where they pulled the hearts out of the living sacrifice, and flayed the flesh of their victims to wear. I read the guidebook, Charlie."

His brother looked at him sharply, then burst out laughing.

"Well, what great city doesn't have its closets stuffed with skeletons, Tom? At least here there was a purpose to it. They honored the dead by wearing their skin an' eating their flesh. Sort of one big, daily communion, you might say, though it's difficult to imagine Francis Cardinal Spellman presidin' over it."

"Oh, I don't know, Charlie. Something tells me His Holiness would've fit in just fine. I could just see him struttin' about Saint Pat's in his human flesh suit every Easter."

For a few minutes they stood and watched the city together in silence.

"I'm sorry about last night, Tommy," Charlie said straight out, at last. "It was just all the talk of home, an' seeing her there . . . Anyway, I'm sorry. What would Dunphy the waiter say?"

"I'm pretty sure he'd say a man is only as good as his friends, Charlie—his friends and his family. He would say no man stands up alone in this world. And he'd be right."

"I know, Tommy, I know it, and I appreciate the sentiment, an' everything you're tryin' to do for me. I don't know that it's worthwhile, dredgin' everything up again, just so I can go back to live among all those damned peacocks."

> "Here lie I, . . . who, alive, all living men did hate:
> Pass by and curse thy fill, but pass and stay
> Not here thy gait."

"Ah, Charlie! Which means *what?*" Tom said, the feeling of disgust growing in him again. "Goin' out to dinner every night to play the stage Paddy? Tragic an' drunk, sittin' around El Ranchito framin' your newspaper clippings? *She's* not going to stand for it, Charlie."

"Don't tell me about my own wife!" his brother said, flaring up. "What the hell d'you know about it, anyway?"

"She won't, Charlie, an' you know it as well as I do," Tom pressed, each word wrenching in his gut, but knowing he had to say them. "She's still in love with you, Charlie. She married you. But not to be buried alive down here. You want to keep her, Charlie, you got to work with me."

His brother put his head down in his hands, rubbing his marvelous thick eyebrows, and for a moment Tom thought he might be crying. But when he looked up again he was dry-eyed, looking a little queasy but nodding his head in agreement. He stared around the makeshift roof garden again in the half-light.

"You know I love the light this time of the mornin'. It reminds me of the evenings back home, somehow, when Da used to take me out to shoot at the lapwings. Did he used to take you shooting, too, Tommy?"

"Yes, he did."

"Ah, that's good. That's when we talked, you know. I remember we were sitting out there with our shotguns across our laps, waiting for the lapwings to come in at dusk, so we could have our shot. And Da asked me, 'What would you like to be when you grow up?' And I—I couldn't have been more than twelve at the time—I told him, 'A schoolteacher,' just like he was."

"I did, too." Tom chuckled. "I told him the same."

"And I remember he told me, 'No, son. A schoolteacher is an estimable enough profession. Your mother was one, and I'm one, and proud to be so, but only because that's all there was for me. That's what it is to live in a captive nation. It's a petty life for a man.'"

Fighting all the time with the village priest, who schemed for twenty years to replace him with a favorite nephew. Peering up the road twice a day to check if the school inspectors were on their way down from Tuam.

He had married his assistant teacher, hitching up the horse and bringing her over to the an beann when it was her time. Bringing his children in one after the other to have the vindictive little priest place his spittle on their lips because it was sacred. His wife held back after Mass with the other new mothers to be "churched"—restored to the purity of the church after having sunk into the world of corruption and carnal sin by the act of giving birth. The life he had to live.

"He told me, 'Charlie, there's nothin' more we can do for you here, son— nothin' compared to the United States of America. There you can find out, at least, what you're capable of. You may be a man, and you may be a bum, but at least you'll find out.' He said, 'All the girls will stay here, and all the boys will go, that's the way of it.' An' then the lapwings come in, an' we had our shoot."

"There was a sadness in the man," Tom agreed.

His whole world a thatch-roofed house, with the mortar made from cow piles and sand and horsehair, mixed by the gobawn *and paid for in Guinness. The slate-roofed schoolhouse on the* baile na carraig, *the one bit of common ground so rocky that nothing at all could be grown on it.*

Winning over the people who became his people. Taking a churn at the butter whenever he walked into a cabin—but making sure never, ever to take a live coal from the fire when someone else did, lest the butter disappear. Listening and nodding as they told him where along the boreens *the ghosts were likely to confuse him, and how to find his way again by taking off his coat and wearing it inside out.*

Wishing them bol o dia an an obair—*God bless the work—as he walked through their fields, and surveying their tiny holdings for them, and having them in to read from the Dublin papers on a Saturday evening. More and more comfortable with it all as the years went by, and despising himself for his comfort.*

"Before that I'd never thought a goin' anyplace else. Oh, maybe runnin' away with the tinkers when they come through, but what boy hasn't? Spend your days hunting and fishing, an' filchin' ducks and chickens from the passin' towns. Your nights in a tent by the road, with your supper bubblin' in a pot over the bright fire, and a tale or two before you eat, an' what boy's life could be better'n that?"

The whole idea of going off anywhere as great and as far as America sticking like a knife in his brain. Poring over the books his father got for him outside of school. Nourishing him on them in semi-secrecy, he knew, beyond the purview of the priest or his mother—the unspoken pact between them. Volumes of Sterne and Swift, and Mark Twain, and Bret Harte, and O. Henry. Complemented by his own dime novels of the Great Plains, of buffalo and Indians, bought in Ballaghaderreen in the few hours they were ever let out from the diocesan high school.

"But you know, Mother was set on me becomin' a priest, an' there was no gettin' around it. How that woman could go up in the air, Tommy! So off to Saint Nathy's I went, an' then to the seminary, with all the neighbors, and the aunts an' the uncles sayin', 'It is a fine thing your father an' mother are doin' for you, takin' you out of the rain an' the mud.' As if we were all livin' like na- ked savages down in Zululand, an' not in County Mayo!"

Qualifying in his examinations for the Irish College in Salamanca. Think- ing if he couldn't go to America, at least he would go to Spain. The old route, from whence the hedge priests had gone and come for centuries. Smuggled out for the preservation of the true church, drilled by the rectors in Latin and Greek, and a little philosophy, then smuggled back in to be hidden and succored by the people, passed along the villages and the hedgerows.

His father always despising it. His father hating all the narrow ways and the narrow brains of the priests. Repulsed by the idea of a son of his hiding behind their black skirts. Or would have been — had he ever believed it would really come off. Had he not known his eldest son as well as he did.

"The evening before, they sent me off to say goodbye to Aunt Mary. And on me way back, I stood on the hill above Kattie Byrnes's, and looked away off at the little thatched huts of Lismirrane, an' the church in Bohola two miles on. From where I was I could see the river, an' the herons flying slow over the water, lookin' for fish, an' beyond that the little island by which the salmon spawned.

"And I looked at all that, an' I thought this time tomorrow evenin', when the trout in the river are snappin' for flies, I will not be here. And it was the same, for every place that I passed on the way home. At the stone steps up to the well, and I thought, when the village women come to draw their water, I will not be here. By the whin bushes where the hares' nest was, and I thought, I will never be here again to see the hares run, an' tease my fat old dog.

"And it was a curious thing, too, for it was an ancient place. I knew that, and yet in the ways of the young I could not fathom the idea of a place I had known — the *only* place I had known — without me.

"But it's good I was young, for the young can slough things off the way peo- ple with too many memories cannot. By the next morning, I was singin' while I dressed, an' I could not wait to be on my way. I remember our da squeezed me, an' pumped me on the back, an' held me before him sayin' he wanted to get one more good look at me, for he didn't know that I'd ever be back. An' Mother scoffed at him an' said, 'Of course he will, as soon as he's taken the orders, he'll be back here to celebrate Mass at Saint Tola's, with me sitting in the front pew, an' we'll just see what Father John O'Grady thinks about *that*.'

"She was giddy with pride, I remember. While the brothers an' sisters couldn't stop laughin' behind their hands, at the very thought of their brother Charlie off to become anything so all-bloody powerful as a *priest*."

The neighbors crowding in, each of them come with a little gift to see the young man off. Putting thirty shillings in his hands before the morning was done. A fortune, he knew, for the seventeen households of Lismirrane, his eyes glistening with their generosity. Then it was time for his father to hitch up the sidecar to old Molly again, and make for Kilfree, and the Sligo-Roscommon line, where the spalpeens would be walking in just a few weeks more, to lift the oats for the English in the back end.

"But then the old horse shied at something, and broke part of the harness. That made us late for the train, but everyone knew we was comin'. Half the town of Bohola came with me, an' Tom Wallace, the town porter, persuaded Pat Snee, who was the engineer, to wait ten minutes. And then when we still weren't there, he finally gave the signal an' rang the bell an' started on down the line. But then Tom Wallace spotted us an' started wavin' the red flag something frantic, so old Pat Snee reversed the engine and come chuggin' the fifty yards back down the track."

The train, he would come to understand later, one in name only — bright wooden boxes mounted on an iron undercarriage with a teakettle for an engine. One that would have been ground to splinters if e'er caught on the same track by a proper American train, a Super Chief or a Twentieth Century, without the engineer so much as noticing. But to him, the grand chariot of his dreams.

"The crowd started cheerin', an' then the passengers started cheerin', too, and the fife-an'-drum band from Dernacartha started up playin' the one song they knew, which was "The Girl I Left Behind Me" — an' quite the proper farewell song that was, too, for a novitiate! And then off I went, the conquistador on his way, quite as grand in his own way as Cortés or Pizarro."

The world opening up before him as he went, traveling on from train to boat, and train to boat, to train. Staring wide-eyed out the window at the vast golden fields of Normandy as they passed. The French farmers' lands larger than anything he'd ever heard of back in County Mayo, ploughed and planted with geometrical precision right down to the very last little copse, and the perfect haystacks. Realizing, as he watched them go by, that no matter what he had read, the world was still far bigger than he ever suspected. The fields going on and on into France, and endless as they were, nothing at all compared in turn to the limitless fields and plains of the United States.

"All of it waiting out there for me — an' growing in me, as I went, the bitter truth that I was to be locked up in a Spanish seminary for years an' years, then spat out again an Irish priest, fit for nothing but the little places from whence I had come.

"You know what Sterne writes about the 'seven wasted years'? How 'the accusing spirit, which flew up to Heaven's chancery with the oath, blushed as he gave it in, and the recording angel as he wrote it down dropped a tear upon the word and blotted it out forever.' That's how I felt, for I knew that I would not complete that vow."

The university like the town around it, elegant but old as time and holed with decay. The rooms and the chapels reeking of old candle wax, and dust, and yellowed paper. He stuck it out for two years, reading still more about Cortés, and Columbus, and dreaming about America. Mooning along the old Roman bridge, high above the river, cursing the vow he had made to God, and above all to his mother.

"The time it came to tell her, I met with apprehension. I put off writing night after night again," he told his brother, who simply nodded at the familiar story, one he had heard so many times before, and let him tell it yet again. "But finally I found the words, and I told her it wasn't in me. What I wanted to say was that I found all the dogma and the theology so much hooey, an' the robes and an' the rituals absurd, and I felt like the biggest hypocrite in the world to imagine takin' someone else's confession and offering him absolution. And that the idea of goin' my whole life without knowing a woman filled me with the most profound depression.

"But I didn't say a word of that to Mother, of course. I told her that I could not feel a calling, and so to proceed would be an affront to Christ, and an insult to the living church. I told her that what I wanted instead was to find a good wife, and raise a decent Christian family like the one I had been brought up in. She wrote back and asked me to pray for guidance. But finally she saw where my heart lay, God bless her, though I know it must've broken hers. By the next post Da sent me a money order with every pound he could raise and a note sayin', 'For God's sakes, boy, *go!*' and I knew exactly where he meant.

"I took that money, an' the thirty shillings the good people of Lismirrane gave me, for there wasn't excuse or time allotted for spending money in Salamanca, and I bought passage out of Cherbourg for the United States. Takin' the train back up into France, through all the green, glimmering fields of the early summer, an' then over in steerage to Ellis Island, where I was claimed by Tom Rouse, who was a dear love of your old aunt Annie—I don't know that you were old enough to know her. And Tom Rouse, who would do anything for her, even collect her spoiled priest of a nephew, took me over to Manhattan on the ferry, an' fed me lunch at a saloon under the Third Avenue el. Then he popped me into the subway an' took me up to a furnished room he'd found for me at a Hundred Sixty-First Street in the Bronx.

"So many amazements in one day, the elevated, an' the subway, an' a real-life saloon, an' then when we come up from underground that whole *rush* that the City has, you know? Steppin' out on the street, with the hurdy-gurdy man playin' "Alice Blue Gown," an' "The Sidewalks of New York," an' little colored girls dancing to it more gracefully than anything I'd ever seen, right there on the sidewalk. And all the horse cabs, an' the lorries, an' the cars, an' the sidewalks—my God! the sidewalks, filled with men an' women at all hours of the day and night, all of 'em walking, walking somewhere. Half running, to tell the truth—nobody ever seemed to walk anywhere in America, not even then. An' givin' a tip of their cap, an' shovelin' a coin to the newsie, and readin' and eatin' and talkin' as they walked, shakin' hands and askin' each other 'How's business?' without a word about havin' to ask the help of this saint or that god, or any concern for the crops, or the weather, or the graces of heaven.

"And I went up there to me room—me own room, where I might do anything I wanted!—and sat on the bed an' took off me shoes. Me, sitting there in the Bronx with twenty-five dollars to my name, an' me own room, without three or four brothers an' sisters, or two or three fellow novitiates to share it. And I told myself, 'It will be all right. I am now at home.'"

"And now you're here."

"And now I'm here."

"Are you at home here, Charlie?"

He stayed where he was, resting his forearms on the roof parapet, studying his brother for a long time, his face seeming to grow still older and less certain as Tom watched him.

"Don't think I don't think about that, too, Tommy! In all the ways I imagine my destiny would've been different. If I shouldn't have come *here* when I left the Jesuits, instead of to New York . . ." His voice trailed off. Testing him, Tom had the distinct impression, probing for something. *But for what?*

He thought again of the piece of paper he had curled up in his pocket. The photographic copy of the note in the medical examiner's hand: *Withhold information by order of DA.* Gripping it, thinking of confronting him with it right here and now.

"What a thing it would've been, eh, to end up here? After two years starin' at the bust of Cortés in the courtyard of the seminary in Salamanca?"

Tom relaxed his grip on the scrap of paper. Thinking it better to dig it out in its own time. When he could get this brother to face facts again, past all his words.

"Maybe it was fated, Charlie," he said.

"Ah, me, maybe it was, maybe it was."

"In any case, it's not your home. And it's not Slim's, either."

"No. You're right there. It's a lovely city, but it's not my own."

He roused himself from the parapet wall then and started to walk away, talking to Tom over his shoulder.

"Get yourself some real sleep in a real bed, then come over for lunch an' I'll have my cook rustle you up somethin' fine."

"Your cook?"

He stopped and gave Tom a broad, teasing smile.

"Oh, you've never seen anything like 'im. But he can cook. Come on over, an' we'll eat, an' you can ask me anything you like. But go get some sleep now. You have to be careful at this elevation. It catches up to you."

12

New York City, 1953

"They were all asleep."

"They were all asleep."

"Mother of God."

"That's what I said."

"Well, I suppose I'm relieved at that," Hogan said, running a hand through his hair, pushing back on the creaky swivel chair in his office. "Good to know, I suppose, that nobody could bribe five New York City police officers into throwing a murder witness out a window. At least, not five specially hand-picked men. All they did was engage in a gross dereliction of duty. Maybe that should be the new motto for the force: 'We're not on the take. Just asleep.'"

"But that leaves the question," Tom said slowly, "of just who did throw him out."

"You do think your Officer Roberts is telling the truth?" Hogan asked.

"Once he talked, I got all the rest to 'fess up," Tom told him. "It only makes sense. You saw those bank records. All the other investigations. We went over them till we were half blind, and there wasn't a single indication that any of those men received a bribe of any kind in regard to the death of Abraham Reles. Once it happened, an' they were banished to the far reaches of the Parks Department, they didn't have even the usual opportunities. No gamblin', no prostitution —"

"Jesus Christ, they must be the cleanest cops in the history of the department," Hogan said, shaking his head. "And you're sure there's no place else they could be hiding it?"

"If they are, they're sharper than Bernard Baruch. And what would they be holdin' it for, the Judgment Day?"

"At least one of them would have quit the force. Taken off for the territory, bought himself a big old boat of a car," Hogan agreed.

"Instead they're all livin' like monks. Just glad to be hangin' on to their homes an' their paycheck. Grateful as hell to Charlie and the Old Man for savin' 'em their jobs."

"So that's what McGrath was doing out there, the morning Reles went out the window. Making sure to put them in the same room together and get their stories straight. That was some quick thinking."

"I imagine he felt responsible," Tom told him. "You know it was he who picked 'em all for the job."

"*Did* he now?"

"I always assumed it was Charlie, or maybe Frank Bals—they were from his special squad. But it was the Old Man, McGrath himself."

"Shows you can never assume on a case. Have you been to talk to him about it?"

"Not yet. You know, he's at Coney Island Hospital."

"I know. How's he doing?"

"Last time I went to see him, they'd cut out half his stomach. He's dyin', Boss."

Hogan grimaced. "I'm sorry to hear that."

"Still in good spirits, they say. I thought I'd wait till he's in a little better shape before I go out there to talk to him about all this."

"I understand. Not that there's much to add," Hogan said, his voice lingering on some stray thought—squeezing at the case now, Tom knew, like a Fifth Avenue maid choosing a melon. "But that is strange, that he chose the men. Why do y'think *that* is, now?"

"What I suspect? That my brother didn't trust Frank Bals. But what I *know?* That's something else entirely."

"Good lad. Don't jump ahead of the evidence."

They looked back down at the piles of paper spread out before them on Hogan's desk. Heads down, almost touching, lost in their concentration as the evening sky turned a steely gray outside the window behind Hogan's chair. Ellie home preparing for a court date the next morning, or she would have still been in the office as well. The back of his hands itching as he thought about whether he would call her later, and whether she would say to come over.

"So—we now know that we *don't* know when Reles went out the damned window," Hogan said at last.

"Right," Tom answered, snapping back to that November morning almost twelve years before. "The question is how long he was lyin' out on the kitchen roof before Mr. Holt comes into his draft board office and spies the body. That was seven sharp."

"When was it Roberts said he saw the little man last?"

"About three in the morning. Which would make him the last one to see Reles alive — the others were already down for the night."

"How nice to know they were getting their beauty rest. All the little killers, tucked in tight."

"He said Reles was up listening to Dr. Brinkley's show, from Mexico — 'the Sunshine Station Between the Nations.' You know, the goat-glands doctor?"

Hogan winced and stood back, taking a sip of his lukewarm coffee as if he were cleansing a bad taste from his mouth.

"I remember him. 'Be the ram what am with every lamb.' Had an uncle who had that operation. What a mess! Sewing in goat balls right next to your own gonads, to improve your virility! They should've hanged him."

"Anyway, the good doctor was broadcasting all right at that hour. But then he was all the time."

"So not conclusive."

"So then I thought, who might've heard a body hit the roof in the middle of the night?"

"Who indeed?"

"Ellie found me the names of the night staff at the Half Moon."

"She's an invaluable asset to this office, that Ellen Abramowitz," Hogan said, giving him a mischievous look, which Tom studiously ignored.

"We couldn't find the assistant manager. The desk clerk bought it on Anzio, God rest his soul. But we did turn up the night bellhop, and the building engineer."

"And did they hear anything suspicious?"

"They certainly did. They couldn't very well have missed it, sitting out where they were, down in the Half Moon lobby. But now who d'ya think was with 'em?"

"Ah, hell!" said Hogan, throwing a pencil across the desk.

"That's right. The two uniforms downstairs. The same two men who were supposed to be out on the boardwalk, walkin' the beat and warding off any lurking gunmen."

Hogan looked up at the ceiling. "Holy Christ. It was only the biggest murder case of the century. Was *anybody* doing their job?"

13

New York, 1953

The narrow little bar was dark as night, though it was still midafternoon outside in Park Slope. This one the same as all the others he had been searching through for the past two hours. The electric sign out front proclaiming PABST BLUE RIBBON, dusty curtains drawn over the two little windows. No name of the establishment visible anywhere, if there had ever been one.

Inside were a pair of booths under each of the curtained windows, the patched seat plastic the color of phlegm in the dim light. A slot machine, a cigarette machine, a jukebox, a row of barstools that matched the color of the booths. One of them occupied by a big man in a porkpie hat and a checkered jacket that reminded Tom of the men on the docks, save for the enormous gut that protruded through it. He was nursing a draft and slowly eating pretzels out of a bowl, his attention given over so acutely to the middleweight fight on the wavy TV screen above the bar that he was unaware of Tom's approach until the bartender gave a quick, almost imperceptible flick of his head while he dried a glass.

The man's enormous torso swiveled slowly around, neck fat bulging. Large moist eyes focusing on Tom but he still said nothing. *Another soldier from the lost brigade,* Tom thought.

"Don'tcha know you shouldn't watch TV in the dark?" Tom said. "Bad for the eyes."

The man on the stool only blinked at him, and the bartender, a trim man with a square jaw, hustled over to wipe down the foot of wood between them.

"What can I getcha?" he said, a challenge in his voice.

"Another for Officer Boyle here, and then a bar's length of distance, if you please," he told the man, pulling out his assistant DA's credential. The barkeep looked at it, looked at Boyle, then poured the beer and moved reluctantly down the bar.

"I ain't on duty," Boyle said, his voice less than confident. "Am I?"

"Hard to know when *you're* on duty or not, Officer Boyle. Who's winnin' the fight?"

"The Mexican's got the jig on points so far. But my boy'll catch him in the end."

"So nice to hear that you don't let your prejudices get in the way of your sportin' acumen."

Boyle said nothing, just sipping his beer and regarding him dully. *An animal resigned to the slaughterhouse,* thought Tom. He sighed, and began.

"I'm not with Internal Affairs, and I don't want your badge, Officer Boyle. I just want to know about things that go bump in the night."

"Come again, pal?"

"I want to know about one of those nights you *were* on duty. So to speak. Your last night at the Half Moon Hotel."

"Oh. That."

Boyle's face curdled and he took another small sip from his beer, casting a quick glance up at the television as if imploring the heavens for something. On the screen, the black fighter had indeed gone on the offensive, pushing the stubborn young Mexican back across the ring. A nothing match on a Sunday afternoon. The spectators on the screen hunched forward like so many toads, peering up at the ring, mouths opening and closing as they worked cigars or cried out barely audible imprecations.

"You bet much on the fights, Mr. Boyle?"

"Nah. Lot more on baseball. The Bums can't miss this year," he said, deigning to give Tom a sardonic, sidelong glance. "You can write it down."

"What's a lot?"

"Oh, I dunno. A finniff here, a deuce there. That's about my speed."

"How about the night of November 12, 1941?"

"That the night he went out the window? Nah, I was on duty, see. Freezin' my ass off on the Coney Island boardwalk."

"But you weren't either, Officer Boyle. You were in the hotel lobby, workin' over the *Racing Form,* tryin' to pick a winner down in Hialeah."

Officer Boyle looked dazzlingly unfazed.

"Is that what I was doin'? Well, Officer Terry Byrnes will tell you different. He was freezin' his ass off with me."

"No, he wasn't. The two of you were inside, by the nice warm fire. You were the first line of defense, for the greatest mob witness of all time. A man with information on eighty-five murder cases. An' you an' your boyfriend were inside, keepin' warm with the hotel help."

"Ah, hell, what's this all about, anyway?" Officer Boyle said, at last stung into mild annoyance. He took another quick look at the television, where Tom could see that the Mexican was trapped in a corner now, bleeding fiercely but still not giving up.

Will all fights of the future be between blacks and whites, he wondered idly, *so they'll show up so nice and clear on TV?*

"If whatch you're sayin' is true, an' I'm not sayin' it is, who the hell cares now? An' what did it matter? They had 'em behind five cops an' a steel door upstairs. Nobody was gettin' past *that* 'less they brought their own tank up in the elevator."

"You didn't think you had an obligation to do your duty?"

"In case you didn't notice, he fell *down*, not up. Me an' Terry didn't do nothin' wrong." He shook his head impatiently. "Jesus Christ, to think I gotta walk a beat out in squirrel territory the rest a my life, just because those assholes up there couldn't keep him alive!"

"But you didn't see anything, you an' your partner. Where you were, *out on the boardwalk,* I mean."

"I told the investigators then. We were both up by the other end of the hotel—"

"No, you weren't. You and Officer Byrnes were both in the hotel lobby. The lobby right next to the hotel kitchen, where Abe Reles landed on the roof."

"So you know everything, what's your question?" Officer Boyle asked, his voice growing steadily angrier. The man's hands were the size and texture of steak slabs, Tom noticed, wondering again at how big all the men assigned to the guard detail were. Remembering how impressive they had all looked taking Reles and the other witnesses to trial, done up in their departmental dress, hats to fresh-shined boots. *A real show.*

"My question is what time you heard the body fall."

Boyle looked impatiently around the bar, then leaned in close to Tom, his breath reeking of days' worth of beer, digested at regular intervals, and rarely if ever relieved.

"Look, I dunno that I heard no *body* fall," he croaked. "An' I ain't sayin' I was in that lobby. But there was a helluva big bang-up about four-thirty that morning."

"In other words, about two and a half hours *before* Reles was so widely reported to have jumped?"

Boyle's eyes seemed to glaze over, looking at him with calculated menace.

"I don' know what you're drivin' at here. I heard about you from some a the others, they said you was pokin' around —"

"Did they now? They were told not to say a thing. Telling you constitutes interference with a criminal investigation."

Boyle retreated, physically drawing back.

"Yeah, well, I dunno what I heard from nobody, or what you want. I just know there was a helluva bump about four-thirty."

"And did you go out to investigate? You and Officer Byrnes?"

Boyle gave a little shrug. "The bellhop said it mighta been a car."

"A *what*? A car? *On the roof?*"

"He said cars jumped the curb an' hit the side a the building all the time late at night. Buncha drunks. Out there on Coney Island —"

"In November?"

"Yeah, well."

Boyle seemed to settle slowly into his beer. A couple walked into the bar, already well lit, and fell into one of the wall booths. The man got up, nickel in hand, and staggered over to start up the jukebox, way too loud.

Is this the future with television, too? Tom wondered. *A cacophony of competing sounds everywhere, negating each other along with any remaining ability to think?*

He moved in closer to Officer Boyle, disgusting as that was. Down at the far end of the bar, the bartender took a step toward them, looking as edgy as bartenders always get when people are talking too much and not drinking enough. Tom halted his advance with a look, then turned back to Boyle.

"And you couldn't tell whether that bump was on the roof, an' not outside on the curb? My, you must be an awfully jumpy man in New York, Officer Boyle!"

"Well, now that I think about it, it was on the roof."

"But you didn't go investigate?"

Boyle sighed. "Do you know how cold it was that night? The way that wind used to come off the ocean —"

"Let me ask you somethin'. D'ya have even the faintest cognizance of your duty, Officer Boyle?"

Boyle said nothing, looking at him lumpenly. Up on the TV, the Mexican managed to bull his way out of the corner, but predictably he found himself more vulnerable when he escaped, the black fighter meeting his flurry of punches with blow after blow of his own, able to fully extend his arms and attack from all angles now. After a couple of swift combinations, the Mexican went down. Got up again, took a right uppercut that knocked out a couple of teeth with his mouthpiece, and went down. Got up again, took a right cross that ripped open an eyebrow. Went down.

"All that extra damage, just to go down anyway," Tom said sadly. "Officer Boyle, you sure can pick 'em."

" 'S'all in figurin' it out logically. Like with that night."

"Do tell."

"If there's somethin' that *ain't* supposed to come from upstairs an' fall on that roof, well, then I figure there's enough guys up there to keep it from fallin'. You catch my drift?"

"And?"

Officer Boyle cocked his head. "If there's somethin' that *is* supposed to come out that window in the middle of the night — well then, I don't wanna know *nothin'* about that."

14

Mexico City, 1953

When his brother opened the door to his little penthouse, standing just behind him was a tall, bony individual with a dull red moustache, wearing a long apron over a suit and a chef's toque on his head.

"This is your cook?" Tom asked.

"Ah, Tommy, I can see now why Hogan hired you, blessed as y'are with such keen powers of observation," Charlie said. "Why, it's a wonder ya didn't go straight to the FBI."

Charlie turned and said something to the tall, bony man in a language Tom didn't know, and didn't know of.

"This is Pishta, Tom," Charlie explained. "He's Hungarian. Understands a little English, but he can speak only one sentence in it."

Charlie turned to the cook again.

"Give him yer one line of English, Pishta."

"Shut up, baby," Pishta said in a high, heavily accented voice. Charlie burst out laughing, while Pishta smiled broadly, his moustache turning up.

"Shut up, bay-bee!" he repeated, more emphatically than ever.

"Oh, that's fine, Pishta, just fine! Now, I think we'll have a scotch before lunch."

Pishta bowed slightly, still beaming, and went off to fetch their drinks while they settled themselves on the awful green couch.

"Wherever did you find him?"

"Hungarian embassy. There was some sort of falling-out amongst our communist brethren over there—I never did learn exactly what. Maybe he said a kind word about Rajk, when Rákosi was in, or a kind word about Rákosi when Rajk was in. In any case, they were goin' to ship him back to Budapest for execution, so I gave him asylum at the embassy."

"Jesus."

"I know," Charlie said, nodding in acknowledgment as Pishta handed them their drinks before returning to the kitchen. "What kind of world are we living in, when someone can bother themselves with killing a creature such as Pishta?"

"How did Slim put up with him?" Tom ventured, unsure if he should mention her name at all.

"Oh, she loved Pishta!" Charlie said fondly. "He was a big help with all those garden parties she liked to throw. My God, we had a five-thousand-dollar entertainment allowance for the year; I think she used it up in three months. Just open up the whole house, and invite everyone for the Fourth of July. You ever see the old ambassadorial residence, Tom?"

"No."

"That's right, you never got down here. Just one story high, but really a beautiful home, full of old-time elegance. It had a long terrace, and then a garden patio that seemed to go on forever, as lush and green as any field in Bohola. Tall trees all around. Lovely, lovely. Slim herself, when she saw it, said right out loud, 'How beautiful!' Just like that: 'How beautiful!'"

"I believe you, Charlie."

"I thought she was happy," he said, draining the rest of the scotch in his glass and jangling the ice plaintively. "Always on the local television, talking about her charities and raising money for this cause or that. First year we were here, she had a society square dance out on the terrace. You've never seen anything so beautiful in your life. All those gorgeous Mexican women, whirling their bright skirts about the lawn! God, I loved those parties!"

Crunching a last piece of ice between his teeth, he put his empty glass down on the coffee table before them, the map of Ireland beneath its glass top. A cloud seemed to pass across his face.

"After the first year or so, though, all she cared for were her bullfight luncheons. Every Sunday, once the cow-butcherin' season commenced in November. She'd have forty, fifty of her aficionados over in the afternoon. Bull breeders and matadors, washed-up picadors an' banderilleros. 'Pickled herrings an' banditos,' I used to call 'em. I remember she had one famous old matador, kept bowing and kissing the hand of every woman in the place. Well, finally I went over an' bowed deep an' kissed *his* hand. That put an end to that!"

He chuckled, then squinted suspiciously at Tom.

"I heard you got over to Plaza Mexico. Did you meet Chu Chu?"

Tom hesitated, decided not to lie, and nodded his head. "I had that distinction."

"So you see what I'm havin' to deal with. For her to associate herself with a man like that—" He cut himself off when he saw Tom's face, shaking his head and crossing his arms. "God, how she loved it, though. All those afternoons in the dry season. She'd have Pishta cook up big platters of *arroz con pollo,* and these hot turkey *tortas* everybody was crazy for then. She put the tables out on the terrace, with one of the little bullfighting puppets she bought in the marketplace on each one. I never saw her so excited. She wasn't nearly so solicitous of me by then, I can tell you that!"

Tom could see her face there. Flushed, with that strand of her blond hair falling down over her ear as she turned to smile . . .

"Then we'd all pile into the big cars an' go over to the Plaza," Charlie kept on, staring down at the coffee table, as if his drink might rematerialize before him. "We'd have to sit ringside, in the box of those damned Madrazos — more of her bullfighting friends. The matador would come over an' make a pretty little speech dedicating the next bull to us, while he winked and licked his lips, an' looked her over like a wolf contemplatin' a lamb. He'd hand me one of those goddamned Mickey Mouse hats, an' I'd have to sit there an' hold it, an' see that it was filled with coins throughout the ensuing butchery."

Pishta reentered the room, and laid out two bowls on a small card table set up across the room, waiting there with a dishtowel over one arm for them to be seated. Charlie pulled himself up from the couch, still shaking his head.

"I never understood how she could love it so much," he said as they took their seats. "I just used to sit there hoping we didn't get soaked in blood. They shove the first spear in between the bull's shoulders, right away, and up it blows like an oil geyser . . ."

He could picture that, too, in the pitiless arena he had glimpsed the day before. The first red streak of blood, splattered across the sand in the dry heat of the afternoon. Then a cheer, and more of it, and more of it.

Of course she would want to see all of it, perched up high on her pillow in that ringside seat. Having all she could do to keep from standing up — daughter of a long line of killers, in their march across the continent. The Madrazos, grizzled bull breeders, no doubt grinning at one another and sneaking looks back at her bottom as she rose off the seat. But she would be oblivious, eyes fixed on the kill. Wanting to see everything, just as she always did, and could Charlie really know his wife so very little?

". . . the rest of it is just the crowd o-layin', an' the matadors prancin' an' posin' till finally they get the poor beast worn down to where it's snortin' foam an' blood out through the mouth. Then they would finish it — an' hand *us* the ears an' the tail. God, I wonder sometimes what she's done with them all!"

The liquid in the bowls before them was a bright orange color, though it smelled familiar.

"Carrot soup," Charlie told him. "You need a stout heart to cook it."

"It's delicious. Spiced like nothing I've ever tasted before."

Charlie said something to Pishta, and he burst into a long spiel of Hungarian.

"He's overjoyed you like the carrot soup. He wants you to know that it's got carrots in it, surprisingly enough, and also onion, garlic, parsnips, and silander."

Pishta's lips and his moustache turned up again, and he turned and marched back into the kitchen.

"Will she be joining us? Slim?" Tom asked, careful not to betray any emotion at all. Charlie looked grim — but before he could answer, Pishta was back with another excited burst of Hungarian.

"The soup again," Charlie translated. "He wanted you to be sure to know there's flour in it, as well. Plus salt and pepper, an' something the size of a nut. At least I think that's what he said. Even after all my years with Pishta, his Hungarian sometimes eludes me. Also bouillon cubes. Also water. Don't forget the water, if yer plannin' to make this when you get back to Manhattan. When the soup starts to boil, mix in an egg. Then throw the shell out the window. Thank you, Pishta."

The cook bowed and retreated again, looking more pleased than ever. Charlie tried to keep his face up.

"I invited her, but she says she's going out of town. She said she'd meet us down in Acapulco. If we want to go down there."

"I see," he said slowly. Wondering if he felt disappointed, and if he should.

"We should go, Tommy," Charlie said, suddenly animated again. "We should get out, see some of the country."

"I dunno, Charlie. I don't know how it'd look, the DA's office funding trips to Acapulco —"

"Ah, the hell with what people say, Tommy!" he exclaimed, the bluff, jovial voice unable to hide the pleading beneath. "You have a dangerous criminal like me, aren't ya supposed to follow me everywhere? We can stay there for free; some of *el presidente's* friends are always very generous about that. Besides, nothing like the open road to free up the mind for reminiscing!"

"Is that what you think we're doin', Charlie? Reminiscing—" he said, but then Pishta was back, clearing away their bowls and bringing in a shoulder of pork, covered with peppers and fried tomatoes. It was even better than the soup, hot and marinated until the meat almost fell off the bone, and when he smiled up at Pishta the cook launched into another extended explanation.

"I think we'll stick with the *Reader's Digest* condensed version this time, Pishta," Charlie said gently. "Suffice it to say, you cook the meat in *agua* for an hour. Then you add a couple thousand herbs of various descriptions, put it on a slow fire, an' let that absorb all the grease. Then, when it's ready, you throw an old *shoe* out the window."

"The carnage below your windows must be somethin' terrible, Charlie."

"Why d'ya think I live in the middle of the roof? Thanks, Pishta."

The Hungarian left them, and Tom wanted to try to find a way back to what he had started to say, but Charlie was already talking again.

"Well, it built up goodwill. We always got a big hand from the Mexican people. But some of the Americans down here started to complain. They wanted their quiet embassy evenings back, playin' canasta around the fire. Slim wouldn't do that, she couldn't stomach that, and so they would complain straight to State, and I would have to hear about it. She was never one for politics, that one. Not the way Claire was, y'know, Tom?"

"Sure, Charlie."

"Oh, but *she* had a head for the game! I used to rely on her for everything, Tom."

"I know you did, Charlie."

"*She* never thought I should've got into politics in the first place. 'Charlie, God bless you, you've got too good a heart, they'll skin you alive,' she used to tell me.

"She worried about me every step of the way up. She'd say, 'I'm glad to see you happy, but I am afraid of it. Are you sure you won't come to any harm?' Oh, she knew me better than I knew myself!"

"Maybe she did, Charlie."

"She had a tongue on her, that one. She was a lady down to her toes, but she had a tongue in her head," Charlie said, chuckling. "D'ya remember when Truman came to break the ground at Idlewild, back in '48, when he looked like he was finished? Neddy Moran told me later, she looked at the two of us comin' up the steps of Gracie Mansion, me an' the president of the United States, an' she said to him, 'Well, here comes Amos 'n Andy'!'"

They were both laughing then.

"It was she that should've been the politician in the family, Tommy. Wasn't a day or a night went by I didn't call her an' ask her advice on somethin'. It was always right, even at the end when all the fight was drained out of her."

"She fought hard, Charlie. Right to the end. She stood it all with a rare grace."

"An' what did *grace* ever do for her, Tom?" Charlie snapped with a bitterness that seemed to come out of nowhere. "What's grace for, what's courage for? What kind of world is this, where a woman like that can die a long, slow death from something like Parkinson's, with the cancer thrown in at the end for a chaser?"

He put down his knife and fork and dabbed suddenly at his eyes with his handkerchief. Tom put out a hand to console him, but Charlie's voice was still bitter.

"Did I ever tell you about the pigeon, Tom? No? It was right near the end. She was up at home, prostrate in bed, an' I was comin' out of some big meeting of all the big men, in midtown. At the Yale Club, or the New York Yacht Club, or maybe just the Big Men Club. It was an evening in the early fall, just after a rainstorm. I come out of the meeting none the worse for wear after a couple scotches, thinkin' all the better of myself after discussin' the great matters of state, and I look up above and the whole sky is golden. Lighting up the Chrysler Building, an' the Empire State, an' all the other high buildings, until it all looked like a gorgeous fairyland we live in."

"I know it, Charlie. I've seen that light myself."

"And then I looked down, an' spotted a pigeon dyin' by the side of a building. It was all tucked into itself, there against the stone wall. Standin' in somethin' that had obviously just come out of it, blood or bile, or its own liquid shit. Shiverin' there, an' waiting to die, or whatever it thought was going to happen to it. I saw that, and it took away any religion I might've had left. I thought, what kind of a God is it, makes the birds of the sky just to huddle and die in their own filth at the end? What kind of a God is it, leaves a woman like that to spend ten years in a wheelchair? Dyin' bit by bit, while her fine peacock of a husband floats around town, full of liquor from the New York fucking Yacht Club? And all the beauty of His golden sky no compensation for their suffering, no compensation at all. Just a gaudy, sham stage, on which to strut in all His cruelty."

"But to *her*, Charlie. Was it worthwhile to *her?*"

Charlie blew his nose and chuckled, despite the tears in his eyes, patting his brother's hand on his shoulder. "Ah, Tom, you always know what to say. Well, I do think she would've been pleased, you know, to see Spellman gave her the big sendoff at Saint Pat's, with all the smells an' bells," he said, softening into his reminiscence, all right. "The cardinal of New York givin' her eulogy at Saint Patrick's Cathedral. I knew he wanted something for it, of course. A tax break for his damned schools, or another raid on some sacrilegious movie house. She would've been the first to tell me that. But even so, it brought tears to the eyes, knowing how pleased she and her whole family would've been — pleased I could do that for her."

"I know she would've, Charlie."

"She was somethin'. They all were. Claire Condon, of the Water Street Condons. What airs that family put on! They lived under the shadow of the Brooklyn Bridge, but they acted like the uncrowned kings of Ireland. Even spelled her name the French way."

"I remember that, Charlie. She was proud of it, too."

"She did have class, though, you could see that from the start. Did I ever tell you how we met, up at the Grand Union Hotel, in Saratoga Springs, before the Great War? She was workin' as a telephone operator at the time, spendin' her week's vacation up there with a girlfriend. I was a barman, in my white apron, handin' out milk punches to the swells, and she come up to the bar to get change for a phone call.

"Right away, she had me so moon-eyed I gave her a Canadian dime by accident. She hung on to it. Years later I saw it in her purse, an' I asked her, 'What joker passed that off on you?' An' she told me, 'You did, the first day I met you.' Did I ever tell ya that?"

"You did, Charlie."

"But you should've seen her in those days, Tommy! You only knew her after she was sick — more's the pity. Back then she was pretty as a picture. Blue eyes, an' milk-white skin. Hair black as a raven's wing. Oh, was she accomplished! You never got to hear her on the piano, Tom, but she had great feeling, great timing, expert finger control —"

"I've heard tell, Charlie."

"All that week, I wooed her in the parlor, or on the big white porch chairs. Sneakin' out there, because the help wasn't supposed to mingle with the guests. Wonderful old barn, the Grand Union was. The Victor Herbert Orchestra givin' a concert out on the piazza, every morning *and* afternoon!"

"That I'd have liked to see, Charlie," Tom said gently.

They resettled on the couch while Pishta cleared the plates. Charlie went on speaking in a voice that made Tom wonder if he was about to cry again.

"She was the making of me, Tommy," he said. "I didn't even wait until the season was over, just threw over that job at the Grand Union and chased her right back to New York.

"It was after I met her that I knew I had to find a way up. Before that, it'd been just one job after another. Stackin' groceries up at a James Butler store in the Bronx, workin' construction over in West Farms. Tendin' bar down at the Ritz-Carlton, an' the Plaza. Racketing around the world —"

"I know, Charlie. I remember the letters."

"The best was when I signed on as a common seaman. Fifteen dollars a month, shovelin' coal aboard the SS *Southern Cross,* an' what I knew about the ocean you could've writ on the head of a pin. They worked me half to death on that boat, but it made a man out of me. Sailin' all the way down to Rio de Janeiro, an' Buenos Aires, an' Montevideo, then up the Río de la Plata to Ensenada. I loved that, Tommy, makin' port in a wondrous new city every other day. I was a good sailor, never seasick for an' hour, and I worked like a mule in harness down in that boiler room.

"But by the end of the voyage, I was broker than I started. To be sure, the purser had taken a shine to me, he promised to sign me up for their next cruise, an' I think if he had, I would've become a sailor, an' what would *that*'ve been like? Sailin' to a new port every trip, all over the world. I never would've met Claire, or Slim. Never would've been mayor. Settlin' down into a whole new place, maybe, with a whole other life — another wife, another family. An' who would *that* Charlie O'Kane have been? D'ya ever think about that, Tommy? How circumstance makes us all that we are in the end?"

"Does it, Charlie?"

He had heard the stories ever since he'd known his brother—from even before, when he still wrote to the family back in Lismirrane. *His father reading the letters around the table along with the papers from Dublin. The neighbors, and all the rest of the family, more interested in hearing Charlie's tales. Lying in glorious comfort in the outshot, the little bed made for him from the wall cropping that stuck out by the kitchen fire. His brothers and sisters all clustered around, picturing as he did the adventures of his brother as they fell toward sleep.*

"But never mind, the purser died of a heart attack, right in the middle of Hanover Square, an' the boat got sold, an' that closed off another life. I was able to get work as a coal passer by then at least. Workin' the night boats up the Hudson, all the way from Christopher Street to the rail bridge in Albany, and back again. That was almost as good as South America; there was never another river like that one in the world! That was where I really learned my trade—cleanin' my fires in the downstream current to Poughkeepsie, well enough to make steam against the heaviest tide into the City. I used to know the old rhyme of the river by heart—*West Point and Middletown, Konnosook and Doodletown, Kakiak and Mamapaw, Stony Point and Haverstraw . . .*"

Tom knew the names almost as well himself, from his brother's letters. He had dreamed of him there, too. Staring from the deck at the Storm King as it emerged through the morning light . . .

"That night I broke the last of all the many promises I made to our mother, an' had a glass of beer at Felix Dolan's Saloon. I suppose that didn't hurt her soul any worse than me becomin' an itinerant fireman, instead of a priest! Besides, I was a regular murphy compared to the rest of the crew—those fellas'd be off on a jake at a moment's notice. The captains liked me. I could always be relied upon to show up for cast-off, and that was another way I could've gone, I suppose, tendin' the boats up an' down the Hudson for the rest of me days.

"But then the river began to freeze up. It was the coldest winter in twenty years, an' I had to get work drivin' a trolley over in Hackensack, an' then it was back to construction. Hod Carriers Local Number Three. We put up the Woolworth Building, don'tcha know—'the Cathedral of Commerce!' Haulin' a load of bricks up fifty stories, with my nose in the next fella's arse. I learned some appreciation for the ancient Hebrews on that job, let me tell you!

"The high steel men used to fascinate me up there. Oh, it was a sight to behold—the best theatre in the world, sixty stories above the ground! I used to slip up to where they were workin' on my lunch break, just to see 'em. They were friendly enough fellas, most of 'em from Ireland, though they didn't tolerate any nonsense. They showed me how it was, taught me how to walk out on the beams the way they did. Nothin' below 'em, no safety net, just a foot-wide steel beam an' eight hundred feet to the ground below.

"God, it scared the life out of me at first! Still does, just to think about it. But they taught me the trick of it—how not to look down, how to judge the wind an' steady yourself. I would sit out on a beam there, an' read westerns an' other adventure stories to them while they ate their lunches. All terrible, dime-novel stuff, but they ate it up. They couldn't understand why I'd waste my lunchtime reading to 'em, but I told 'em I was tryin' to lose my accent so I could go into politics.

"It wasn't true, though—not yet. What I really wanted was that view up there, Tommy. You could see the great bridges over the East River, and the other skyscrapers, and that quaint little building known as City Hall. You could see all the ships in the harbor, an' the little figures swarming over the docks. You could see the curvature of the earth, Tom, where it moved along the blue line of the sea. And I stood up there, where all the winds of the earth blew right through, and I thought like Archimedes that here was a place to stand on to move the world."

He was silent then for a moment, picturing again how the world had looked, sixty stories up in the air. Giving voice to his ambition at last, so Tom let him talk. Staring up toward the ceiling of the little beige room as if he were still out on the beams, dazed by the sun and the wind and the curve of the earth.

"I was young still, but growin' tired of myself," he said, speaking in a lower, almost chastised voice now. "I was tired of how I lived, in my neat little boardinghouses up in the Bronx. Goin' downtown to have Dunphy teach me to use the correct knife an' fork. Goin' out to make eyes at the ladies along Broadway, or maybe watch the athletics over in Celtic Park on a Sunday afternoon.

"I wanted a home, I wanted a vocation. I just didn't know what it was yet. So when the big building was finished, I let my feet take me again. I went up to Saratoga for the summer, and that's how I met Claire Condon, of the Water Street Condons, an' suddenly I had it all — that home, that life, that way forward.

"None of it happened right away. But the Condon Colony of Dreamers wasn't about to countenance a hod carrier, or a barman, no matter if he was a spoilt priest from the Irish College at Salamanca! I put in three years of night school up at City College, studyin' English, an' civics, an' American history, and shorthand an' typing. Then I got my citizenship, an' joined the force, an' started on my law degree at the same time, until finally they ran out of objections to us gettin' married.

"I'd put aside a little money by then, enough to take her on a honeymoon. We sailed out on the *Southern Cross,* the very same ship I shoveled coal on, an' don't think I wasn't proud of *that,* as we cruised down to Rio de Janeiro, and up the broad River Plate. It was the same as I remembered it, the wild jungles, an' the beautiful cities, and it was still a place of wonder. But I had no thought of what it would be like to stay there anymore, or to sail from port to port. I had a purpose now, and a wife by my side, and even a passel of in-laws bound to me, however grudgingly, and I thought then that at last I did belong.

"But you know, I often wonder if she got all she hoped for from *me,* Tom. Besides that grand funeral, I mean —"

"I'm sure that she did, Charlie. Why wouldn't she?"

"She had a great head for the politics, Tom, but I don't know that she liked the game."

He paused while Pishta brought them coffee. It was dark and thick, and spiked with something that tasted like chocolate to Tom, as astonishingly strange and delicious as everything else he'd been served.

"I think she thought it was below her, a rough, vulgar sort of profession. And indeed it was, Tom, indeed it was," he said sadly. "I think she would have liked me to be in somethin' more refined. But you know, she never complained. Not even after we got the final diagnosis.

"God, but that's a strange feeling! I hope you never have to endure it, Tommy. Sittin' in a doctor's office, feeling more or less like you always do, an' having a man tell you how an' when you will die. What use is the brain, will you tell me, then, Tommy? What is consciousness but a curse? That pigeon at least, it may've suspected it was in trouble. But nobody sat it down in a clean, sterile office, an' told it that it was doomed to a long, cruel death. God*damn*it, Tom! It's as if we're God's special whipping boys — if there were a God.

"We come out of the doctor's office at Bellevue, and I was about all done in by the news. But Claire, she looked up at me with her eyes shining, an' she said, 'Thank God, Tom, we didn't have children!' That was her explanation as to why God had been so cruel as to deprive us of a child of our own, and give us young Jimmy instead. To her, this was *good* news, a chance to make sense of life, and forgive *God.*"

He stood up and began to pace agitatedly around the little living room.

"Can you imagine that, Tom? A woman as smart, and talented, and loving as that, *relieved* to get the news that she's going to die a long, horrible death because it *explains* the Almighty to her! And isn't that the ultimate cruelty of havin' a mind at all, Tom? Of bein' condemned to *think.* To excuse even the sight of a bird shuddering to death in a golden light — just so we can forgive that God we made in our own image, and so want to love. The stories that we tell ourselves to get through to the end —"

"God bless, Charlie, but take it easy now," Tom said, alarmed to see the state his brother was suddenly in. Pishta stuck his head in, too, but retreated immediately to the kitchen, his face solemn.

"I didn't know her well, but I knew her long enough to know she loved life, and she loved you, an' she stuck it out right to the end," Tom said quickly, almost babbling in his eagerness to calm his brother.

Tom's memory of her still mostly as a shadow, in those back bedrooms of the attached house in Bay Ridge, and then at Gracie Mansion. Already confined to the chair. Always dressed up nicely, in prim hats and well-cut dresses. But her hair was lank and oily under the hats by then, and there were piles of white flecks on the shoulders of her new outfits, no matter how repeatedly Neddy Moran flicked them away. Her face a rigid mask, the drool running out one side of her mouth, no matter how alert Neddy was with the handkerchief. By the end, though he tried not to think it, she reminded him of some sort of ancient oracle, wheeled out in her chair with that mask of a face, speaking in a soft monotone they all had to lean in to hear.

"And what did I do? Did I devote myself to her in her dyin' days? No, I went right on with my political career, sheer vanity that it was, and for all the joy it would bring me!"

"You had to work, Charlie—"

"Yes, I had to work!" he said viciously. "But I could've stayed on the bench in Brooklyn, helpin' the people with their problems. I didn't *have* to be the crusading DA. I didn't *have* to be the mayor. And for chrissakes, Tommy, I sure as hell didn't have to go off to war!"

"We all did that, Charlie."

"No, no. Are ye that dense, you don't see what I'm talkin' about? You don't see the difference. That was another part of my *political* ambitions, such as they were," Charlie said furiously, still pacing the floor. "God knows, it was all of a piece—and I knew it then, too, in some part of me head. I didn't go to stop the damned Germans, or the Japanese, halfway around the goddamned world. I did it for me! *Me*, Tom, *me!* Vanity, all vanity! Standin' in his office with the Great Man while I got a medal pinned on my chest. Listenin' to him tell me how I should run for governor or senator! And all with her dyin' back home."

He sat back on the couch and seemed to sink into a reverie. Sipping at the last of his coffee, staring straight ahead.

"Thank God for Neddy Moran. That's all I have to say. I know you don't want to hear it, Tommy, but it's the truth! Thank God for Neddy, he was the one stayed home an' took care of her, while I went gallivantin' out across the USA, and over to Italy. He was the one who always looked after her—well, he and poor Jimmy. But after Jimmy was gone, it was always him. Never complained, never asked for a thing."

"He betrayed you, Charlie."

"No, Tommy, no. It wasn't like that. If anything, I betrayed *him*, the poor man. Stickin' him with a job like that."

"He got his pound of flesh," Tom said grimly. "He got what he wanted out of you, and through his actions he blackened your name in return."

"I won't speak ill of the man, Tommy. He was there for her. He was there for her when I wasn't, and that's all that matters."

"Damnit, Charlie, don't ya see?" he said, his frustration brimming over despite himself. "Men like Moran have used you. They've taken your good name an' flung it in the gutter."

"No, no, I'm not God, I won't judge the man!" Charlie said, turning away from him and walking across the room to stand under the framed picture of himself as the bold mayor of New York, face floating serenely over the vast tangle of trains, and planes, and skyscrapers. "He was good to Claire all those years. He took such care of her when I was in the army —"

"God bless, Charlie, he could've joined the Sisters of Mercy. But when he was at the fire department he was liftin' two thousand dollars a week, I don't care why he did it —"

"If he did what he's accused of doin', then he's wrong, and I feel sorry for the man," Charlie said, holding up a hand. "He knew I wanted him to be clean. I'd heard rumors about him before. Your boss, Mr. Hogan, warned me off him. I remember he told me Neddy Moran's a man who trades in favors. But that's like sayin' the man who follows the circus parade sweeps up a little shite from time to time. That's what politics is, Tommy."

"You should've listened, Charlie," he said, standing now and half pleading, his hands held out toward his brother.

"You have to understand, Tom, Neddy's a narrow, untutored man. He rubs people the wrong way, but I'da been lost without him. He'd been with me ever since he was my stenographer on the magistrate's court, an' then he was my clerk at the DA's office. Besides, the job I ended up givin' him wasn't so important —"

"Deputy fire commissioner?"

"I had to do it, Tom, so he could educate his children. You should've seen him when I told him — the tears were streamin' down his face —"

"Goddamnit, Charlie, it wasn't the first time! He'd already betrayed you! Pullin' those wanted cards on Anastasia. Makin' those union files disappear —"

Charlie sighed and sat down in a chair. Running a hand over his forehead as if he were back under the blazing television lights.

"Well, now, there was that," he said in a small voice. "There was that."

15

New York, 1953

He caught the train for Sing Sing at Grand Central. Crossing the great hall under its floating turquoise zodiac, begrimed almost beyond recognition by cigarette smoke, and still uncleaned since the war. Thinking of Charlie standing up in one of the galleries around the vast room. Watching Slim Sadler walk a beam of white light in a shimmering gown. The golden daughter of America, right there for the taking.

The image he had never seen, replaced by one he had. The first time he had taken the prison train, more than twelve years ago. A lifetime ago, before war, and return, and all the things he hadn't wanted to know. A beautiful spring day, when they took Buggsy Goldstein and Pittsburgh Phil Strauss, the first two men convicted by Abe Reles's testimony, up to the Dance Hall to die.

The crowds surging about the station just to get a glimpse of them. The uniformed guards bulling their way through, shotguns held out before them, eyes wild as they scanned the crowd for hit men. The whole situation on the verge of flying completely out of control — the festive, mocking crowd, pushing and jostling to see the killers. The guards with their guns spooking every time they heard the rattan-fan shuffle of the departure board. Everything sloppily planned — the way his brother did so much so sloppily, letting his concentration slip.

But there proved to be no hit men in the crowd. Everybody knew Buggsy and Pep would never squeal — and that they'd be useless as witnesses if they did. They let themselves be pulled along, smirking at the raucous crowd. Clapping their cuffed hands over their heads from time to time, Pep Strauss making barking noises like a trained seal — a menacing, shuffling figure, still wearing the wild hair and the full beard with which he'd to try to play crazy during the trial. Goldstein immaculately dressed and groomed as ever, walking and talking like a duck, his wide face a series of creases when he smiled, reminding Tom of a friendly Chinese laundryman. Asked if there was anything he wanted to say after his death sentence was handed down, he had addressed the court in a somber, quiet voice: "Yes, Your Honor, there is. Before I die, there is only one thing I would like to do. I would like to piss up your leg."

"Which is another reason why it's wrong to put a man to death," Charlie said afterward. "It frees him from all earthly considerations, and imbues him with a heroism that he has not earned."

The crowd had followed them right onto the platform, gawking in the train windows, leering and pointing at the condemned men. Pittsburgh Phil grinning back, putting his face up against theirs on the other side of the glass—then suddenly spitting, laughing to watch the rubberneckers jump back in revulsion. He flipped them the bird, then took off his shoes and hurled them at the photographers when they tried to take their flashes. Goldstein still smiling, playing to the reporters, giving them line after line to scribble furiously in their little notebooks.

"Just tell that rat Reles I'll be waiting for him. Maybe it'll be in hell, I dunno. But I'll be waiting. And I bet I got a pitchfork."

It was like a convention train the whole way up to the Dance Hall, which was what they called the Death House at Sing Sing. Everyone talking too loud. The reporters nipping openly from hip flasks, the commuters trying to barge their way into the car to take a look at the killers. Goldstein still smirking, Strauss farting and belching as loudly as he could, starting to unbutton his fly before one of the bulls stopped him. Tom sure this was why his brother had wanted him to see it—appointed a special deputy for the occasion, ostensibly to report back to him. Really there to observe as the restraints of civilization slipped away. It was a warm day, the air unbearably close and rank by the time they reached the prison platform, the men pulling off their jackets, sweat puddling on their necks and forming dark blotches under their arms. Then the doors opened, and the funereal smell of early lilacs and magnolias filled the air, reducing them all to silence for a moment. Pep Strauss just laughed.

A few weeks later, they put them to death on the same night. Pep first, now clean-shaven and dressed in his best suit. The insanity act abandoned, almost contemplative at the end. Goldstein issued into the chair just minutes later, the chamber still crackling with electricity, redolent with the smell of burnt flesh.

"Hey, it's still warm!" he said, laughing, when they sat him down, before the leather bit was shoved between his teeth. "Too bad I can't hold Reles's hand while I go!"

"A barbaric ritual," Charlie said afterward. "Telling a man exactly when he's going to die, weeks in advance. Shave him an' clean him up, an' give him a priest and his favorite meal. Show him all the kindness and humanity that might've kept him from arriving there in the first place. Then pull the switch, and watch him shit all over himself!"

* * *

The train pulled in as reluctantly as its human cargo. Tom staring up at the four iron walkways above, the watchtowers and the pretty, incongruous Victorian turrets. It was spring again, but cold, and the trees in the lovely, rolling hills above the village of Ossining looked threadbare and poor — not even the lilacs blooming yet. The sky low, and as gray as the stone prison walls, the only smell in the air this day the smoke wending slowly out of the prison workshop chimneys.

He held back for a minute, pretending to light a cigarette while he waited for a brace of detectives to march their prisoners through. Then he flashed his credentials at the gate and was led into an ancient, red-brick cellblock, the walls covered with dead brown veins of ivy. From there was shown into a small, ancient room, one of the oldest in the prison, where across a scarred wooden table sat Neddy Moran.

It jarred him to see him there, much as he'd tried to prepare himself for it: Neddy Moran in prison grays. The man he had watched at his brother's side so many times before, in one of his shapeless blue suits, or his court officer's uniforms, phlegmatic and stern. The same man leaning down tirelessly to wipe the drool from Claire O'Kane's face. His hulking body angled forward now over the table, like an aged oak bent down at last by its own size.

"Hello, Tom," he said with a softness that surprised him, so that he had to start fiddling with his briefcase to steady himself.

"Hello, Ned. Here, for you."

He slid the carton of Lucky Strikes he'd brought across the table to him. Moran smiled at it contemptuously.

"Always the considerate prison gift, useful as cash on the inside," he said, his voice again as surly and laconic as Tom remembered it now. He opened it up nonetheless, accepting the light Tom proffered and taking his first drag as gratefully as a man pulled from a river sucks in air.

"Ned, I need to ask you some things —" he started, pulling the great stack of paper from his briefcase.

"That the transcript from the trial?" Moran asked, cutting him off.

"Yes."

"Then you got it already. It's what I wrote you: I don't have anything to say to anybody."

Tom stared at him across the table. The huge, craggy face looked slack and unhealthy now, what hair he had left turned white. But the eyes were still bright and combative.

"How you gettin' on in here, Ned?"

Moran took another drag, idly glowering at him for a little while, then gave a slow, mountainous shrug.

"I can't kick. They have me in isolation from the general prison population here. For my own protection—or maybe theirs. What did Senator Tobey call me at the Kefauver hearings? 'That colossus of crime'?"

"That so? You know, I'm workin' for Hogan now, so—"

"So what?"

"So he can put in a word, get some time taken off your sentence. Maybe make it so you can serve your whole time down in the Tombs, where you can see your family every day . . . " The hard, dark eyes looked uncertain for just a moment. Then a mask of defiance descended again. "No thank you. You tell Mr. Frank fucking Hogan that I came into this world a man, and I'm going out a man."

"You know it works both ways—" Tom snapped in his frustration.

"Meaning what? You'll revoke my privileges? Put me in the general population, with the perverts an' the killers?" Moran sneered, crossing his arms defiantly against his chest. "Go ahead. You think you can still hurt me? You think anything could be worse already than having Mary an' the boys see me in this place?"

He took a last, deep drag, then stubbed out the cigarette on the bottom of his shoe and dropped it into his shirt pocket. He shoved the rest of the carton, including the opened pack, angrily back across the table.

"It's not like that!" Tom said hastily, scrambling now to keep the interview from ending. "It's not anything to do with Hogan, or anything else but Charlie. I need you to help me for *Charlie's* sake, Ned."

"You want me to help Charlie O'Kane? Haven't I done enough already?" he said, holding up his hands. But he pulled the carton back to himself, rustling out another cigarette. This time Tom flipped him the book of matches and he lit it for himself.

"This where you always knew I'd end up, Tom? Being such a terrible, corruptive influence on your brother? I know you never liked me, and to be honest, I never much liked you. I always thought you were a goo-goo phony with a bunch of high ideals that would only get Charlie into trouble. But I tell you this much: I never looked out for anybody else like I did your brother."

He half turned from Tom, sucking angrily on his cigarette, this huge man, like a petulant schoolboy sent to sit in a corner.

"Ned—"

"Did I ever ask for anything?" he burst out, turning back around. "Did I ask to have so much as a day taken off? Five years for perjury, another thirteen years on the rackets charge. *Eighteen years.* As much time as a man gets for an armed robbery gone bad. And all for doin' what it was they used to make men senators an' judges for: followin' orders and keepin' quiet."

"You don't think you belong here?" Tom asked him, thumping the trial transcript with his hand. "You made three hundred thousand dollars off the deputy fire commissioner job my brother gave you. A half million dollars of the public's money, all in all, skimmed off the top in inspection bribes *every year.*"

"Don't believe everything you read in the papers. The feds tried to get me on that, too. Income tax evasion—I don't have any money! We had to take eleven thousand dollars out of the pension fund an' mortgage the house, just to get through the trial."

"How much more in little envelopes from the Uniformed Firemen's Association, that Mr. Crane testified about?"

"John Crane is a fucking liar. He skimmed a hundred thirty-five thousand out of that fund by my count, and he had to do something to make it look right to the boys. Claiming he gave your brother ten thousand dollars in an envelope right out on the steps of Gracie Mansion!"

"Maybe he gave it to you instead?"

"That's what I was there for! Jesus, why would anyone ever hand OK Charlie ten thousand dollars? You know what your brother's like! When he was a magistrate he used to borrow haircut money from the clerks because he carried so little cash around."

"Then where did the rest of the fire inspection bribes go? To the campaign?"

"Some of it," Moran conceded. "You have to understand, I wasn't just tryin' to cut myself in. It was tryin' to regularize it."

"Regularize it?"

"Look, the fire inspectors get greased every time they give the okay to someone who wants to put in a new oil burner, or an oil tank," Moran said slowly and distinctly, as if he were explaining things to an especially dim child. "Been that way for goin' back to Boss goddamned Tweed, an' it'll be that way when we're dead an' gone. Twenty, thirty, fifty bucks, just to let 'em turn on the pilot light. Or didn't you know that, what with all your bleedin' heart plans to help the Jews get a homeland?"

"No, I didn't," Tom admitted. Wondering what else he didn't know, but trying not to show it.

"But you see, it was a dangerous business. Each inspector could charge whatever he liked, do whatever he wanted to pass for an inspection. I put a stop to it."

"*You* did? How?"

"I made 'em keep a log, and turn in every penny. There were *rules.* They had to do a real inspection. No money until they made sure the tank wasn't leakin' an' the burner wouldn't blow everyone on the block to kingdom come in the middle of the night. There was a sliding scale for what they could ask, dependin' on the size of the building, the size of the burner."

"You were takin' in five hundred thousand a year. That's some slide."

"There's about a thousand contractors who install oil burners in New York," Neddy said with that long shrug again. "That's five hundred dollars apiece — not so much. Call it the price of doin' business. And meanwhile, we get somethin' to keep the machine running, so the bankers an' the Wall Street boys can't just buy the City back."

"So you're doin' the people's business now, is it?"

Moran glared at him from across the table. "That's *always* been the people's business. Restoring order out of chaos. That's how things are done in the world of men. This is practical politics we're talkin' about. Not your boy's adventure story, shippin' off guns to help the poor Hebrews, or suing in court on behalf of every stray spic or nigger who gets roughed up by a cop."

"Is that how it works, Ned? Is that why you put my brother in the same apartment with the most notorious mobster in New York?"

The gangster's hands, fidgeting, interlocking, folding that piece of paper over and over again. Frank Costello, the Prime Minister of the Underworld. Indelibly associated with his brother now.

Moran paused in his anger, the massive, ruined face eyeing him warily now, Tom thought — uncertain again about something. *But what?*

"Going up to see Frank Costello in his apartment. Still dressed in the uniform of his country."

"It was himself, put him in that apartment," Moran said slowly, staring closely at Tom as if he were trying to pick up some signal, some visual clue. "I only made the arrangements."

"Did you? How was that?"

Moran drew out another cigarette, tapping it at the thick court transcript.

"You were at the trial," he said. "You have it right there. It was during the war, when he was with the army procurement office, investigating waste and racketeering."

Tom could have sworn he looked uncertain now, his rasping voice suddenly softer again. "That was his idea," Moran repeated. "I only set it up."

"Did you? Or did you put the idea in his head to start with?"

"It's like he testified. Read it yourself; it's all there!" Moran said, reaching across the table to push scornfully at the mound of paper Tom had brought. "It was when Charlie was still in the Materièl Division with the Army Air Corps, down in Washington. Around Christmas. The year after we got into the war, an' he was comin' up for the weekend to see Claire. He told me he wanted to set up a meeting with Frank Costello."

"He did? Why?"

Moran crossed his legs, pulling up the loose, shabby prison material and puffing away at his cigarette for a few more seconds before he answered.

"It's all in the transcript. He said he got an anonymous letter about racketeering out at Wright Field, in Ohio," he said carefully, like a led witness trying his best to follow a tricky cross-examination.

"Who was that?"

"Fella named Irving Sherman. He supplied shirts to the navy. Charlie used to talk to him all the time."

"Why would a man who supplied shirts to the *navy* brief him on an Army Air Corps base?"

"Call it interservice cooperation. Anyway, he knew Costello, so I gave him a call an' set it up. The Century apartments, twenty-five Central Park West. Charlie said he'd meet me at Columbus Circle, by that restaurant across from the park."

"And you didn't think that was funny? Go an' talk with the Prime Minister of the Underworld in his own apartment? Why not drag him down to Washington, or at least downtown to give him the third degree?"

"He said that would be a mistake. He said an old pro like Frank Costello would just clam up, an' haul along a dozen lawyers. Tip everybody off. Charlie said it was best to keep it low-key, so he asked me to set it up."

The two of them huddling together in their overcoats, out on the bitter corner. Out in that wartime city Tom had only known in transit, or on short passes. A city of shadows. Of dimmed lights and packed dance clubs. People out everywhere, all the time, finally with a little money in their pockets for the first time in years, and nothing else to spend it on. Everybody laughing a little too loud, talking a little too fast. The streets full of staggering drunks, couples groping and pawing at each other in doorways. Men in uniform passed out in the subways, their pockets turned out.

"It was Charlie's idea to show up in uniform. I told him then an' there, I didn't think he should be seen in a mob boss's apartment, dressed in the uniform of a U.S. Army general," Moran said. "I told him I thought he should at least change into his civvies, keep a lower profile. But you know Charlie. He said he wanted to keep it all open and aboveboard. He said he had nothin' to hide."

"He didn't. He *had* nothing to hide; you knew that," Tom said indignantly. Moran looked at him for another long moment before resuming.

"I took him up from there. The Century was one of those fancy new places. You know, all that art deco junk in the lobby, and a doorman to announce you. We went up in the elevator, and Costello had his butler meet us at the door. Nice place, like somethin' you'd see at the Translux."

"Big, was it?"

"Big enough to fit half the politicians in New York."

"Who was there?"

"Just all of Tammany Hall. Plenty of Republicans, too. The aforementioned Irving Sherman —"

"Fresh from supplying fresh shirts to our boys at sea?"

"I suppose. There was Generoso Pope, strutting about telling everyone how he was going to take care of that goddamned Tresca once an' for all. Carmine De Sapio, the little creep, lookin' like a vampire with his sunglasses on inside. More goddamned guineas everywhere. All of 'em four sheets to the wind already, the hypocrites — boozin' and laughin' it up like the war was the best thing that ever happened to 'em. I'm just surprised they didn't have some girls up there, too."

"What was the occasion?"

"Nothin' special. I think they were all goin' to a show afterward — or maybe it was the fights. This was just a little warm-up action."

"Who did my brother talk to?"

"A few of the guests, just to say hi. Then he went into a back bedroom somewhere, to talk to Costello. It was a helluva big apartment."

"How long were they there?"

"Not long. Maybe fifteen minutes. It felt like a goddamned lifetime to me, I can tell you that," Moran recalled with real feeling now. "The boys kept offerin' me somethin' to drink, but I didn't want it. I just stood by the door, wantin' to get Charlie away from there as quick as possible."

"Why?"

"Because it didn't look right. Because you know Charlie. He could charm the ears off a jackass, but then he'll just wander off an' say the first damned thing that comes into his head to the wrong person."

Tom thinking of the bantam senator from New Hampshire, shaking his finger at his brother for the cameras: *It seems to me you should've said about Costello, 'Unclean! Unclean!' and left him like a leper!' The Greek chorus of heads in the audience behind him nodding in unison while Charlie fumed and tugged at his collar . . .*

"What did you think he was liable to say?"

"I didn't know. There was an evil air in there. I thought maybe the whole thing was some kind of setup, you want the God's honest truth," Moran told him, leaning forward emphatically. "I thought, we're gonna go up in this goddamned art deco piece of shit, and there'll be ten nude girls there, an' the next thing you know Westbrook Pegler and a couple hundred photographers will come bustin' down the door. You know what I mean?"

"Sure."

"In short, to answer your question, I didn't think it was a good place to be. I was about to go take a hunt for him in Mr. Frank Costello's palatial apartment when out they came."

"With what?"

"With nothin'. He said exactly what he did to the Kefauver committee. That Costello told him he didn't know a thing about the Wright Field contracts, that he stayed away from anything to do with the military."

"That was all?"

"All that I ever knew. They went off to their fights, or their show, an' me an' Charlie went home to Brooklyn. All those ward heelers laughin' their asses off, while the maid brought 'em canapés on a tray! I remember we stared out the window at the view Frank Costello had, while we waited for the butler to bring us our coats. It only took in about half of Manhattan. And your brother gave me a wink, an' that OK Charlie grin of his, an' he says, 'This is the problem with virtue.' You had to love the man."

Tom trying to picture them there. The two of them, each raised from nothing. Still just getting by on their public-service salaries, while the big party went on around them. Staring out at the blackened expanse of the park, and the towers all around it. Darkened for the blackout, too, but still shimmering in the moonlight, and all the more alluring for it. Standing in the foyer of a rich man's home, waiting for their coats, and looking out at everything their gangster host could see every day . . .

"And that was it?"

"That was all I heard. You have to remember, that's when we were separated, during the war. I saw him sometimes when he came up from Washington to see Claire. But most of the time, he was off all over the country, then over to Italy."

"Why didn't he take you with him?"

"My job was to stay here, and keep an eye on things. He was still the district attorney of Kings County. I had to look after the office. And Mrs. O'Kane, of course."

"Was that a chore for you?"

Instantly, Moran's face was a bright, furious red. "It was an honor!" he exclaimed angrily. "It was a privilege, to help a woman like that. She had such class, Clairey O'Kane . . ."

He trailed off, tears brimming in his eyes, and Tom was astonished. Revising instantly his memories of the hulking man in his court uniform, leaning down to wipe her mouth, or dust away her dandruff in the wheelchair. Doing it now not as a drudgery to curry favor but carefully, as an act of love. Could it be?

"I saw more of her than I did me own wife an' boys in those days, but it was never a chore. She had such refinement! She was such a kind woman, even when she was dying. Never had a hard word for anyone. Never blamed Charlie for goin' off to war an' leavin' her stuck in that chair.

"'Charlie's the sort, has to go off and see the elephant,' she used to say. 'It would be cruel to try to deprive him of that. Probably unsuccessful, too. Charlie does what he wants to do, in the end.' She was so understanding. Half the time, she'd end up comforting *me* with all my little complaints and troubles. God, but she was a good woman!"

"She was that," Tom said, still surprised.

"You know, she could hardly even smile by then. But she'd do it with her eyes. How much that woman could convey by her eyes alone! And it was always kindness. It was always good cheer, even mischief. She worried about all of us. She cared about me an' my little problems, an' she worried about you away in Italy, and of course she was heartbroken when she got the telegram that Jimmy died. So was I, so was I.

"But the one she worried about the most was Charlie. She never *stopped* worryin' about him. But not for why I thought."

"What d'ya mean?"

"I thought she worried about what I worried about. Which was gettin' Charlie's nose out of his books, an' gettin' him through the day without some farmer sellin' him a load of magic beans."

"But that wasn't it?"

"No! She was always afraid Charlie was *too* ambitious for his own good. 'He's always gettin' ahead of himself,' she would say. 'That's what you must be careful of once I'm gone. You must make sure he doesn't get too much ahead of himself, for one day he'll get his head an' run right over a cliff. That's my Charlie.'"

The tears running freely down his cheeks even as he related this. Tom remembered now how he had wept at the funeral. *The big man looking down at his lap during all the grand pomp at Saint Pat's, his shoulders heaving, his wife trying to console him. Still bawling into his handkerchief as he helped carry her out as the lead pallbearer, carting his share of the coffin easily with one enormous paw. He'd thought at the time it was the overweening tears of a courtier, but he could see it all now, how bereft he really was.*

So if he wasn't the schemer — and it wasn't Charlie . . .

"Did you know that Frank Bals didn't pick the guard detail at the Half Moon?" he asked abruptly, Moran's head jolting back as if slapped.

"No? Who did, then? Are you accusin' me —"

"It was Jack McGrath. Or at least that's what the cops say."

"The Old Man," Moran mused affectionately. "How's he doin'? I heard he's not long."

"No."

"I can remember him up in the Rats Suite that morning, helpin' all those idjits get their stories straight —"

"You mean, obstructing a police investigation?"

"Ah, come off it, will ya? Reles was stone dead already, an' there was no use gettin' seven fine officers in trouble for the demise of a punk like that, just because they fell asleep!"

Tom stared at him. "You *knew* they were sleepin'?"

"What else would they have been doin'? Dancin' the gavotte down in the Oceana Grille? Those were good men. They made a mistake, it shouldn't've ruined their careers."

"How did Reles die, then? How'd he go out the window?"

"Oh, for Christ's sake, if I knew *that* —"

"But you did know who Reles was going to testify against next. Didn't you?" Tom struck home. "Once he put all of Murder, Inc., away. The next guy was Albert Anastasia, the Camardas' chief enforcer down on the docks."

"So?" Moran snorted.

"So when my brother went to the war, and you were left in charge of the DA's office back in Brooklyn — why did you have Albert Anastasia's wanted card pulled from the police files?"

"Because there was no case! Not after Reles died. It was a clerical procedure. Besides, what cop in New York couldn't spot Albert Anastasia —"

"A clerical procedure? Taking the wanted card for the most-wanted man in New York out of the police ID files?"

"What're you drivin' at?" Moran said, his tone angry and bewildered. "What d'ya want from me now?"

"How about the files my brother got from the Camarda locals? On all those thugs over there? You got John Harlan Amen, the state special prosecutor, to hand you over their files on the Camardas, and their boy Anastasia. But they went missing, too."

That whole weird movie set along the piers. The Old Man standing atop a customs shed with his bullhorn, Charlie snapping orders. The detectives carting off their armloads of ledger books. The faces of the longshoremen and their wives and children, staring blank and spectral in the white klieg lights . . .

"How the hell should I know what happened to 'em? That was over twelve years ago! We had good information; we made a raid. Hauled in every gangster we could find, every one of their ledger books, every document we could get our hands on. Amen was so impressed, he gave us his evidence, too."

"And there it stayed. Buried away somewhere in the Brooklyn DA's files during the war, while you quietly let those cases drop, too —"

"There *was* no case! You think those thugs would let us take their real books? They'd already burned those — probably the minute that little bastard in City Hall got Governor Lehman to name Amen the special prosecutor. You know that as well as I do!"

"That's not what Charlie said the night of the raid," Tom persisted. "He told the papers the raid broke the case against the Camardas wide open. He said he had proof that night they'd extorted six hundred thousand dollars from the longshoremen. He said he had a perfect case against Anastasia —"

"But don't ya see, that's your brother all over? The perfect moon calf he could be? He did a fine job in the DA's office, never saw a man work like that in my life. But then he'd get ahead of himself, start promising what he couldn't deliver. We didn't have a case, we had to bluff our way through as best we could."

"Who killed Peter Panto, Neddy?"

"You know the last as well as I do! You read Reles's testimony —"

"I mean who put him on the spot. Who gave him the orders?"

"Say, what is this?" Moran said, drawing himself up in his chair, his eyes dark pools of suspicion. "How's this supposed to help Charlie? What're you tryin' to pull here?"

"Just answer me. Just tell me what you know — tell me what you think. What was Bill McCormack's part in it? You know — 'Mr. Big'?"

"I think I've done enough for Charlie O'Kane to last a lifetime, that's what I think," Moran said, stubbing out his butt. It followed the other two into his pocket. He snatched up the rest of the carton and went over to bang on the door.

"I'm not confessing to a capital crime for him or anyone else, I don't care what he did for me. Especially a crime I didn't commit."

"Goddamnit, Neddy, that's not what I'm talkin' about —" Tom cried, not even sure what was happening. But the guard had already appeared to take Neddy Moran back to his cell.

"You tell Charlie O'Kane he wants another favor, he can come ask it for himself. That's if he's ever man enough to come back from Mexico. You tell him he can't buy me anymore," Neddy said, his face flushed and contemptuous again. "Tell it to Mr. Frank Hogan, too. I'll do my time an' I'll keep me mouth shut. But they can both go to hell."

He waved the carton of cigarettes sarcastically at Tom as he left.

"Thanks for the smokes!"

16

New York, 1953

"Don't get discouraged."

Hogan uncuffed his French sleeves and folded them slowly, fastidiously up his arm before picking up the chalk. Then he began to print names on the blackboard they'd rolled in from the conference room, writing in meticulously straight, precise little letters. When he was through, he pointed to each of the names in turn as he spoke. Tom listening slumped in the chair where he had thrown himself as soon as he got back from Sing Sing. Certain that he was missing something and even more frustrated that he couldn't figure out what it was.

"Albert Anastasia. Dear Albert was chief enforcer for the Camardas on the docks — among others."

Hogan drew a line from Anastasia to the next name: King Joe Ryan.

"We know the Camardas had the blessing of King Joe Ryan, president-for-life of the International Longshoremen's Association. But we also know that King Joe Ryan is no king at all, just a smarmy little puppet of" — he drew one more line, to a name that read only, "Mr. Big," then put a question mark next to it — "Mr. Big. Who may be Bill McCormack."

"Who else?" Tom said bleakly. "You can read that in *Life* magazine."

"That's not good enough. We're in the proof business here," Hogan corrected him. "What we want to know is how Frank Costello fits into all this."

"Moran explained what they were doing there —"

"I'm not buying any of that. *Yet*," Hogan said, cutting him off. "Certainly not on the word of Neddy."

"What *could* Costello have to do with it?"

"I don't know." Hogan weighed the question, rubbing a hand over his cheek as he studied the chalkboard. "He's run Luciano's outfit since we first shipped Charlie Lucky upstate. But Costello's really more of a politician than a mob boss. A fixer with Tammany. He doesn't have anything to do with the docks, from what I know of, doesn't like the strong-arm stuff. For all that 'Prime Minister of the Underworld' hooey in the papers, he's just a glorified gambler, with his card games, his race wires, and his slot machines. Keeps the boys happy by spreading the wealth around. Had the good sense to get out of town, go down to New Orleans when La Guardia was in."

"What're you sayin', Boss?"

"Just this. Costello does a lot of favors, carries a lot of messages for his friends. And one of his friends is Albert Anastasia. He's part of the muscle that keeps him in power."

"Maybe," Tom said tersely. "But by the time my brother went up there, Anastasia was already off the hook."

"Sure."

Hogan made a pair of annotations along the line he had drawn.

"Albert lams it the minute Reles turned himself in and started blabberin'. March 1940. He stays out of sight for over two years. Then, Neddy Moran pulls his police ID card from the files of every precinct in the City, and — *mirabile dictu* — he resurfaces, almost on cue. Then Albert joins the army for the duration. Even makes sergeant!"

Another mark on the chalkboard.

"Your brother and Mr. Moran don't visit Costello until Christmastime, over six months later."

"And the whole of that time, my brother was in the army, travelin' all over the country with the inspector general's office," Tom told him, his jaw set hard.

"That's true. But Charlie was still keeping in touch with Ned Moran enough to have Neddy set up his meeting with Costello," Hogan pointed out. "Yet we're still supposed to believe he didn't know anything about Moran pulling Anastasia's wanted card. Or how the state prosecutor's case — John Harlan Amen's case — got made to disappear in the first place."

"There must be a reason," Tom insisted.

"I'm sure there's a reason," Hogan said drily. "The question is whether it's a good one. And what does it have to do with our Mr. McCormack?"

New York, 1940

He met Mr. Big the night of the racket for Joe Ryan. Standing in the back of the ballroom at the Commodore Hotel, looking as unobtrusive as possible for a man over six feet tall, with the shoulders and chest of a linebacker, a chin like a destroyer's bow, and a pair of clear blue eyes that promised merry mayhem.

Tom was still in mourning for Peter Panto then. Going back and forth in a daze from his law school classes to his new job clerking for Natie Cohen in his brother's old firm. Barely able to force himself to the giddy celebration at the Saint George Hotel when Charlie won his race for the district attorney's office a few days later. Duly nodding his head when his brother took him aside, assuring him that now that he was in charge, things would be different.

Things were too late already, he wanted to say.

The words by then beginning to appear all along the Brooklyn waterfront: DOVE PANTO? WHERE IS PANTO? Chalked and painted along the walls and the dock sheds and the warehouses, on the railroad cars and the loading trucks and inside the dark holds of the ships they worked. This strange appeal, pleading and demanding at the same time. Spreading slowly out from the waterfront and into the daylight city, to baffle the commuters and the housewives and the office workers. Written on subway tiles, and the sides of Manhattan office buildings, and the sidewalks up on the Heights and Park Slope. In leaflets in Italian and English, blowing along with the winter trash in the streets: *Where is Panto? Where is Panto? Where is Panto?* Still threatening enough that the *shlammers,* sleek as seals in their overcoats, paused long enough to get their hands dirty and reach down into the gutters for them, balling them up and throwing them into the ashcans before hurrying away.

DOVE PANTO?

But everybody knew where he was. In a quicklime pit somewhere, or a building foundation, or a rusting oil barrel bobbing among the buoys out past Seagate. The strikes were over now, the Rank-and-File Committee shut down. The old halls along the waterfront gathering dust again, as they had for so many years. Tom hadn't gone back to the docks at all, unable to bear looking at the defeated men in their shabby loose clothing crowding in for the morning shape. Too cowed to tell the cops and the newspaper reporters anything more now than "We are men with families, and want to live."

The last thing he felt like doing was putting on black tie and going to a big can racket for King Joe Ryan, but Charlie had insisted on taking both him and Jimmy, saying he wanted to teach them a lesson in practical politics. When they got there, Tom was astonished by the enormous size of the room, packed as it was to the walls with hundreds of tables, each one topped with an immense, silly floral centerpiece. Red, white, and blue bunting streaming from the balconies as if it were the upper deck of Yankee Stadium during the World Series. Blown-up photos of King Joe Ryan's pug's face—a face that always looked as if it were taken unawares—strung up in between.

He turned over the menu card on his plate, his eyes skimming in astonishment over the words there: *"Petite marmite Henry IV... prime sirloin with mushroom sauce... bombe praline..."* The whole event had a starchy, well-heeled air, more like a society function than a smoker. There were only a few women in attendance, but they were dressed in formal gowns and gloves and being shuttled slowly around the dance floor to the tunes of a somnambular orchestra.

All around him he could make out the faces of some of the worst *shlammers* from the docks, struggling with their salad forks and their *marmite* cheek-by-jowl with the most powerful and respected men in the City, business executives and elected officials, civic reformers and financiers. The goons and the statesmen all but indistinguishable from one another once they put on their tuxedoes.

Charlie sat between him and Jimmy, pointing out all the big men in attendance: Al Smith and Jimmy Walker sitting up on the dais, along with Archbishop Spellman, and Monsignor "Taxi Jack" O'Donnell, from Guardian Angel.

"Why do they call him 'Taxi Jack'?" Jimmy asked with his usual innocence, enjoying himself, pleased to be away from his law studies for an evening.

"Because every year, King Joe Ryan and the waterfront businessmen chip in and put a brand-new, chauffeured limousine at his disposal," Tom interjected. "They keep him in his little toy parish down by the docks, just so long as he goes along and does as he's told."

"Over there is Mr. Hague, the boss of Jersey City, and his boys. Happy Keane, and Connie McKeon, and the Little Man, John Kenny," Charlie said, smoothing over his words, as if they had never been said. "And over at that next table is George the Fifth—George V. McLaughlin, president of the Brooklyn Trust."

"Who's the one next to him with the ham for a face?" Jimmy asked.

"That's O'Malley, his flunky," Charlie said, his voice amused. "George the Fifth's got him trying to turn the Dodgers into a paying proposition, if ye can imagine that one. He says O'Malley even counts how many peanuts there are in each bag, poor idjit."

"Why don'tcha tell him who else is here?" Tom asked him. Surprising himself with how furious he felt.

"What's that?" Charlie asked amicably, sawing away at his steak.

"Only some of the worst killers on the docks. Cockeye Dunn, who runs another of the pistol locals for King Joe. Socks Lanza from the fish market," Tom said, jabbing his finger openly about the room. "Mike Clemente from the East Side, Alex DiBrizzi, who's uncle of the Three D's over in Staten Island. Men who beat and crush and murder workingmen every day, Jimmy—"

Charlie admonished him mildly, hooking a thumb behind him. "Now, Tommy, *every*body's here tonight."

Following his gaze to a far corner of the ballroom, Tom could make out Mayor La Guardia at a table with Governor Lehman and Robert Moses, the three of them sitting glumly over their sirloin.

"What's the mayor doing here?" he asked out loud, truly astonished.

"King Joe Ryan controls the union; the union has the votes," Charlie told him patiently. "If he wants the votes, he has to come to the union. That's the way any city is run, Tom. Especially *this* city, which was the first one ever to be run by the people."

"And where do the people come in, exactly?" Tom shot back, struggling to keep his voice down—to keep from saying something that would hurt his brother although he felt at this moment he would very much like to. "With King Joe Ryan, president-for-life? The monsignor he pays off in donations and a chauffeured car? The killers and muggers, breaking bread with us as if they were decent men?"

But by then the waiters were removing the red meat and the speeches had begun—the same sorts of speeches that always accompany free dinners, indulgent, witless, and long. After an hour or two they worked their way around to Taxi Jack O'Donnell, who was to introduce King Joe himself. He opened with a prayer and closed with a blessing, performing in between the not inconsiderable feat of looking down his nose and up to heaven at the same time.

At last he brought on King Joe, whom he praised for "bringing the return of a man's world to our docks." Unfathomable as his introduction was, it reduced Ryan to real tears, sliding down the long accordion folds of his florid, expressive face. Tom had never seen the man this close before. He had a fighter's cauliflower ears and high, thick eyebrows, and his hair so dark and tightly plastered on his head that it might have been shoe polish. He had a barrel chest, and thick, flat fingers with jeweled rings that sparkled on both pinkies as he tapped them up and down. Blubbering out the gripping story of · how he had risen from nothing in the world, interspersed with the usual one-liners.

"Now, I know many lies have been spoken about how we use union funds, an' what the boys think of us, but I want to tell you right now — next to meself, the thing I like best is silk underwear!

It got a big laugh from the stewed crowd, the killers and the executives alike now stuffed with *marmite* and glazed in scotch. One of them yelled out drunkenly, *"Behind ya all the way, Joe!"* and Tom would have walked out then and there, but Charlie grabbed the end of his jacket.

"I was an orphan boy at nine, but this union has seen fit to make me a leader of men, and to sit in the halls of power. I especially want to thank Monsignor O'Donnell, who I rely upon as my advisor in all things having to do with the spirit, an' William McCormack, of the Mooremack Lines, who has always looked out for me, and who did so much to organize this event tonight—"

"Bravo! Bravo!"

A paunchy, twinkly old man with a pair of grandfatherly spectacles on his nose was standing and applauding fervently a couple of tables away. Tom had noticed him talking and laughing raucously the whole night, oblivious of the other speakers, and now his bow tie was undone, his tux splattered with large soup stains. He looked down at one of his tablemates while he clapped. The man with those linebacker's shoulders and chest, and jutting chin, who seemed genuinely embarrassed by all the attention, smiling gently and trying to wave the excited grandfather back into his seat. Instead, the old man grabbed McCormack by his lapels and planted a big kiss on the top of his head — the rest of the room laughing and applauding while King Joe Ryan gestured dramatically from the dais, a last tear running out of one eye.

"Who's that?" It was Tom's turn to ask, the faces vaguely familiar though he was unable to place them.

"Why, that's the Holy Trinity over there," his brother told him. "Subway

Sam Rosoff, William McCormack, an' Generoso Pope — a Jew, a Mick, and a Dago. They must've built half the City. Sam alone's dug out fifty million dollars' worth of the subway —"

"And three years ago he had the sandhogs' union rep killed. I remember. Less than twelve hours after he broke off negotiations —"

"That's just hearsay —"

"And Pope? Who runs that fascist sheet, *Il Progresso*?" Tom blurted, staring over at the third man — a handsome, fussily coiffed and dressed individual who sat with his arms crossed and his chest stuck out as if he were Il Duce himself.

"Well, now, that's another country —"

The *bombe praline* arrived, a perfect tit, complete with a nipple of a cherry on top, and they all dug in enthusiastically. When the brandy and the cigars came out, Tom excused himself to wander at random between the tables, watching all the shmoozing and the glad-handing of the great and the useful.

Nobody has anything against anybody anymore, he thought, marveling, *and nothing means anything. Reformers and crooks, bosses and union men. Killers and human beings — it's all the same in here.*

He saw his brother head toward one of the long corridors leading off the grand ballroom and went after him, wanting to get out of this place as soon as possible, but he lost him in the crowd of identical black coats. It was there, searching about, that he found himself face-to-face with William McCormack, standing back by a pillar and still looking for all the world as if he did not want to be seen. But neither one of them was able to move away in the crush, and McCormack nodded politely to him.

"You're the brother," he said matter-of-factly. "It's good to have a brother who looks out for you."

"It is," Tom said warily, unsure what this man could possibly want from him.

"God knows, my brother did it enough for me. He's always had the heart of a lion, Harry."

He nodded toward a man a few yards away who looked like a cruder, rougher version of himself — short and squat, with an even broader chest and shoulders, and hands that looked like paddles and seemed to hang nearly to his knees.

"I remember, there was one time back in the Horseshoe over in Jersey City, when I was gettin' the worst of it from a couple a teamsters. Harry come after them with a cooperage adz. That was the end a that," he said in a pleasant voice, a faint smile playing around his lips.

"You seem to know how to make your way around the docks," Tom said deliberately, but McCormack only gave a soft chuckle.

"Well, let's just say it's not for the poor in spirit, or the pure of heart," McCormack told him. "There used to be some hard lads down there — men like Tanner Smith and Rubber Shaw, who ran with the Hudson Dusters. I remember the night when Shaw shot Tanner, back in July of 1919, just after the Great War."

He gave another light chuckle, like a man reminiscing over a good hand of pinochle, and looked Tom in the eye.

"The man Shaw really wanted to kill, though, was *me*. He come into the Avonia Club, where I was playin' cards. Oh, that was a warm night! The perspiration was already drippin' off our necks, so he couldn't see me sweat. He come right up behind me, and I knew he had to have a piece on him."

"What'd you do?"

"There was nothin' I *could* do. He had me if he wanted me. All I could do was keep playin' cards, an' hope he wouldn't have the balls to shoot me in front of ten witnesses."

"And?"

"And he didn't. He stood there watchin' me play poker for a little while. Then he went out without a word, and went over to the Marginals' clubhouse on Sixteenth Street an' shot Tanner Smith." McCormack paused significantly, the merry blue eyes dancing. "Two weeks later, he wound up dead himself over in Hoboken, where he was tryin' to hole up. Things have a way of comin' back around."

"Am I supposed to take that as a message, Mr. McCormack?" Tom asked.

"Take it any way you like!" McCormack told him with a laugh that was almost charming but fell just short.

Tom didn't know if he'd ever met a man who radiated more aggressive, animal energy — not even the *shlammers* who had surrounded them like so many wolves back on President Street. It seemed to all but burst from his chest, his jutting chin and jaw.

"I know you were raising hell down on my pier, and I don't mind," McCormack told him. "I respect a man who can stand up for himself."

"Like Peter Panto?"

McCormack's eyes flicked downward, as if politely ignoring a grave social gaffe. "Ah, I was very sorry to hear about that," he said. "There's another man who could raise some hell, and I respected him for it, too. I blame myself for not getting down there an' makin' everyone work it out. But there was hot-heads on either side."

"You would've settled it?"

"That's what I believe in. Get right down on the job, talk it over with the men, and work it out face-to-face! That's how the Holy Father says it should be done. We have a doctrine for it in the church; it's called subsidiarity. Men of faith settling their differences as equals and Christians, with no one else to interfere."

"Which is why you're sitting at table tonight with Generoso Pope? Because you're a good Christian?"

"Oh, Genny's a right guy! He's just what I'm talkin' about, worked his way up from nothin', same as me an' Harry. When he first come over here he got his start haulin' water for the hod carriers. Now he's the biggest sand-and-gravel man in New York!"

"He runs a fascist newspaper."

"That's about Italy. Here in America, he's a regular Democrat. As are we all."

"And Sam Rosoff? He only does his killing over in Jersey?"

"Sam never killed anyone," McCormack scoffed, " 'cept maybe a few people he bored to death talkin' about his subways. You should see him at his dinner parties! He gets so worked up he drags his guests down to one of his digs in their evenin' clothes!"

"How about King Joe Ryan? Is it true what they say?" Tom asked.

"What's that now?"

"That he doesn't scratch his ass without gettin' your written permission?"

But McCormack just laughed at him again. "Whattaya think, that I run this whole town myself? Joe's an old friend; we have lunch sometimes over at Toots Shor's. Just to share what we know an' see what we can both do to keep the port runnin' smoothly."

McCormack regarded him coolly now, his eyes narrowing.

"We all make our way in this world. Genny, an' Sam an' your own brother, and what's wrong with that?" he asked. "How else would ya have us do it? You know, my old man, he was famine Irish. He worked down the Washington Market haulin' fruit and vegetables for thirty-nine years. Then he got sick an' missed a day of work. *One day.* They gave him the sack, sent him home with half a week's wages. Thirty-nine years, an' it's seven dollars an' goodbye!"

"So—"

"So you talk about fascism, that's what fascism is to me! Some big boss, some power nobody ever elected who makes all the rules, and no appeal. What you see here tonight, this is the alternative—all of us together sayin' what goes. The good and the bad, an' the strong an' the clever. Not relyin' on some big, faceless power like the Port Authority they're always pushin' to have take over the harbor. I'd just as soon have Harry with his adz to even things up—"

He stopped talking abruptly as another man joined them, this one about Tom's age. He slipped a horse's neck into McCormack's hand with the obsequiousness of a butler, and Tom noticed that he was holding one himself, the two of them contentedly sipping their ginger ales with lemon slices when nearly every other man in the room had brandy and a cigar in hand. He nodded at Tom but said nothing until McCormack introduced him.

"This is my son, William Junior," he announced with a pride and a warmth that surprised Tom.

Junior was a little slighter and finer boned than his father, and more serious-looking, his hair still dark and his deep-set eyes studying everything closely. Bill Senior, he noticed, kept his eyes on him the whole time.

"Bill here is taking over our new gas station chain, Morania Gas and Oil. Just two years out of college, and already he's my right-hand man. I don't know what I'd do without him."

William Junior demurred—"You'd do every bit as well as you always do, Da"—but the pride he took at the compliment was evident in his voice. He looked at Tom. "I'm just trying to learn what I can from him."

"We was just havin' a bit of a chat about church doctrine an' the New York waterfront," his father told him, a note of warning in his voice that Tom decided to ignore.

"And what happens to the likes of Peter Panto in subsidiarity? Where does he fit in? Or does he just fall through the cracks?"

"That was a shame," McCormack said, his great predator's jaw snapping shut. "Nothing of that sort should ever happen."

"How could it not happen? Have you seen the men who run things on your piers, Mr. McCormack?"

McCormack nodded grimly, still looking at his son more than Tom.

"It's true, there's too many of these boy-oes gettin' beyond themselves just now. That's the trouble after all these years of labor an' management fightin' one another. Each side bringin' in their gangsters. We're goin' to clean 'em all out now that we've elected an honest, decent man like your brother district attorney. You have my word on that."

He said this last with such gravity and sincerity that Tom could almost believe he meant it. Before he could think of how to respond, McCormack thrust a hand out, and Tom grasped it despite himself, feeling the power of his grip, the rough, horned palm and gnarled fingers of the old teamster. McCormack staring him straight in the eyes as he did so, his gaze steady and riveting.

Bill Junior spoke up then, breaking the spell. "Mr. O'Kane, I believe I saw your brother just down the hall. He was talking with the governor."

McCormack dropped his hand and clapped him on both shoulders, grinning a wide, lupine grin at him. "That's what I mean! Man to man. Don't worry, lad, you'll see things change!"

At that moment Charlie reappeared, his brow furrowed. Governor Lehman veering off behind him looking, as always, as serene as an Italian cardinal.

"He's gonna name a special prosecutor," Charlie said, walking up and talking to them at once. "That goddamned Lehman! He's going to appoint someone to look into Panto, and all the waterfront locals."

"Who, Charlie?" asked McCormack right away.

"John Harlan Amen."

"He's a good man. Completely incorruptible," McCormack answered, making each word sound like an indictment. Tom could only look on — stunned by just what good terms his brother seemed to be on with McCormack, how intimate they were with each other. He noticed as well that Bill Junior had already receded somewhere into the crowd.

"He can't do this to me!" Charlie said, turning to Tom, his face red with anger. "I just got in, and now he wants to take my biggest case away from me!"

"Maybe it's for the best, Charlie—"

"The hell it is! It's cutting my balls off. It's caving in to that goddamned Dewey because Lehman's scared the man'll beat him the next time out!"

"He can't just appoint some uptown reformer like Amen," McCormack put in. "He doesn't know Brooklyn; he doesn't know the docks the way you do. They'll screw the whole case."

Charlie pulled himself up straighter, tugging down the lapels of his tux jacket.

"We've got to head him off," he announced to Tom. "We've got to find a way around him."

"Whatever you need, Charlie," Bill McCormack said, quietly as a prayer, before Charlie nodded a terse goodbye, pulling Tom away with him.

There was a sudden swelling in conversation around them, and Tom had the distinct impression that he had been subjected to some kind of performance, though what and why, he could not for the life of him imagine. But before they could leave, a familiar, frog-like figure with slits for eyes brushed hard past Tom. *Emil Camarda.* Pausing only long enough to pump his distracted brother's hand and bestow on Tom a knowing, gold-flecked smile.

"See?" he said. "I told you I'd be glad he was elected!" And then he was lost again in the world of men.

The following night they made the raid. Tom had just reached the DA's office when the black, armor-plated sedan sped up out of the garage and jerked to a stop at the curb beside him. The back door popping open, and a voice commanding tersely from within: "Get in."

Tom bent down to see his brother in the back seat, Captain Frank Bals, in full dress uniform and regalia, there beside him.

"What, you were going to leave without me?" he said, trying to joke, but both men's faces were rigid. He saw then that the police captain was holding something by his side, pointed at the floor.

"Jesus, Frank, is that a Tommy gun?"

"Just get in the damned car. Now!" Charlie barked, and Tom did as he was told and slid himself in.

"Why all the mystery, Charlie?" he said, trying to joke again, but one look at Charlie's unsmiling face told him not to.

Just then more long, dark official police cars began to speed out of the underground garage like bats startled from under a bridge. They poured out over the hump of the driveway, then gunned their motors, accelerating noisily away. On many of them, he noticed, still more cops resplendent in full-dress uniforms were clutching tightly to the running boards. After them came the white, red-crossed ambulances, and the boxy black Mariahs, the whole scene reminding him of nothing so much as a gangster movie about Chicago.

They roared off with the rest, a motorcycle escort falling in around them. Neddy Moran, phlegmatic and morose as ever, was behind the wheel. A pair of assistant DAs up there beside him, leafing hastily through thick piles of warrants on their knees. They didn't have far to go, just a slight hitch from the courts down through North Gowanus to the docks, but through all their urgent rides together over the years — all their *adventures* — Tom had never seen his brother look so agitated and fidgety. He was dressed as splendidly as the cops, Tom noticed — new, dark-gray alpaca coat, a Borsalino with a gray silk band on his head — but he couldn't seem to keep from rubbing his hands together, crossing and uncrossing his legs.

"We just got word — Governor Lehman's special investigator is about to make his move. We put this little flying squad together on the fly," Charlie told him.

"What? You were serious about that?"

"Of course!"

"But *shouldn't* we let them have it? They're the state, after all. John Harlan Amen, he's always been on the up-an'-up. Why —"

"Because it's *mine*, don'tcha know it, Tommy!" his brother snapped at him, so vehemently it made the heads of Frank Bals and the two ADAs swivel about — Neddy Moran even checking in the rearview mirror. "Because it's my territory, my jurisdiction, my case! How else d'ya think a DA makes his way in the world — by letting other men make his cases for him?"

"Is that what this is about? Territory?" Tom asked, his voice soft with disappointment.

"No, of course not," Charlie said, less harshly, in a low, urgent, confidential voice that made the other heads in the car swivel away again. "It is about me bein' able to do my job. Jesus, Tommy, don'tcha see it? If Dewey can get Lehman to supersede me with some special prosecutor, if he makes me look like I'm one more machine hack, I'm finished."

"I see that," Tom admitted glumly.

"We can't afford to let 'em louse it up," Charlie continued. "A buncha special cops an' special lawyers from Albany! If they blow it, the Camardas can do as they please."

"The Camardas? We're raiding the Camardas?" Tom asked, his head reeling. Charlie grinned at him.

"*Now* will you trust your big brother?"

They drove into Red Hook and pulled up by the Atlantic Basin, making only about the noise a small mechanized army would make. But to Tom's surprise there was no sign of any activity from the docks or the pier sheds before them—the Camarda headquarters where he had gone with Peter Panto just months before.

There was instead a silence so sudden and complete, he could hear the water lapping at the pilings, the way he used to love to hear it early in the morning. Then, all of a sudden, a great bank of white klieg lights snapped on, as if someone had shouted *Action!* on a movie set. Just as abruptly, there was the noise of car doors opening and slamming shut, men running past them and shouting orders, toting shotguns and rifles and Tommy guns.

The Old Man was on them then, rushing up to the door before Frank Bals even had it opened, and Tom felt a rush of relief. He, too, was in his best dress uniform, but all business, speaking quickly and succinctly to Charlie.

"Nothin' moves in or out of Red Hook tonight! We got roadblocks up all along Hamilton Avenue. We even got the harbor patrol out in the channel!"

As if on command, a new bank of dazzling white lights opened up on a row of little police boats, out over the water.

"'One if by land, and two if by sea,'eh, Jack?" Charlie crowed. "But then, I can't imagine the Camardas travelin' by sea! What about the state's men?"

"They're holed up in some warehouses over on the Bush Terminal. Just waiting for the word," the Old Man said with a smirk.

Charlie turned back to Tom, giving him a dazzling grin. "Just make sure to smile for the cameras!"

Even as he spoke, a herd of reporters and news photographers were leaping out of their cars and racing after the cops, flashes already popping brittlely in the cold, late-March night.

"Is that why all the dress uniforms, Charlie? And the new clothes?"

His brother shrugged, gave a mischievous boy's smile. "Well, you have to give them a little of the show business, Tommy!"

He turned and walked toward the docks, where literally hundreds of cops were swarming about the piers and the Camarda locals. The Old Man had already taken charge, leaping up on a customs shed with a bullhorn, loudly directing his squads of cops as they hauled in anyone in sight for questioning. The uniforms striking dramatic poses with their big guns, dropping down to one knee or even their bellies and aiming, like doughboys firing on a German trench. Special detectives emerging from the Camarda sheds with armloads of fat ledger books they hauled ostentatiously past the news photographers, depositing them with a flourish in the armored cars Charlie had ordered up for that purpose. The assistant DAs trotting around waving their warrants like priests sprinkling holy water at anyone who seemed likely to resist arrest.

There were precious few of them. Plenty of likely-looking *shlammers* came staggering out of the pier sheds, all right, blinking and squinting into the harsh lights. The papers reported more than a hundred arrests before the night was over. But none of them the Camardas themselves, or the Anastasias. The men they did find strangely passive, none of them giving the cops even the usual lip on an arrest.

"That's the way, spare us the kid gloves!" Charlie was exulting anyway as they were wrestled roughly into cuffs and hauled away.

All of it still reminding him of a movie he had seen once, or maybe a movie about a movie — the blinding klieg lights, giving everything an otherworldly glow. The photographers running here and there, flashing their pictures, the cops bustling about striking poses and barking orders to no one. Everybody moving, everybody shouting, and the car doors slamming and the sirens blaring, and all of it so coordinated that he was tempted to look around for the director.

Instead, he turned his gaze back toward the shabby streets that butted up against the docks, where the people of Red Hook had come out to see the show. The longshoremen who lived in the worn brick tenements and the sagging wooden boardinghouses just off the docks. Standing with their wives and children, old coats and robes wrapped around their pajamas against the March-night chill. All of them watching the scene silently, hands shoved into their pockets or up in their armpits, faces unreadable as the water before them.

The raid went on all through the rest of the night and well into the next day. The whole drill just as loud and contrived back at the DA's office. Lawyers and secretaries striding purposefully up and down the halls. Shouting out instructions to prepare indictments, pulling rap sheets and mug shots, while the reporters and photographers scrambled after them, scribbling notes and popping still more pictures.

Tom all but giving in to it himself, he knew. Unable to keep from grinning as he watched all the *shlammers* and the Camarda thugs being hauled in — thrown into cells, dragged downstairs to be given the third degree. And Charlie — Charlie moving tirelessly back and forth between his assistant DAs and the reporters, issuing statements and squelching rumors. A squad of huge cops under the Old Man's direct supervision carrying in the union books at one point, where he had them locked away in the office vault for the photographers. Frowning as sternly at the ledger books as if they had kidnapped the Lindbergh baby.

Tom walked among it all in a near daze, wanting to believe, but not quite able, somehow. The whole moment like a dim newspaper cliché, by way of the funny pages and *Dick Tracy:* CAMARDAS' EMPIRE BROKEN IN A NIGHT!

"I halfway expect Flat-Top to surrender himself next," he joked to his brother.

Charlie didn't laugh, and Tom supposed he couldn't afford to do so, with the flashing cameras all around him. And the next day, sure enough, there were the pictures, along with the headlines three inches high, blotting out even the news of the war. Before the week was out, Charlie was in charge of the whole case. Governor Lehman and John Harlan Amen, the special prosecutor from Albany, confident enough in his work to hand over all the files, and that was almost enough to make him believe, too. The idea that such high and mighty individuals would trust in his brother, even if the people of Red Hook reserved judgment.

But then . . . nothing. Little by little, week by week, month by month, it all fell apart. No indictments passed down, no trials held. All the petty goons from the docks quickly and quietly released.

"The books were fakes, phonies," Charlie told him when he couldn't comprehend it. Just shaking his head when Tom still refused to believe it. "To look at 'em, you'd think they were running the ladies' junior league."

"What? How?"

"Those feckin' Camardas set us up, that's how. They had a dummy set of books ready an' waitin' for us. I should've seen it coming, but I was in such a hurry to keep the state from lousing it all up."

"I don't understand. What about the witnesses, all those arrests?" Tom said helplessly. "Didn't anyone tell us anything?"

"They all dummied up, every last one of 'em. Most of 'em were small fry anyway, hangers-on. Maybe *they* were a setup, too," Charlie said, red-faced, and gave him a small, embarrassed shrug. "This is the waterfront. I warned you: it's a different world."

"So what now? What do we do?"

His brother shrugged again.

"I dunno. Whattaya got?"

Mexico City, 1953
They drove down in the early evening to Cuernavaca, where Charlie said the air was eternally like spring. They traveled south first, along the Avenida de los Insurgentes, past the slab monoliths of the new University City and the fashionable new homes and the black lava soil of El Pedregal, before they began the long climb up the pass between the two mountains, Popocatépetl and Iztaccíhuatl, the Raging Man and the Sleeping Woman.

He had wanted to meet earlier, but Charlie assured him that the light was at its most beautiful at dusk, and he was right. The setting sun glinting spectacularly off the snowcapped mountain peaks, blue sky fading into flotillas of gold-tinged clouds. They were traveling on yet another brand-new, four-lane highway—this one, too, somehow named for Presidente Miguel Alemán—in a big new Lincoln Charlie had dug up somewhere. Beneficio, the same stocky, good-natured young Mayan who had picked Tom up at the airport, behind the wheel. The two of them lounging in the huge back seat, Charlie wearing a blue blazer and gray dress pants now, the air cooler in the evening, and growing cooler still as they climbed.

"Look at it back there!" Charlie said, exulting, pointing out the back window to where the Valley of Mexico receded behind them. "Did you ever *see* such a setting for a great city? You know, this is the way Cortés came, over four hundred years ago: '*And some of our soldiers even asked whether the things that we saw were not a dream.*'"

Tom nodded, his ears popping painfully as they continued to climb. They were driving along a desolate, rock-strewn stretch of the mountain pass that reminded him, all at once, of Italy.

Where the Germans had kept them stuck below that goddamned hill for so long. Where he found out about Jimmy . . .

"I strongly urge you to read Bernal Díaz del Castillo, *The Discovery and Conquest of Mexico*. It's great source material—" Charlie was prattling happily, unbearably.

"Where'd you get the car, Charlie?" Tom asked, cutting him off.

"Hmm? It was a loan from Jorge Pasquel—"

"A loan? Or a gift?" Tom asked sharply.

"Well, he did tell me I could keep it as long as I want!" Charlie said, grinning sheepishly. "He's a real gentleman. We're going to do *some* business together—"

"You think that's a good idea, Charlie? How d'ya think it's gonna look? A man like that who has his fingers into everything."

"Ah, don't be that way, Tommy," his brother told him, moving closer and looping an arm playfully around his neck. "It's all on the up-an'-up. Besides, we're on our way to Cuernavaca, where the air is ever like wine!"

They passed through a pine forest, the air suddenly crisp and fresh, then started down the pass to the next valley—"ten thousand feet up, and forty-five hundred down," as Charlie made sure to tell him.

"You know, Dwight Morrow used to come out to Cuernavaca, back when *he* was ambassador to Mexico. You remember, Lindbergh's father-in-law? He loved it out there. So did Josephus Daniels, who was ambassador under FDR," he went on. "They stoned the windows of the embassy when he first came down, because Josephus was an old Wilson man, and they remember things down here. But he won them over, too.

"He used to love to sneak away to a *festiva* in some little village or other, an' dance and dance. Already in his seventies by then, but there he'd be. The people would look around, an' there was the American ambassador, dancing their village dances with 'em!"

He paused, then said reflectively, "You know, they're not a hard people to love. And such a country."

"It was reminding me of Italy," Tom told him abruptly.

"Oh, God, Tommy, I'm sorry. That was a helluva time for you," Charlie said, softening his exuberance.

"It's not your fault."

Trying to restrain the irrational anger growing in him toward his brother's equally overweening sympathy. Unable to shake the feeling he'd had ever since he'd first arrived at El Ranchito — that somehow, he was being played.

"A helluva time for us all," he said.

"It was a disaster right from the start," Tom said grimly.

The part that stayed with him, that he could never quite believe, was how long it went on. From his first minute on the beach at Anzio, he was almost laughing in his horror and shock. Thinking: They can't be serious. They can't possibly expect this to continue. But they did. That was when he understood there was no natural end to it. That men would fight forever, that they would go on fighting until every one of them was dead, and the whole world destroyed.

Keeping his face flat in the muck for months, the shells falling incessantly. Then the endless slog up into the Apennines. When Charlie found him they had been trying to take the same hill just south of Bologna for two weeks. The Germans keeping them pinned down with their M34s and their eighty-eights — better weapons than anything they had. The shelling going on every day and night now, taking away any ability to sleep, driving them all mad . . .

"They were holed up in some ancient Etruscan temple on top of the hill. At least that's what we were told it was: an ancient Etruscan temple, though I can't say we ever got close enough to inspect its provenance. We called in the flyboys and they flattened it for us, but that just made it easier for them to defend the rubble."

The aerial bombardment more terrifying and immobilizing than even the worst of the artillery barrages he had endured already. The ground bouncing and vibrating with each load of bombs, his eardrums nearly bursting. Unable to move, unable to shout out to the men right next to him, only to stare straight ahead and pray that the next bomb didn't miss by a few hundred yards and blow them all to pieces. And when it was finally over, and all the smoke and dust had died down, and the noise had cleared a little . . . they could see the bright pin-points of the German machine guns still flashing up the hill, like the twinkling lights on a Christmas tree. Firing at nothing, really. Just sending them the message that they would still have to come and get them, sooner or later . . .

"Each night, they would collect the dead if there wasn't too much moon, and take them back down the hill by mule. The Italian muleskinners didn't want the job. They wouldn't walk next to the dead, so *we* had to do it," Tom remembered. "We had to take 'em all the way down, men we had known an' loved, dumped over some mule's back like a sack of meat. Then pull them off for the burial detail, once we got back to the bottom of the hill. Men dead three, four days. Men we had known, pulled up face-to-face before us, so we could put 'em on the stretcher. Goddamn, but it wouldn't stop. Day after day, the Jerries were still there, an' we couldn't get to the top of that hill, and it wouldn't stop."

"I know. I remember how you looked, kiddo," Charlie said softly, patting his shoulder. "President Roosevelt sent me over the same summer you were there, an' Jimmy was in France. Brought me into his office, made me a briga-dier general *and* a minister in the State Department, all in the same day. *Me,* Charlie O'Kane from Lismirrane! A general and . . . a minister of state! Read me a letter from my boss at the investigation office: 'In a nation of one hun-dred thirty-five million, why deprive me of Charlie O'Kane?' "

Tom smiled weakly at him. He would've found the boastful words unfor-givable, if he had not understood they were said in genuine wonder — Char-lie's wonder that he could ever find himself in the company of presidents and generals.

"Oh, let me tell you, that kind of praise is heady wine, especially when it's bein' read to you by the president of the United States in his own office. Then

I went over there, an' saw the mess he'd given me to clean up! The railroads torn up, mines in all the fields, so you couldn't bring in the harvest. Ports wrecked, so you couldn't even ship food in. Half the population starvin', or without a home. And the things the Germans did! Whole villages packed into churches an' burned alive — men, women, an' children. Machine-gunned, an' sealed into the sacred catacombs, God help us. There was no purpose to it by then, not even the purpose of terrorizing the population. Just random madness.

"I telegraphed the President an' threatened to resign. I told him, 'I have no heart to preside over a national funeral!' But bad as I felt for the poor Italians, my main idea was to find *you*. That's all I wanted. And that's when the word about Jimmy came."

He remembered when he got the order. Wanting to feel guilty as he saw the savage looks from the other men in his platoon, but not really caring. Half of them replacements anyway by that time, but not caring what anyone thought by then. Certain he would never get out of the war alive. Just wanting a respite from that hill, for any reason, and no matter what happened to any of them in his stead.

The jeep from the staff headquarters took him directly to the villa where Charlie was staying, the driver in a crisp, new uniform and unstained boots, face daily shaven. Giving Tom the usual, cringing support-staff stare of shame mixed with revulsion. Tom knowing how he must have looked, how he must have smelled without a bath for weeks, covered in dried mud, his hair and beard grown wild. It was the first thing that made him smile since he'd gotten to Italy.

The staff corporal drove him up to the gates of the villa, not even trying to make any small talk, no doubt able to read the sheer exhaustion in his face and the slump of his body. Pulling up to where Charlie stood in his newly pressed general's uniform and jacket, in front of the gorgeous, half-wrecked villa and grounds, and he would've laughed at the sheer ludicrousness of it, at the absurdity of his brother a general, and going halfway around the world to war and meeting up like this with him. Except that he saw the look on his brother's face, and from that he divined at once that Jimmy must be dead, because he didn't think that he himself quite was yet.

"The villa wasn't my idea, you know," Charlie told him. "That was our dear cardinal—then still only a mere archbishop. I never liked those things, I refused to stay in 'em, even though all the other Allied liaisons did. Livin' like the lord of the manor, when half the population would kill for a potato! It wasn't right, but dear Francis was ridin' high just then. He'd come over to help the cause, an' he insisted on havin' a villa everywhere he went, even if it belonged to one of the lesser Sforzas, with half the roof caved in."

All he could remember was that it seemed like a cathedral, after so many weeks on the line. Wandering through it in a daze, after Charlie had greeted him at the gate, hugging and kissing him on both cheeks and telling him they'd talk later, once he got himself cleaned up and had some sleep. He staggered up to the second floor, where some ancient, desiccated servant who seemed to come with the place helped him out of his gear and into a hot bath—the plumbing still working, apparently, which was all that mattered. He didn't know how long he lay in that tub, but when he got back to the little maid's room the hollow-eyed butler guided him to, one of the few not ruined by their artillery, his uniform was there, miraculously brushed clean and pressed, mounted carefully on wooden hangers.

He had fallen into the maid's bed, not big enough for him to sleep in without curling up his knees, but he lost consciousness instantly, nevertheless. Only his hunger awakening him, he didn't know how many hours or days later. It was dark out now, and as if in a dream he carefully dressed himself and made his way back downstairs. Walking toward the smell of meat roasting on an open fire, the most enticing food he ever had or ever would smell in his life. Following it at last to a huge, open room.

It was a sumptuous, ancient room, rimmed with dark wooden panels, and bookcases, made to look all the larger because half of it had been blasted away. Closed up again only with makeshift wooden pilings—a thing once perfect in itself, now ruined, and never to be the same again, like so many of the ruined things and men he had seen. A huge room, a Christmas fantasy room, even in the summer heat. With a row of perfect toy soldiers lined up across one side, and a pig roasting on a spit over the fire, and Santa Claus himself, a little red, round beaming creature, sitting at the head of the table with a great gold cross around his neck, smiling benignly.

* * *

"You should've seen the look he gave you when you came down, the little fag. I thought he was gonna come all over his nice red robes," Charlie said, chuckling. "Not that I wasn't affected, either. You looked like a recruitin' poster, lean an' hard, an' murderous, but I could see the pain of it in your eyes. It went to my heart, to see you there. The only thing I could think of was how much you looked like Jimmy."

"Like the dead?"

"Ay, like the dead. So better idealized than the living."

His own recollections of the moment were still clouded by the haze he was in at the time. He remembered his brother looking tired and wary, the same expression he usually had in the presence of the cardinal. Spellman beaming cherubically at him. A short, fussy man, plump and bald, save for a faint gray laurel around the top of his head. Sharp, restless eyes taking in everything through his gold wire-rimmed glasses.

He got up from his seat at the head of the table and walked straight over to Tom, guiding him into a massive, carved wooden chair from the Renaissance. Fat little fingers sharp as talons on his arm, seeing him into his chair, pouring him a glass of wine the color of his splendid robes. Still beaming like an idiot as he announced, "Now, here is our American fighting man!"

"It was his big moment," Charlie remembered. "They'd always took him for a fool in Rome — when they thought of him a'tall. You remember what Cardinal O'Connell used to say about him? 'Francis is what happens when you teach a bookkeeper how to read.' They thought he was just one more idiot American.

"Then, all of a sudden, everything's gone to hell and here he is: head of the richest archdiocese in the world, with the great army on earth behind him! It must've been the most frightening thing what ever happened to the Holy See since Alaric showed up with his Visigoths. Which is why I'm sure Roosevelt sent him over as an emissary. Who better to make a point about power than good old, tactless Frankie Spellman?"

The slices of roasted pig were as good as they smelled. So were the roasted potatoes, and some kind of real green vegetable, like nothing he had tasted in months. All served by the same hollowed butler he had seen before, with the help of some mess men tending the fire. The MPs on guard standing the whole meal with their legs spread, arms behind their backs. It made him sick, to see them all waiting on them, himself and his brother and the archbishop, like they were so many house servants. But he didn't have the strength to do anything but keep slowly eating what was put in front of him. The glass in his hand the finest crystal. Their plates finely wrought silver, the utensils gold, the great table they were sitting about large enough to feed an army, and probably support one, too.

The archbishop dominating the conversation, as usual. His mood exultant, as he went on about his audience with the pope a few days before.

"Before the war, I wouldn't have got the time of day. Now His Holiness and the papal nuncio were hanging on my every word! They came to me as — as . . . supplicants! With a hat full of requests and respectful questions about what I thought the president was going to do, and how the postwar world was going to look."

"That's terrific, Your Eminence," Charlie told him glumly — but with his usual obliviousness Spellman failed to pick up on the mood in the room.

"Don't you see where we are right now, Charlie?" he demanded instead, in his flat, grating Massachusetts accent. "We're what Spain was for the Church, back in the sixteenth century. We're the young Catholic nation on the march, the sword of the Church for *this* century. Taking over for the crumbling empires, holding back Russian communism, the next big fight —"

"A Catholic nation, Your Eminence?"

Spellman waved a hand furiously in dismissal. "Just a matter of time! Another generation — less! — and we'll see a Catholic majority in the United States. We've been the outsiders for so long, but now we're the young, virile, manly faith! The Protestants have had their day — all dried-up old bones. *We* are the faith that binds all the vigorous new races of the nation together. The Irish, the Italian, the Pole and the Latin and the Eastern Europeans!

"And like Spain was, we're the richest country in the world. And it's not a wealth that rests on some Mexican silver mines, or the gold of Peru. It comes from our ingenuity, our inventiveness, our minds," he said, tapping his temple with a forefinger just in case someone didn't understand.

"We were already the workingman's faith, Charlie. Now our people are rising! Becoming doctors and lawyers, taking over whole corporations. And there's only the Church to bring the workers and capital together. Just like this!" he said, standing up in his agitation, moving around the enormous table toward them and clenching his fat little hands together.

"You should see the investments we've made for the archdiocese over the last few years," he said, gloating. "General Foods! Procter and Gamble! Westinghouse! Thirty million alone in aircraft stocks — Boeing, and Curtiss-Wright, and Lockheed! These are the companies of the future, in the nation of the future, and we've tied our fate to them."

"You've done splendidly with the archdiocese, Your Eminence," Charlie said politely. "You know they call you 'the Great Builder.'"

"Ah, well, I don't know about that," Spellman said, sitting back down, obviously pleased. "I attribute it to all of the brilliant Catholic laymen we now have in business, whose expertise I can call on. You know, my father used to say, 'Son, always associate with people smarter than yourself, and that shouldn't be hard to do.'"

"Wise advice," Charlie said. "Was he a scholar?"

"He was a grocer," Spellman said contemptuously. "And my grandfather Patrick was a bootmaker, from Clonmel, in Tipperary. But this is a new generation, a new time for us, Charlie."

He tore into a haunch, waving a golden knife at them.

"That's what I'm trying to tell you, Charlie. We're entering a new age, where America is the hinge of the world! And New York is going to be the capital of that world. Don't you see what we need there is a good Catholic mayor? Not some red, half-Jew Episcopalian like we have now! Not a libertine, like Mr. Walker. But a good, pious, Catholic family man. A man who's risen up from the working class and got himself an education. A man like yourself, Charlie O'Kane!"

"You flatter me, Your Eminence," Charlie told him, smiling weakly. "Last time I was in Washington, the president told me I should consider running for governor, or senator. Seems everybody has a place picked out for me but myself."

"All in good time, all in good time for that, Charlie," Spellman said, waving his meat at him. "But don't you see where the *real* power is? It's right in the

City, *our* city, the greatest city that ever was! The new Rome, the new Jerusalem, the new Byzantium, all rolled into one!"

"Yes, Your Eminence," Charlie said wearily, but by then Tom wasn't able to take any more. Lurching to his feet as the archbishop went on hectoring his brother. His head spinning from all the talk of the hinge of the world, and the new Jerusalems, and the young Catholic nation on the march, while Jimmy was dead, and he would have to go back out to that hill. Or maybe it was just the fresh roasted pork, turning in his stomach. All eyes on him now, his brother asking what was wrong and even Spellman's attention turning to him now, the candlelight blurring and spinning, as he stumbled on over toward the fire and vomited into an exquisite Renaissance vase.

19

New York, 1953

"It gets worse."

"Worse? Worse than half the New York Police Department falling asleep when they're guarding the most important mob witness of the century? Worse than officers hearing a body fall on the roof—and not wanting to go see about it because it might mean having to go out in the cold? *Worse than that?*"

Tom spread the letters out across his desk for Hogan: two of them never sent, the third paper-clipped to the envelope it had been mailed in. Hogan stared at them—crude, handwritten scrawls on stationery from the Half Moon Hotel.

"Somebody surely didn't learn penmanship in a Catholic school."

"They're from Sholem Bernstein, one of the rats in the suite with our Mr. Reles."

"I remember. How'd this happen to come to light?"

"Ellie found them, after about ten straight hours of digging. They were buried deep, but she came up with them."

"Good work, Miss Abramowitz."

"Thank you, sir."

Ellie glancing at him over Hogan's shoulder and shooting up one triumphant eyebrow. The three of them working the late shift together now. Ellie beaming quietly, Tom saw whenever he caught her eye.

They were more strictly correct than ever with each other, around the office. Working longer hours than before, due to some indefinable sense of guilt over their affair. Rushing back up to the Village only when they felt their brains would crumble to ashes if they went through one more box of documents. Sometimes they might go out to the White Horse to hear the Clancys, or the intellectuals blabbing, but more often they went straight to her apartment in the basement, Ellie pouring them each a finger of Black Bush in the dim yellow light of her living room. Still excited, still talking about anything and everything until they wrestled each other into bed. Taking great pains to come to the office separately, from different directions, the next morning. Ellie careful to place herself just ahead of him, hips swaying more wickedly than ever as she walked.

"What's it say?" Hogan asked, staring down his nose through his glasses at the sixth-grade scrawl.

"It's a bit of loan-sharking," Tom told him. "A gentle reminder to an individual who had fallen behind on the matter of a few dollars he borrowed from Mr. Bernstein—at a rate of twenty percent interest, compounded weekly."

"'Why don't you get wise? Do you know what I can do to you? I could have you pinched tomorrow if I want to,'" Ellie read aloud. "'Don't kid yourself. I'm going to give you EXACTLY ONE WEEK to give my wife two hundred and five dollars every week. If you don't, I'm going to put you in with me. My wife gives me a visit next week, and if you didn't give it to her, as true as my mother (may she rest in peace), you will be right in here with me.'"

"Well, at least he thinks highly of his mother," Tom said.

Ellie handed the note to Hogan, who peered at it for a long moment, then let the piece of paper drop back to the desk in disgust and picked up a mug shot of the man. Bernstein slight and dark. A young thirty at the time, with a long, straight nose and big ears on a thin face, his eyes large and dreamy.

"Looks like a member of the junior faculty," Hogan said, studying a mug shot of the man in his best testifying-go-to-court clothes, a suit and vest and neatly knotted tie. "How'd he happen to end up in the Rats Suite?"

"He was born in the borough," Ellie rattled off. "A small-time gambler, a carny shill—"

"Another little man, trying to be big," Hogan sniffed. "What was his connection to Reles and the rest?"

"He started borrowin' from the shylocks. The usual vig, six for five, just to pay off his markers," Tom put in. "Then all of a sudden he got big. Started callin' himself a real estate man, an' borrowed fifty thousand in one go."

"Who would ever give him *that?*"

"The Food Dealers Association bank."

"Another mob front?" Hogan asked rhetorically.

"Next he popped up in Bensonhurst," Ellie continued. "Set up in a candy store with Al Glass. It became a popular hangout for undesirables of all sorts — burglars, second-story men, stickup men—"

"Sure, I remember Cherry Glass." Hogan nodded. "That was his specialty. Setting up employment bureaus for felons."

"Bernstein himself did a little bit of everything. Making book, loan-sharking, breaking and entering, safecracking. Strong-arming down in Florida. He was involved in at least three murders that we know of," Tom listed.

"A one-man finance company, with muscles and guns!" Hogan snorted. "What sort of time did he serve?"

"Nothing," Tom told him. "He was arrested on three different occasions, but he walked each time. Got caught red-handed on a burglary job, and a larceny charge—got probation. He was even picked up in a stolen car with two known stickup men. All of 'em had guns. Sholem pleaded guilty to auto theft—"

"And let me guess—he got more probation," Hogan finished, and Tom nodded. The DA gave a low, speculative whistle. "Some serious money must've changed hands on that one. Somebody really wanted to keep our boy on the outside."

"He was the best car thief in Brooklyn," Tom explained. "Best in the City. They even used to farm him out, just like the killers. He was spotted in Florida, California, the Catskills in the summer — though he used to say he was just on vacation."

Hogan gave a short, mirthless laugh. "Yes, I suppose even murderers must need vacations. What was his secret?"

"The usual," Tom told him. "Quick hands, delicate fingers. He could pick any garage lock, boost any car. Move 'em from this garage to that street corner, switch their license plates. Make 'em appear and disappear at will. He'd trace the route of a getaway the night before, learn every possible exit by heart. The next day, they'd pull a hit, or a stickup; he'd make the gunmen disappear before anybody knew they were there."

Ghosting his cars back and forth over the sepulchral streets of Brownsville and Ocean Hill, unseen but seeing everything. Scouting the far reaches of the City, the lonely places by the bay and the high sea grass, where a body might be dropped in peace.

"His real sin was helping Pep Strauss and Tick-Tock Tannenbaum bury one of Lepke Buchalter's old business partners, up by the bonny, bonny banks of Loch Sheldrake."

"Which one?"

"Hyman Yuran, and no, that's not a joke. Back when it all started to come apart—when Lepke first went on the lam and made himself crazy thinking anybody he ever knew might rat him out."

"What did the euphoniously named Hyman Yuran do for him?"

"He was his front in the Garment District, ran a dressmaking shop there."

"What a thing to die for. How'd they do it?"

"Pittsburgh Phil's weapon of choice, the old reliable ice pick," Tom said, consulting the file. "It was August 1938 — Yuran was on vacation up in the Ambassador Hotel in Fallsburg. They made a call, sent a blonde in a car to pick him up."

"Ah, the tried-and-true methods."

They could all see it. *The middle-aged dress manufacturer, perspiring in his underwear and dark socks, under a slow-moving fan in some dump of an upstate hotel. A phone call from the blonde he had met that day in the bar, or maybe out by the pool with its hordes of screaming kids, parents lying comatose and sun-blistered in their pool chairs. Throwing on his other suit, the one he hadn't worn that day. Picking out his best silk tie, splashing on the bay rum. The last stand of Hyman Yuran.*

And then, out in the car, had they been waiting in the back seat? Or in whatever little tourist cabin, deep in the woods, where she finally pulled over? Watching her eyes lift just as he reached for her. Her expression changing effortlessly from sultry passion to a steady, level-eyed curiosity so that for the first time—for that one moment—he could see how truly hard she looked, and how old. Barely flinching as the first thin line of blood fell across her cheek. His blood, seeing it even as he felt the stunning pain of the ice pick striking home again at the top of his neck, heard the grunt and laughter of his killer behind him.

"They tried to bury him in a cemetery—" Ellie volunteered.

"How genteel."

"—but the ground was too rocky. So Tannenbaum took them to Loch Sheldrake—a hotel and cabins his parents owned. He knew they had just finished digging a pool drain there."

The body not ten yards from where more legions of families and kids would lie and jump and scream all about the pool. Maybe the same ones who had given Hyman Yuran such a splitting headache on his last afternoon alive.

"Buried him right in his parents' backyard, did he? What would Dr. Freud's head doctors have to say about *that?*" Hogan shook his head mournfully. "And Mr. Tannenbaum, Mr. Bernstein—who's the other one?

"Mickey Sycoff."

"These were the state's witnesses?"

"They came in when Lepke started killing everybody who ever knew him, just like Reles himself," Tom said. "I guess they thought they'd be next."

"Yes, that's the trouble when you go killing anybody who ever worked for you. Sooner or later, even the executioners start getting antsy."

"We chased Bernstein all over the place, afraid his old friends were going to catch up to him first," Tom told him. "Down to Miami, then out to L.A., up to San Francisco. He told us he knew the syndicate was looking for him everywhere. He took a bus all the way to Dallas—they spotted him nine hours later. Went up to St. Louis; they were on to him in two days. We even had word they found a corpse in Chicago. Then, a week later, he walks into our office."

"Funny, isn't it?" Hogan frowned. "A man as resourceful as all that—a man familiar with the whole country—getting found so easily when he didn't want to be found."

Tom nodded. "All he told us was, 'They can't get me if I'm with the law.' Still, even then he wouldn't talk. Bernstein kept insisting he wanted to see Reles, that he couldn't believe he was singing. He wouldn't say a word until we put him in with the little man himself. Then, fifteen minutes later, he comes out an' tells us, 'I will become a rat and tell everything.'"

"Strange choice of words. But an understandable choice, I guess, when you consider he could keep his loan business going while in the state's custody."

Hogan picked up Sholem Bernstein's extortion note again and turned to Ellie.

"Young lady, this is the one trouble with having women working in the office now. I can't curse like a sailor when I really need to."

"I understand, sir. I felt like cursing myself when I found that."

"I'd like to hear that someday." He tapped the threatening letter. "Were these missives ever mailed?"

"That one was," Ellie told him. "It was turned in later by the individual he sent it to—a grocer named David Bellel. The other two were found up in Bernstein's room after Reles went out the window. They were much the same—a threatening note to a headwaiter who got his girl in a family way. A house painter who was out of work. He told the investigators he wrote them with a detective standing over his shoulder."

"This case stinks six ways to Sunday, and the more you stick a finger into it, the worse it gets," Hogan said with disgust. "Who knows how many of these he sent out—or what other information he might've passed on? They had a phone, too, up in the Rats Suite—didn't they?"

"That they did," Tom confirmed. "The guards let 'em make calls out on it."

"Faith, Tom, why didn't they just let them send telegrams and semaphore signals, too? What were they *thinking* of, letting those jokers communicate freely with the outside world?"

"The guards were told to keep 'em happy," Tom said, bristling a little under the implied criticism of his brother, but forced to admit it. *Oh, Charlie, why couldn't you have followed up on a single detail in your life?*

"*Happy,* is it? They should've been happy enough your brother didn't let Lepke and Anastasia cut their throats!"

"Charlie was afraid they'd go stir-crazy," Tom stuck up for his brother. "Cooped up there twenty months—with Abe Reles. There'd been an incident the year before, the ice pick went missing. Reles was sure one of the other rats palmed it to use on him. He kept raisin' a rumpus about it, until it turned out a cop took it to chop ice an' forgot to put it back."

"So they let them do whatever they wanted? Make phone calls, run their shyster rackets —"

"The idea was to keep 'em talkin'. No matter what it took."

There had even been beach outings that first summer. Tom had gone along on one of them. Driving out to a deserted tract of Hecksher State Park, on Long Island, using a battered old school bus to call as little attention to themselves as possible. Everybody jumpy the whole way out, expecting an ambush. Thinking how easy it would be for one of the squealers to simply walk away down the beach, or even make a run for the Great South Bay and swim for it. The whole afternoon more than a little unreal: the uniformed guards standing along the edge of the sand in the hot sun, holding their shotguns across their chests. Forming a perimeter around the haimish little grove of picnic tables and metal grilles where the four killers gamboled and cavorted.

Yet nothing happened, and after a couple of hours out there, they began to relax. The guards laying down their guns and stripping off their blue tunics. Joining in with their prisoners until it began to resemble the annual company outing — men playing ball in their T-shirts and flopping suspenders, laughing and shouting. Reles fat and sleek as a well-fed pigeon by then, whatever his lung ailment was under control for the time being. Slamming a softball into the gnarled beach trees and chortling like a little boy as he ran around the bases. Whipping the ball at the guards' heads with his huge hands and braying with laughter. Frying up hamburgers on the little metal grilles, flipping them onto buns and holding them out to the guards — then spitting on them just as they reached out to take them, and laughing and laughing some more.

The other rats not nearly as jubilant, Tom noticed later, once the softball game was over and they settled down to their hot dogs and hamburgers. Churning through it methodically, eyes flickering about as if they were in a prison commissary, keeping a constant lookout.

Tick-Tock Tannenbaum, the resort owner's son, continuing the ceaseless stream of patter that earned him his nickname. Thin and immaculate, with a dark face, a high brow. A long nose that crooked at the end and hooded, Asiatic eyes that could look impish and merry one moment, infinitely sad the next. He'd had some college even, before settling in with the mob. A cheap *shlammer* for easy jobs, specializing in letting stink bombs loose in stores and waylaying strikers in back alleys, but an accomplice as well in at least six murders.

Next to him Mickey Sycoff, stolid and pudgy, his face as round and bland as a vanilla pudding. Ploughing through his potato salad with mechnical efficiency. He looked as placid and imperturbable as a tie salesman, though Tom knew he was another loan shark, famous for his vicious beatings, an accomplice in three more murders. And then Sholem — his whole aspect morose and paranoid, even when the others were enjoying the games. Tapping his foot nervously, barely eating, his dreamy eyes clouded and resentful now.

"He gets like this whenever he knows he's about to testify against his old pals," Reles had told him, sidling up to his elbow. His breath like fouled grease itself on his neck and ear. "He don't like it. Anybody tries to talk to him, he curses 'em out, won't listen to reason. He don't like me, neither."

"Can you blame him?" Tom told the little man, glancing down his nose at him. Reles's second-banana face fell in mock surprise, then lit up again in its usual, vicious glee.

"What's not to like?" he said. "I'm just tellin' ya, you better be careful with that one."

"How so?"

Reles shrugged. "Sholem likes to mull over things in his life," he said. "When he does, it's a sure sign he's about to crack. You just better be sure you keep him away from me when he does."

Reles's thick lips twisting malevolently.

"I'll kill him if I have to. I'll break his goddamned neck an' throw him right out the window."

"So *did* Bernstein's wife bring him the money he wanted from his correspondent?" Hogan was asking now. "Did he have cash in there, too?"

"Wait — that's something we missed," Ellie said, touching his arm, Tom smiling involuntarily at the feel of her hand.

"What is?"

"The note says his wife was coming to see him —"

"Sure. Once a week, same as Reles's wife did. Mrs. Kid Twist always brought Abie a bottle of Rémy Martin brandy. I'm thinking that must be where the alcohol in his stomach came from."

"What did they talk about? Did any of the guards report it?" Hogan asked, catching on.

"No. They went into Reles's room and shut the door," Ellie told him, consulting her notes without the blush, Tom was proud to note, that one of the Seven Sisters ADAs would have summoned up.

"Of course. Conjugal visits. Why not? Room service, a seaside hotel, trips to the beach — they must've thought they were on a second honeymoon!"

"The night before Reles went out the window, Mickey Sycoff told the investigators Reles and the missus were in there much longer than usual. Three hours, he said," Ellie continued triumphantly. "And — when she left she was very upset."

"Upset?"

"Crying, even. Sycoff said it was the first time she'd visited that she didn't ask him or Tick-Tock Tannenbaum how their families were. She just rushed out of the suite."

Tom remembered vividly the night she'd first come in, to arrange her husband's surrender. A short, plump woman, with a childlike face and a superior air, and a tendency to go to pieces when she was crossed. She had shown up one evening in March unannounced, while he was waiting to go home with Charlie. Sweeping dramatically into the DA's office like some cinematic grande dame, dressed in a fine beige coat with a wolf collar and a matching turban on her head, much to the amusement of the cops downstairs at the desk.

They were at an ebb then, the big raid on the waterfront locals having fallen to pieces. The truth was that they were floundering until Rose Reles swept through the door. Demanding to speak to his brother alone, refusing to substitute even Burton Turkus, the prosecutor whose picture was in all the papers. Her fine-boned face scrunching up hysterically, dropping the grande dame pretensions and screeching like a child when she was denied: "No, no! I wanna speak to District Attorney Char-lie O'Kane!"

Mad, over-rouged face staring imperiously around the room until at last Charlie came hurrying down from his office, so she could look up at him with tears in her eyes and a voice as throaty as any movie heroine's. "I want to save my husband from the electric chair," she pleaded, showing them for the first time the protrusion of her stomach under her coat. "My baby is coming in June. *I want to save him!*"

Charlie turning and looking at him then, his eyes wide. Wondering, Tom knew, just as he was, if it wasn't another setup. But thinking, too, as Charlie told him later, *Well, well, look what just dropped into the lap of Charlie O'Kane.*

Tom recognized her easily when Hogan brought her down from Utica, where she was living under another name and another husband. The teasingly plump body gone shapeless and heavy now, the fine, baby-doll face sagging. The wolf's collar and the turban replaced by a plain cloth coat that was the color of nothing, really, and a cheap bandana wrapped around her disheveled hair. But there was still a haughtiness bordering on madness in the way she carried herself, the same air of entitlement mixed with incipient hysteria.

The three of them met her in a small room in the Roosevelt, another one of the looming brick hotels that surrounded Grand Central like a castle keep. Hogan didn't want the press picking up a whiff of her around the office, so he'd brought her down on the train and registered the room under Ellie's name. Once inside, he treated her with his usual antique respect around women. Carefully hanging up her shabby, mottled coat, making sure she had some water, offering to send the detective stationed out in the hall to get something to eat. But she only shook her head, spooked and jumpy from the very beginning of their cross-examination, answering everything in as few words as she could get away with.

"Now, when did you an' Abe get married, ma'am?" Hogan tried first, asking his questions in as gentle a voice as he possessed.

"I can't remember," Rose told him, sitting up stiffly in her hotel chair.

"You can't remember your own wedding date?" he asked, incredulous.

"That bum? I blotted out everyt'ing t'do wit' him!"

"He was the father of your children. You must remember that."

"Sure," she sniffed disdainfully.

"So then you must've been married to him at least seven years before his death."

"I suppose."

Hogan made an impatient movement in his chair, one Tom had seen a few times before in the office — always preliminary to his bursting into rage.

"How long after you and Abe married did you have your first child?"

"About a year an' a half."

"So that means you married him *ten or eleven years* before he died."

"I imagine."

"You imagine." Hogan ran a hand slowly through his hair. "So let me ask you this, Mrs. Reles: How did you *imagine* he was making his living all those years you were together?"

"I don' go by that name no more," she protested. "I'm Mrs. Lewanda now. The neighbors found out that name, an' they wouldn't stop askin' me about 'im."

"How did they find out, if you don't go by it anymore?"

"I dunno."

"All right, *Mrs. Lewanda.* How did you *think* Abe Reles made his living?"

"He was a bookmaker an' a shylock, I suppose. Then he decided ta go straight, an' become a gambler an' opened a luncheonette," she said, as if reciting something she'd memorized long ago.

"You never had any inkling that he was a professional killer? You're sure of that?"

"I am almost sure," she replied, looking haughtier than ever, though Tom was sure he could sense a deep fear beneath the words.

"You didn't know that your husband was the most notorious criminal in Brownsville? In Brooklyn? You never knew that even though everybody else in the neighborhood knew it?"

"*I* never felt that way."

"I didn't ask how you *felt.* I asked, didn't you *know* that your husband, Abe Reles, was considered the most notorious killer in Brooklyn?"

"How would you know somethin'? I mean, is somebody supposed ta tell it to ya? Nobody ever said nothin' ta me about Abie," she insisted.

"No, I don't suppose they would. So all you knew was that he was a book-maker and a loan shark?"

"I suppose."

"Mrs. Lewanda, next time you *suppose* something, I suppose I might put you up before a grand jury."

The edge of hysteria suddenly flicked across her eyes again, and she pulled her pocketbook up in front of her.

"He used ta bring home every paper there was, an' when he was t'rough readin' 'em I'd pick 'em up. But I could never find anyt'ing in 'em because he'd cut out pieces an' I could never find the next page," she blurted.

"He used to cut up all the newspapers he'd bring home," Hogan confirmed, his voice heavy with incredulity. "And he'd cut out everything in them about himself—is that what you're trying to say to me?"

"I guess."

"For what, his scrapbook?"

"He didn't keep a scrapbook. Not that I knew about—"

"All right, Mrs. Lewanda!" Hogan held up a hand to stop her. "Let's get to the last night you saw Abe—the last night he was alive. How long did you spend with him that evening?"

"I dunno. Not very long. I just came an' went."

"Everybody who's talked to our investigators said you were there at least three hours—a very long time indeed."

"I dunno how anybody can say that. They're just guessin'," she said, her voice low but dogged.

"I'm trying to make this as easy as possible for you, Mrs. Lewanda. But I don't know what I can do if you don't want to cooperate. Our information is that you were there for a much longer visit than usual."

"That's not true. That is absolutely not true!" she insisted, Hogan rising to stand over her, slapping a piece of paper in his hand.

"Mrs. Lewanda, why aren't you being truthful with us? I have a copy of the visitors' log right here in my hand. You were there over three hours!"

There was a pause as Rose stared wildly up at him. Then she dropped her eyes and shrugged. "Well, it was a long time ago. I didn't mean ta lie."

Hogan sat back down. "So what did you talk about during that time?" he asked, forcing himself to modulate his voice.

"I didn't talk."

"You didn't talk? In three hours?"

"He did all the talkin'."

"All right. What did he talk about?"

"He talked about how he was in the hospital, an' how sick he was."

"That's it?"

"Yup. Far as I remember." She looked around the room as if she'd just emerged from a light coma. "Anybody got a cigarette?"

Hogan ignored her request.

"Did he say *anything* — anything at all — that might shed some light on his going out the window the next morning?"

"What? No, no."

She continued to look around the room, fingers fidgeting with her pocketbook clasp.

"Nothing at all?"

"Nah."

"Did he seem agitated in any way? Despondent? Frightened?"

"Nah, nothin' like that." She gave a little snort. "You didn't know Abie."

"Nothing at all?"

"No. Well, he was mad at me. Because of the divorce."

"*What* divorce?"

"I went there ta ask him for a divorce that night," she said, her eyes suddenly misting over. "I wanted ta get his signature."

"You wanted to get his signature on divorce papers?" Hogan asked, incredulous again, but Rose nodded vehemently, before pulling a clot of half-used tissue out of her bag and holding it to her face.

"You brought him divorce papers? From your lawyer?"

"They wasn't full divorce papers. I didn't go ta no lawyer," she said as she blew her nose.

"What do you mean, not 'full' divorce papers?"

"Well, it was more like I brought 'im a blank piece a paper. I asked Abie just ta sign his name an' said I'd fill in all the particulars, grantin' me a divorce. But he wouldn't hear nothin' about it. So I didn't talk ta him no more after that."

"Let me get this straight," Hogan said through gritted teeth, sure he was being toyed with. Tom wasn't as certain, looking over at Ellie. Her face was neither exasperated nor amused, but she was leaning forward in her chair, concentrating on Rose, her chin in her hand as if she were trying to figure something out.

"You wanted your husband to sign a blank piece of paper," Hogan recounted. "You told him you were going to fill in the rest of it, granting you a divorce and listing 'the particulars.'"

"That's right. I thought then when I got started, I'd have his signature, an' the rest would take care of itself."

"But he would have none of it."

"Well, no. He just looked at me like he was sick — he *was* sick, comin' out of the hospital then," Rose said hurriedly, then lifted up her head dramatically. "He looked at me an' he said . . . he said, 'At a time like this, you would do a thing like that?'"

"What did he mean, 'at a time like this'? Did he elaborate?" Hogan pressed.

"What?"

"Did he *explain* in any way?"

"Nah."

"Nothing at all?"

"Nah."

"He must've given you *some* hint of what he was talking about. 'At a time like this — '"

"Nope."

"Did you get his signature on your homemade divorce decree?"

"No."

Hogan's face was so red now that Tom was sure he was about to start screaming at the woman. But just then Ellie moved her chair forward, actually daring to place a restraining hand gently on his forearm.

"Do you mind if I ask Mrs. Lewanda something, Boss?" she asked quietly, all the while keeping her gaze focused on Rose, now sniffling away behind her clump of tissues.

"Be my guest," Hogan said, disgusted.

"Rose, may I ask you something?"

"Sure. Why not? Ya got me locked up in here, ya can do whatever youse want!"

Ellie produced a couple of cigarettes from her purse, taking one herself and handing the other to Rose, who accepted it with a look of deep trepidation but went ahead and lit up, pulling in a long drag of smoke. Ellie took a draw as well, then put the pack and an ashtray on a table near her, and smiled.

"Rose — may I call you Rose?"

There was another terse nod.

"Rose, my name is Ellie. I work with Mr. Hogan. Thank you for coming down here today."

The woman gave a slight nod but said nothing, looking at her almost as suspiciously as she had regarded Hogan.

"Rose, did you really go to ask your husband for a divorce? At a time like that?"

She continued to look at Ellie suspiciously but gave a quick, fierce shake of her head. "*No!* I would never do nothin' like that, not with 'im locked up."

"You never wanted a divorce, did you, Rose? Not with the kids still little and no money coming in. You wanted him out so he could help you run the luncheonette. Didn't you, Rose?"

She sniffled vigorously. "Yes," she said, in so piteous a voice that Tom almost felt sorry for her. "He told me he was goin' straight. That's how Abie convinced me to go to the police in the first place."

"So he talked you into it then, Rose? It wasn't you going on your own," Ellie confirmed.

"No. I didn't wanna do it at first. But Abie told me it was best, what with Lepke havin' everybody who knew anyt'in' rubbed out. It was the only way he could stay alive."

"In fact, it was *he* who asked *you* for the divorce. Wasn't it, Rose?" Ellie asked, her voice so warm and maternal that the nervous, agitated woman sitting in the chair before her burst into sobs, nodding her head vigorously up and down.

"Ye-es," she squeaked. "He wanted it. After I stayed with 'im through all that! The no-good bum. After all that!"

She sobbed quietly for a little while more, and they let her, saying nothing. Then she put her head up, blinking back the tears and looking around for another cigarette. Ellie had it already lit and waiting.

"He was just out outta the hospital, an' he looked terrible. He had me lie down with him again, the bum. I didn't wanna, but he looked so bad. His hair was thinned out, an' his skin was pale, an' he said his lungs was real bad. He had me lie down one more time, an' took the bottle I brung him. Then he tells me that's it, he's decided he wants a divorce."

"Did he say why?" Ellie asked.

"He just said with the deal he cut, he would get off free, an' he wasn't comin' back ta the old neighborhood. He said he was takin' off, an' he didn't want no more *baggage* with him."

"I see," Ellie told her softly. "And you tried to argue with him."

"I told him I was the only one who could take care a him," Rose said, her voice breaking, arms stretched out in front of her as if appealing to them. "I said he was sick, an' I was the only person who really knew what he was — the only one who could really take care a him."

"And what did he say?"

"He just laughed an' said he was fine. He laughed an' said he could take care a hisself, an' if he got divorced, the government would put him someplace I could never find 'im."

"And how did you feel about that?"

"How would *you* feel?" Rose snapped bitterly. "I told 'im he was a rotter. I told 'im he was a bum. But he wouldn't listen."

"But that was the only plan he mentioned to you? Just to let the government move him somewhere? No plans to escape?"

Rose shook her head and wiped her eyes, the tissues smearing the thin lines of mascara. But she looked straight at them now, the hysteria and the grief and the hurt subsiding.

"Nah. He was afraid a those guys. That's why he turned hisself in. He was afraid Albert Anastasia an' his *shtarkers* would kill him for Lepke, an' he didn't wanna go back ta jail. Besides, he was sick, he couldn't run or go climbin' outta windows. He couldn't go nowheres. He was sick, which is the only reason why he ever asked me for a divorce. He didn't know what he was doin'."

Ellie pulled her chair back, deferring to Hogan with that motion, and he cleared his throat.

"Thank you, Mrs. Lewanda," he said, his voice almost contrite. "But tell me, why were you reluctant to talk to us?"

"How do I know what's gonna happen to me?" she said, leaning forward, the fear bulging her eyes. "How do I know, maybe I say the wrong thing about 'im goin' out the window, they knock me off, too."

"Mrs. Lewanda, you're under a full police guard, in a locked hotel room, under the protection of the district attorney's office," Hogan told her.

Rose leaned back, shrugging, and Tom thought he saw the ghost of a smile around her lips.

"I know," she said. "So was Abie."

After it was all over and Rose put safely back on her train to Utica, he strolled with Ellie down to the main concourse of Grand Central. It was the evening rush hour by then, and as they came down the stairs they gazed out over the thousands of commuters with their hats and suits and briefcases, hustling for their trains. The haze of their cigarette smoke wafting slowly up toward the ceiling, where the once magnificent blue, celestial map there was all but obliterated by the same tar they were now pumping into their lungs.

Among the oblivious Westchester crowd, the porters were laying out the crimson carpet for the Twentieth Century Limited. Passing out the usual corsages and bottles of perfume to the women and boutonnieres to the men — the excitement of many of them palpable as they strutted up the carpet, ready to be whisked across the country to Chicago with the night.

It was a scene he had always enjoyed watching, yet he couldn't help thinking how tonight everything somehow seemed a little weary, even grim. The great red rug looked frayed and faded, the hall and even the celestial blue ceiling darker and grimier than he had seen it since the war.

Why don't they ever clean anything? he wondered to himself. *Isn't the City rich enough for that?* Remembering how, when he was mayor, Charlie was always bemoaning the lack of money in the City coffers. *But how could that possibly be, in so rich a city — the wealthiest place on earth?*

Beside him Ellie seemed just as pensive, having said almost nothing since they'd left the hotel.

"You did well up there — very well," he told her. "The boss was impressed."

"Thanks," she said, but to his surprise her voice sounded glum and flat.

"You didn't think so?"

"No, I knew it was the way to get to her," she conceded as they continued down the ramp to the lower hall and into the Oyster Bar, where they took two seats at the counter. "I just felt bad for her."

"The former Mrs. Reles?" Tom asked, surprised.

"I know she's a silly old woman. But think of how it must feel — to be that close to someone and not know what they are," she said, looking down.

"You really don't think she knew exactly what Abe Reles was?"

"Oh, I know she must have — at some time, in some part of her brain," Ellie agreed. "But not right away. Not when they got married."

"I suspect Mr. Reles always had *hoodlum* writ large on him."

"But not like this. Sure, she thought he was another wise guy around the neighborhood," she explained. "Making a little book, fencing stuff that fell off a truck. Someone exciting to be with, flashing his roll around. A guy who could take care of himself, if it came to that. But not a professional killer. Not some animal, killing anybody for the money, without an ounce of remorse."

They ordered up a couple of bowls of the clam chowder and some coffee, then sat in silence for a few minutes, while the ebullient evening crowd swelled up around them. The bar and restaurant packed with people greeting one another loudly after work or after a journey of a thousand miles, filling themselves with lobsters and steaks, and cocktails.

They sat almost huddled next to each other among all the happy people, and an errant thought gripped him: of Slim gliding along the main concourse upstairs, in a shining gown. Of the first time Charlie had introduced her to him, right here in the Oyster Bar.

Sitting there in her flawless rose suit, with matching hat and matching bag. This woman like none either of them had ever met before, exquisitely composed, and sensuous, and knowing. He had taken one look at her and thought, consciously, *Charlie, you're in trouble.* But he knew, even then, that he was really the one in trouble.

"I suppose Reles could dissemble the same as the rest of us," Tom said, turning to his coffee. "Even to those closest to him."

"*Especially* to those closest to him," Ellie corrected, stabbing at the small bowl of chowder with her spoon. "Doesn't it always seem that's how it is, Tom? We lie the most to those nearest to us, and why is that?"

"I don't know. I guess it's because those are the people we're *afraid* will know us best. They're the ones we need to fool the most."

"And isn't that sad," she said, looking up at him in the crowded bar, her dark eyes lovely and a little moist.

"Yes, I guess it is," he said. The words wrenched from him, him feeling like she was reading his thoughts. What he said then surprising even himself: "But are we capable of showing anybody exactly who we really are? Wouldn't we rather die of shame?"

"Spoken like a true Catholic." She smiled. "I don't think I'd die. I think I'd rather know everything."

"That's because you're a good prosecutor," he told her, putting an arm around her shoulders, breathing in the scent of her and the warmth as he brought her close. "And because you have nothing to be ashamed about."

"And what about you?"

"Ah, that you'll have to find out on your own," he said, letting her go and wagging a finger at her, trying to sound playful. He stared out at all the drunken, happy, shouting people around them.

"Tell me, do ya still have that hotel room?" he asked her.

"What? I guess so. Mr. Hogan put Rose on the train back to Utica — she was too frightened even to stay the night," Ellie said, startled at first, the realization of what he was saying just beginning to dawn in her eyes. She started to grin that smile he loved. "Why do you ask?"

"Whattaya say we take advantage of it?" he asked. Picturing them wrapped up in the hotel sheets and each other, two anonymous souls, hidden away from everything and everyone in the middle of the City.

"Don't you mean, take advantage of *me?*" she asked, her eyes glinting merrily. He smiled back at her, thinking a hundred different things, but only wanting her.

"C'mon. I'll treat you to room service."

And so they went, making their way up through the throngs and past the red carpet now being rolled back up by the porters, the train dinging its way slowly out of the station toward Chicago. Up through the dimly lit halls of the hotel, arm in arm, her head on his shoulder. They were starting to undress each other before they got the door closed.

20

Mexico, 1953

They came down through the pass into the valley just as the light was fading. Indian women were walking along the side of the road, returning from the markets with goats and pigs at their feet, and iguanas they held aloft on strings as the car drove by. The air smelled of roses, and tortillas, and the wet burros they guided, weighed down with more goods and tents, and giggling children.

They crossed a vast, wooded plateau, fissured by one long ravine after another, as if someone had scraped a giant rake across the land. In between, there were fields full of corn, and red roses, and waxy white tuberoses. Along the ravines, he could see the roots of the high trees wending their way down along the cliff face like desperate fingers, trying to seize a chokehold on the land.

"The *barrancas* — ravines. They were a natural fortification," Charlie explained needlessly as they passed over a bridge, prattling happily again. "When the Spanish came, they cut the bridges, and threw everything they had at them — arrows, lances, rocks."

"But it wasn't enough?"

"No. It never is."

Beneficio pushed the boat of a Lincoln up a last hill and into the narrow, serpentine streets of Cuernavaca, as carefully as a captain navigating a new harbor without a pilot. Tom could smell incense now, and just underneath it the rank scent of the garbage floating in the open sewers. But in the windows of the little shops he could make out the names Westinghouse, and Frigidaire, and RCA, and there were signs for Coca-Cola everywhere. They passed a small, pink jewel of a movie house, with a marquee advertising Lana Turner and Kirk Douglas in *The Bad and the Beautiful,* and something with Cantinflas. Then they turned onto a walled road that opened out into a tawdry cluster of bungalows, arrayed around a dance pavilion and a big, filthy swimming pool.

A lean, athletic man in his sixties, his sharp face turned a deep brown by the sun, was standing out front. When they pulled up, he grinned and broke into a quick little soft-shoe, then stuck out a hand to Tom.

"Welcome to Shangri-La!"

"Welcome to Cuernavaca, the City of Eternal Spring!" Charlie boomed behind Tom, climbing out of the car. He pumped the man's hand enthusiastically, and the two of them embraced and beamed at each other.

"Tommy, I can't believe I never introduced you to Henry Fink back in New York. He's only the greatest vaudeville man who ever lived! Used to run the Club Samoa, with Leo Bernstein. You remember — that great Tiki place on the Street, just across from the Onyx, and Jimmy Ryan's?"

"I know it."

"Best supper club in the Latin Quarter!"

"Ah, c'mon," Fink said, waving him off, though he was clearly delighted. "I been outta New York a long time. Everybody's forgot about that stuff."

"Never, Henry, never!"

"Your brother's too kind to me. Besides, I hear now it's just another bust-out joint, with the girls givin' juksters hand jobs under the tables," Henry Fink told him, latching onto his arm with a callused hand. He was wearing a white linen shirt and white pants, with a robust growth of white chest hair sticking out through the unbuttoned top of his shirt. "Let's go sit by the pool an' have somethin' refreshing, before I show y'around this dump —"

"Whattaya talk? Did you know this is where the emperor Maximilian and the Mad Carlota used to have their summer place? Right here!" Charlie burbled up just behind them.

"Really? Which bungalow?" Tom asked.

"This whole place, plus all that on the other side of the wall. It used to be the Borda Gardens — their own little private Shangri-la, where they could go to escape the heat in the summer."

Peering over the wall, Tom could see only a jumbled green ruin of stone and jungle.

"You can almost see 'em there, can't ya? The emperor and his lady at their trysting place, walking alone along the torchlit paths." Charlie sighed. "Did ya know Henry here talked the governor into lettin' him lease half of the gardens, an' set up this place?"

"It's what lettin' a Mexican win at golf will get ya," Henry Fink said, giving them a broad show-business wink.

"I wonder what letting a Mexican *lose* at golf'll get you," Tom said, but Fink was too busy ushering them into a pair of cushioned rattan chairs around a small table with an umbrella staked through the middle. They were the best set by the pool, but even so the red plastic cushions were cracked and faded, the chairs swaying uneasily under their weight. On others the rattan bottoms had all sagged through, like an old man's gut, or broken out altogether, the legs pocked with hundreds of visible termite holes.

The pool looked Olympic sized, but it was covered with leaves and rotting fruit from the mango trees that bent over it, and enormous water bugs skittering across the surface like vacationing water-skiers. A very dignified, white-moustachioed man who looked as if he could be left over from Maximilian and Carlota's time was working at cleaning it, netting the mangoes as deliberately as if he were searching for portents in the water, and tossing them into a rising mound of green and yellow slush on the lawn.

Henry Fink called over an equally ancient waiter named Gabriel and ordered them up a round of Negra Modelos, and the man bowed and retreated to the covered rococo bar just off the dance floor. The bar was another fabulous ruin—at least forty feet long, most of it coated in dust, its garish gold brocade lying in tatters. Herculean spider webs filled every open space, even between the countless brands of rum and tequila behind the bartender, and sitting off to one corner, as gaudy and unexpected as a shipwreck in a desert, was a grand piano.

Fink gestured with his head in the direction of the dignified old man spooning at the pool.

"All I've got to work with right now is Gabriel an' Guillermo over there, the fucking Gold Dust twins. But you should come back on the weekend; it'll be jumpin'."

"No need to apologize, Henry! This is the best joint in Mexico, far as I'm concerned. You really have to see it on a Saturday, Tom, when they have a band in. All the Big Crowd is here, all the expats, down from Mexico City. Oh, but you should see it!"

He could see it well enough. The same types he'd glimpsed back in the ballroom of the Hotel del Prado. More aging American exiles like his brother, or copies of the ladies from El Ranchito, unable or unwilling to go home. Bored to death, sitting around the pool drinking themselves stupid in their white dinner jackets, the women shrieking with laughter as the bottom slowly gave out of the night, like one of Henry Fink's rattan chairs. Tom wondering: *Did he bring Slim here, too?*

He wanted to walk away. He wanted to tell Charlie that he had a headache or a stomachache, or some kind of ache, and excuse himself and go into one of the little bungalows and sleep for about a hundred years. Or maybe go down the hill and get a taxi somewhere, if such a thing existed, and go back up forty-five hundred feet, and down ten thousand, and fly out of Mexico City and back to Ellie.

He was thinking of doing all those things. But instead he made himself take another swallow of his dark Mexican beer, and leaned back in his chair, gazing out into the night, and the massive hodgepodge of churches below them. Some adorned with statues and gold, like something out of the Philippines. Others with red-tipped cupolas and Romanesque domes, looking as ancient and massive as the cathedrals they had blown up in Italy —

"How far back do we go, Henry?" Charlie was almost shouting the few feet over to Henry Fink at his table.

"That Saint Patty's Day, Charlie. I remember they had you standin' in the back of a flower car, up at a Hundred Tenth Street an' Fifth Avenue."

"Christ, no, Henry, it's further back than that! I seem to recall it was that Saturday night, down in Bay Ridge. You was with a fella named Pete Reilly."

"Pete Reilly? Nah, never knew the man. Didn't he manage prizefighters?"

"That's right. He had a fighter called himself Jacques de LeHand, said he was the champion of Quebec. In fact his real name was Jack Delahanty, but Pete bought 'im, an' he made a pretty fair livin' off Jacques de LeHand until he run into Tiger Ward one night in Hoboken, an' that was the end a that."

"D'ya remember what he said after that fight? Ol' Jacques? He said, 'Ward was throwin' so many punches I thought the ref had joined in!'"

The two men hooted with laughter, and Charlie slapped the table.

"I think it was Bill McCormack started callin' 'im 'Jacques de No-Left-Hand'," Charlie said, and roared again.

"William McCormack? You saw the fight with him?" Tom cut in, something pricking at him.

"Sure, sure. He was always gettin' the boys together, givin' out tickets to the fights, an' afterwards there'd be a beefsteak, or some such. All on him!" Charlie churned on without blinking. He turned to his friend. "How about your greatest hit, Henry?" Charlie proposed. " 'The Curse of an Aching Heart'!"

"That old thing? Oh, God, no!" Henry laughed, but Charlie persisted.

"Here, you've never seen us together," he told Tom.

The two of them stood up and harmonized skillfully enough that he realized they must have done it many times before, and he wondered again if Slim had been sitting where he was, night after perfect spring night in Cuernavaca. Just over the wall from the magic trysting place of Maximilian and Carlota — listening to two white-haired men sing a song written before the First World War.

> *You've shattered each and every dream,*
> *Fooled me right from the start.*
> *And though you're not true,*
> *May God bless you,*
> *That's the curse of an aching heart.*

The light was gone completely now, and the stars were out, which brought a few couples and some ragged-looking individuals filtering into the Shangri-La. Guillermo, he noticed, had put away his net and changed into a red-coated waiter's costume, napkin over one arm, guiding them to one or another of the least battered tables, while his brother and Henry Fink sang on, oblivious.

When they were finally done there was a smattering of applause from the scattered patrons, and then Henry suggested they go inside the pavilion. There Guillermo pounded the dust off one of the cracked cushions and with a kindly smile under his white brush moustache gestured for them to be seated. They ate some chicken soup that Henry said he had been saving just for Charlie, and then some fried chicken, and tried to figure out again just when it was they had first met.

"No, no, it must've been when I was on the force, Henry," Charlie told him.

"Did ya know, Tom, I passed the examination on July 7, 1917? Seven-seven-teen-seventeen, now there's an auspicious date for you!"

"So you've said, Charlie."

"Started at Fordham Law the same year, and they put me a-way out in the Seventy-Deuce, over in Brooklyn. Sunset Park, at Forty-Third Street an' the Fourth Avenue. Had me on all hours — day, night, midnight. God, but what a place for a rookie cop to start, between Green-Wood Cemetery and the docks!"

"Tough, was it?" Tom asked.

"Tough!" Henry Fink said, and snorted.

"You don't know how raw it still was out there in those days," Charlie told them. "It was barely a city. There were still little dirt farms, an' squatters' shacks all over the place then. I walked my beat at night, between the water and the dead."

"Gives me chills," Fink chimed in.

"Believe me, the dead was the least of my concerns. I don't know how I woulda made it out of there without the Old Man."

"That's where you met McGrath?" Tom asked.

"Sure, an' thank God. James Brannan, the captain down at the Seventy-Deuce, was a swell-headed little tyrant. We used to say, 'If Brannan owned the lake in Prospect Park, he wouldn't give the ducks a swim.' Oh, he was some-thin'!"

Charlie's reminiscences were voluble enough to attract the attention of some of the patrons, and they sidled over closer to the moldy bar to listen. One man in particular, Tom noticed peering in closely at them — or at least as much as he might in his condition. He was an American, wearing a rumpled seersucker suit, who looked as if he might have been dragged in behind a car. His eyes kept crossing and uncrossing drunkenly, but he was determined to listen to them in the way that only drunks can be determined.

"You're a great man, Mr. Ambassador!" the drunk said suddenly, leaning precariously toward them on his ratty barstool, flecking them all with the li-quor spittle of his tribute.

"Thank you," Charlie said without looking at the man, his voice suddenly cool and sober. "It was Jack McGrath, the Old Man, what got me through

Captain Brannan, and all the rest of it—who helped me *survive*. McGrath was already a legend out there. They were already tellin' the story all over the precinct about how he drove all the perverts out of Brooklyn. He'd go around to the station houses on his days off, an' get the names of all the known child molesters in the neighborhood. Then he'd go to their homes an' just give 'em a beating, tell 'em they had twenty-four hours to leave the borough. Cleared every single one of 'em outta the borough, by God, like Saint Patrick driving the snakes outta Ireland!"

"You are a great man, and a great American, Mr. Ambassador!" the drunken man interjected again. "Ev'body in Mexico loves you, sir."

"All right now. We've heard about enough of your love," Charlie said, and Henry Fink rose slowly to his feet, looking questioningly at Charlie.

"Michael Finn is coming, Michael Finn is coming," he repeated, but Charlie just shook his head.

"The Old Man got me through down there, he really did," he continued instead. "There were some hard men on the waterfront then. The Kilduffs, who stole whatever they could, even boats if they were small enough. But the worst was the Kid Cheese gang. They used to terrorize the night watchmen, cut their throats an' throw their bodies in the water, just for the sport of it.

"They wouldn't hesitate to do the same to a cop. Early on, they got it in for me because I had the effrontery to arrest a couple of 'em while they was cleanin' out a boxcar on a rail siding. They decided they would teach me a lesson, so they lured me into an apartment hallway with the oldest trick in the book, pretendin' there was a mugging goin' on.

"I walked right into it. They'd smashed the hall light bulb, it was pitch-black in there, an' before I even knew what it was about, they had me down on the floor. It was a narrow space, an' I was helpless. I woulda taken a terrible beatin', been stamped an' kicked an' punched senseless at the very least, an' maybe even thrown in the harbor to drown. There was other cops down there by the waterfront, went out on their beat an' never came back, an' nobody ever found what happened to them."

Charlie spoke calmly, with a gentle smile on his face, but Tom could imagine well enough what it must have been like: the terrifying feeling of being trapped, unable even to extend his arms. Twisting about helplessly, while blow after blow rained down on him. Pounded with fists and blackjacks and brass knuckles, the breath growing heavier and heavier in his chest. The fear that he was going to die, right there and then —

"But God's grace, the Old Man was out again lookin' after his pups. He heard the commotion an' come runnin'. Didn't even spend time to whistle up reinforcements, or bang on the manhole covers to spread the word: *Policeman in trouble.* No, he just ran to the sound of the battle, with nothin' but his pocket billy in those close quarters. By the time I was back on my feet he had 'em all spread out in the snow outside. Eight members of the Kid Cheese gang, lyin' there out cold. An' Jack McGrath lookin' at me with a rare smile of satisfaction, sayin', 'That'll teach 'em to respect an officer of the law!'"

Just then the drunk in the seersucker staggered off his stool and took a determined step toward them. But his legs got tangled, as the legs of drunks will, and instead he dropped down with a loud exhalation on his backside, stilling what crowd there was and drawing all eyes to their table.

"Anyt'ing happen to you in Mexico, the populace'd be *grief-stricken,*" he told Charlie from his seat on the floor. "Absolutely *grief*-stricken. But answer me one thing — just *one* t'ing. Why'd she leave you? Why'd she walk out on a great man like you?"

Henry Fink was on his feet now, dancing behind where the drunk was sitting, chanting, "Michael Finn is coming, Michael Finn is coming" again. The pavilion went very still, Guillermo and Gabriel looking over, along with the handful of tourists. Tom noticed that his brother's face had turned the color of ash, but once again he shook his head at Henry — who shrugged, and gave over his dancing. Instead he helped the drunk in the seersucker carefully to his feet and walked him slowly out of the Shangri-La. Somebody put money in the jukebox, and those who remained turned back to their higher interests in alcohol and sloppy, late-night passes.

"Henry is so kind. He is so very kind," Charlie said softly, turning to his brother.

"So that's where you met Jack McGrath," Tom said. "And you were friends ever since?"

"Jack stood by me, and when I got elected DA, I saw to it that he got every promotion he'd been denied over the years," Charlie told him. "It wasn't easy, let me tell you—he wouldn't play ball with the clubhouse boys—"

"Did you have the Old Man pick the detail to guard Reles?" Tom asked him.

"Hmm? Oh, I don't remember," Charlie said, sounding preoccupied. "I thought that was Frank Bals. But it could've been McGrath. Maybe it was."

"D'ya know the next morning he had all the guards together in the same room? Before you or anybody else could get up there," Tom told him. "Gettin' their stories straight."

"Did he now?" Charlie chuckled and held out a hand, palm up. "Well, I suppose that was him all along, lookin' out for his men."

"Except that you took the fall instead."

"Ah, Tommy, for chrissakes, don't you see?" Charlie asked wearily. "I was the one in charge no matter what happened. So we could've nailed up a few poor cops for catchin' some sleep on the job, like every policeman's done since the Crucifixion itself. It still woulda been *me* takin' the blame, once Reles went out that window."

"But then who did it? Who threw him out?"

His brother started to laugh, a dry, hard chuckle that sounded as rueful as anything he'd said since he'd come to Mexico.

"Well, if we knew that, Tommy, why the *fook* would we be sittin' in some bar in Cuernavaca?"

"But Charlie—"

"You know, you really oughtta go back to New York, clear your name, Charlie." Henry Fink had returned, and slid into a chair at their table with a quiet grace that belied his years. "They could use you up there. Everybody tells me the goddamned City is turning into a sewer!"

"Return, and be dragged from one investigatin' committee to another? Return to make headlines for every schemin' pol, every prosecutor who'd like to run for office?" Charlie said, looking meaningfully at Tom. "How could I ever clear my name, when every question is an accusation, even from me own brother—"

"You know that isn't true, Charlie."

"—an' every accusation is a headline that convicts you all over again, in the eyes of the people?" he went on. "Go back? To what? What job could I even get? Not a dime to my name, an' every hand raised against me —"

Tom realizing that his brother was drunk again. *You have to be careful up this high* . . . Putting a hand on his back, trying physically to calm him.

"There's plenty that only want to help you, Charlie," he said. "Who just can't stand to see your old friends fob off the blame on you, while they go free."

Charlie seized hold of his hand over his shoulder, nodding and patting it. "You're right, Tommy, you're right, God forgive me. I know you only mean to help. I want to come back, God knows. Maybe later, when it's all died down more."

"That's the spirit, Charlie!" Henry Fink crowed. Guillermo appeared at his elbow, with two blood-red daiquiris on a tray, complete with straws and paper umbrellas, and Fink passed one of them to his brother.

"Hell, maybe I *will* come back an' run for office. Governor, or maybe mayor again!" Charlie said, his face brightening as rapidly and as fully as a child's after a good cry. Beaming happily at them as he sipped from his daiquiri through its straw.

"What I meant, Charlie —"

"Run just so I can get it all out in the open, win or lose!" he said, spreading a hand over the table as if he were laying out his vision. "Sure, I'll come back. And I'll make an entrance, all right! You can stage-manage it, Henry —"

"Love to, Charlie!"

He had risen up out of his chair now, drawing the bemused stares of the few remaining patrons at the Shangri-La.

"I think Ebbets Field would be the place to do it. Sure, they'll boo me. There'll be a whole storm of boos!" He grinned beatifically down at them — welcoming the boos — then cupped a hand over his heart, as if saying the pledge of allegiance. "But I'll stare 'em down! Like this. And there'll be the Brooklyn Symphony there. I'll have 'em play 'The Sidewalks of New York' when I come in. There'll be boos. But I'll win 'em over!"

"Speaking of booze —"

The drunken man staggered, and Tom moved quickly to catch him, guiding him back down into his rattan chair. There Charlie blinked, and shook his head, the smile fading from his face — as if he were awaking from a dream.

"Ah, no. Forget it. Wouldn't be right to Slim. To make her deal with all that."

The rest of the bar gazed disappointedly down at their drinks again, while Charlie stared off toward the wild, green world beyond the walls, doubly shrouded by the darkness now.

"Y'know, if only we'd had a little trysting place for our own. Someplace to get away to, like what the old Aztec emperors, an' Maximilian and Carlota had here—"

"It may've been their trysting place, but not with each other," Henry Fink said, laughing.

"What're ya talkin' about?"

"Don'tcha know that story? Ol' Max had a hot little Indian number he kept in town. They still talk about it around here—La Bonita India. And when he was away, the missus was *shtupping* one of the horse guards. The rumor is she even got knocked up, gave birth to that shmuck general who lost France to the Nazis—"

"No, I didn't know that. So this is just where he kept his girl on the side," Charlie said, pondering, sounding disappointed. Tom looked away. "Well, I guess romance is dead. Still, it's beautiful, don'tcha know—the two of 'em walking in their moonlit garden."

The last few guests began to leave, and Henry Fink stood up to excuse himself. Charlie seemed to become suddenly conscious of himself again—sitting up straighter in his rickety chair, looking over guiltily at Tom.

"I'm sorry, Tom. But I can't blame Jack McGrath for lettin' some good men down easy," he said, placing a hand on his shoulder. "He saved my life more than once down there in Red Hook. I told you about the docks, Tommy. Nothing is as it seems.

"Those days, after the Great War, men were comin' back from the fighting, but they couldn't leave it behind 'em. There were housebreakings all over the precinct, an' I don't mean cat burglars, or second-story men. It was gangs of veterans. They'd go right in, an' somebody got in their way, they'd cut their throat. We worked hard to keep it outta the paper, how many times we found an army bayonet at the scene of the crime.

"That's how we got Jimmy, y'know. The poor fella, his parents gone from one war, an' him in the next."

"I didn't know that," Tom said. "I mean, I know the story, but —"

"But not that part of it. I know. It was a house up along Thirty-Ninth Street, by the BMT yards. One of those old wooden double-deckers that used to grow like toadstools in Brooklyn. There was a family on the first floor that was always trouble. One or t'other of us was always in there, tryna stop the man of the house bashin' his wife's head against a wall.

"She was a sweet woman, too. Not one to put a tongue on a man until it drove him mad," he reflected, staring out at the black nullity of the pool. "Hair the color of Jimmy's — that's where he got it, that sort of ginger shade. A little thing, always cheerful. Not like the mister, a big brute of a man. Quiet as a parson most a the time, workin' the docks with his crew. But he'd get into the growler on a Saturday night, and then the whiskey, an' everything would change.

"He'd blacken her eye for her, put out a tooth. Broke her nose so many times, until it was tilted over permanently, like some cheap pug's. That sweet woman! He'd hit her until the neighbors couldn't stand it anymore, an' they were not a squeamish lot, believe me. We'd have to go in an' restrain the *duid raibead*, the raging man. We'd get 'im settled, with the tap of a nightstick if need be, an' somebody would send for the priest to talk to him, while she sobbed in the next room. But the priest never told 'im anything but to mind his temper, and he never told *her* anything but to stay with her husband, an' so there you were."

"So there *you* were. And Jimmy?"

Charlie kept staring out at the pool, putting his big, red drink up on the table like Guillermo discarding a waterlogged mango.

"He come out to me of a Saturday evenin' in the summer. It was a hot night, but not the hottest. That's the worst, as the Old Man warned me it would be. When it gets *too* hot, the way it can, nobody has the energy to do anything. The City becomes almost peaceful, as peaceful as it ever is, because everybody's too exhausted to move. But when it's *just* hot enough to prick an' itch at ya, an' keep ya from sleep . . . when it turns the beer you drink sour in yer stomach — that's when it's bad. We'd have half the women in the neighborhood walkin' around claimin' they run into doors.

"This evenin' Jimmy come out to see me, so I knew it was somethin' very wrong. He was about seven then, as fair a little boy as you'd want to look at.

When we had to come into his place, he'd just stay down the hall, peekin' out at what was happenin' with those big brown eyes of his wide as two moon pies, but never sayin' a thing.

"This night he come out into the street, an' he asked me would I please come, his mother was in trouble. That's just how he put it, too: 'Me ma is in trouble.' We tried to go into family fights at least two at a time, that's how dangerous they were, but I knew from the look on his face, there was no time for me to find a partner. He wasn't even wearin' shoes, just dressed in his pajamas, an' so I followed him right back into that house."

The whole scene already a hell. He could tell from the moment he walked through the open front door, half off its hinges. (Where she tried to flee, before being hauled back in?) What bare sticks of furniture there were tumbled over and broken, the lacework she'd done to make the house as much of a home as it could be thrown on the floor.

"She was in a corner of the kitchen, a mass of blood. The long hair covered her face—praise God, it spared her son that, at least. But she wasn't movin' an' she wasn't breathin'. The brute standin' over her in his undershirt an' suspenders and his army-issue pants. The blood coating his hands, but still standin' over her, his fists cocked. Like it was a prizefight, an' he was just darin' her to get up again."

When he came into the narrow, broken kitchen the raging man turned on him at once. Moving across the room in two quick strides, without bothering to say a word. He hadn't had time to say anything himself, or even get his nightstick up. Just able to push Jimmy back behind him, down the hall, before the husband was upon him.

He got his stick up in time to block the first blow, but the raging man only shoved it back into him. Sending him stumbling back down the hall, falling over. It was madness, his strength a force like nothing else Charlie had ever felt in his life, not even from the gang who ambushed him by the docks. His eyes, in the moment he'd seen them up close, like two pools of tar, black and impenetrable, inured to all reason and care.

He tried to get to his feet, watching as the man grabbed up a bayonet from the kitchen table, the blade as bloodstained as his hands, and came back at him. Scrambling for the pistol in his belt holster then, knowing as surely as he knew anything that if he did not get it out, he was going to die . . .

"I shot him right in the chest, dead center, when he come down that hall-way after me. It just slowed him down. He didn't even drop the bayonet. So I shot him again, right over the heart this time, an' he dropped close enough for me to smell his breath, an' damn if I didn't shoot him again in the head, just to make sure the son of a bitch was finally dead.

"An' the worst of it was, I turned around an' there was Jimmy standin' there, with those big eyes of his. He'd seen the whole thing; I killed the boy's father right in front of him. But you know, he never said a word.

"I walked out on the porch of that double-decker, and a lot of the neighbors were already there, wantin' to know what happened. Most of them were al-ready keenin' like idiots, an' goin' on about what a good man the deceased was, an' how could I a shot him—the same lot that heard him bangin' his wife's skull off the woodwork every Saturday night! But little Jimmy, he just took me hand, an' led me over to the porch bench, an' there we sat, him lookin' up at me as if to see if *I* was all right.

"It was then that the Old Man arrived, thank Christ, with a troop of the lads. He told all the righteous citizens to disperse immediately if they didn't want to get their heads broke an' turned in for public riotin'. They moved away right quick. Then he knelt down an' asked me if I was all right, an' he asked Jimmy how he was, while the rest a the boys went in to take care of the scene. And I couldn't get a word out. It was the first an' last time I ever shot a man, even if it was in self-defense, and I couldn't say a thing. But Jimmy just turned to McGrath an' told him, 'He saved my life.'"

Charlie stabbed idly at the slushy ice and the few pieces of fruit remaining in the daiquiri. The bar at the Shangri-La empty now, save for the two of them.

"You know the rest of it," Charlie said in a flat, even voice, still looking away. "She was dead, just as I knew, the poor woman. They said in the papers he'd been buried alive for ten minutes over there when a shell hit his trench. They said he was always a well-tempered man before he went over, but I didn't care about any of that. He was dead, and I was glad he was dead.

"To me he never seemed human. He seemed like the wrath of God itself, Tommy, d'ya know what I'm sayin'? He seemed like some force of destruction greater than any man, an' I knew I'd come within one slip on the trigger, one uncleaned barrel from bein' gutted myself, right there on the floor. He was all the chaos an' bloodlust he'd brought back from the war, all that we released into this world, and have kept spewin' out ever since. I knew then I had to get out, I couldn't face it anymore. I knew I had to get through Fordham an' pass the bar as soon as I could because this was not the work I was cut out for: openin' up every can a worms there was in the borough of Brooklyn, New York."

"I know, Charlie."

"But the Old Man was. That was just what he was built for, makin' order out of chaos, like the hand of God Itself. He took control of the whole situation. He made sure to get the bodies out without me or Jimmy havin' to look at 'em again, and he threatened the gabbling neighbors within an inch of their lives if they dared to come into court an' make up lies, and he got me back to Claire's arms that night. The inquest cleared me without any trouble, an' it wasn't long after that he saw to it that I was transferred to work as a driver for the borough inspector, an' then to work plainclothes out at Coney Island, trackin' the touts an' the policy runners, an' the palm readers, and all the other raffish merchants of illusion.

"But one day before I left the Seventy-Deuce, he brought in Jimmy to see me, and he told me, 'Take him and raise him as your own.' I told him I couldn't do that, there was the Book of Rules, an' City regulations, an' they'd need to search for next of kin. An' he told me, 'There is no next a kin, not in this world, an' screw the Book of Rules. He's already been forgotten, far as this city is concerned, so take him home an' give him a good life, an' ease the pain for the both a you.'

"An' so I did. And so Claire took him in just like the fine mother I always knew she could be, and he was everything you'd want in a son. Never gave us any trouble, an' he grew up to be a big, fine lad, a fighter when he had to be, gentle as a lamb the rest of the time. They put him in the Airborne, an' he made it through D-Day even with his glider crashin', and havin' to walk back ten miles through the Jerry lines — only to get shot in the hedgerows, three weeks later. A good, quick death, they said, never knew what hit him. And they told me, an' then I had to go tell you."

Tom remembering the rest of that night in the ruined Italian villa. How after he threw up, the archbishop had become surprisingly solicitous, even tender, running his chubby hands over his face as he held his head. Blessing him, and Jimmy. Saying a prayer for him right there by the great Renaissance mantel-

piece of the vanished Sforza. The MPs and the butler, and the cooks dropping down to their knees, to hear Archbishop Francis Spellman give his thanks for the fallen warrior of the Faith, and he had made it seem like it almost meant something . . .

"But what I always remember—how I'll always see Jimmy—is that day in Sunset Park. The dear boy. Walkin' off with me hand in hand, a little packet of his things an' his clothes clutched to his chest. Headin' with me to the subway, an' the ride back to his new home, and his new life in Bay Ridge. And short as it was, and cut off as it was, that was the greatest blessing of my life, Tommy. That was the best of it, and it was the Old Man who set it up, just as he always put everything to rights."

21

New York, 1953

He wasn't going to bother the Old Man, not even for his brother—not since he'd heard he was dying. Instead it was he who got the summons, to go down and see him at Coney Island Hospital, where Jack McGrath was coughing and spitting out his life a day at a time.

Tom borrowed a car from his old partner, Natie Cohen. Taking Ocean Parkway down to Avenue Z, the same way they'd passed that morning with his brother almost twelve years before. Down the lovely broad, tree-lined boulevard, with all the brick homes full of good citizens, with husbands who waved goodbye to their wives before a day of honest labor. He took Ellie with him because she wouldn't take no for an answer, trying to explain to her the whole way down how she'd have to spend most of her time cooling her heels in the waiting room.

"So I'm just along for the ride?" she asked, half teasing, her mouth a dark-lipsticked pout.

She was looking particularly beautiful today, he thought, her black hair pulled back from her face and tucked under a small red hat cocked jauntily to one side. Her eyes large and inviting, with the usual hint of mischief in them.

"Mmm-hmm. Nice ride," he said, and she smiled and put her hand in his coat pocket, and moved in close against him.

"What do you think he wants to tell you?" she asked him, for about the fifth time since they'd started out.

"I don't know. He was only on the scene after it happened, and he was never called before any of the grand juries, or Kefauver. I don't know what there is he *can* tell me. But whatever it is, he'll want to tell me alone."

"Be careful of that, Tom," she said, to his surprise.

"Hmm?"

"Be careful what he *does* tell you alone — that it's not something that makes you complicit."

"Complicit in *what?*"

"In . . . in all of *this,* whatever it is. Make sure he's not dragging you into anything," she told him, and he leaned over to kiss her forehead reassuringly.

"Whatever it is, it's past time it all came out."

"That's fine to say. Just make sure you don't get blindsided."

Two blocks north of the Shore Parkway they pulled into a complex of drab institutional buildings, built out of brick the color of sand, with a couple of tall smokestacks for exclamation marks. Next door, workmen were clambering all over a massive new building, two huge, steel-frame towers with a connecting slab, creating a constant din of pneumatic drills, and hammers, and clattering pipes.

"How do the patients sleep with all that?" Ellie wondered.

"It's New York. They probably find it comforting."

They went to the main building, where the Old Man was out on the fifth-floor sun porch, tucked into a wicker wheelchair under a double swath of blankets, even though it was an unseasonably warm fall day, the sun basting the porch in light and heat. Reminding him of Charlie there, his last days in New York, when his health was breaking down. *How little he knew then . . .*

Alongside the Old Man was a row of new mothers in wheelchairs and blankets, gingerly rocking their newborn babies, most of them with their eyes closed and their heads held back to reap the sun. They reminded Tom of a picture of atomic scientists he'd just seen in the paper, faces bent back, glowing in the light from another test blast. On the floor around them were a few children, some of them with their heads shaved, playing with blocks and dolls with the obliviousness that only kids could manage.

"I don't know why they have me out here frightenin' the mothers an' babes," Jack McGrath said when they walked in, "but if they can stand it, it does my heart good."

Tom smiled and told him not to be silly, and hoped the Old Man couldn't tell how badly he was lying. He hadn't visited since he'd been admitted for his latest operation, and it stunned him now to see much he'd changed.

The powerful, iron-rod physique was completely wasted away, until he was curled up in his hospital chair like a boiled shrimp. His hands and forearms, the only part of his body outside of the blankets, were mere liver-spotted sticks extending from his pajamas. His face was blotchy, with only a few tendrils of mouse-gray hair left, and the skin pulled back tight around the skull. As close to a death's head as it could be, right down to the brown, rotting teeth that leered at Tom and Ellie.

"This is my partner on the case, Miss Ellen Abramowitz," he said to the Old Man, and McGrath smiled and nodded as charmingly as he could while he squeezed her hand.

"And what a beautiful addition to the district attorney's office she is," he said, while Ellie smiled back at him.

"Tom's told me a great deal about you," she said, taking his hand. "I think outside of his brother, he admires you more than anyone else in the world."

"Isn't that a pretty thing to say?" he replied, still smiling with his tumbled, brown teeth, but the eyes suddenly hard as crystals, even as he patted the back of her hand.

The hammering outside suddenly picked up, the sound invading the tranquil sun porch, and the Old Man pulled his hand away and coughed heavily. He reached out for a pitcher of water and a glass on the little stand next to his chair, but Ellie anticipated him gracefully, pouring him a glass and placing it in his bony hand.

"Thank ye, darlin'," he said.

There was the distinct sound from outside of a hammer falling twelve stories to the ground, and hitting a steel strut on every one of them. The Old Man gave a little chuckle and slowly shook his head.

"I picked this hospital specific fer the cool ocean breezes, an' now it's become a construction site."

"Doesn't all of it keep you awake?" she asked solicitously. "All the noise from the parks, and the parkway—"

"Not until those lumpers started up," he told her, smiling again, and tilting his head in the direction of the construction site. "The parkway's more like a background noise. A steady hum—lets me know that the City's still out there. All the people out on the rides an' the boardwalk, that's a different sound. More like the waves themselves, risin' an' fallin'. But I love it. Even the kiddies screamin' on the roller coaster—you can tell the whole ride by how they rise an' fall. It tells a story by its sound."

He coughed again, and took some more water, then looked up sweetly at them both.

"Speakin' a stories . . ."

"It's been a pleasure meeting you, Captain McGrath," Ellie told him, taking her cue. Squeezing his hand once more before she left. "I hope you get some rest."

"I will, dear, bless yer heart," he said, and watched her all the way out, the smile fixed to his lips. But when he swung his head around again it was gone, and his eyes were grim.

"Whattaya doin', bringin' yer girl into this?" he rasped.

"Miss Abramowitz works with me—"

"Ye think I was a cop in Brooklyn forty years, I can't tell when two people are in love?" he scoffed. "Ya shouldn't be bringin' her into it. Ya shouldn't be diggin' this up at *all*."

He emphasized the last word as decisively as a man crushing a cigarette butt under his heel, then dissolved into another coughing fit, followed by a series of wheezing gasps that left his whole wasted chest convulsing visibly. Some of the mothers sitting near him turned about apprehensively. But Tom was alarmed mostly by the stark hostility in his voice, even in its diminished state.

Just like that day out on the roof at the Half Moon, grabbing the hospital doctor by his lapels.

"I didn't dig it up," he told him as evenly as he could manage. "Senator

Kefauver and Rudy Halley dug it up. Now that it's out there, I'm not willing to let it go — not until my brother's name is good again."

One of the stick-like arms shot out from the loose hospital pajamas, and a hand seized his wrist — the grip still that of the young man who could wield a pocket billy like no one else on the waterfront.

"I'm tellin' ya, " he said, his eyes as fierce as Tom remembered them. "*Don't* go diggin' too deep into this. You don't know what ya might pull up."

"How could it be any worse?" Tom said, suddenly enraged at the Old Man's intransigence. "My brother all over the television as some murderin' mob stooge! He's a half a step from indictment, can't even show his face in this country. And now you're tellin' me I need to be *careful?*"

"That's *exactly* what I'm sayin'. You don't know what yer dealin' with here —"

"My brother always said you saved his life! He said he could trust you with anything, you'd always have his back —"

"Yes, and what a hard man he was to keep out of trouble, too! Without enough sense in his head to know even when his own brother was sniffin' around after his wife!"

Tom took a step back, despite himself. Trying desperately to keep his equilibrium, the death's head stare of the Old Man burning into him. Just then a nurse bustled out to the row of young mothers, telling the most attractive one that it was time for a feeding. She had long chestnut hair and an angelic, pale face, and the Old Man watched openly while the nurse set up a high bamboo screen around the woman's chair.

"Sometimes they forget I'm here, an' they just put 'em out, right in the open. Ah, what I wouldn't give just to see a full young breast again!" he said in a wheezy whisper, turning back to face Tom — as if they had just been hanging out on a street corner, watching the girls go by. "That's the crazy part, how these desires linger on even when you've got one foot in the grave. The older I get, the more I think a man is made out of nothin' but his appetites."

"Was it that obvious?" Tom asked.

"To me. T'others, who knows?" The Old Man gave a little snort. "Certainly not to *him*, more's the pity of it."

"He didn't know."

"I don't think so. Though he's a tough one to read sometimes, your brother. He dissembles more than you'd think."

"You know, it was just me. We never —"

"Oh, spare me the lady's virtue! It's a little late for that now, don'tcha think?"

Tom sat down on a chair next to McGrath and pulled off his light overcoat. Unable to help himself, drenched in sweat beneath his jacket, in the glare of the late-afternoon sun — under no further illusion that he would be running this interview.

"Sometimes I think I can almost see it," the Old Man said, sounding philosophical now, his eyes trained on the streaked yellow glare of the windows. "The Half Moon Hotel, over there to the west, past the parkway. But it's too far. I know. I was the one who checked every possible line of fire for your brother when they put the rats out there — includin' this hospital."

"Afraid they'd have a gunman fake a case of appendicitis, get him in here?"

"Somethin' like that."

"You were the one who picked the men for the guard detail, too," Tom said, attempting to gather himself somehow, and get back to what he wanted to ask.

"Did I?" McGrath shrugged and closed his eyes, leaning back into his pillow. "I don't remember. I suppose it was either me or Frank Bals."

"It was you."

"So? What's it to ya?"

"So you picked the biggest collection of empty uniforms ever assembled by the New York Police Department."

"Every one a those men had a perfect service record," McGrath said calmly, with his eyes still shut. "Men of pure muscle —"

"Includin' that between their ears," Tom told him. "Sure, they looked good on paper, and in the newspapers. But to protect the most wanted mob witness that ever was?"

The Old Man's eyes opened, calculating as a lizard's, and vaguely amused.

"Most criminals are idjits. That's why they're criminals. They don't possess the brains to steal legally, like everybody else in this blessed country. Cowards, too, without an ounce a courage in 'em when they don't have a drop on ya with a pistol, or ten a their pals waitin' for ya in a dark hallway. I knew if I put enough big-chested men out there, it would intimidate them, and I was right. They never dared to take so much as a potshot at the witnesses."

"But your men fell asleep."

"Sure they did. Tired men at night, near the end of a twenty-four-hour shift. You would, too."

"Why were they on twenty-four hours at a stretch? Who made that rule?"

"Who knows?" The Old Man slowly shook his head, a tight, contemptuous smile stretched across his hard face. "Blame that one on me, too, if ye like. But never underestimate the role of stupidity in human affairs. It wasn't the men's fault."

"So that's why you covered for them?"

"That's what you do for yer men, you look out for 'em when they get into trouble," he said as fiercely as he was able to now. "Those men were too good to go down for a piece a filth like Abe Reles. So was yer brother."

"You were the one who put them together in a room, before Charlie got there. Warned them they'd better get the story straight. How they patrolled up and down the suite hall, all night, every fifteen minutes. All the doors of the squealers kept wide open—"

"Sure. Maybe I fed 'em that. You can put that on me, too, if yer dear Mr. Hogan needs someone."

"But the rats didn't get the word. They told the press the guards were sittin' up right in their rooms, next to their beds."

"Wise guys, every one of 'em. Jokers. They had to go embellish it." The Old Man shook his head. "Before the reporters got there, Frank Bals put 'em in separate rooms. It wouldn't a done to have the squealers right in there with the guards. But of course they had to embroider it, beyond what we agreed on. All about how the guards sat up in chairs in their rooms every night. Watchin' over 'em till they went to sleep, like their faithful Irish nannies."

"In fact the rats went to sleep alone in their own rooms. Isn't that right? With their doors closed—and locked. And their radios on, if they wanted them. Isn't *that* true?"

The Old Man turned a gimlet eye upon him again. "Yer brother said to keep 'em happy. They were gangsters, kept locked up in a hotel suite for twenty months. Whattaya want? We even took 'em out for picnics on Long Island in the summer."

He could see that afternoon again, in his mind's eye—would never be able to forget it. The squealers playing their game of ball with the guards out at the Hecksher State Park campsite. Reles running excitedly about the dusty clearing in his shirtsleeves, gut hanging out over his belt. The apelike arms dangling past his knees. Working the hamburgers on the little charcoal grill, with his wide, flat fingers, eyes glinting with rancid mischief.

"And Sholem Bernstein? Allowed to run his shylock business right from the hotel? Having cops deliver letters threatening to break men's arms if they didn't pay the vig."

The Old Man rolled his eyes. "You think he ever collected a cent? You seen what these people are. Like dogs. Like carrion birds! The moment one goes down, the rest fall on 'im an' eat out his entrails. And on it goes, over an' over again."

"So who wanted Reles gone?"

"Who didn't?"

"Who threw him out the window? Or are you gonna tell me it was all an escape attempt again?"

"Who would you guess, with all your college smarts?" the Old Man answered him right back, mottled teeth mocking him with a smile now. "A locked hotel suite, where half the inmates are sleeping policemen, an' half are known murderers an' felons. Who do *you* think killed him?"

"But *why?* On whose say-so?"

The hammering sound picked up considerably again, the faces of the resting mothers on the porch looking up. Then there was a terrible crashing noise, hard enough to make the children's blocks on the floor bounce, the sound reverberating across the floor. He could hear voices arguing furiously, then another, smaller crash, and a few seconds of silence. Then slowly, the hammering and drilling sounds resumed. The children with the shaved heads looked up, a whole new sense of foreboding in their eyes. The babes in arms began to squall, triggering a new rush of nurses with bamboo stands.

"Bunch a lumpers," the Old Man said caustically. "They're puttin' up a whole new wing, y'know. I guess they expect sick people to be a big growth industry in the future."

"The more people there are," Tom said slowly, "the more will sicken, an' the more will die. You know they turned the Half Moon into an old folks' home?"

"I heard that. An' now that bastard Moses's tryna close down all of Coney Island. Shuttin' down Luna Park, ripping out most of the Gut. You know that's where I had my first beat, walkin' the Gut? They were good people, too. Not just carnies, though they were all right, but all sorts of folks. Poor as dirt, but happy an' good-natured as ya please, never gave me a lick a trouble. Not like the waterfront."

"No."

"But then, it was yer brother who handed over the City to Bob Moses—"

"That's not true."

"It is and you know it. He turned it all over to him. Hell, if Macy's wanted to condemn Gimbels, it would be okay, so long as Robert Moses says so!" The tough brown cop's eyes searching Tom's face, his voice taunting. "Yer brother has an enormous capacity for gettin' himself into places beyond where he belongs, wouldn't ya say?"

"What's that supposed to mean?"

"You figure it out. Just ask yourself how it is a man like OK Charlie got to be DA, then mayor—"

"He worships you," Tom said, sounding brokenhearted, he couldn't help it.

"Then think again about where your investigation's likely to lead. Think about how much you brung out just today."

"Is that a threat?"

"No, just a warning. Not even that."

The blotched death's head fell back against the pillow, all the tautness seeming to go out of McGrath's face and body until he looked like just a little old man again, shriveled up on a hospital chair. His eyes drifted over in the direction of the sick kids, playing again but shooting glances periodically out the window, wary now of all the crashing and banging outside.

"I don't have the strength or the ability to back up any of it anymore, which is a bad place for a street cop to be."

He paused for a moment, trying to clear his throat. His words almost a whisper when he spoke again: "You heard how I chased all the child molesters out of Brooklyn?"

"Who didn't?"

"Like Saint Patrick his own self, chasin' all the snakes out of Ireland. Well, it's a lie. I chased out plenty, but there's always more comin' in. Always more snakes. They're all yours now."

His voice faded away altogether then, and Tom could see that he was sleeping. His breathing heavy, hands twitching, not stirring even when the nurses came to take down the blinds one by one and wheel away the young mothers.

The sun skulked on toward the west, the room suddenly cooled, and the windows cleared again. Tom went over to look outside, and watched the long, blue slice of the sea reappearing. The moribund honky-tonks and penny arcades emerging once more along the boardwalk, looking shuttered and sad out of season—just as they had that November day twelve years before.

Tom walked back toward the hallway, trying to pick at everything the Old Man had told him, the way he knew Frank Hogan would. Walking until he got out to Ellie, who looked up at his face with a dozen questions, and was immediately stifled into silence.

"I need to tell you something," he told her.

22

New York, 1945

He stood at the bow of the ship and watched as the great white City came to him. Most of the other men had gone over to the port side to see the Statue of Liberty, but he stayed where he was, watching the skyscrapers emerge as he used to watch them appear from the Brooklyn docks. Many of them really gray or brown, he knew, or the color of rust or sand. But all of it shimmering whitely now in the afternoon sun as it rose before him.

Just as he had imagined Charlie watching the white cities emerge along the River Plate down in South America.

There was a low buzzing sound coming out of the sky that made him start, as such things did now. Looking up, he saw that it was a navy blimp, and a couple of biplanes circling lazily through the sky around it. There was a great, ragged shout, running up and down the boat, and he looked back down again, blinking at the sight. Ships of every possible description were steaming toward them, as if they were in some kind of mad race. Steel-gray destroyers and battleships, and even two huge, open-decked aircraft carriers maneuvering ponderously about. All of them strung from helm to stern in flags and pennants, ringing their bells and blowing horns — a whole New Year's Eve, making full steam for them.

A powerful little fireboat sped up alongside and fired a salute from its water cannons, the flumes cascading over even the upper decks of the *Queen Mary,* soaking the soldiers next to him, who yelled and laughed. A pair of motor yachts hove up, and to the astonishment of everyone on board, they saw that their decks were filled with young women. They were wearing flowers in their hair, like some fantastic cinematic vision — waving and blowing kisses, wiggling and twisting their hips as they called up to them from the rail. Behind them, still more girls were jitterbugging wildly with each other, to an all-WAC band banging away at chorus after chorus of "In the Mood."

"Oh, baby!" a soldier was shouting next to him, leaping up and down on the rail. "What kind of holy-moly, motherfucking place is *this?*"

There were crowds waving and shouting to them from all around the harbor, from along the Battery, and the promenade on Brooklyn Heights, and all up and down the docks that jutted out into the water. The captain blew the foghorn, and every other boat in the harbor answered back, a cacophony of sound that was so loud and vibratious that he had to put his hands over his ears, sure that it was the corniest thing he had ever seen in his life, and one that sent a chill down him all the way to his toes.

After the tugs closed in and corralled them slowly into the West Side piers, after the men had shouted themselves hoarse making completely filthy proposals to the women in the yachts who smiled and waved obliviously back — after they had all screamed and howled, and banged on the pots and pans they'd requisitioned from the ship's mess, and waved and whistled, and held up their handmade signs saying things like WE MADE IT MOM and CHEERIO MATES and OVER HERE! for the newsreel cameras — after they blew up balloons out of condoms that they batted toward the City, and that hung in the air like so many gaily floating, flesh-colored udders, and after they waved and waved their hats until their arms gave out — all they could do was stand there with their hands on the rail, just as Tom did throughout, a smile frozen on his face, taking in the great city before him that he had convinced himself he would never see again.

Along the pier someone, somehow, was throwing confetti all over them. The gangways went down at last, and a mob of people, most of them women, gave a wild cry and stampeded down the pier. Forcing their way past the MPs, who were grinning helplessly, throwing themselves into the arms of the men as they descended. All of them shuffling and pulling one another down the dock together, arm in arm, as they sorted themselves out in a gigantic, improvised dance.

Someone shouted out, "Hey, what town did you say this was?" and then everybody laughed, and the reporters scribbled their notes, and the press photographers flashed their pictures from the bottom of the gangway, and then everybody had to get into the act — telling them all about their adventures, unable to stop talking.

Tom pushed his way gently past, moving down the pier with the flow of the crowd. His duffel bag held carefully to his side, instinctively blocking access to his pockets as he did in any close crowd — he had remembered that much. The docks beneath his feet seemed to be in terrible condition, he noted as he walked into the City. The pier sheds unpainted and rusting, the windows broken here and there. There were gaping holes in the wood and the concrete, some of them big enough for a man to fall through.

But at the end of the dock was a long row of Red Cross carts, all of them holding half-pints of milk. Without a second thought, he picked one up and peeled back the paper covering, drinking it down in one continuous gulp. He placed the empty glass container carefully back into the cart, wiping his mouth as genteelly as he could with the back of his hand. All around him were dozens of other soldiers doing the same thing, guzzling their own half-pints of milk like it was so much beer. And then he spotted the big official car, and Charlie striding toward him in his general's uniform, a huge smile on his face.

"By God, *that's* the way to come back," he was saying, "ridin' on top a the *Queen Mary,* instead of huddlin' in the hull like the wretched masses!"

"Hello, Charlie," he said, smiling a little sheepishly as he looked about him. The noise still drowning out almost everything around them — even the noise of the rushing City, just beyond the docks. "Do you do this every day?"

"Only for the last four months or so," his brother said, and laughed, taking Tom's bag from him as he guided him over to the car. "You know there's still a waiting list of five thousand girls who want to go on the yachts to greet the soldier boys? Of course, the venereal disease rates have gone through the roof. But then what's the penicillin for?"

Tom smiled again — then caught a glimpse of some of the longshoremen, waiting out the wild arrival scene by a line of trucks. Some of them leaned against the vehicles in their undershirts, hooks stuck over their shoulders, while the rest were seated on discarded wooden crates, smoking and playing a desultory game of cards, ignoring the whole commotion.

"I was even trying to remember if this was the same dock I first came in on," Tom said slowly, watching them. Thinking again of how rotten the piers looked.

"How about them?" Tom said, gesturing toward the men. "They finally got theirs during the war, I hope."

Charlie smiled indulgently and threw his bag into the trunk, clapping him on both shoulders. Neddy Moran came out from behind the wheel to shake his hand, and for once Tom was glad to see even him.

"If it's not the same pier, it's close, and you done it in grand style," Charlie was saying as they got into the car, ignoring his question.

Tom had seen his brother just a few weeks before in London, where they had taken him to heal. He'd gotten his due at last, and it wasn't too bad, considering: a through-and-through in the leg, a clean wound, and some grenade fragments in his shoulder that would make it ache when there was rain for the rest of his life, both when they charged up yet another hill along the Gothic Line. It was near the end by then, and after they'd shipped him off to London there was no need to go back. Charlie had tried to arrange a seat for him on his plane back to the States, but Tom was just as glad to go back with the rest of the men, taking the crossing slow and easy, on a real boat this time.

It was a decision he regretted by the first day out. There were fourteen thousand men on board, packed four and five to a cabin. Half of them seasick in the rough weather, including himself, wondering how the hell he could've forgotten what it was like on the way over, as he vomited off the side. But after that the sun came out and it wasn't so bad, and in the end he got what he secretly wanted, which was to sail into the great harbor this time like a conquering hero. *Like his brother had written, from down in South America.*

Neddy Moran pulled the official car, a big old Studebaker, away from the curb, and they drove through streets that looked strangely wide and clean. Everything around him—the buildings, the rushing elevated overhead, and all the cars—seemed fantastically large, or new, or fast. Almost as much as it had the first time he'd come to the City. Almost so much so that he felt amazed anything like this could still exist, after the wreckage of Italy, and all the smashed-up streets and buildings of London.

"You'll get used to it all over again," Charlie said, laughing next to him in the back seat, slapping a hand on his knee. He looked bigger, more powerful, too, somehow. "They all do—trust me. One week, and it'll seem like you never left!"

"I don't think so." Tom smiled, unsure of what to say to this grinning, amiable giant anymore. "My God, what's happened to the place?"

"The money's back, boy-o," his brother told him. "It's more than back, it's here like it's never really been here before. And now you're gonna see what this town can do."

"What are *you* going to do?"

"Well, that's the thing," Charlie said, grinning at him. "We're runnin' for mayor."

The campaign went like a dream. La Guardia had decided not to run again, and the good-government types were divided between the reds and the Republicans and the liberals. The unions came around as soon as they saw there was no alternative, and then most of the newspapers. There was even an endorsement from Eleanor Roosevelt.

" 'General O'Kane knows his enemies and the enemies of good government well, and I think the future will prove that he knows how to fight them,' " Charlie read to him, bursting with pride, on their way to a campaign event.

There were still rides through the night in the big black car—all through the City this time—but everything seemed less fraught and urgent now. His brother looking and acting more confident than Tom had ever seen him before, telling him all about how he had brought the clubhouse boys into line.

217

"Some of the county leaders were squawkin'," he informed him. "But they got nobody else, that's the God's honest truth. They wanted to drop Frank Hogan from the ticket for Manhattan DA, but I said no dice. I told 'em he stays, an' so does McDonald out in Brooklyn."

"That's bold of ya, Charlie."

"Well, that's just the way it's gonna be. I told Frank Hogan I was keepin' him on the ticket, an' he said, 'Thanks, Charlie,' an' I told him I was almost sorry the bosses gave in so easy. I would've enjoyed takin' it to the voters in a primary!"

"So it's all in the bag, then, Charlie?" Tom wondered aloud. "Just like that?"

"Why not?" his brother said almost smugly. "We got the slate all set—Lazarus Josephs on for comptroller, an' Vincent Impellitteri for council president—"

"*Who?*"

"He's a clerk for Judge Gavagan; somebody picked his name out of the *Green Book*. It's a perfectly balanced ticket: a Mick, a Jew, and an I-tie. Brooklyn, the Bronx, an' Manhattan."

The big car wheeled onto the Brooklyn Bridge, headed down to Manhattan and his next stump speech. This, too, had become oddly complacent and indolent, Tom thought—delivered now not to crowds of fevered workingmen in dark little Brownsville halls but in bright new high school gymnasiums, and hotel function rooms full of polite, receptive crowds. Mostly a recitation of the glory that was Charlie, though he could hardly blame him.

I know our city. It has been my school and where I have learned the meaning of American democracy. It has strengthened my faith in democracy and has made me keenly appreciate its blessings. I have worked in this city as a laborer. I have patrolled its streets and its waterfronts. I have lived in its tenements, and have come to know the problems of its slums, of poverty, of social conflicts, of labor and industry . . .

When it came time to take questions, he alternated between more patriotic aphorisms and maudlin displays. Bantering with the press:

"Charlie, Mrs. Schiff says Newbold Morris's drawing room manners are superior to yours—"

"Boys, the lady well knows, there are more rooms in the home than the living room."

A burst of surprised laughter.

"Did ya have any particular room in mind, Charlie?"

"I did indeed. The kitchen, of course. As the president says, that's where the heat is, and where the real work gets done."

"Charlie, are you the candidate of the bosses?"

"Which bosses are those? Surely, boys, you can see that this is a modern metropolis we live in today," he scoffed. "No one is going to come back from the great global crusade we just fought for freedom and let themselves be bossed. It's a new day, gentlemen!"

Tom stayed away from the campaign for the most part. Charlie even offered him an official position, but he declined, sure he wasn't needed. He made some desultory efforts to study for the bar and set up his shingle, but he couldn't concentrate on that yet, either. He knew he should go down to the docks, to look up his old friends and try to do something useful, but he didn't.

For the most part he drifted, living off his 52-20 checks. Walking up and down the wide avenues of Manhattan, still marveling at how rich and fat the City seemed. Staring into the windows of the old mansions along Fifth Avenue, now converted into stores — the Venetian palace that was Tiffany, the Tudor townhouse and turret that housed Finchley, the little jewel box that was Scribner's.

It was as if it were a new city altogether, as if the shabby, grimy city he remembered from before the war had been shrugged off like a snake's discarded skin. The crowds moving past were dressed better than he ever remembered them, just out to shop or lunch on a weekday afternoon — women in gloves and hats and veils, nylons and high heels. He began to spot, too, a number of other men browsing and window-shopping, in suits they were still too lean for, serviceman's button in the lapel. He began to think of the City as full of hard-eyed men in ill-fitting suits, all of them with an eye to case the joint.

Sometimes at night he might take a girl out to one of the new bebop joints on Fifty-Second Street, where the music was very good, or maybe down to Café Society in the Village, which everybody said was run by a communist. It made no sense, and no one cared — communists running the jazz joints, capitalists making money hand over fist in the shiny new towers they were putting up all over midtown. The entire City out on the town, it seemed like sometimes. Sometimes he even got laid.

It all seemed to be moving too fast, but somehow it never cracked up. Everyone was in a hurry, delighted, impatient, laughing and yelling. Whole tribes seemed to be moving through the City together — herds of tourists and commuters, day-trippers and new arrivals. Half-starved European war refugees, and wide-eyed college graduates, and whole families of colored people up from Florida and North Carolina, still in their Sunday-meeting straw hats and flowered dresses — all elbowing their way along with the rest, all plunging in. Buffeted by the crowds one day in the Times Square station, fighting his way toward the stairs, he looked up and saw a large warning sign, and he took it as a prophecy: HOLD ON TO YOUR HAT.

One evening in the early fall he got a message from Charlie to meet him at Toots Shor's restaurant, at 51 West Fifty-First, just around the corner from Swing Street. It was at that perfect moment during the New York summer's long digression into fall, the weather still warm enough to skip an overcoat, but with just enough of a sharpness in the air to put a snap into every step. He had heard of the place by then but he'd never been, and he approached it with real anticipation despite himself — that eagerness to see what any night out in the City might bring, as drunken and tawdry as it was likely to end.

The joint was perfectly pedestrian on the outside, so much so that he nearly walked past it at first. It was the sort of bar one might see in a thousand small towns — a converted old vaudeville house, with a faux-*haimish* entrance shaped to look like the doorway to a typical home, for some unfathomable reason. Just inside he was intercepted by a gigantic character, a massive, shambling individual with a face that looked as folded as a racing form. He took one glance at Tom, then enveloped his right hand in his own slab. Pounding him on the back with a left so heavy that it nearly sent him through a wall.

"Hiya!" the man said with a crooked grin. "I'm Tootsie, the pretty Jew."

"Hi, I'm—"

"*I* know who you are, ya krum-bum! The mayor's brother."

"Not yet."

Toots snorted like a horse. "You know of any action against him, lemme in on it. I could use the kale!"

Inside, once his eyes adjusted to the late-afternoon saloon darkness, Tom was surprised at how stark the place was, with everything cool and slick and modern. The main room consisted mostly of an enormous round bar, with the drinkers stacked up four and five thick around it. There were a few booths around the walls and then another room, a hangar-like dining hall, with a low, wood-paneled ceiling and small, simple tables covered with checkered table-cloths, assembled in five straight ranks.

It was a place for men to drink. Everything else — the food, the furnishings, the atmosphere, even the women — was merely tangential. That much was clear from the outset. The few ladies on hand stood off to the side of the scrum around the bar, most of them blond, nearly all of them pneumatic, every last one of them openly bored and annoyed.

The men, with their highballs, stood and yammered away, laughing and poking belligerently at one another's chests with their fingers. Tom was impressed, he had to admit to himself after he safely hauled a tall scotch back through the crowd, by just how many famous individuals he recognized — congressmen and judges, ballplayers and singers, actors and writers. At the bar, a comedian whose face he knew from the nightclubs — a great whale of a man, who was nonetheless terrifically light and graceful on his feet — was drunkenly braying something at Toots, questioning his ancestry. Toots croaking the same insults right back at him, the two of them competing like a pair of combative walruses in mating season. But then Tom was distracted by another face he knew even better, one gaunt and somber as an Italian saint.

"Jesus Christ, is that Joe DiMaggio?" he murmured, and was immediately embarrassed when he felt a powerful hand on his shoulder.

"Shouldn't you ask it the other way around: 'Joe DiMaggio, is that Jesus Christ?'" a voice that he knew but couldn't place quipped, and turning around he found himself looking into the twinkly blue eyes of William McCormack.

"Mr. McCormack! How is the subsidiarity going?" he asked spontaneously, and McCormack gave a sharp, pleased laugh.

"That's good, son, that's quite a memory you have. You should go into politics like your brother, with a memory like that."

The big man looked much as Tom remembered him from before the war, only haler and heartier, if that were possible. His hair was turning silver, but his face, with its sharp, protruding nose and chin, looked more alert and belligerent than ever. He still carried himself in a fighter's stance, broad shoulders pulled back as if ready to take a swing, pigeon chest thrust forward aggressively.

"Actually, I expect it to be a golden age of subsidiarity now, with your brother about to take over in City Hall," McCormack continued, still grinning at him. "What did I tell you about how he'd clean things up in Brooklyn, and rid us of all those wild boys over there?"

"Almost all," Tom said quietly. "How are your docks doing out there? Still run by the Camardas?"

"Alas, someone did away with Emil Camarda a while back," McCormack said, sounding very steady about it all. "Shot him dead at his desk at the local, in broad daylight. Quite a loss to the knights of labor, I should imagine."

"I hadn't heard," Tom admitted, nonplussed for the moment.

Thinking of Camarda's piggish, slit-eyed face. How ready he had been to kill all of them that day down on President Street. Lying now on his own desk, blood trickling down his fine camel's hair coat. Eyes wide in surprise, this was supposed to happen to suckers . . .

"That's right, you've been away at the wars, God bless you," McCormack was saying. "But that's always the way with that sort — they get carried away with themselves. In the end, they're only a minor hindrance in the great scheme a things, to be swept aside once you have a man with a firm hand in charge."

"Is that right?"

"It's a trice, a speck, a nothing," McCormack said, ignoring the irony in Tom's words. "I remember when my brother Harry an' meself were runnin' the Teamsters Local 449, over the West Side. We'd meet in this little saloon at Hudson an' Tenth — there wasn't a single meeting somebody didn't leave in an ambulance. Once Dan Tobin his own self, soon to be the president of the International Brotherhood, come down to remonstrate with us. They had to take *him* out in a wheelbarrow! It's all just the lads sorting things out."

"How *is* Harry with his adz?" Tom asked amiably, enjoying McCormack's racket despite himself.

"Dead!" he snapped, his whole expression falling, and the tears welling up instantly in his eyes. "Dead a year now. It was his heart, of all things – and Harry a man with the strength of a lion!"

"I'm sorry," Tom found himself saying, almost wanting to console the big man in front of him, he seemed so suddenly bereft.

"I only wish he could've lived long enough to see the golden age we're comin' into now, thanks to the sacrifice of boys like you," McCormack said, nodding his head. "Nothing's going to hold us back now! And it's your brother who's will lead us to the promised land, once he's mayor."

"With you right beside him?"

"I'll do what I can to help. As always," he said, half turning to place his empty glass of ginger ale with the usual slice of lemon back on the bar. "I only wish I wasn't so old myself, so I could live to see more of it. But at least my boy will."

He leaned back a little then, and pulled forward Bill Junior, whom Tom hadn't noticed in the crush – realizing now that he'd been hovering just back of his father the whole time. He was another of the hard-eyed men in ill-fitting suits, Tom noticed, his serviceman's pin firmly in his lapel. The reproduction of his father's face more finely chiseled than ever. But at the same time there seemed to be something stronger, more assertive about him, too.

"Welcome back," he said to Tom, and the two of them shook hands with real warmth, while Bill Senior excused himself with a smile and faded into the crowd. "Where did you do yours?"

"Italy. You?"

"The Pacific. Guadalcanal, Guam, Okinawa. How was it?"

"Not so bad." Tom shrugged at first. "Awful, actually. How 'bout for you?"

"The worst. But not too much to complain about. Just some jungle rot and a little shrapnel in the knee. They kept everything attached, at least."

"Same here. That was the main objective." Tom smiled. "Just enough to know you been there and back."

"How are you making out? Going to go work for your brother when he's elected?"

"I don't know," Tom said, realizing for the first time that he really didn't know for sure. "What about you – back at the gas stations?"

"For now," Bill Junior said, jiggling the ice cubes in his scotch and looking down at the drink—a real drink now, but one that Tom saw he had barely touched.

"Da would like me to," he went on. "He'd like me to take it all over one day."

"But you're not sure."

"No," McCormack said, his voice doleful. "That's Da, he's got a hand in everything, more than ever. He has four sand-and-gravel companies now. Still running his piers. The cement business with Sammy Rosoff and Genny Pope, his ships and his trucks. He says this is our moment. I'm sure he's right. Everyone's going to make money now like they've never seen before."

"But?"

"But I don't know if it's for me," Bill Junior said with a nod, sounding frustrated. "It's . . . it's as if everything's different now, being back. Do you ever get that feeling?"

"Just every day," Tom said, his gaze flicking over the booths, trying to search out where his brother might be.

"It's like everything here's bigger and better than it ever was—bigger than I remembered, anyway," Bill Junior was saying. "But at the same time, it's like it's never enough. Does that make any sense?"

"Completely," Tom told him. "It feels as if the biggest, best dream you ever had isn't good enough anymore. Or like it isn't the *right* dream—"

"Like you need something different," Bill Junior said. "Something you still can't quite imagine."

"And how can that be?" Tom asked, but just then he caught sight of his brother, talking over by one of the far booths with Bill Senior and another man, whose face he also knew from the papers.

"Excuse me," he said with real regret to the younger McCormack, who shook his hand warmly again, giving him a significant look, and his hand an extra squeeze that surprised Tom.

"One more thing," Bill Junior said, his eyes watering. "I was very sorry to hear about Jimmy."

"Thanks," Tom said, the name a jolt to him, and he lingered for a moment, still holding on to his hand. "It was a great loss. I tell myself I'm glad it was quick at least—he never knew what hit him. But that doesn't make it any better."

"No. No, it doesn't. It never did for any of the friends I had."

"We should talk again sometime," Tom said, dropping his hand at last to move toward his brother. "Let me know if you find out what it is you can't imagine."

"I will," Bill Junior said, smiling, lifting a hand in benediction. "You do the same. It's gotta be out there somewhere."

By the time he reached his brother and Bill Senior, the other man — the man with the Jimmy Durante face he remembered so well from the papers — had left them, headed toward the door. Tom pointed a thumb at his retreating back.

"Was that Frank Costello?" he asked straight out.

"It was," his brother said evenly.

"Why?"

"Why what?"

"Why the hell would you be talkin' to Frank Costello?"

"Now, Tom, don't go starting that again," his brother said reassuringly. "Me an' Bill were just finishin' up a little piece a business from the war, tryin' to get to the bottom of some contract jobbing. It's all friends here, all open an' aboveboard—"

"Don't worry, Tom, the goo-goos have all left an' gone away," Bill Senior said patronizingly. "La Guardia will be the last of 'em. Then this town will be open for business again. Nobody's gonna care that you happen to run into a bad man in a bar."

He wanted to say something, but Toots Shor was bearing down on them then like a force of nature, herding them toward the dining room with a lot of the others.

"C'mon, c'mon, get to dinner if you're dinin', ya krum-bums. I got a little surprise for everybody!"

Bill Junior joined them again, and the four of them sat awkwardly at table, trying to make small talk. Ordering up the standard steakhouse fare—a shrimp cocktail, a salad of stacked tomato and onion slices with blue cheese, a New York strip steak with home fries—that Charlie assured them was the only safe choice at Toots's. Tom aware, as they ploughed through the piles of food, that something was hanging in the air, though it was hard to discern just what it was. The dining room was filling up with people — and at the same time a giddy, almost tangible sense of heedlessness, and self-satisfaction. The laughter and the conversation rising headily, the big blondes engaged now. There was a constant punctuation of glasses smashing, of corks popping and the clatter of empty plates as the steaks were devoured.

"Tommy, I want you to come work for me," Charlie told him at last, though by then he could barely concentrate on what his brother was saying.

"Charlie—"

"No, no, think about it before you decide! I'm serious now. You're still awfully young, but that doesn't mean I expect you to start at the bottom. You just name it, the post is yours—"

"Charlie, I don't think that's a good idea."

"That's a big opportunity, Tom," William McCormack, Sr., said, finishing up yet another horse's neck, no doubt the only person in the room who had remained stone sober, Tom thought. His big, blue eyes openly scrutinizing him. "Think of what you could do with it. The things that need to be done with housing in this city, with education—"

"Why, Bill, I think you could do those things just as well as I could. Much better, really," Tom said, pretending to smile.

"No, no, Tom, that's not what *we* do," McCormack told him, squeezing his son's neck—Bill Junior looking guardedly at Tom, then dropping his eyes. "We're the business end of things. You an' Charlie are the government side. Mr. Inside an' Mr. Outside, as it were. Think of how much we could do for this city—for this country, the four of us, all here right now. Then pass it on, one generation to the next."

"Who would be Mr. Outside," Tom asked slowly, "and who exactly would be Mr. Inside? And which one would devour the other?"

Bill Senior's big face turned slowly into a stony ugliness that Tom thought must have caused so many men's hearts to drop into their socks, over in the Horseshoe. Even more alarming was to see his son—his father's hand still around his neck—shoot him a warning look. *Is he that much of a terror?* Tom thought, wondering if he really understood William McCormack at all. For his part, Charlie was looking from one of them to the next, not sure of what to do or say next. McCormack opened his mouth to speak — but just then Toots strode into the dining room and clapped his huge slabs of hands together.

"Ladies an' gentlemen, krums an' bums," he announced. "I have a little surprise for you tonight, just to thank you for your patronage, and to celebrate the fact that the war is over and our boys are back home!"

An expectant buzz, punctuated by a few mocking laughs, ran through the room, but nobody put down their knives and forks, much less their glasses. Toots turned on his heel and left the dining room. But just as quickly he was back, walking slowly down the center aisle, this time with two men on each of his arms — their faces the most recognizable of all. They strode down the rows of tables with the beaming Toots trying to seem nonchalant, but before they got very far, a big, crooked, child's grin was creasing his face, and then all the others were smiling as well. The room falling slowly into awed silence at first, as everyone recognized them. Then there was a dramatic gasp, then a shout, and even the most jaded among them were on their feet, looking amazed and delighted.

On his right side were Babe Ruth and Jack Dempsey — and on the left were Bing Crosby and Frank Sinatra. The faces, the names they had all seen, all known for as far back as any of them could remember — the ballplayer, the champ, the crooners, all gathered here for *them*. And as they paraded down one aisle of tables, then back up another, the applause rose, and rose, their reception almost hysterical, hard and triumphant. The applause of the diners, Tom realizing as it went on and on, for *themselves* as much as for the great men among them. Applauding the honor due them, to be here on this night, and in this city.

His brother took City Hall that fall by the largest majority anyone could remember. When Charlie went down to pay a courtesy call a few days later, even La Guardia was gracious about it, grinning and clasping his hand for the press, pushing him down into the mayoral chair and exclaiming: "Sit down! Now *you* have inherited a perpetual headache! Patience and fortitude, Charlie — you'll need all you can get!"

When it came to the inauguration, though, Claire was in such a bad way that Charlie announced he was canceling the usual celebration, holding only a simple swearing-in ceremony out at her sister Anne's home in the Rockaways, where she had been staying since the summer. It was a small gathering, just family and a few close friends, but Tom sneaked out an idealistic young priest from the Carmelites to give the benediction, just to make sure he stayed humble.

"Mr. Mayor, I have just prayed that God will give you guidance to solve the many problems that you face in your new task. Much will be written and said about the problems of the subways, and of Idlewild, and of arterial highways and of adequate parking space, but Mr. Mayor, these are really minor problems. The *real* problems that confront you are how you can bring about better conditions for the poor, the humble, the lowly, and underprivileged. Then there is the Negro problem . . . " the young priest went on fervently, the benediction turning into a long political sermon as Tom, on his knees across Anne Condon's living room, shot Charlie a small, impish grin.

"That was very funny," Charlie said, cornering him in the kitchen afterward. "I'm surprised he didn't go on as well about Chiang Kai-shek, an' all the starvin' babes in China."

"Congratulations, Charlie," Tom told him, and meant it. "Da woulda been very proud of you. Ma, too."

"Mmm, even if she'd rather have Francis Spellman for a son."

"Never. You climbed all this way on your own, an' I couldn't be prouder myself," he said, and meant that, too. "You understand about me not coming to work for ya?"

"No. But I suppose it's just as well. You'd just fill City Hall with more of your pinkos." Charlie smiled, gesturing back toward the living room, where the fervent young priest was still holding court. "Six months in, we'd be blackin' each other's eyes."

"Aye. *You* be Mr. Inside, Charlie, an' I'll be Mr. Outside. It's task enough doin' this without havin' to deal with your relatives."

"True, true," Charlie said, looking out through Anne Condon's kitchen in the dying light, to where the sluggish gray waves were lapping up on the shore of Rockaway Bay. As they watched, a bent old man in an ancient suit made his way unobtrusively to a chair in her backyard and sat himself down, gnawing contentedly with the side of his mouth at one of Anne's fine biscuits.

"Who's that one?" Tom asked, remembering him as the one person he couldn't identify at the swearing-in ceremony.

"Tom Rouse. You remember, our aunt's old suitor? The same one what met me at the boat, took me up to my first lunch in the New World."

"Ah. But you're a sentimentalist, Charlie!" he teased.

"God, but it's a task," Charlie said, his voice suddenly sounding frightened. "You don't know, Tom, but what a thing it is!"

"What did Claire say to you about it?" he asked, knowing the answer — remembering her barely able to reach out a hand to him in her wheelchair in the living room. Scarcely able to move or talk now, rasping a whisper in his ear that brought a smile to his brother's lips and tears to his eyes at the same time.

"She asked if I was happy," he said, repeating her standard query, turning to smile at his brother with a look that at the time Tom thought contained fathomless depths of both hope and sadness, but later wondered if it were anything of the sort — "and she asked if it would get me in trouble."

"Well, there you go, then."

"Here I go."

23

New York, 1947

He would only ask later if it wasn't what he deserved. Finding himself at the end of an evening, seated in a rich man's apartment. Dressed in his best dinner clothes, with a good cigar in one hand and a glass of hundred-year-old brandy in the other, when in walked the most beautiful young woman he had ever seen, and he thought, *Why not?* Widowed now. Powerful and respected, the mayor of the City. Surrounded by other powerful men, hovering about to pay court to him. He saw her face and thought, *Why not?*

"My, it looks like a speakeasy in here," he heard her say, taking in all the silly, baronial frippery as she stood there in her designer gown. The voice rich, amused, sardonic.

Knowing what she'd look like before he even turned around, which one she had to be. A face and a form like some classic Greek huntress. *Like a fable embroidered on a tapestry, Diana with her hounds.* But it was the voice that made him turn. Husky and self-assured, the confidence alone enough to send chills up his neck. It was the voice of country clubs, and summer houses, and the knowledge of horses and sailboats. Or at least what he wanted them to sound like.

He was already on his way to her by then. Walking across the Persian carpet of the dead railroad mogul, in his fabulous lair hidden away in the upper reaches of Grand Central station. The thick beams supposed to look like a medieval lord's hall. Arched fireplace big enough to roast a boar on at one end of the room, a very modern bar along the side, under the stained glass windows. Literal crests, bought up and carted off from all over Europe, displayed along the oaken paneling, broadswords and maces and morning stars piled up in umbrella stands on either side of the fireplace.

The silliest robber-baron imitation of old wealth imaginable. Empowering him to go up to her and show her that he knew it. That he knew his way around now, Charlie O'Kane from Lismirrane. Saying to her as he came up behind her, so that all she knew of him first was his own rich voice, pitched deep and low to the setting: "Young lady, you are too young, and too well bred, to know anything of speakeasies."

Then watching to see how she turned, her green eyes flickering as she looked upon him. Thinking when he saw that face close up, *Why not? Why not, why not, why not?*

Up in the rail baron's apartment, the green-eyed goddess of America winked at him.

After he was sworn in, he had a small elevator put in at the mayor's mansion to accommodate Claire. But she called the place "the Museum," and stayed there as infrequently as she could get away with. Complaining about how the old wooden house creaked at night, and how much noise the ships' horns and the bells on the buoys made out in the river. Most of all, she didn't like how the police guards and the pedestrians on East End Avenue would stare at her, when Neddy Moran was helping her from her wheelchair into the car for a drive.

She preferred to spend the last summer of her life at her sister Anne's house out in Rockaway, warm-weather capital of the Condon Colony of Dreamers. They both knew she was dying by then, and she tried to make a joke of it, even though she could barely speak, or even move her face. Forming a rictus grin that he could barely stand to look at but forced himself to for her sake — knowing that she was trying to get across her little jest.

"See how it'll extend your political honeymoon, a dying wife," she rasped raggedly at him, her breath warm and rancid on his cheek as he leaned in to hear what she was saying, forcing himself to keep smiling. "See how good it is for you, what sympathy you'll get!"

"Ah, God, Clairey—"

"No, no, I'm serious. A little," she told him. "You weren't made to live alone, Charlie. See you get yourself somebody when I'm gone."

"What makes you think I'll outlive you? Sez who?"

"Get yourself—" She made a rattling sound, deep in her throat, one that made the hairs on the back of his head go up. "Get yourself . . . one who . . . will . . . hold . . . you on the ground. You can get into an awful lot of trouble, Charlie, when you get above yourself."

"Enough of this morbid talk now, Clairey," he said, trying to soothe her. "Let me tell you what they tried to put over on me today . . . "

She died at last in October, when the weather was just beginning to turn into another glorious New York fall. She passed at the old Holy Family Hospital, on Dean Street in Brooklyn, and after it was over, Tom could remember only the harsh smell of antiseptic everywhere, and the pale green linoleum out in the hallways. Natie Cohen raised a fund among Charlie's many friends, and the next spring they donated a sparkling new ambulance to the hospital in her name.

"How can I tell you in a few words . . . it is sweet of you to remember Mrs. O'Kane" was all Charlie was able to get through at the dedication ceremony before his voice broke, burying his face in his handkerchief while Natie led him off.

Tom worried about him after Claire's death, though he tried to keep his distance. Hearing he was putting in twelve-hour days at City Hall, shuttling between his office and Gracie Mansion. Whenever they did meet, though, they argued about housing, and taxes, and the poor, all the everyday horrors of the world, and he wanted desperately not to be a burden to his brother.

Thus he was pleasantly surprised and intrigued when he got the call from

Charlie to meet him up at the Powerhouse, which was what they called the cardinal's residence behind Saint Patrick's. It was coming on another summer, and Charlie was still basking in his greatest triumphs — the settling of the tugboat strike and the removal of a late snowfall from the streets.

"The quotidian tasks of government," he liked to say, "but it's what people see, and hear, and feel every day."

Things were running well then, the City humming along. Growing steadily fatter, richer, higher, than he had ever seen it. Tom had noticed that most of the hard-eyed men back from the war were gone — including himself. They fit more easily in their suits now, or even bulged out. Their eyes no longer looked so ravenous, their service buttons tucked away at home, forgotten in the bureau of the new bedroom set.

It was about this time that the *Time* magazine article came out, Charlie on the cover. Painting him as the unflappable tribune of the people, the poor boy made good. Spouting what had fast become all the usual, fantastic statistics and claims about the City since the war. Tom wary of the whole triumphalist tone, but secretly swept along by it, too — thrilled to think his brother could be running such a place:

"It is the biggest, richest city the world has ever seen — its wealth greater than all of Europe's combined! . . . the greatest port, the greatest tourist destination, the greatest manufacturing center, the greatest marketplace! . . . along Manhattan's great avenues the women shop like stalking tigresses, they dress like foreign spies, and they strut like courtesans . . . here half-a-million Irishmen like Mr. Mayor mix every day in more-or-less perfect harmony with 2 million Jews, more than a million Italians, another half-million Negroes, a quarter-million Puerto Ricans . . .

"The city that every day takes in and spits out a billion gallons of water, 23,500 tons of food, a billion gallons of sewage, 8,000 tons of garbage. One that requires 20 million gallons of fuel in the winter, subways and elevated railroads that glide 6 million people a day to work; where a train arrives from out of town every 50 seconds, morning, noon, and night. A city with 150,000 municipal workers. And at the head of this great army, one man: an immigrant success story as great as any in America today. The blue-eyed boy from Bohola, the former cop on the beat, Charles C. O'Kane.

"The city is a great organism, an organism without a memory, but OK Charlie refuses to believe it. "The Big City is the work of man," he says, and like all of man's creations, he believes, it can be controlled, and made an instrument of good . . ."

"Of course, sillier words were never wrote," Charlie told him, grinning modestly when Tom congratulated him on the article. "And everybody knows, the City is all memory. It may sleep for a spell, but it all comes out, sooner or later. You can count on it."

His brother looked tired, but Tom was very pleased to see there was some color in his face, even a little spring in his step. He was wearing the best suit Tom had ever seen on him, cleaned and starched to a knife edge. When he came up to him, on the corner just below the Powerhouse, at the back of Saint Pat's, he seemed to be studying closely the shut-up buildings across Madison Avenue.

"What's it about?" Tom asked him, but Charlie just shook him off, smiling mischievously.

"Oh, you'll see soon enough. I have a couple surprises for you today, me boy!"

"Is that so? And how is it with you, Charlie? How are ye gettin' on?" he asked, the concern obvious in his voice, and Charlie smiled again and ran a hand over his hair.

"Oh, it's all right. There are moments when it scares me to death. Suddenly I'll think, 'My God, I'm mayor of the City of New York,'" he admitted. He shook his head, but to Tom's relief gave a little chuckle. "Ah, but I have missed ya, lad. It's been too long, Tommy."

"I know it, Charlie."

"That's why I thought I'd treat ya to this piece of business with our old friend the cardinal. Make you believe I'm still fighting on the side of the angels. I have been summoned by my spiritual prince, you see."

"Is this about his fight with the gravediggers?"

"In part. Did you see him in the papers today?"

"No, what now?"

The archdiocese's gravediggers had gone on strike the month before, and the cardinal was having none of it. Already, he had denounced them as communists — to their wives.

"He brought a busload of seminary students out to dig the graves."

"Ah, Jesus!"

"Yep. The press had a field day: 'Turning Priests into Scabs!' All those soft-handed little seminarians in their street shoes and brand-new overalls, laborin' mightily to dig a hole in the ground. The dear cardinal took his own turn with the shovel, and every paper got a picture. I showed it to Red Mike Quill when he came by with *his* latest demands, an' I asked him, 'Whattaya think?'"

"What'd Quill say?"

"He said, 'I think that poor bastard is not going down very far!' And now he's got himself in a big row with Mrs. Roosevelt!" Charlie added, when they had both stopped laughing.

"Oh, yes, I did see that! That open letter he put in the *Mirror:* 'I shall not again publicly acknowledge you' —"

"Mm, called her anti-Catholic for saying the public shouldn't have to pay for religious schools —"

"Goin' on about the rights of the innocent little children, an' Cardinal Mindszenty being tortured by the Hungarians. All it lacked was the poor missionaries being boiled an' roasted by cannibals."

"Frankie Spellman's not one to leave out the kitchen sink if he can get somebody to lift it for 'im," Charlie said, ruminating. "Course, she gave it back to him as good as she got. She's quite the street fighter at heart, is our Eleanor. Now I've got to rescue the poor man, before she eats him like those missionaries."

He picked up the hefty brass knocker at the back door of Saint Patrick's and let fly — Tom feeling as though they were asking permission to enter a castle keep, or maybe the Vatican itself. A very pretty young Irishwoman with black hair and blue eyes let them in, blushing a little to see the mayor. Inside, more young women bustled about, cleaning and dusting, setting the dining table and hauling bags of food into the kitchen. All of them just as pretty, and young, and Irish.

"If I didn't know his predilections, I'd say the cardinal was running a seraglio," Tom whispered to Charlie while they waited, hats in hand.

"It's precisely because of that he hires these sweet young things," Charlie whispered back with a wink. "He must be the only prelate in the world lookin' to *start* a rumor."

The cardinal kept them waiting for a solid ten minutes, then emerged beaming like a big, jubilant baby — his face more cherubic than ever, a last wisp of gray hair settled along his head like a perfect halo. To Tom's surprise, he was wearing not the red robes of his office but an old black cassock, gone rusty with age around the edges and tied with a simple rope.

"Mr. Mayor! And Thomas, too! Well, this is an occasion," he said, his eyes twinkling benignly behind his Santa Claus spectacles.

"Excuse me, Your Excellency, if we've interrupted you at your ablutions," Charlie said with a perfectly straight face.

"What, you mean this old thing?" the cardinal said, gesturing expansively at his robe. "It's what I feel most comfortable in. You know, I'm really just an old parish priest at heart."

"Yes, I've read that many times," Charlie remarked.

"I tell you, it's just such a relief to get back here, and relax a little among my flock after all the traveling I'm required to do these days," Spellman said, chatting on as if he hadn't heard him. "I have to go back to Italy again next month, and then there are some speaking engagements on the West Coast, and there's another interdenominational conference up in Albany. It seems I'm constantly in demand these days!"

As if to underscore the constant bustle of his life, he led them through one magnificently appointed room after another, as he spoke. There was a parlor with red velvet chairs, and a Persian rug, and paintings of all the previous archbishops, and gold curtains draped from ceiling to floor. The "throne room," for formal church ceremonies, with the simple country priest's chair deliberately mounted above everyone else's. A study full of more well-stuffed chairs and a fireplace bigger than the one Tom remembered back in the Sforza villa in Italy. The dining room full of impossibly heavy, dark wooden furniture — its table set with fine china and crystal for a meal to which they were pointedly not invited.

At last they entered the heart of the Powerhouse, an enormous, well-appointed space that, despite its twenty-foot-high ceiling and its carved walnut panels depicting scenes from the lives of the apostles, was still unmistakably a boardroom, dominated by a long conference table polished to a dazzling shine. Spellman gestured them coolly into a couple of plush, cushioned chairs, then sat across the table with all the benevolence vanished from his cherub's face, his hands folded and lips pressed tightly together.

"Thank you, Your Eminence," Charlie said, pulling the handkerchief out of his jacket pocket and pretending to mop his brow. "I thought we might be goin' around by way of the Panama Canal."

"Charlie, I won't beat around the bush," Spellman said, using the mayor's first name as condescendingly as possible. "I called you here to talk about the descending moral tone of this city, and how our Mother Church is under attack."

"How is that, Your Eminence? Is there another salacious film that's opened?" Charlie asked piously.

"Have you seen this magazine? It's outrageous!" Spellman cried, producing a copy of *The New Yorker* from the sleeve of his simple country priest's cassock and smacking it down on the conference table.

"Your Grace, I think you are best off ignoring the yellow press —" Charlie tried, but the cardinal had worked himself up to a storm now. Standing up out of his plush chair, banging the magazine repeatedly on the table.

"*Did* you see the doggerel in here?! The effrontery! It's time you took a moral stand, Charlie, instead of trying to straddle the middle between the church and its enemies!"

"I take it you mean the MacLeish poem —"

"'I Shall Not Again Publicly Acknowledge You.' Outright mockery of the church, and people of faith!"

"With all due respect, Your Grace, he was flingin' your own words back at you —"

"'Consider, Prince, your place and nation —' What is that, some sort of *threat?* How he can be allowed to write such things in a public magazine —"

"Look, Francis, that's what happens when you call the First Lady unworthy to be an American mother," Charlie snapped at last. "You're out there every week pickin' a new fight an' cryin' anti-Catholic bigotry when somebody punches back. Last month it was Planned Parenthood. Now you picked yourself a beauty."

"I'm right and you know it!" Spellman insisted, though his voice sounded shrill and more than a little desperate. "The public *should* pay something toward our schools. We lift a considerable burden off the taxpayer—"

"You'll never convince anybody of that by goin' after Eleanor Roosevelt. You're punchin' above yer weight with this one, Frank, an' we both know it. The public's on her side, an' we can't have all this disturbance with a tough election comin' up. It doesn't matter who stands with you, if we all go down to defeat."

The cardinal resided into his chair, arms crossed against his chest. Tom amazed at how genuinely angry he seemed. His face still red, his voice snippy, he asked Charlie: "Well, what do you want *me* to do about it? Apologize?"

"That's exactly what you'll do. Ed Flynn's arranged for you to stop by Hyde Park on the way to that interdenominational conference of yours. You'll take tea with Mrs. Roosevelt, an' tell the gentlemen of the press it's all been a misunderstanding," Charlie dictated in rapid-fire order. "You'll find she's quite gracious, though I'd eat a good lunch before you go, if I was you. And you might say something nice about Mr. Truman while you're there."

"I will not!" the cardinal still protested, looking shocked.

"You will, or that commercial rent control bill is goin' to pass the city council next week, an' I just might forget to veto it. Let's see how your Mr. Reynolds will like that."

Tom knew that John J. Reynolds, another one of the businessmen Spellman courted so assiduously, was said to have made the archdiocese at least a hundred million dollars, just since the war. A heavy-drinking rail fly most of his life, he had discovered in himself a capacity for investing in oil wells, and making real estate deals, which he brought the church in on. *The money that was coursing through the City now,* Tom thought, marveling to himself.

"You can't do that!" Spellman ranted, freshly outraged.

"Can't I? Reynolds is gouging half the shopkeepers in this town till the blood comes out their ears. But you've got him living up there on a church estate in Riverdale, complete with a tennis court an' a swimming pool for that new chorus-girl wife a his—"

"It's all perfectly legitimate!"

"Sure, what's not legitimate in a sacred cause? Whatch ya do, give him another of your papal knighthoods? Or was it fixin' him up with Joe Kennedy?

Yes, I know about that, too. Kennedy gets the whole Chicago Merchandise Mart for a song — and you get all those buildings just over t'other side of Madison Avenue. How d'ya think that deal will look in the papers?"

"Are you through?" Spellman said icily, but Tom could see, to his amazement, that he was stymied, at least for the moment.

"Not quite," his brother continued. "There's the matter of the United Cemetery Workers —"

"That's strictly diocesan business!" Spellman exclaimed. "Those men put their union above their church!"

"From what I heard, they were just quotin' the pope's encyclical. About a family of four deservin' sixty-eight dollars a week to live on —"

"That's those Passionists! They shouldn't listen to that bunch of bandits —"

"So instead, you pay them fifty-nine dollars to work six days a week, eight hours a day. And then you call their wives communists."

"I told them, I felt as badly for them as if they were my own mother in the same circumstances," Spellman objected. "In the end, though, they had nothing to offer me, and I had nothing to offer them."

"Well, I'm sure that you'll find something to offer them, Your Grace. Maybe Johnny Reynolds's tennis court."

Spellman stood up indignantly, and they slowly stood with him.

"I'm sorry I can't stay here and listen to any more of these indignities. I'm entertaining Lester Cuddihy and some of our other, *faithful* associates for lunch."

"Then I shall not again detain you, Your Eminence," Charlie told him with a slight bow and a grin. "I'm sure we can find our own way back out. Tom here left some bread crumbs."

Without another word, Francis Cardinal Spellman turned on his heel and strode out of the Powerhouse boardroom. Leaving the chancery, Tom and Charlie passed his lunch party of contractors and self-made businessmen coming in, each of them ripe with toilet water and eau de cologne, making an unconscious genuflection and bow as they acknowledged him.

"It's all right, boys. I'm just the mayor, not the prince of the church," Charlie cracked as they passed, but this only drew wary frowns.

"Jesus, there they go. Frankie Spellman's very own Knights of the Golden

Fleece, or whatever he calls 'em," Charlie remarked when they had passed. "Did you catch all of 'em?"

"Sure. There was Murray McDonnell, an' Joe an' Tom Murray. And Cuddihy, of course—"

"Did you notice the fine white choppers Lester has now?"

"How could you not? I thought I'd been blinded like Paul on the road to Damascus."

"Did ya hear that Spellman pointed them out, over at the Hoguets?" Charlie said, grinning like a mischievous child himself. "When Cuddihy goes up to kiss the ring on the reception line, he says, 'Ah, Lester, I see you have some new teeth!' And Lester says, 'I'll teach you to call attention to my new teeth!' Instead of kissin' the ring, he bit Spellman right on his finger, so hard it drew blood!"

"That's not bad. An' you, Charlie—boxing the cardinal's ears right in the Powerhouse! You were magnificent!" Tom said, exultant.

His brother grinned at him, and maybe it was Tom's imagination, but he almost seemed to kick up his heels.

"Sometimes, I dunno, you just have to have a bit a the devil in ye to do this job! Ah, he'll never forgive me, but I was just savin' the poor man from himself."

They were back outside and striding down Madison by now, toward Grand Central. Charlie checking his watch, evidently headed somewhere with a purpose.

"By God, Charlie, it's good to see you lookin' so strong—so full of purpose," Tom told him.

"Well, there's a reason for that, too, maybe. I want you to meet it today."

"What's that?"

They were in the Oyster Bar by then, the waiter ushering them over to the corner table. Faces on all the diners lighting up to see him go by, grinning as if they were in on some great joke together.

She was already at the table. The most beautiful woman he had ever seen close up, and dressed like no one he had ever known dressed. Sitting right there in the Oyster Bar, wearing a rose suit with matching hat, stole, and bag. Looking as though she'd be every bit as comfortable waiting for them there as at the Automat, or the palace of Versailles. She turned a warm smile on them, and he was lost in it right away. Charlie talking for no apparent reason, apologizing for them being late, telling him: "—but you must have seen her in the paper! Slim, I'd like you to meet my lout of a younger brother, Tom O'Kane. Tom, this is Slim Sadler, who I'm sure you've read all about—"

Reaching out a rose-gloved hand, which he took as Charlie beamed at them both, and held on to for dear life.

"Oh, you're sure to get on. You're two of a kind!"

24

Mexico, 1953

They left Cuernavaca early the next morning, before Henry Fink was up, which Tom was just as glad to do. The bungalow he had eventually dragged himself to at the end of the night proved as filthy as the rest of Shangri-La. When the sun woke him through the uncovered window he discovered a gang of enormous insects and a couple of small, bright lizards scuttling across his mosquito netting, not to mention the pulpy remains of slower bugs he'd heard himself crunching the night before but hadn't wanted to turn on the light to acknowledge.

Yet by the time he got himself dressed, and washed as well as he could with the few rusty drippings that emerged from the showerhead, Charlie was already up and waiting for him. Looking little the worse for wear, having a cup of the strong local coffee. Watching Guillermo, back at his Sisyphean labor of netting the mango droppings in the big pool.

"Hi, Tommy, how'd you sleep?" Charlie called out, and took a deep breath, pushing his chest out.

"All right, I guess."

"Smell that air! Air like that could keep a man perpetually young!"

"Yes. That's why they call it Shangri-La."

Beneficio was already waiting for them as well, and they traced their way down through the narrow streets, past all their riotous hedges and crumbling walls. Heading west, they passed little, grass-roofed houses, and wooden shanties, and a grim, stone-gray fortress. On the next corner, Tom noticed a cluster of vultures, hunched on the high branches of a cypress tree like petty hoods occupying a street corner, the ammonia stench of their vomit spoiling the spring air.

They moved through one valley after another, as the sun rose higher and the big Lincoln grew hotter. The highway deteriorating with each mile they moved away from Cuernavaca, the signs with Presidente Alemán's name on them growing scarcer, the land between the mountain passes rockier and starker.

They pulled into the bare trace of a village about noon, with the sun beating down and the inside of the big Lincoln truly sweltering. Beneficio cosseted the car off the crumbling highway and into the gravel and dirt of the shoulder so carefully that Tom could barely feel the difference beneath their wheels. Rolling it to a perfect stop by the antique pump, the gas bubbling languidly up in its clear, glass circular head topped by the image of a flying horse.

There they waited with the motor off and the windows open, eyeing the whitewashed brick garage and office. After a long minute a yellow dog emerged through its open door, plodding slowly forward, seeming too ener-vated by the heat to bark. It merely raised its snout at them, then turned back toward the garage, where a mechanic presently appeared in an oil-slicked pair of tanned leather overalls, nodding and smiling and wiping off a wrench. As he approached, his eyes grew wider and a smile spread across his face.

"Señor Embajador!" he chortled, walking to the back-seat window and sticking out a hand to Charlie — then quickly pulling it back to wipe it on his rag, then proffering it again.

"*Señor Embajador! Bienvenido!*"

"How are you, my friend?" Charlie said, pumping his hand while he turned to shoot Tom a look and a quick, delighted wink. "How good to see you!"

There was a rapid exchange of Spanish, and then the three of them were out of the car, walking down the one dirt street behind the gas station. The mechanic walking ahead, announcing their presence with calls and whistles as he went. Weary-looking people emerged from the square adobe homes, or walked in from the fields behind them, grinning and waving their hats and calling out, "*Señor Embajador! Señor Embajador!*"

"They seem to know you, Charlie."

"Well, now, it may just be that Slim and I stopped here a time or two on our ramblings," Charlie allowed, blushing a little but still looking completely delighted by their welcome. "How nice to see *some*body remembers me with kindness."

They let the mechanic lead them into a little box of a *pulquería*, a cool, dark place with tiled floors and green shutter doors. There Charlie talked and joked and laughed with the villagers, seated around them, and they downed *nochote* in smoky green glasses, and ate goat burritos just off the grill with their fingers until they were sated. Charlie leaning back in his chair with a sigh — all his previous edginess from their talk the night before gone now, Tom thought.

"It was like this all the time when Slim and I used to tour," he said, tapping his hands on his full stomach. "Did you know, when we used to drive into these places they'd greet us with brass bands an' confetti — *confetti*, Tommy, real bits of paper they'd ripped up from somewhere."

"Yes, Slim told me."

"They'd throw them over us like it was rice on the church steps, and we'd just got married all over again. You shoulda heard her laugh those times, Tommy. She'd get out of the car an' walk into these little towns with her blond hair and a shimmery white dress. They'd go mad for her."

He patted his stomach again, looking a little sad. The people he'd been talking to so enthusiastically drifting discreetly away from the table, headed back to their work as the worst heat of the day slowly relented. Leaving them to their talk.

"Maybe I could get her to come back out and tour around with me again," he said speculatively. "Those were the days. No cares, not tied down to anything. It was like a permanent honeymoon."

Someone dropped a coin into the new-looking jukebox in the corner, and to Tom's surprise what came up was not the sound of a mariachi band but a slow, plaintive number.

"The 'Muchero,'" Charlie said, then burped sadly. He reached out to grip Tom's arm, muttering, "Where is she now, where is she now?"

"In Acapulco, Charlie. That's why we're headed there."

"You know she used to love to play this song," he said, ignoring him. "This, and the 'Lisboa Antigua' — all those sad songs. That was her music phase. She learned to play guitar, an' started bringing all her musician friends back from the cafés. I would lie in our bed lookin' at the ceiling, an' listen to her sing all these old tunes. She thought I was asleep, but of course I wasn't."

Charlie looked directly at him then, and for some reason Tom felt a chill go through him.

"I never was asleep," he said.

"How d'ya mean?" Tom asked.

"Oh, nothin', nothin' really," he said, waving off the question and looking aside. "Only that's how maybe all this started. D'ya remember that time when I was mayor, and the intruder got into Gracie Mansion?"

"Yes. Of course," Tom said, a small, hard lump forming in his stomach.

"I woke up at six in the morning, an' there he was, sittin' on the side of our bed. Perfectly ordinary-lookin' fella, wearin' glasses and a sweater."

"I remember."

"He asked me, 'Are you O'Kane?' So thinkin' faster than I ever did on the stump, I told him, 'No, but I'll take you to him.' And you know, the funny thing was, all I could think of right then was my fear that he'd killed poor old Joe Previtel, the overnight guard at the mansion."

"Sure." Tom stared down at the tiled floor of the *pulquería,* unable to look his brother in the face anymore.

"Well, as it turned out, he hadn't, a course. I put on my robe an' took the lad down to the kitchen to get some coffee, an' once down there I was able to buzz the guard booth. Turned out he'd penetrated our crack security team through the ingenious method of climbing over the iron fence an' comin' around the back entrance. Might've walked off with half the heirlooms of New York City, if he'd had a mind to."

"They took him off to Bellevue, didn't they?"

"Yes, the poor lad. His one statement was, he'd only wanted to talk with me for a few minutes to discuss juvenile delinquency. God knows, he was probably the most reasonable petitioner I saw durin' all my time as mayor. Just wanted a few minutes of my opinion, as opposed to the keys to the City treasury."

He looked at Tom again, his face almost beseeching now, and Tom felt compelled to look back.

"But the thing I never understood, the thing I didn't think about at all until much later, was why I was worried about Joe Previtel — and not my wife. And why she wasn't in my bed."

Tom could only sit there, not trusting himself to say a thing — trying not to betray any emotion at all.

"And then, you know, she came in, with all the excitement and the cops runnin' all around," Charlie said contemplatively. "I remembered she'd been out late to some benefit gala or another, an' she come in still wearin' the dress she'd had on the night before, and in her bare feet, holding her shoes in her hand. She said she'd got in a while before, but hadn't felt like sleeping and had just been out wanderin' the grounds. And it was a miracle, I thought, that she hadn't encountered this young lunatic climbing his way over our stout iron fence, but then it's a big grounds, and as he had demonstrated, he could certainly move about with great stealth an' quiet, this young madman of ours, who had already evaded the best of our police force."

"Yes," Tom said listlessly.

"But I always wondered why I didn't think first of her, when I woke up that morning."

"Maybe," Tom said slowly, "you just knew she could always take care of herself."

"Maybe that was it!" Charlie laughed suddenly, startling Beneficio where he was still finishing his goat burritos at the end of the table. "She certainly could, you know. But it weighed on my mind, how I didn't think of her first — and how I just expected that she had left my bed. So when she'd go out late to the cantinas and the dance halls with her music friends, I always made sure to stay awake till she got back, an' keep my ears open."

"Jesus, Charlie," he said, sweating in the cool little *pulquería*, unsure if it was for himself or his brother. "You'll drive yourself mad."

"No, no, just the usual madness of an old man with a young wife. It was my own fault, for not keepin' a better hold on her in the first place. But I could deny her nothing."

"Who ever could?" Tom said, despite himself.

"She made things lively around the embassy; I can't say I didn't like it. We invited more Mexicans than Americans over to those big receptions she liked to throw. No ambassador had ever done that before, and it was very popular.

The press loved her — at first. They called her *La Embajatriz*, even named her "Woman of the Year."

"But then the older American expats started to complain. You know, the old oil an' mining boys, and their wives. They wanted their quiet evenings back, playin' canasta around the fire with the ambassador, and they had to be catered to. Slim couldn't stomach that, and so they would complain straight to State, an' then I would hear about it."

"Is that why she's out in Acapulco?"

Instead of answering, Charlie drained the last of the milky white *nochote,* then sat staring at the green glass.

"Amazing people. To make a drink like this out of maguey and cactus juice!"

Beneficio, his lunch finished, stood by Charlie's side in his chauffeur's uniform, hat tucked jauntily under one arm. Charlie nodded to him, and they rose and headed back out into the broiling sun.

The village was very quiet now, the only sound an occasional barking dog somewhere far away, its yelps halfhearted and surrendering gradually to the engulfing silence. Tom walked along making his legs go forward, not sure if he should feel like a relieved man or one still on his way to the gibbet.

"Ah, the civilized thing to do would be to settle in and nap away the rest of the afternoon heat," Charlie remarked, dabbing at his red face with a handkerchief. "Really, the civilized thing to do would be to sleep here in perfect contentment, like this village has been doing for the past three hundred years. But that's not for us, eh, Tommy?"

"No."

"No, we're Cortés. Or Balboa, pushing on to the sea. But sometimes you have to wonder, what in Christ's name for?"

Back at the gas station, they found that the mechanic had washed and waxed the big Lincoln for them while they were at lunch, and now it gleamed like an obsidian blade in the sun. The mechanic and his dog standing next to it, the man beaming away at them, the dog looking haggard on its splayed legs.

"My God, what a generous people," Charlie said, insisting in Spanish through all the man's strenuous protests on paying handsomely for his work, and the gas, and the lunch.

"A visit like this, it could be half their income for the month, especially if it's

not the tourist season," he said as they pulled away, waving back at the gas station owner and the village, which was quickly shrinking again to a dot in the
immense and desolate landscape. "Yet somehow, they live within their means,
unlike those of us who pass by."

"You never answered my question," Tom said. "Why's she in Acapulco?"

"It was me who got her out there." Charlie sighed. "I thought it best, with
all the complaints from the expats. The Big Crowd adored her—they'd have
her come out to spend weekends at their mansions, or on their yachts. She
loved it, too. Golfing, water-skiing, swimming—she'd go all day. You know
how she always liked the sports, Tommy."

"Yes."

The golden girl, finally reaching the empire of the Pacific.

"In between there'd be lunch with daiquiris at two, an' mariachis at five, an'
cocktails at seven, an' dinner and dancing from nine until who damned well
knew when."

His brother's face looked suddenly fearful, his chin wobbling slightly.

"I couldn't keep up, ya see, Tommy. I went out there a few weekends with
her, an' I thought it was gonna kill me. I'd fall asleep at lunch, snorin' away like
some damned old man, everybody smiling at me when I woke up! I begged
off after that, told them I had official business. I let her go stay out there with
Parada, and Melchior Perusquia, who's a friend of mine, we do a little business
together, he must've built ninety percent of Acapulco, an' I figured it would be
all right."

He gave a little bitter laugh and cocked his head.

"Next thing I know, she's in the papers bein' squired all about by this hotel heir—some Princeton grad, if you can believe it! Must be twenty years
younger than me, the son of a bitch—"

"All right, Charlie, I get it."

Charlie settled back in his seat, looking drained.

"That was the end of it, then," he said, in a dull, flat voice. "I called her up
and asked her to come back to town. She refused, point-blank. I asked her if
she was in love with him, an' she just laughed at me. An' then all the papers
picked it up, an' the next thing you know, it was a big scandal. Thank God we
were near the end of our ambassadorship by then, or the New York papers

would've laid that on me head, too. But it was a humiliating thing, Tommy, still made me a laughingstock."

He put his face in his hands then, and his shoulders shook, and Tom wondered if he was actually crying. He didn't say a thing, because there was nothing to say, and so he sat back in his seat and looked away to give his brother what privacy there was in the back seat of a car, talking about the infidelity of his wife.

They were rising again into more mountains. But now the entire landscape was beginning to transform itself back into something lush and fecund, and more tropical. The road was not even finished here. There was just a layer of bedrock laid down, the one sign he saw that paid tribute to *el presidente* lying broken along the shoulder. The Lincoln twisted along the gravelly mess like a snake, delving down through deep green gorges, through valleys with orange and green and red parrots sailing back and forth between towering trees.

He was about to look over to see how Charlie was doing, but then he heard a noise, and to his surprise he saw that his brother was asleep again, after all the burritos and *nochote,* his face as calm and untroubled as an infant's in repose. He found himself beginning to nod, too, in the rain-forest humidity. The scenery passed in a daze — not quite a dream, but not quite real, either. And in the dream he was with Slim again in the little boat off Hobe Sound, cruising slowly through the inland waterways. The same lush, green vista, dappled with sun through the tall, ancient trees, the two of them watching it all pass as they stood silently next to each other. Tom trying not to admit to himself how aware he was of the brush of her arm against his, her breath against his neck, her tanned legs in their white shorts . . .

He came awake just as they swung around the last bend down the mountain, and the great arc of Acapulco Bay and town opened up before them. The beach below them like a crescent moon that had been pulled down to the earth, gleaming white and spotless, and a sea that was a startling bright, cerulean blue — colors he had never seen before in nature, in any part of the world he knew. There was not a cloud in the sky, just beginning to give over to evening, and he was sure that he had never seen anything so brazenly beautiful.

Yet he could also see the cranes again. There were at least half a dozen hotels going up, slabs of white and beige layered one on top of the other all along the rim of the beach. Many more, obviously brand-new mansions stuck chock-a-block in the hills, lavender and white and aquamarine, littered with pillars and white plaster statues of cherubs and naiads at play beside swimming pools the size of football fields.

"It'd be lovely," he said, "if you could just get rid of the people."

"I know, but it's progress. This is part of the New World, too," Charlie said. "Where men can pull themselves up outta nothing."

"Yes, but I'm beginning to wonder if that's enough of an excuse for all the terrible things we do," Tom said, and pointed to the largest, most ostentatious mansion of all, a massive white building jutting out from the Indian laurels on the cliffside like a hawk's beak.

"That's Perusquia's place," Charlie answered in a small voice. "That's where she is."

25

New York, 1953

Tom left the hospital with Ellie and walked her the few blocks left to the boardwalk, into the wind off the ocean. There were a few people strolling the boards, despite the hour and the season. Men with lunch pails coming back from the subway and work, walking quickly toward home. Older women wrapped up in layers of shawls and walking slowly, staring out at the breakers. A couple of schoolkids laughing and thumping the boards as hard as they could as they ran off to dinner. Out on the old Dreamland pilings a single fisherman sat perfectly still near the end of the pier, his line swaying in the water as he turned into a silhouette.

Off to the east, they could see where the Gut once stood, the old year-round neighborhood—most of its wooden bungalows and its low brick tenements now pulverized into rubble by Robert Moses's crews. Among the wreckage three big yellow bulldozers sat stilled for the night, like burned-out tanks Tom remembered in ruined Italian villages.

"The lousy bastard," Ellie said ritually, with no real vehemence.

They walked on in silence, arm in arm, until they reached Lulu's, the only place still open off-season. It was no more than a long bar, a hot-plate counter, and a collection of salt-battered wooden chairs and tables, with a few carny games off to one side. It was completely open to the sea, and every time a new breeze swept in, the bartender looked apprehensively at the ketchup bottles and the napkin dispensers where they jangled along the tabletops.

He sat her down at one of the tables as far back in the joint as he could find and went to get two coffees from the bar. There were only a couple of other patrons, pounding diligently through their beers while standing at the rail, as if they were being made to drink as a punishment. To the side, a pair of teenagers were fooling sullenly with the Skee-Ball games, the thunk of the ball the only sound in the bar the wind didn't make.

She looked up at him when he brought their coffees over, her eyes wary and expectant. There was still a hint of mischief in them, he noticed — the exuberance of a woman still in the first throes of love. He knew that he would never see that look again after he told her what he was going to tell her, and already he regretted it more than anything he had ever done.

"So, we're alone. If we get any more alone, we're going to be swept out to sea," she said, her every joking word tearing him up inside. "What's the big news? Something the Old Man told you?"

He took a first, slow sip of his coffee, still too hot, letting it scald his tongue and the roof of his mouth. Shivering anyway in the wind at his back.

"I slept with my brother's wife," he said, telling it all at once, the only way he could get it out. Making himself watch her face fall as he said it. The eyes uncomprehending at first, the glint in them frozen there, then stunned, then falling in disappointment. The small smile that was on her lips vanishing.

"I see," she said.

"No, you don't," he told her. "Because I still can't see it myself."

It started down in Florida. Late in Charlie's first term, when the sheen of the office was gone and he was being worn down by the job more every day. By how everything was an emergency, all the time, and the strikes and the threats to strike, and the endless budget meetings and speeches. The papers hounding them all around town, even when he tried to take Slim up to Saratoga for a weekend. Charlie screaming at the reporters from the porch of the Grand Union Hotel, "It's the end of this circus! We're cutting short our stay!"

Actually, Tom knew, it had started long before that. It had started the first time he saw her, in that rose-colored suit at the Oyster Bar in Grand Central station. *A stupid boy's crush,* he'd told himself, and he'd tried staying away to get over it. Busying himself out at his law offices in Brooklyn, and with his "children's crusades," as Charlie liked to call them. Not trusting himself even to speak when he was around her, beyond the most perfunctory noises — so much so that she joked about it during the depleted Sunday dinners they still had in Bay Ridge, just frequently enough to keep the tradition going.

"I think your brother Tom hates me," she'd tease him, and Charlie would laugh and tell her, "No, no, he's just tongue-tied by yer beauty," and then she would laugh, too, and Tom would smile, wanting to say that it was true. Her green eyes shining, blond hair drawn back behind her in a ponytail, maybe still in her tennis whites after an afternoon spent trying to teach Charlie the game. He'd watch Charlie watching her, and he knew that he was thinking the same thing, unable to fathom how anyone could be so confident in her own skin.

"It was lust, pure lust, that was all," he swore to Ellie. "And all the more shameful for it."

"But lust for what?" she asked, looking at him closely above her coffee cup.

He knew she was right — knew that it was always more than just the beautiful, green-flecked eyes, or the blond hair, or the slender, aristocrat's body that drew both him and Charlie. It was the past, as well. Everything that she was, and that she had been molded and shaped to be, through three hundred years of her family's history.

The golden girl of the golden land. Her forefathers' empire reaching all the way to the Western Sea, at last — and beyond. Selling the kerosene to light the lamps of China. Carrying the flag forward, and a cash box under one arm ...

He had seen her in the papers, bits and pieces here and there, more of course after Charlie started squiring her around. Out on the town with her sister, a matching, sloe-eyed, black-haired beauty to Slim's blonde — *Those Fabulous Sadler Girls at 21!* Her companions the likes of Grace Kelly, Wallis Simpson, foreign princes, and Hollywood producers. Laughing, smiling, gazing with alarming frankness right into the camera. Never vulgar, never drunk or overexcited, but carrying herself always with perfect aplomb in the highest of high society.

It was the one thing he never found mysterious about his older brother. He understood perfectly why he had to have her. The only trouble was that he did, too.

He swore he would stop accepting invitations to the Sunday dinners at the Bay Ridge house, and for a time that worked. They weren't the same, anyway, haunted now by the absence of Jimmy, and Claire, even in her wheelchair. But then Charlie went into the hospital for the second time for heart palpitations, after the debacle in Saratoga. It was then that he finally got Slim to agree to marry him. She was at his bedside every day while he complained, telling him finally, "Look, if you want some privacy, why don't you make it? You're the mayor."

"There's nothing so private as a married couple," he told her.

The plan was for Tom to take her down to Florida in secret, on the plane, while Charlie went alone by train to draw away the press, telling them he just wanted to rest and recuperate. Tom was supposed to stash her away before the wedding, at a place on Hobe Sound owned by a retired doctor and his wife Charlie knew from back in the City — a mossy old Spanish villa surrounded by a small state's worth of lush, green lawn on every side.

Their hosts gave them a motor launch to use, and they would pack a lunch and take it out every morning while they waited to hear that the last reporter had given up and it was safe to come out now. Cruising slowly in and out of the inland waterways around the Sound, staring at the sheer fecundity of the world around them. The huge, primeval trees. The swift black and white and brown birds with long orange beaks that darted over the water and the high marsh grasses. Sometimes he even noticed an alligator move grudgingly into the black, algaed water and trail noiselessly after them for a little while, with only its hooded, reptile eyes above the water.

She treated him like a little brother at first when they were together, although they were almost the same age. Driving him wild with the clothes she'd wear, high-fashion trousers as soft as pajamas, taffeta skirts so light they'd lift in the faintest breeze, constantly revealing a glimpse of leg. Teasing him over the stiff city clothing he was wearing, and how little he knew about boats, even though he insisted on driving.

"Charlie would never forgive me if something happened with a woman at the wheel," he told her, titillated though he was to find himself with a woman who knew of boats — and tennis, and no doubt horses and high tea, as well. He let her take him into town to buy him some proper boating whites and deck shoes, blushing furiously as she marched him up and down the sleepy little department store in front of a bemused clerk, insisting that he try on the pants in the curtained dressing room.

"Can I come in and see?" she asked, and stepped in through the curtain before he could reply. The clerk was off across the store at the moment, and he was very aware of how close they were in the little room. Her hand on his belt, pulling up the pants a little, both of them looking him over in the mirror.

"Now, there's a sight for ya — the Irish navy!" he told her, though he could see only her at his side, svelte and tanned in a pair of white shorts and almost as tall as he was. Holding a hand to her mouth while she giggled and poked at him — but both of them still looking at each other in the mirror.

"You look wonderful. Like a regular commodore," she told him, though the next morning when they went out to the launch again, she surprised him by tripping him, then jumping on top and rolling him over across the wet green lawn and the loamy dirt.

"Hey! What about my beautiful new boat clothes?" he said, laughing.

"Don't you know that being rich is all about not looking the part?" she said, mashing a handful of grass into his shirt. Laughing as she straddled him, her long bare legs against his hips — then jumping up just as quickly and running for the boat, Tom jogging sheepishly after her.

"You know, Charlie's the same way," she told him when they were deep into the sluggish, winding creeks and rivers that made up most of the waterway. "I know it sounds fantastic, but he's never even set foot on a pleasure boat."

"There wasn't much call for them around Bohola, we being landlocked an' all that."

She slapped his shoulder playfully.

"You laugh, but it's true! I don't think he's ever worn a pair of shorts in his life. He's never had a real fishing pole in his hands, never so much as *tried* to swim. He's a man who has known only work."

"What else is a man supposed to know?" he said, keeping his eyes ahead for half-sunken trees and vines.

"A lot. We're borrowing a yacht for the honeymoon, from another friend of his. I want him to get to know what pleasure is. I'm scared he's going to work himself to death in that job."

"I am, too," he said, looking at her gravely. "It's a good thing you're doing for him. *You're* a good thing for him."

"Well, thank you, sir." She laughed, but to his surprise he saw that she was blushing.

They stopped at an abandoned old pier for lunch, the only sign of the house it had belonged to a pair of crumbling brick chimneys up the hill. There she spread the contents of the picnic basket genteelly out along the rotting, gray-green planks. Making an entire meal of it, laying down a checkered tablecloth first, then delicate china plates, and cloth napkins, and finger sandwiches of cucumber, and chicken and lettuce. They ate and drank a little white wine, and he watched her across the pier where she sat in another perfect, organdy blouse and her white shorts again, long, tanned legs folded beneath her. She caught him staring at her and smiled as if to say it was all right, and this time it was his turn to blush, and turn to his sandwich.

They talked about this and that — Charlie, and mutual friends back in New York, and their hosts, and Charlie again, and after that they were out of conversation and could only look at each other in the quiet of the green world around them. There was nothing for it, then, but to get back onto the boat and head for home. Both of them saying less now, aware that this interlude together was coming to an end.

"I just want this one to work," she said at last.

"Why wouldn't it?"

"The last one didn't."

"Why was that?"

"It's a cliché. We were both too young. We didn't know what we wanted. Or rather I *did* know what I wanted, which didn't include being married to him."

"Why *did* ya marry, then?"

"Because we were supposed to. Because we knew each other our whole lives. His father and my father charged up San Juan Hill together, you see."

253

"You're pulling my leg," he said, turning from the murky green channel ahead to frown at her.

"I'm not, I swear. His father was a Rough Rider."

"What did *he* do?"

"He was a polo player, from Teaneck, New Jersey. Carleton Carstens Hopp. That was his name, I swear."

"God help us," he said, chuckling, and she laughed with him—a nice, full-throated laugh, and he was very conscious of her next to him, her long, bare legs, and the smell of her hair and her neck very close.

"He wasn't so bad. But I had only been working for a little while, and I didn't want to give it up," she said, looking off ahead of them where a bird suddenly burst out of the underbrush. They were headed into the late-afternoon sun, and she put a hand up to shield her eyes, standing radiant beside him in the glow.

"You were able to support yourself?" he asked, surprised she had ever really worked at all.

"I was the best damned millinery model in the City," she said proudly. "I made twenty-five dollars an hour, working for John Robert Powers."

"Jesus. I wouldn't a given that up, either!"

"Mr. Powers used to say that I wasn't just a beautiful statue, I was always playing a part—that I was a true actress."

"Was it true?"

"Sure. I'd go out to some charity benefit, or some lunchtime showing at the Waldorf-Astoria, and I'd put on the best show I could for the ladies there. Trying to think how they'd like to see themselves in the clothes I was wearing—"

"And you liked all that?" he asked.

"I loved it," she said defiantly, looking straight at him. "I loved being on my own in the City. I loved the openings every season, when they brought out the new lines, and all the press were there, and the buyers from out of town. They let me keep the outfits, just so long as I'd wear them out in public, and I loved that, too. I loved going everywhere dressed in the best clothes in the world, and I loved making my own living, and I know I wasn't supposed to, but I can't help it, I did, I loved it."

"He never stood a chance."

"No. Poor guy. But we went ahead and got married because everybody assumed that we would. It lasted five years. I'm not proud of it. Nobody in my family ever got divorced. Thank God it was a civil ceremony, so we didn't have to have it annulled, and go through all that."

"Yes," said Tom. "Frankie Spellman would only have asked that Charlie turn over Central Park to the church for that."

She gave a small laugh and blew out a last ring of smoke before throwing her cigarette into the water.

"Was it the war?" he asked.

"What?"

"Was it the war that ended it?"

"Oh, no. I think if he *had* gone away, we would be married still. I would never leave a man who went off to war," she said with surprising force. "I never understood the women who did. I would have worried over him like crazy, maybe convinced myself that I loved him."

"Good girl."

"Unfortunately, the farthest away he got was Fort George on Staten Island, doing some sort of thing with logistics."

"What were the grounds?"

"'Mental cruelty.' On the idea, I think, that it was cruel for two people to completely ignore what their poor brains were telling them all along."

He laughed out loud at that, and she smiled back at him, putting an elbow on his shoulder to support herself. Her arm was sun-soaked and warm, with just a trace of her perspiration and her perfume.

"And then?"

"I took the train out to Reno, the usual story. Then I came home and went back into modeling."

"And back to the society pages."

"That's not what I am, Tom," she said, her voice serious.

"No?"

"*No.* That's the image; that's how you get jobs. But it's not me. I can't tell you how boring the nightlife is. That's the part of it I never liked."

A cloud passed across her, a hint of melancholy he hadn't suspected in her before.

"That was my mother. She never forgave my dad for going off to the First World War. How could he take her to all the cotillions, if he was in some trench over in France?'"

"That would present a dilemma."

"He was gassed over there, and when he came back he had tuberculosis. While he was trying to get well, the business fell apart, and then she divorced him while there was still something left," she said, letting the words fall out into the heavy air between them, as if they tasted too rotten to keep in her mouth. "I went back to live with him in Highland Park, Texas. Just the two of us, in a nice little brick house on Abbott Avenue."

"Doesn't sound too bad."

"It was the best. Because we didn't have money anymore, I had to forego being sent to some awful finishing school in Switzerland, or Connecticut."

"Quite a hardship."

"Instead it was Highland Park High School, just like any other fortunate girl. I joined a sorority, went to dances at the local country club and the American Legion hall. Stood in the bleachers and cheered my boyfriend every Friday night."

"Was he good?"

"He wasn't a benchwarmer."

"But the bright lights beckoned."

"That was Daddy." She sighed. "He wanted me to have something of my own. He used to sit about at night, still unable to believe he lost all that money. I used to laugh at him. 'Don't worry,' I would tell him. 'There will always be more money.' That's how much I knew."

She gave a small, embarrassed laugh, about having been young.

"I would've gone to some Texas cow college, or just gotten married, it didn't matter. Or stayed with him in that little brick house. But he knew he didn't have much longer. He was the one who told me to go the Powers agency. And that led to everything else."

"And now you want to marry my brother."

"Yes. Yes, I do, Tom," she said, and to his surprise her face began to quiver, her delicate lips trembling.

"What's the matter? Don't you love him, then?" he asked.

"Oh, I do, Tom, I do. Sometimes I even feel like I'm madly in love with him," she said, the tears coming now, and she put her hands up to her face, rubbing her palms into her eyes like a little girl. "It's just that he's so much older than I am, and a serious person, and I don't want to disappoint him."

"You could never disappoint —" he started, but then his mouth was on hers. He was never sure just who reached for whom first, but he could feel her arms around his neck, and he was leaning down into her, kissing her fervently.

"Oh, Tom, oh, Tom," she was saying, running her hands down over his head while he kissed her again and again, just as he had been wanting to do for all those months. Kissing her on her soft, pink lips, then on her neck, her cheek, her eyelids, anywhere he wanted to.

He took off her clothes while she still stood before him — first the fine lacy blouse, then her adorable white shorts, and her underwear, too — just wanting to look at all of her there, for a moment, in the light of the sinking Florida sun. They made love slowly, with her sitting on his lap on the boat's bench, facing him. She would push back to look at him for a moment, then embrace him and pull herself to him again, coming finally with her arms around his neck as he ran his hands up and down her ribs, and her small, high breasts, and kissed her mouth again.

She didn't say anything for a long time after they were finished, and he could have sat there all evening, with her skin against his, listening to her breathing. But one of those swift, orange-billed birds dived low over their boat, squawking raucously and startling them back to life. They started to get dressed then, because there was nothing else but to go back. She cried some more, but then she got ahold of herself and went to stand next to him again at the wheel, putting an arm around his waist while he steered them home to Charlie's friend's house in the gathering darkness.

It was the last time they went out in the boat. Two days later word came from Charlie, and they were married in an old Spanish chapel in Stuart. There was only Tom, and Slim's sister and mother, and the doctor and his wife in the whole wedding party, but there was a small local choir that sang an Ave Maria beautifully. Charlie looked tanned and ebullient, and more rested than Tom had seen him in months, and Slim wore a perfect, navy-blue designer suit. At the end of the Mass she looked at him teary-eyed, and Charlie grinned

257

and pumped his hand, and told him, "Wish us luck, Tom!" and so he did, and meant it, and went off to the long train ride home.

"But that wasn't it," Ellie said, looking at him, their coffees gone cold and mostly untouched.

"No. How did you know that?"

"Because I know you — a little, anyway. If that had been it, you'd have gone and done a hundred penances, or whatever it is you do as a semi-lapsed Catholic, and never said a word, to protect her reputation and his."

"You're right," he said with a bitter smile. "You do know me."

"So it didn't stop then."

"No, it didn't stop," he said after a long sigh. "I saw her again, back in the City, and not just once, either, and it went on and both of us hated it."

"At least that's what you told yourselves," she said, an edge to her voice for the first time — something he was almost relieved to hear.

"It diminished us. It took more and more away from how we thought of ourselves, and there wasn't enough to replace it," he said sadly. "Not all the thrills in the world would've been enough."

"But you were in love," she said.

"What? No —"

"You were. Otherwise it wouldn't have gone on."

He sat looking at her for a long few seconds. "I suppose . . . I suppose we might've thought . . . yes. Yes, I guess we were," he said finally, the words moving like mud through his mouth. "I guess we *thought* we were. But no more."

She was silent for another minute, looking past him and out to the boardwalk, and the long bar where the last remaining drinker braced himself and took another mournful pull at his beer.

"Well, what do you think?" he asked when he couldn't stand it any longer.

"I think it's more wrong than ever that you're on this case," she said, looking at him somberly. "I think it's my duty to go to Mr. Hogan and tell him what I know. But you know I won't do that."

"No."

"But I hate the fact that you knew that."

"Sorry."

She stood up then, and he stood up with her, and the two of them walked out of the open bar and back onto the boardwalk. They made for the hospital parking lot and the car, walking with their hands in their pockets, while the riled night sea pounded the beach behind them. In the ruins of the Gut, the yellow bulldozers looked like sinister creatures, huddling over a moonscape now — everything altered beyond recognition.

"So the Old Man knew," she said abruptly.

"Yep. He picked it up," he told her.

"Or he said he did. Maybe he just took a wild shot, but you fell for it."

"Maybe," he conceded.

"Damnit, Tom, you should've had me stay," she said, sounding angry at last. "He would never have dared to bring it up with me in the room."

"No. But he wouldn't have said anything else, either."

"Oh? And what did he say that was so important?"

"Mostly, he just warned me off it," he said sheepishly.

"So he put you on your heels, then said just what he wanted to say to you."

"He played me like some rookie cop," Tom admitted, and had to laugh and shake his head despite himself. He looked over at her, and to his surprise Ellie was smiling ruefully, too. They had reached the car, almost alone now in the visitors' section of the lot, and he reached out his hands and held hers, looking into her face.

"So, now you know the worst thing about me," he told her. "I'm more ashamed of it than I can say. It was a rotten thing to do, it was a betrayal, and if you want to have nothing else to do with me, I can't blame ya. All I can say is that I didn't know you, and I can't feature ever having done it if I had."

"I know that." She sighed. "Or at least I'd like to believe it. I know I'm not your first girl, Tom, and you've been to a war, and lived half a lifetime before you met me. I just wish it hadn't been an affair, and I wish it wasn't your brother, and I wish I didn't think you were still half in love with her."

"I'm not. I'm not, and I'll prove it to ya—"

"No, Tom, that's not—"

"I'll prove it to ya. Marry me, Ellie. Say you'll marry me, right now."

"Ah, Tom. That's not it! That's not what I was trying for—"

"Marry me. I mean it."

He pulled her to him and kissed her on the mouth, and she resisted at first.

"Marry me, marry me," he murmured to her, and stroked her hair, and after a moment she gave in and embraced him, and kissed him back.

"Ah, Tom, how's this supposed to work? With her your brother's wife still?" she said unhappily, her hands against his chest, pushing him back a little but allowing him to fold her in his arms.

"It'll work. You'll be there."

"We'll see," she said, kissing him quickly, then pulling away again. "He's going to send you down to Mexico, you know."

"He is? The boss?" Tom said, jubilant. "When?"

"When we have enough. One way or the other, he'll send you — if you'll go."

"I'll go."

She looked at him sharply. "You go and come back without falling for her again, we'll talk about marriage."

He grinned at her. "God bless you, Ellie."

"Just come back."

In the car she asked him, "So did he say *anything?*"

"Who?"

"The Old Man. Besides how you better drop it, I mean."

"He strongly implied the other rats might've had something to do with Mr. Reles's demise," he said, wheeling the car back onto Ocean Parkway, now dimmed and peaceful and quiet, a thousand lights shining in a thousand kitchens.

"That's not exactly a revelation," she said.

"No, it's not," he said. "They're about the only ones left. But even if they did it, they wouldn't try anything like that on their own."

"So, go talk to them," she said.

"The other squealers?"

"Why not? It's where the Old Man wants you to go. So, go there and find out what he wants you to find out. It will be taking away one more piece, hiding what he *doesn't* want you to find out."

26

Brooklyn, 1940

There was something about the man that made you want to hit him in the face the moment you laid eyes on him. *Abe Reles, AKA Kid Twist II.*

He was a short guy in a loud suit, no more than five-two, but he had arms that hung down to his knees, with huge hands and fingers that could only be described as spatulate. He had a clown's face, or more precisely the face of a second banana in a cheap burlesque house, with a big nose and big ears, thick red lips, and big, brown doe-like eyes that could turn instantly from mischief to pathos and back again. There was something innately grotesque and corrupt about him, like a six-inch cockroach or a water rat, that made you just want to stomp and smash him out of existence.

He came in towed along by Frank Bals and the Old Man, picked up from the luncheonette where his wife had said he would be waiting. Grinning from ear to ear, as if it were *he* who had caught *them.* His eyes fixed triumphantly on Charlie.

"I can make you the biggest man in the country" was the first thing he said.

They took him into the interrogation room on the first floor, where they sat him down, still handcuffed, in a metal chair. There were no outside windows in the room, the blinds drawn over the one-way glass in the hallway. The four of them — Charlie, Burton Turkus, Jack McGrath, and Captain Bals — gathered around him, standing or slinging a leg up on their chairs.

And Tom with them, too. Not because he had any kind of official position, but because Charlie said he wanted him there. So he could witness that he was making good on his pledge to find out what happened to Panto, he knew — something he thought about over and over again, later on, after everything began to come out.

Five men in a semicircle. With Reles smirking back at them.

"I can make you the biggest man in the country," he repeated, his eyes still focused only on Charlie. "But I gotta walk clean."

"You're dreamin' if—" snapped Captain Bals, but Burt Turkus cut him off.

"That depends. What can you give us?'" he asked.

"What can I *give* you?" Reles smirked some more. "I can give you anything you want. I can give you guys who go all the way to the top. Guys you'll never get any other way. I can give you any murder you want. Brooklyn, New York, New Jersey, Chicago. California, Florida. *Any*where, all over the country. What can I give you?" He lifted his chin, grinning exultantly. "Just ask me."

"We can get you a cell in the highest-security prison in the land. Put you out in Leavenworth, maybe Alcatraz, if you prefer. Someplace no one can get to you. Meanwhile, you have my personal promise that we'll get you the lowest possible sentence—" Burt Turkus said, but Reles waved him away like a man shooing flies from a piece of pie.

"Anywhere you put me — any prison you can name, even in solitary confinement — they'll find a way in. That's why once it's all over, I gotta walk. Or it's no deal."

"These days, we have men like you coming in every day to spill their guts, terrified that Lepke and his pals will knock them off," Turkus tried. "Why would we need *you?*"

"Because you got no corroboration," Reles told him calmly, his gaping mouth expanding into a jack-o'-lantern's smile. "According to the laws of the State of New York, you need somebody who's got firsthand knowledge of a murder but wasn't involved in it. All you got now is stoolies, tryna rat out their partners before they rat on *them*. I can tell you how every hit in this city was done, even the ones I *didn't* do."

"Why should you know about all of this?"

"I dunno, people tell me things. I guess it's because I got a face they can trust." He directed his grin at Charlie again. "Like I said. I can make you the biggest man in the country."

Tom caught the look that Turkus shot his brother. Burt had already started toward the door, assuming they would go to confer. But Charlie never budged. Staring back at the prisoner for a long moment, one leg up on a chair, elbow propped on his knee, chin propped in his hand, rocking a little back and forth while he pondered whether or not to become the biggest man in the country. He looked at Turkus, who had stopped halfway to the door, and shook his head.

"Give the little man his deal," Charlie told him, then turned to Reles. "But if you should tell me one single lie, Mr. Reles—just one little, goddamned white lie, about anything at all . . . so help me God, I'll send you to the chair and pull the switch myself."

"Oh, you won't never hear no lie from *me,*" Reles said, grinning, then held his cuffed hands up before them, like an organ grinder's monkey. "So now that we're all good friends, how's about takin' the cuffs off, an' let's get started?"

It went on and on, deep into the early-morning hours. His voice never flagging, never halting: *the little man who wouldn't stop talking.* Filling up notebook after notebook, seventy-five of them before he was finished. Giving them everything in exacting detail—names, addresses, accomplices, eyewitnesses. Descriptions of crimes that would visibly sicken the women stenos and secretaries—Abie grinning lasciviously as they asked to take a break. Reciting the whole epic story of life and death in Brooklyn, New York.

"How did you get into this? You came from a decent home," Burt Turkus asked first, trying to elicit the thread of his life from him. Already planning how it would go in court, the story of the witness as important as the story he would tell.

"My old man used to go sell neckties from a pushcart on Shlamazel Avenue," he said with a shrug, and grinned again. "That wasn't for me. Me an' Buggsy Goldstein, we wanted somethin' a little more outta life."

"What was that?"

"I dunno." Another shrug. "A little money in our pockets. Broads, good food. Maybe a nice car. We were kids, we didn't know from nothin'."

"How did you go about it?"

"We left school, we did a little shylocking, cigarette machines, pinball. Some stink bombs, nothin' serious—"

"Running whores. Breaking strikes," Turkus added, but Reles only grinned some more.

"I lost count," he said.

"You did two years for assault and battery, up at Elmira."

"Yeah, that was nothin'. That was useful, it was only after that we knew enough to get our troop together. Me an' Buggsy. Dukey Maffetore, George

Defeo, Blue Jaw Magoon. That little punk, Tick-Tock Tannenbaum. We brought over Dasher Abbandando an' Happy Maione from the Ocean Hill Hooligans. But when Pittsburgh Phil come on, that was like adding a whole other troop, just by himself!"

"You did another stretch," Turkus said coolly, still leafing through his files. "One Charles Battle, a colored attendant at a midtown parking garage in Manhattan. Told you an' your pals to pipe down when you wouldn't stop honking for service."

"Well, we had a little altercation. He gets on his high horse —"

"You beat him half to death with a bottle. Next day, they found another attendant, a man named Snider, who looked an awful lot like Charlie Battle, stabbed to death behind the garage."

"Yeah, well," said Reles with a weak smile, spreading his hands out before him. "*You* go tell spooks apart."

"But Battle testified anyway. Got you two more years, this time up in Sing Sing," Turkus said, putting the file aside and directing a level stare at Reles. "Is that what this is really all about, Abe? Too old? Afraid to do any more time?"

Reles hesitated, surprised, a shadow of uncertainty flicking across his face for the first time. "I ain't afraid," he said. "You go ahead an' ask me anything you want."

"How many men have *you* killed? I mean personally?"

Reles's face brightened.

"There was Irving Shapiro, back when we was chasin' the Shapiros outta Brownsville," he began. "Me an' Goldstein shot that son of a bitch eighteen times in a hallway, then dragged him out on the sidewalk an' shot him again in the face. I did Willie Shapiro with a wire, an' dumped him by the beach. Meyer Shapiro I shot through the ear. He looked fine, except for the blood. Then Joey Silver, I blew his head off against a tree with a shotgun. Then there was Rocco, Jack Paley, Ruben Smith. Somebody by the name a Mummy. Moe Greenblatt, an' Jake the Painter. How many is that, ten? Oh, yeah, Whitey Rudnick, that junkie floater . . . "

The voice was almost mesmerizing as he gladly recalled his crimes. Not flat, or dulled, but animated, almost jubilant, like that of someone remembering well-loved friends and family.

"Did it ever bother you to kill all these men? Did you feel anything?" Turkus asked.

"How did you feel when you tried your first case?" Reles grinned back at him.

"I was rather nervous."

"An' how 'bout your second case?"

"It wasn't so bad, but I was still a little nervous."

"Still a little nervous . . ."

You could almost see it in his eyes. The little man thinking, *What a schvantz! This fucking guy still nervous over his second trial. But willing to go on, to work with him. A natural from the beginning . . .*

"And after that?" he asked the prosecutor.

"Oh, after that I was all right. I was used to it."

"You answered your own question. It's the same with murder. I got used to it."

The rest of them standing around, impressed despite themselves. Thinking how well he was going to do on the stand.

"How did you plan these killings?"

"We didn't need any plan. We are experts," he retorted. "You just get some kid like Sholem Bernstein to ghost you a car, change the plates on it. Then ya do the job, stash the stiff in the car, an' leave it in some vacant lot. Maybe take it out someplace like the wood shacks in Neponsit. Canarsie or Plumb Beach, if it ain't summer. Bury the body, or torch it in the tall grass, if you don't got time."

Listening to it, Tom couldn't help thinking: *Is that where Panto ended up, too?*

"Sometimes they'd put up a fight," Reles conceded. "With Whitey Rudnick, that junkie, Pep strangled him some, then he stabbed 'im with an ice pick. We wrapped 'im in a rug, but when we was gettin' him in the car it looked like he moved a little bit. Who knows, but Happy Maione says, 'Here, lemme hit him once for luck!' an' he picks up a meat clever an' beats his head in with it. Then we had to break his legs to get him to fit in the trunk —"

The metal legs of a chair squealed as the stenographer leaped up, asking to be excused for a minute. Reles followed her rigid form avidly as she hurried out of the room and wheezed with laughter.

"Boy, did she ever look green! You never know with women, how they're gonna take it. Did I tell you yet about Ladies' Night?"

They shook their heads and leaned in closer, looking almost conspiratorial. Six men in a room for the moment, their jackets off, shirtsleeves rolled up. Sitting close together, the air thick with their cigarette smoke and the smell of stale coffee, to hear the story of a murder.

"It was when we hit the Ambergs for killin' Hy Kazner. Mendy Weiss got Pretty Amberg, who he was friends with, to meet him up at Yiddel Lorber's. You know — that joint by the on-ramp for the Williamsburg Bridge?"

"We're familiar with Mr. Lorber."

"He gave Pretty Amberg over to us, an' we took him into the back room an' cut him up with little knives, until he wasn't so pretty anymore. Then we put him in the back of his car, an' left it in some empty lot over in East New York.

"We was all goin' out that night, an' the girls was always on us about wantin' to know what we did, what we was up to when we wasn't spendin' all our money on them, all that hoo-ha. So we decided to drive 'em out to that lot an' let 'em take a look."

He shook his head, laughing.

"We thought they'd scream, or get sick or somethin', once they got a load of Pretty Amberg cut up like that in the back seat a that car. But they couldn't keep their eyes off him! Starin' an' starin' into that window, like they was at the freak show on Coney Island. They even drew straws, see who would burn him up. Pep's girl, Evelyn, she won an' got to drop the match inside the car, once we doused it with gas. We never got such tail like we did that night —"

"Enough of that!" Burt Turkus cut him off at last, as the steno came back into the room, a young, slender woman with her brown hair pinned up tightly on her head, looking pale but determined.

"You'll keep a civil tongue in your head when you talk to us, especially when there's a lady present. Now, we need to know why. What made you decide to kill these men?"

Reles shrugged again, looking baffled. "What made us decide? Mostly, we'd just hang on the corner outside Midnight Rose's, an' wait for a call."

"Rose's?"

"You know, the candy store. On the corner a Saratoga and Livonia, just under the No. 2 tracks."

"A fetid little hole in the wall," the Old Man said with a snort. "Rose Gold's shop. Nasty old hag, claims she can't read or write a word of English. She bails out these mutts, takes their phone calls for them."

"We had her up before the magistrate's bench, for a public nuisance," Charlie said, smiling faintly. "I asked her, 'Why do you let so many criminals frequent your store?' An' she told me, 'Why don't the police keep 'em out?' Pretty good comeback, I have to give her that."

"It's open twenty-four hours, only place in the neighborhood," Reles told them. "She let us use the back room, leave rods in the toilet for fellas to pick up. She would take phone calls for us, so's we'd get our assignments."

"Your assignments?"

"Sure. When somebody in some other gang wants us to knock off somebody? We didn't have no phones. We used Midnight Rose's."

"A city of a million schemes, most of them formulated around lunch counters and newspaper stands," Charlie said softly.

The grimy little corner store tucked under the long black line of elevated rail track. The yellow light out its door and its grimy windows the only thing visible for blocks in the late-night Brownsville darkness.

The gaunt, rigid-mouthed madwoman standing behind the cash register, lank hair the color of a rat's coat. After dark would come the older men, shuffling down to get copies of the Racing Form *and the early editions, to read about the Dodgers, or the war, or whatever else might distract them through the Brooklyn night of longing and trepidation. Watching the gangsters come and go, listening to the trains rushing by up above. Waiting for something, anything to happen . . .*

"What assignments?" Turkus asked — most of them still not quite understanding it yet.

"You know — *as-sign-ments*," Reles told them, carefully enunciating each syllable. "Somebody'd call. Usually Lepke, or Albert, but sometimes it was somebody from Luciano's troop, or from Frankie Costello, or Longy Zwillman, over in Jersey. They'd tell us who it was they wanted taken care of. An' we'd do it for 'em."

"So anyone — *anyone* high enough in the New York mob could call you and order up a murder," Turkus said, almost in disbelief.

"Not just New York! *Anywhere*," Reles told him. "Anywhere around the country. Someone wants someone dead, they call up an' clear it with one a the big boys. Then they pass it on to us."

"Just like that — you order up a murder the way you would a hamburger!" Turkus said in wonderment.

"It's better that way. You don't have no hard feelings in your own backyard. An' if you're from outta town, they don't see you comin'," Reles explained, his eyes gleaming. "Pep loves goin' on the road. He says it all the time: 'Like a ballplayer, that's me. I figure I get seasoning doing these jobs, then somebody from one a the big mobs spots me. Then, up to the big leagues I go!'"

"Pep?" Charlie asked, consulting Turkus's notes. "That's Pittsburgh Phil Strauss."

"Sure. He got it down to a science. He got this leather kit bag — just enough room for a pair a pants, his silk underwear, an' a fresh white shirt. Underneath, he's got his gat, a rope, an' a ice pick. Oh, he's a genius with a rope, Pep Strauss! Even so, he ended up havin' to kill this one *schmohole* in a Jacksonville movie house with a fire axe," Reles said, laughing. "You gotta learn to roll with the punches!"

The hard stranger who brushed past you on the platform at Grand Central, or Penn Station. Anonymous as every other passenger. Neatly dressed in a suit and tie — his little leather kit under one arm. A junior executive, off on an overnight. Arriving in a strange town, unknown and unnoticed, vanishing into the station crowds. Running into him on the way back. Nodding to you in the smoker or the observation car, the same cunning leather kit in tow. His job completed. Quiet and uncommunicative, nursing a highball while he looked out the window, watching the miles of telephone poles flash by. Maybe flicking you a quick, penetrating stare when you weren't looking, just to make sure you weren't some kind of cop, or someone from another mob. Then returning to his magazine before you even noticed . . .

"And for this you got money?"

"Sure. Few hundred bucks, plus expenses. It added up. More'n that, though, it kept the big boys happy," Reles explained. "They'd throw a few more rackets our way, made sure everybody left us alone. We was like an exterminator service for 'em, keepin' down the vermin."

They took a break, to order in more coffee and sandwiches and let the uniforms haul Reles out to the bathroom. None of them even sure what time it was anymore, but too het up to go to sleep yet, still absorbing the ramifications of what they had just heard.

"A murder business, pure an' simple," Charlie said, marveling. "Putting men you've never even met down like goddamned dogs. I knew these guys were punks, but —"

"Sure, but it's the way of the world now," the Old Man told him.

"This is going to be big," Turkus said, already anticipating the headlines. "If he's telling the truth, we can crack open every mob in this country. Lepke, Luciano's guys — everybody."

"None of this gets out to the papers just yet," Charlie ordered, smoothing his hair back with his hands. "We have got to make sure he's on the up-and-up, haul in some more corroborating witnesses if we can."

"We have to find a place to *put* him," Frank Bals added, shaking his head. "My God, he's right — there won't be a prison in the world where he's safe!"

"But think of it! Any case we want, anywhere in the nation! He's right, you *will* be the biggest man in the country," Turkus told his brother.

"First things first, gentlemen! Let's find out exactly what he really knows."

Tom moving close to him then, as more cops brought in the cardboard boxes stuffed with cups of coffee and sandwiches in wax paper. Saying it to him alone, almost in a whisper, but making sure he caught his eye as he said it.

"You know what's *first,* Charlie."

"We'll get to it all, Tommy."

His face, Tom noticed up close, looking more tired than he had thought, even haggard. Looking down now, as if he were trying to avoid his eyes. Still he persisted.

"You know what we have to ask, Charlie."

"All right, Tom. All right, then."

The uniforms brought Reles back into the room, and it was then, when he was in the middle of his tuna salad sandwich, that Charlie asked him about Peter Panto.

"Panto? The guy makin' all the trouble on the docks? Yeah, I know all about *him,*" Reles sneered, as jubilant as ever.

"Do ya now —" Tom started, leaning in over the man, but he felt his brother's hand on one shoulder, holding him in place.

"Sure! Mendy Weiss told me all about it."

"What did he say?" Charlie asked this time.

Reles leered up at their faces, still chewing his way through his sandwich as he answered, bits of bread and mayonnaise sticking to his stubbled face, mulched into thick white gobs in his open mouth.

"I met Mendy out in Prospect Park just after. He liked to go there, walk around the lake where no one could hear his business. This time, I notice he's got scratches an' bite marks all over his hands.

"I asked him, 'What happened to you, wha'd you do, get in a fight with some frail?'

"And Mendy said him an' Albert's brother, Tough Tony, was waitin' out at the house at Jimmy Ferraco's chicken farm in Lyndhurst the night before. Somebody s'pposed to bring some wop out there they was gonna take care of. He said, 'The guy just stepped through the door, an' he musta realized what it was about, an' he tried to get out—'"

"Repeat that!" Tom cried out before he knew he was saying anything. Lurching over the chair toward the little man, his whole body trembling. Charlie and the Old Man holding him back. Reles looking up at him, startled but amused. Still chewing the tuna into blobs of white in his fat face, until Tom wanted to pick up the chair and crush his skull with it.

"I *said,* Mendy told me they was waitin' half the night out at the chicken farm for somebody to bring this wop they was supposed to kill. An' when he got there, an' got in the door, he knew what was up an' tried to get out."

He could see Panto's friendly, smiling face, trying to appear as brave as ever as they drove and drove. Through half of Brooklyn, and into Manhattan, and then through the tunnel and across the Jersey flatlands. The conviction growing steadily—how could it not have?—that this was all wrong. The men beside him and up front growing quieter and colder after their earlier, forced jollity, as the houses and the possibilities of escape fell away. Their presence as large and unyielding as boulders around him. No fool, knowing somewhere deep down that he had made a mistake but still hoping somehow it wasn't so—trying to tell himself they were just trying to frighten him, soften him up for negotiations.

Relying, still, on that absolute guarantee someone had given him. Someone big enough to get him into that car in the first place . . .

Then they would have been out past where the streets and the sidewalks ended

270

altogether, moving through another desolate industrial wasteland. *Hearing the wail of a freight train passing, the only other sound of man deep in the Jersey night. Relieved, at last, to see them come to a stop before a lonely farmhouse, a light on in an upper window. Not quite the middle of nowhere, where there could be no doubt: a gravel pit or an old construction site, with a hole in the ground dug and waiting.*

At least they are sparing me that — *did such an awful thought cross his mind? Banishing it immediately for a remaining, furtive hope. The big men in the car letting him out, suddenly talkative and smiling again. Telling him politely enough that they were right upstairs — whomever he was supposed to meet. The sound of the car speeding off, his hand on the railing in the dark stairway.*

Surely it would all be right now, *he must have thought, legs wobbly with relief. Giving him another last, lethal shot of hope, to carry him over to his death. Adjusting his tie, composing himself before he went any farther after putting that one hand on the crude wooden banister. Anxious to show them they hadn't intimidated him.*

The fear rising again in him. All the worse because, Tom knew, he had been through it before already — been trapped there, on President Street, by the Camardas' thugs, thinking surely he was going to die.

All the worse, knowing that fear before. Thinking he should flee, he should just run out into the darkness. Hide himself down along the railbed, from where he'd heard the wail of the freight train rise. Run down into the swamps, and the dumps of scrap metal and junked cars they had passed a few miles back. Grab onto the back of a freight, or just jump into a ditch and stay there until the danger had all passed, until no one could get him anymore. Flee, hide, live.

And why not? Did he just delude himself till the end? Or was he unwilling to flee from them? To be caught at the end gaping up in terror into their faces, their flashlights?

Was that it? *What led him into that house and up those steps, after the car sped off? His hope, his pride, his dignity? Or couldn't he believe that he was really betrayed. Was it self-delusion after all? His inability to finally accept that one man — a man he must have known and trusted — would do this to another? Would leave him out here like this.*

It must have seemed impossible. But at the end, he knew. When he opened the door with the light behind it and saw the men inside, he must have known right away. One look, and he must have known that his worst fear was right, shocking him into action at last . . .

"Mendy told me, 'If I wasn't there, he woulda got away. I grabbed him an' mugged him.' He said, 'I mugged him, got my arm around his neck, and he tried to break the mug an' get away, an' that's when he scratched me, an' bit my hand real bad.' He said he fought like a real man. He fought with the heart of a lion, with everything he had. Right to the end."

"I guess he would've," Charlie said in a low voice. All of them looking down, hands in their pockets. Save for the little man, who kept merrily eating and talking away.

"Mendy said, 'I hated to take that kid. But Albert asked me to do it, an' Albert's been a good friend to me.' He said he hated to take him, he fought so hard. He almost made it outta there —"

Reles gobbled down the last bite of his sandwich with relish, then wiped his hands of it and looked up at them all again, oblivious, his imp's grin spreading across his face. Full of an animal contentment.

"Almost."

27

Brooklyn, 1941
They brought a steam shovel out to Jimmy Ferraco's chicken farm, and there it scratched and banged at the still-frozen earth while the press photographers roamed the property, snapping pictures of the abandoned farmhouse, and the dead chickens where they lay in the yard after they were left to be ravaged by raccoons and packs of feral dogs. Tom spent the long days huddled with the cops and the assistant DAs against the wind off the Passaic, stomping back and forth to get some feeling in their feet, smoking continuously to cover the smell from the slaughtered chickens and the fetid sink of a river.

After three weeks of the cold, and the stench, and the wind that swept the desolate ground up into stinging eddies of dirt, and pebbles, and dried chicken droppings, his brother brought Reles and some of the other squealers out to see if they could narrow down the search. The little man chuckling and smacking his hands together, proclaiming in a voice loud enough for the reporters to hear: "I'm tellin' ya, there must be six or eight stiffs planted out here. It's like old home week!"

"Just pipe down an' show us where," the Old Man told him, and he skittered back and forth across the farm before finally pointing happily to a slight rise near the river.

Tom had brought some of Panto's men from the old Rank-and-File Committee, and when the steam shovel made its initial cut they jumped in, carefully digging out the fetid marshland around it, until at last the steam shovel was able to gingerly lift up a single, gigantic block of frozen earth and quicklime. Chunks of it fell away as they raised it toward the wintry sun, and suddenly the bones were visible — half a skeleton still wrapped in scraps of clothing, and a skull grinning obscenely down at them. The dockworkers dropping their spades and tearing off their caps at the sight, and even the cops and the reporters taking a step back when they saw it, the remains of Peter Panto, rising above them into the light.

"That's him! That's him — see the gap in his front teeth!" one of the longshoremen was shouting, but Tom had already seen all that he needed: the remains of that silly black hat. Half eaten away by the quicklime, but enough of the hatband still there, where one of his killers had tossed it in, idly or contemptuously, next to the strangled corpse of his friend.

"The little man was right. They had all kinds of bodies out there," Charlie told him when they were trying to get warm back in his office, over endless cups of coffee and a little brandy. "The morgue's still tryin' to sort it all out, but it looks like they've been dumping 'em out there for years — maybe decades. One outfit passin' it on to another."

"Jesus."

"I know. Can you imagine it? Going back out there, night after night, all those years?" Charlie said, looking more drained than Tom could ever quite remember seeing him, as if something more than sheer fatigue had gotten under his skin. "Going back to that same evil fucking place, like an animal returning to its lair."

They had loaded the great block of molting earth onto a flatbed truck, and they drove it slowly through the tunnel and back into the City with an escort of police motorcyclists and whirring prowler cars, out of the official fear that some gangsters might try to hijack the evidence. But there was no chance of that. Panto's friends standing along the flatbed, linking arms to balance themselves and make a protective ring around the frozen cube of ground. Holding their shovels fiercely out before them and glaring back at any gawkers while they shielded his opened grave from their eyes.

That was how they brought Peter Panto back to Brooklyn. And a few weeks later, when it was warm again, they walked up from the docks to carry his casket from the Scotto funeral home over to the Church of the Sacred Heart. The men bearing it along through the crowds in the streets like they carried the statue of Saint Anthony on his name's day but still in their work clothes this time, their box hooks slung over their shoulders.

And when it was all over, when the pallbearers took the casket back down the aisle to the hearse, and the ride to the cemetery, they crowded around Charlie. Eager to pump his brother's hand and squeeze his shoulder and thank him for bringing Pete Panto back to them.

"They were so grateful, we brought the body back, at least," Charlie had marveled afterward, in the car to the graveyard. "Just to have something to hold on to, so they knew he wasn't disappeared in the middle of the night, just like that."

"You did it—and you'll do much, much more, that's what they're thankin' you for in advance," Tom said, punching his shoulder in his pride.

"We're all proud of you," Jimmy said on the other side of him, in the broad funeral limousine. "And now you'll go clean out all the rest of the bastards."

"We'll see, boys," Charlie said—a note of real fear in his voice that unsettled Tom for a moment. "We'll see if I possibly can."

"You can, Charlie. If anybody can, it's you."

He shook his head.

"All these little monsters. Pittsburgh Phil, an' Blue Jaw Magoon, an' Tough Tony this an' Buggsy that. A whole other world, going on right under our noses."

"It's them that are the illusion, Charlie. That's why they can't last against men like you," he said, trying to reassure him, but his brother was hardly listening.

"Living amongst us like they were real human beings—when they're . . . *something else*. Standing around their candy stores an' their poolrooms like real people—*imitating* the rest of us. Waiting for the call to go back to that swamp."

"People aren't bad, Charlie. Not most of 'em. They're just scared, want someone to lead 'em. . ."

Charlie looked at Jimmy with his head half cocked then, as if he were about to say something but changed his mind—a gesture Tom would remember all the rest of his life.

"Or maybe just someone to frighten them," he said instead of whatever it was he'd been thinking of, "and is that the same thing in the end?"

But by then they were all singing. All the rats, scuttling in—the wheelmen and the bookmakers and the *shtarkers*. Anyone who had done business with Lepke Buchalter, willingly or not, up in the garment district, or in the unions, or even driving a truck, now that they knew Abe Reles was talking. The Old Man coming up with the idea to stow the most important witnesses out in the Half Moon, the newspapers going crazy over the idea of the "Rats Suite."

There was a new rumor circulating every day—that the syndicate was bringing in a special team of assassins from the Purple Gang, or the Mayfield Road Gang out in Cleveland, or maybe all the way from L.A. They were going to storm the beach in speedboats, put snipers with high-powered rifles up on the Wonder Wheel, or the Parachute Jump. Frank Bals sending out squads of uniforms to search through bathhouses full of old Russian men, or the crumbling fairyland towers of Luna Park. Back at the DA's office it became a standard joke, the kind used to build camaraderie in war, which is what they felt they were all in now.

In court, everything went easier than they could have imagined. The old clubhouse judges replaced by the governor, or browbeaten into giving them a fair shake by the papers, and Dewey's office over in Manhattan. The defendants' high-priced legal talent suddenly discovering that none of their old ploys or stalls would work any longer. The papers amazed and titillated by the contract killings, dubbing Reles's troop *Murder, Inc.,* in huge block headlines. The tales of their exploits—of that unimagined world, existing in the same city, all around them—filling the front page.

The gangsters could barely believe it, even snared in court. Falling perfectly into their parts. Speaking out of turn, sneering and growling threats at the state's witnesses, declaiming their innocence or swearing vengeance like the villains in some old Bowery theatrical.

Buggsy Goldstein ranting and raving at Reles during his testimony, shouting out, "For God's sake, that's some story you're telling! You're burning me!" Happy Maione lunging at the little man in the hallway outside the courtroom, yelling, "You stool pigeon son of a bitch! I'm gonna kill you! I'm gonna tear your throat out!" Flinging a water glass from his lawyer's table at Reles when he dared to mention his house: "You son of a bitch, leave my home out of this! You was never *in* my home!"

Pittsburgh Phil faking insanity, refusing to shower or shave or cut his hair, answering every question in non sequiturs:

"Did you kill him?"

"Over easy, please. Plenty of toast."

"It's a circus out there, every day," Charlie admitted. "But it's trials like people think they should be—like they see them in the movies, or hear them over their radios. They understand them this way."

And still, the little man kept talking. Closing the books on eighty-five murders, the papers calculated. Sending one of his old pals after another up to the chair, Lepke and Louis Capone, and the Dasher, and Reles's oldest friend in the world, Buggsy Goldstein. All of them leaving the court quietly enough, looking stunned and uncomprehending when the verdicts came in.

Back at the suite in the Half Moon, Abie helped them line up each case. Giving them names of witnesses, telling them how to get to the defendants. When he wasn't testifying for him, Charlie loaned him out to DAs all over the country, for their unsolved murders. Tom flying with him sometimes, to make sure it all went according to Hoyle. The guards bundling him off the plane when they stopped to refuel at some tiny airstrip out on the Great Plains. Hustling him out to the edge of the tarmac. Brandishing their shotguns while Reles smoked and stared out forlornly at the illimitable expanse of prairie.

* * *

Tom had never seen his brother work so hard, or so concertedly. He seemed to have command of everything, every detail of every prosecution. The papers already full of speculation about him running for mayor, though he didn't let it throw him off track, refusing questions about anything but the cases. Toiling into the early-morning hours, night after night, until his face began to take on a dull gray sheen. Tom and Natie Cohen begging him at last to take some time off, spend at least a full Sunday back in Bay Ridge with Claire.

"I can't, Tommy, much as I'd like to, much as it kills me to neglect her," he told him — a certain air of serenity, of satisfaction about him beneath the fatigue. "But she's got Jimmy, an' Neddy Moran to look out for her, and I've gotta do this *now*, Tommy. If we don't — if we don't sweep it all clean right now, who knows if it can ever be done again?"

The key to it all was the rapport between the little man and Burt Turkus — suave and dynamic in his slick, shiny gray suits, with his pencil moustache and his skill at seeming to hold a conversation with the jury. The mobsters and then the papers calling him "Mr. Arsenic." Every eye in the courtroom on him when he was up from his chair, weaving dramatically back and forth from the bench to the jury box. He and Reles worked together with the ease and the timing of a vaudeville team on its thirtieth swing around the circuit. Turkus anticipating each of the jurors' silent objections. Reles, his big, second-banana's eyes turning instantly wounded and sincere, punching home each line they expected, before they knew they expected it:

"Are you a stool pigeon, Mr. Reles?"

"I am not a stool pigeon." Gesturing out toward the scowling prisoners. "I didn't just talk to get out of jail. I did it because I knew I had to change my life."

"What made you decide to change your way of life?"

The big brown eyes going soft and bewildered. The words coming out rambling and a little confused, as if he were just articulating them now, no matter how many times he had said them before: "I was expecting another child, and I had one already. I was disgusted with the way I was living. It was my life: I was fed up with my life."

"Your *conscience* told you to make this change?" Burt Turkus prompted, putting a touch of the sneer into his voice, preempting the defense attorney and the jury's own skepticism. Reles looking up at him with puppy dog eyes.

277

"Conscience? That is too deep for me. I just made a change."

"Why should we believe you? Why shouldn't we believe you'd say anything to save your life?"

The eyes slightly smaller then, fearful, with their awful cunning dimmed. "Because Charlie O'Kane told me if he found out that I told so much as a little white lie, he would send me to the electric chair the same as the rest of 'em, and that is why I am telling the truth."

The meaningless tautology, spoken with convincing, childlike simplicity. The better defense attorneys, the men living in Park and Fifth Avenue penthouses who came over to defend Brownsville's killers, forced his crimes out anyway, as Turkus knew they would. One judge so appalled by them that he felt obliged to rant to the jury: "For the record I will say this man never had a conscience when he killed men. He killed men as a business. He had no sympathies. He was killing other men for money. He is a living tiger."

Reles staring blankly back out at the courtroom, Tom noticed. Eyes flaring only when he registered on the word *tiger*.

They won their cases on attrition. Wearing down the jurors, taking them past their initial revulsion with Reles by repeating the pitiless, petty cruelties of the killings and the men who did them. The people who were just like them: a newsstand owner gunned down when he was out on the curb, picking up the Sunday papers. A union truck driver, shot while crossing the street at midday. A pair of middle-aged bachelor plasterers, shot to pieces because they refused to murder another plasterer, their pet bulldog killed next to them. Lured out of their basement apartment by a thug dressed up like a blonde, complete with a wig.

The killers killing because of an unpaid debt, a slight, a suspicion — a whim. Killing because they were told to. Killing men who didn't even know why they were being killed. Killing without question, but with verve and enthusiasm. Whacking away with hammers and meat cleavers, slipping in shivs and ice picks. Strangling a man in any number of inventive ways — so close they could feel his death gasp on their cheeks, watch him cough up his blood on their overcoats.

Putting across always the visceral, sexual release of the act — if never quite spelled out in so many words. Communicating it to the jury nevertheless, that this was what they lived for, their one escape around the tedious hours spent pawing through comic books and racing sheets at Midnight Rose's. The dull routine of stink bombs and shakedowns, stickups and beatings, petty jobs done for petty cash that was their regular operation. Broken only by the orgasmic release of these all but random murders, followed by postcoital orgies of food and drink.

"We all went down to Sheepshead Bay for a shore dinner," Reles told the jury in a climactic recitation, describing the aftermath of the killing of Puggy Feinstein, an ex-boxer whose murder was what sent Pep Strauss and Buggsy Goldstein to the chair. Feinstein left to choke himself to death on what Reles called "the rope trick," a way of binding a man so that the more he struggled, the more he strangled, leaving him finally in a bloody mess.

"A shore dinner?" Turkus pressed it home.

"You know. Lobsters, steamers. Corn on the cob. The works."

"Did you talk about it there?"

"Not much. I give Pep some grief for lettin' that bum bite his hand, an' he give it right back, tellin' me I shoulda helped him."

"After that talk, what happened?"

"Then the lobsters came. We ate."

"All these Puggies and Buggies, and what have you." Charlie shuddered in disgust afterward, back in his office. "What little monsters they all are, all around us. Can't wait to get back an' stuff their faces after it! They're not natural—"

"That they ain't, and it's a great thing you're doin', Charlie, puttin' 'em all away," Tom interrupted. "But is this all of it?"

"What do you want from me, Tommy?"

"When are we going to get to the big boys, Charlie? The men who *had* Panto killed?"

His anxiety growing, too, ever since he'd seen how ill Reles had begun to look. His lung problems worse than ever, the guard detail rushing him up Surf Avenue to the Coney Island Hospital on more than one night.

"Patience, Tommy, we still don't have Mr. Anastasia in custody! Once they bring him in, that'll be the moment, I promise ya."

A month later, the little man got Mendy Weiss convicted for another killing, this one the murder of a truck driver in the garment district. He left the courtroom raving, "All I can say is I'm innocent!" while Captain Frank Bals hissed at him as he was walked past, "Peter Panto is waiting for you!" and Tom squeezed his hands behind his back in triumph, until he felt his knuckles pop.

Sure, then, that it couldn't be much longer before someone gave up Anastasia, and they started in on the real work. On not only convicting one more hired killer, but getting down to the bottom of it all, to who had set up Panto in the first place.

And then came the call that Abe Reles had gone out the window.

Acapulco, 1953
She moved to the door like a vision, crossing the floor so silently and elegantly that he thought he must be watching a reflection, some trick of the dying Acapulco sun along the glass of her mansion on the cliff. Flowing toward them like some piece of rear projection, real but not quite real, wearing an after-swim gown nearly the color of the midnight-blue sea below. Her head held high and her eyes hidden behind dark glasses, moving with such grace that Tom could fully understand at last what it must have been like to see her gliding along the great hall of Grand Central station in a spotlight.

Charlie and he stood at the door like a couple of chastened schoolboys, holding their overnight bags in their hands. When she saw them there she stopped for a moment in her glide across the floor, her mouth tightening in irritation.

"Jesus, Charlie," she said after she slid the glass door open with a luxurious whoosh. Brushing the dark glasses up on her forehead, her green eyes flashing disapproval at the both of them. "You brought the original stage Paddy show on the road."

"You should've seen us in Cuernavaca," Tom said, while Charlie tried to grin.

"Good to see you, too, Slim," he said.

* * *

The house was set up in the cliffs above all the other flamboyant mansions, like the one real jewel in a garish tiara. It was enormous, white and glassed in, and wedged ingeniously into the cliffside, just below the Indian laurels. There were little gardens of rock and cactus leading into the laurels, and a patio the size of a ballroom, paved with slate-blue stone, and a drained, blue-bottomed pool to one side. The winding mountain road they had followed up to it ended at a garage built for a dozen cars, and a turnabout that was roughly the size of Columbus Circle.

Inside, the house was dark and cool and cavernous, their shoes echoing along the ochre tile work, where Slim glided noiselessly in her bare feet. The place seemed barely furnished, and what couches and chairs there were looked faintly ridiculous, gilt-edged or glass or overstuffed and white, like the kind of things they sold to not-overly-bright tourists along Fifty-Seventh Street. Slim left them to sit uncomfortably on a very slippery white leather couch, while she fixed a tray of scotch and ice.

"Servants' night off?" Charlie tried, but Slim just scoffed at him.

"What servants?" She lit a cigarette and blew the smoke out slowly. "There's just Mercedes, who comes in once a week to make sure I haven't burned the place down, smoking in bed. Melchior usually shuts the house this time of year. He offered to have them stay on, but I told him I liked the isolation."

She laid the tray with its cut-glass scotch decanters and glasses on the ridiculously ornate glass coffee table in front of the couch and sat in front of them so they could see her face. A beautiful blond woman wreathed in smoke. Just behind her, through the panoramic front windows, they could make out almost the whole of the deep-blue bay and the white crescent beach.

"Where's dear Melchior off to? Europe, with the rest of the lammisters?" Charlie asked, and Slim stared at him, even more incredulous.

"What are you talking about, Charlie? That's your Big Crowd —"

"You used to like them well enough."

"It's they who don't like me anymore," she said, turning to address herself to Tom. "Not much company here, in case you haven't noticed."

"No? Not even Princeton?" Charlie goaded, his voice almost a snarl, surprising Tom in its fury.

"Ah, Jesus, Charlie, really? You're really going to make us go through all this again, in front of Tom?"

"He's family," Charlie said evenly, weighing his scotch in both hands, down between his legs. "And maybe he *should* hear about it."

"Goddamn you, Charlie. God*damn* you," she said softly. "I tell you it's done, and you come all the way out here just looking to start this up again."

"Why, don't you want him to know about it? It was nothin'—nothin' at all, that's what you told me."

"Damn you, Charlie, don't do this to me—"

"Don'tcha know why she's up here all alone, Tommy?" he said, half turning to face him on the couch. Looking every bit his age just then, Tom couldn't help but notice. His face broad and red in his indignation, the slack jowls wagging as he worked his jaw. Thick legs planted in a bulldog stance on the tiled floor.

"Didn't she tell you anything about it? Didn't you read about it? No, I'm not surprised you didn't. It took our big friends, the ones she despises now, a lot of money to keep it out of the New York papers. C'mon, Slim, tell 'im all about it—tell 'im how you divided the whole town of Acapulco—"

"Stop it!" she screamed at him, drawn at last out of the low, cool voice she had been talking in. "Stop it! Why are you being so *hate*ful?"

"Because that's the way it was. While I was on the phone three, four times a day *pleadin'* with ya to come home, you were out on the beach with Princeton, becomin' a scandal again in still another town—"

"Do you know what he told me? Do you know what he told me in the end?" she said, pointing at Charlie, her voice miserable and teary and beyond control now. Both of them were on their feet, snapping at each other across the coffee table. Tom stood, too, more startled than anything else, not even sure what he was witnessing.

"Slim—" He tried to cut her off—too late.

"He told me, 'You're embarrassing a high officer of the United States.' Those are the exact words that he used! Jesus Christ, what kind of a man would say such a thing?"

"That's *enough!*" Tom shouted. He moved toward her but was looking back at his brother, in time to see a curdled grin creep up over his face.

"'*Me gusta caballeros.*' I like to ride men. I guess that wasn't so wrong after all." He turned on his heel, striding across the room, heading for the door.

"Charlie, what the hell—"

Charlie kept going, as if he hadn't heard him, hurriedly snatching up his overnight bag, then sliding back through the door to the car in the turnabout, and Beneficio, who moved obediently into the driver's seat.

"I thought you came here to bring her back!" Tom called after him.

"It's no use!" Charlie said brusquely. "All she's intent on is humiliating me. It was a mistake to come."

He looked around for his own bag, but Charlie was already climbing into the car, banging on the door for a confused Beneficio to start moving.

"Charlie—wait! Don't be a damned fool—" Slim called, running up after them in her bare feet, but he ignored her.

"I'm going back tonight. Slim can give you a ride tomorrow, or I'll send Benny here back with the car. I'm sorry, Tom—I just can't spend a night under the same roof where I've been insulted like that!"

Then the big Lincoln was gone, speeding down the serpentine cliff road they had just climbed up. Tom in shock watching it go.

"What was *that?*" he asked no one in particular, but Slim only shook her head and padded back to the front room, where by now the stars were beginning to appear over the perfect sea and the perfect beach, as if all the big white mansions along the cliffs had been fired up into the distant sky.

"It's this place. It makes him crazy," she said, shaking her head as she slipped another cigarette into her mouth and lifted a hefty silver lighter in the shape of an egg off the coffee table.

"What? How?" Tom asked distractedly.

She gave a half shrug.

"It's a young man's town, Tom—and he's old."

"Who's *Princeton?*" Tom asked, and she seemed to deflate then, letting herself fall back into the couch and looking out toward the darkness where the ocean had been. Even that movement she managed to make seem elegant and sexual, her body dropping weightlessly. He noticed that she already had something of a tan, a light browning over the past couple of days that made her skin glow all the more radiantly against her blond hair.

"Nobody," she said miserably. "Just a . . . *boy*. He's the son of one of the big hotel owners here, a friend of Melchior's—"

"Another member of the Big Crowd? And an Ivy Leaguer at that?"

"Well, that would account for why they call him Princeton, now, wouldn't it. You'd be surprised, Tom, they can read and write here, too, now, as well as in Ireland," she snapped at him, and he realized that what he was feeling was a twist of jealousy.

"And?"

"And what?"

"And is there anything between you?"

She stared at him so hard that he thought she might hurl the scotch glass at his head.

" 'Is there anything between you?' What are you now, my father confessor, Tom? Jesus Christ, have all the O'Kanes lost their brains on the same night?"

"I'm just saying—"

"I know what you're saying, and I don't care for it." She stood up and began pacing before him, furious now. "I told you, it's *over* between me and your brother. And you gave up any claiming rights a long time ago."

"All right—"

"Ah, Jesus, Tom!" she said, stopping in front of him and putting the palm of her cigarette hand to her head. "Ah, Jesus, but I messed up! I messed everything up."

He stood up then and went to her side. Taking her into his arms despite himself, despite everything that he'd told himself he wouldn't do. Rocking her gently there, while she cried and shook her head.

"I made a fool of myself. It's just that I couldn't stand it anymore. Did he tell you about how it was—back in Mexico City?"

"Just a little," he admitted. "He said there were complaints from the ex-pats—"

"Those old carrion eaters and their wives!" she said with a snort, pulling away from him and sitting down again to pull at her scotch and gesture vehemently with her cigarette. "Retired oil men and mining engineers, the red glint still in their eyes. Wanting to know what Charlie was doing to de-nationalize the oil companies. Just waiting for everything to blow up, so they could grab it all back again! You should've heard Charlie talk about them — but now *I'm* the one to blame for not wanting to spend my evenings with them!"

"You had your bullfighting afternoons —"

"Yes, did he complain about those, too?" she asked, her voice bitter. "Oh, he liked them well enough at the time! He used to love it when we walked to the Madrazos' box and the whole Plaza de Toros stood up and cheered him. He would bow to the crowd, hold up the matador's hat to them. He *loved* it, Tom, he *loved* it. You can't believe how many lies he tells. It's another one of his goddamned *fantasies.* Did he tell you about his dream of coming back to Ebbets Field and having all the *little people* cheer him?"

"No," Tom lied. "Now just tell me what happened."

He leaned down to hold her hand, and put an arm back around her shoulders, and she clung to it.

"I couldn't take it anymore, I told you. The only times I could stand were those bullfight luncheons in the fall, and nights with my music friends. We'd get back to the embassy late, after going to the cafés, and I would play the guitar with them, and sing a little. I know he didn't like that, either, but it was the only time I had to relax. At least I was home, right downstairs; he could've come down anytime he wanted, and I would've sung to *him*!"

"It's all right, Slim —"

"But it wasn't, don't you see that?" she said, looking up at him anxiously. "I had to do something, I had to get out, I was *trapped* there. The songs only made it worse, singing sad love ballads in my living room. I was still a young woman, Tom! Going around acting like I was *wrecked,* like I was wrecked just the same as he was —"

She put a hand to her mouth as soon as she said it, looking at him for forgiveness.

"I didn't mean it that way, Tom. I don't mean he's *wrecked,* or that he didn't get a bad rap —"

"I know, Slim, I know."

"But that's the way *he* acts, isn't it? Like he's goddamned Napoleon on goddamned Saint Helena! Like he's a church martyr — and I was supposed to do that with him! I wouldn't, Tom. I just *couldn't* anymore."

"I know you couldn't."

"I think I lost myself then, Tom. I have to admit, I really think I did. We started socializing all the time with those awful friends of his. You saw them. Second-rate crooks in a third-rate country. I lived in society all my life, Tom. I know what a social parasite looks like. I know what a crook is, too — I lived in New York.

"But I told myself I loved them. I told myself I was as crazy about them as Charlie was — Charlie O'Kane, still and evermore the Barefoot Boy from Bohola! Impressed by anyone who could flash some money and a little style in front of him —"

"Don't say that, Slim. It isn't fair."

"No, no, I suppose you're right, Tom." She sniffled, shaking her head. "I won't blame him for what I know better myself. I knew what they were, and I threw myself into it. God, it felt like such a relief after suffocating in that embassy! Just to be out and about, *doing* things! No more bridge nights with the mummies. No more evenings down in Cuernavaca, watching Henry Fink do his goddamned softshoe — did he really take you there?"

"He did," Tom conceded grudgingly.

"So you know what it was like. This was our *life*, Tom! I couldn't take it any longer. Even the Big Crowd would do, if that's all there was. And it was such an easy life, Tom. There was always a hotel suite available — always a mansion like this. No money necessary, no obligation. I got too deep into it, Tom. I got too deep, and I lost myself."

"Not from where I'm sitting, Slim."

"Ah, you don't know, Tom!" she said, writhing in his arms. "I started staying out here in Acapulco. I knew he wanted me back, Tom. I knew he needed me back. His term as ambassador was ending, and he'd just been up to testify in front of Kefauver, and I knew he was at low ebb — as low as I've ever seen him.

"But I couldn't go back. Instead I stayed here, even though he was calling me three, four times a day. He started ordering me to come back, pleading with me. Going on with that god*damned* silly stuff about how I was embarrassing *a high officer of the United States! Je*sus, have you ever heard anything so stupid? How the hell did I marry such a man?"

"Easy, now," Tom warned. "He wasn't himself —"

"Yes, yes, I know it," she said sadly. "And I wasn't myself by then."

"And there was this boy . . ."

"There was this boy," she said, her voice leavening as she thought of him. "And that's all he was, really, a boy. It was just a flirtation, really. *Princeton.* I was staying in his daddy's hotel. He was married already, and I knew that. I knew it couldn't last. But we'd be seen together. We started water-skiing together across the bay every morning, and people started to talk. It's quite a prudish little Catholic country still, for all its airs."

"Were you in love with him?" he asked quietly.

"No, nothing like that," she said, swiping a hand at the notion. "But I loved being with him. I loved the whole feeling of being free again, of being with a man who adored me."

"But you weren't free."

"I know that. But it felt so *good,* to be away from Charlie, and all that gloom. I was out there in the sun with him one afternoon, just lying about, talking and flirting, nothing more serious than that. When I came off the beach I just felt so good, so strong and radiant with the sun. My *flesh* just felt so good, you know how that is? And I came back into the hotel lobby feeling like I loved everything and everybody in the world, and there was his wife."

"Jesus—"

"She was furious, I could tell. But it was like I was drunk. I was feeling so good that I thought I could make anything right, and I went right up to her, smiling, and kissed her on the cheek, right there in the lobby. Just as a way to say, you know, *there's nothing very serious going on with your husband, I love you, too.* I kissed her right there, in front of about half of Acapulco—and then she exploded."

"Ah, Slim—"

"I know. It was a damned foolish thing to do, but it seemed so right at the moment. I kissed her, and I guess she thought I was patronizing her, and she made a scene. The next thing I knew it was all over the papers down here. Charlie managed to hush that up, all right, before it hit the States, anyway, but it was all over for me!" She laughed bitterly.

"It was the kiss that divided a country—both here in Acapulco, and back in Mexico City. Everybody was on his side or hers, but nobody was on mine. I was a marked woman."

"Jesus, Slim—"

"And all these hypocrites with their mistresses, and their back-door lovers!"

"Why don't you just get out?"

"I'd like to just get out, Tom. I'd love to get out, but I don't know where to go. Back to Charlie, and El Ranchito? Back to New York, where he's already queered it for us? Back to *you*, Tom?"

"You know that's not possible, Slim."

"Isn't it, Tom? Then you tell me what is."

"You know I'm trying to fix it. But he won't stand still. I can't get anything out of him —"

"But that's how he's always been, Tom. You know that. He's the most evasive man in the world, when he wants to be."

"But why, Slim? Doesn't he want to get out, too? Out of all of this?"

"What makes you think so, Tom?" she said, turning that same ironic smile on him again. "Has he ever said so?"

"Not exactly —"

"What makes you think he isn't perfectly contented to stay down here, flirting with all those Kansas City divorcées who come through El Ranchito, or the local talent Henry Fink provides? What makes you think he wants for one minute to give up playing the martyr down here — the wrongfully accused exile, the cuckolded husband — when he can get such beautiful sympathy for it?"

"But *why?*" Tom asked, almost pleading. "*Why* wouldn't he want to clear his name?"

"You saw how he was as mayor. There's something in Charlie that gets right up to the starting gate, but then he shies away. There's something that's almost great about the man, and that's what's worst —"

"Don't *say* things like that about him!"

"It's true, and you know it. It's like there's no foundation to him, he just crumbles in the end. He's not the man we want him to be. He's not the man we think he is. Surely, he's told that to you with his own lips. I know he's said it to me."

Tom slumped down on the floor, looking up at Slim in her chair, astonished.

"You know," he said, "I believe he has."

"Ah, Tom," she said, reaching out to put a hand under his chin. "You know, for a prosecutor you don't listen very well."

29

New York, 1949

When they got back from their honeymoon, Tom decided the only way to handle things was to contrive never to see her again, and to stick to it this time. It wasn't easy, putting off his brother so often, hearing the hurt and the puzzlement in Charlie's voice. Pleading always too much work, between the office and all the causes and what Charlie liked to call the fracases that he threw himself into.

Instead he followed them from afar—as afar as he could stand to get. She was in the press all the time by then. It was when she got *her* big cover, on *Life*. The Eisenstaedt Charlie would frame and hang on his wall in Mexico. Slim smiling adorably, sensuously, somehow, from under the brim of a Stetson some visiting delegation of Texas mayors had insisted she try on. Pulling it off even with the pearl necklace and earrings, and the stunning, black and white Jacques Fath dress she was wearing for a lawn reception at Gracie Mansion.

The headline inside proclaiming HOW SHE RUNS HER BRIDE'S HOUSE, with more pictures of her—in pearls and a hat—moving the furniture to make sure everyone got a chance to sit close to the mayor. Arranging flowers, opening the mail, looking over what seemed to be some kind of report. Gliding down the mansion stairs, past the oil paintings she had borrowed from the Metropolitan in a black Schiaparelli cocktail dress, her face beaming—laughing, it seemed, at herself, aware of what a grand joke this whole life was.

"Friends say O'Kane is thriving under new management!" The camera capturing the thrill of her up close, the boldness and warmth of her look, capturing it so well he had to put the magazine away.

He thought he might be safe when Charlie invited him to a weekday lunch in midtown. He knew from the papers that Slim had a fashion benefit that day at one of the big hotels, and so he decided to risk it. Meeting his brother on the curb in the Latin Quarter, Charlie all by himself for a change, without Neddy Moran or the big black official car. Tom hadn't seen him in person for months, and he was shocked by how tired and frail he looked—his face haggard, suit badly rumpled.

When Tom walked up to him, Charlie didn't have a word to say, as if he were too exhausted to do anything more than shake his hand and clap him softly on the back.

"It's no good, Charlie. You got to get out, get some relief," he told him as they strolled slowly uptown—Tom afraid to go any faster—but Charlie just shook his head.

"We all need relief," he said softly. "This whole city was neglected for four long years durin' the war, and now the bill's comin' due. The hospitals need x-ray machines, an' the piers are rotting, an' every time somebody flushes a toilet, it backs up into the North River."

Tom expected some joke or ironic remark, but instead Charlie just went on with his grim analysis, looking straight ahead.

"Any trouble you wanna name, we got it. We're chokin' to death on our own smoke, in case you haven't noticed, an' the subways're fallin' apart. The transit workers are threatenin' to go out, an' so are the teamsters, an' maybe the cabbies. We're still housin' people in Quonset huts, but I can't get the Bruckner Houses finished because the plumbers are havin' a dispute with the hod carriers."

"Charlie, you're just eatin' yourself up with this!"

"Never mind *four* years—this city's been left to wrack and ruin for a century. We're lookin' at a billion-dollar budget next year, but we're goin' broke. Why? 'Cause we're still payin' off the debt service from Boss Tweed's time. I mean it. The other day I came across an item in the budget, an' asked what the hell is that? It was the vig on some 1870 bonds, to build a plank road in the Bronx. I told Neddy Moran, I said, 'Jesus Christ, Neddy, you mean we still don't own the goddamned *Bronx?*'"

Tom was almost relieved by the passersby who recognized Charlie as they walked up Fifth Avenue—most of them friendly, smiling or shouting a greeting, shaking hands or tipping a hat. Tom saw that his brother took each acknowledgment like a tonic. His face reviving a little after every exchange, even playfully chasing off a boy in knee pants and a propeller cap on his head, who had the audacity to ask the mayor for a nickel after he shook his hand.

"Go on with ya, ya little beggar!"

The boy scampered away, laughing—with strangely familiar rectangles of silver glinting around his neck.

"What was that?" Tom asked.

"What was what?"

"What he was wearing. If I didn't know any better, I'd swear it was dog tags."

"Prob'ly is," Charlie confirmed. "They pass 'em out in school now. Orders of the Civil Defense. Along with teaching 'em how to duck under their desks to dodge the atomic bombs, an' run for the basement, and all the other nonsense that won't make a bit of difference when we're turned to ashes in the flick of an eye."

"But nobody else even *has* the bomb," Tom said, shaking his head as he watched the boy disappear up the avenue. "Do they?"

"They will. And when they do, we're first. Didn't you see the cover of *Collier's*? Big hole, right in the middle of Manhattan, with a mushroom cloud over it. 'Artist's rendering'—of our mass incineration! As if I didn't have enough to worry about."

"Jesus."

"Jesus is right," Charlie agreed. "You saw it for yourself as well as I did in Europe—better. And now we're ready for another round. What did the poet say? 'Mere anarchy is loosed upon the world.'"

"Surely it's not as bad as all that, Charlie."

"Look at them all!" Charlie said, ignoring him. "They have no idea what goes into keepin' this so nice for them."

They were standing now in the Plaza, next to the fountain, its waters spraying merrily onto the cobblestones. Across the street the park was in full, riotous bloom, streaked with swaths of yellow and pink and green. Mothers with young children were flocking to the zoo, past the glowering green statue of General Sherman and his horse. All around them, Tom noticed, were the towers of great hotels, and the windows of the most lavish department stores in the world. All his brother's dire talk felt more than a little unreal.

"I was a fool, Tommy," Charlie said abruptly, pushing a hand through his now thoroughly gray hair. "I didn't really know a goddamned thing about running this town. Everybody thinks he could be mayor, and I thought so, too. But I was no smarter than the rest of 'em."

Tom saw a glint of real fear in his eyes.

"Charlie—"

"Don't worry, I get over it. Any fool learns something in time, if he sits at his desk long enough." Charlie hooked his arm around Tom's. He led him across the street, then down the sidewalk along Central Park South. "C'mon— there's some people I want ya to meet."

"Who?"

But his brother was already pulling him into the Oak Room, in all its sullen splendor. There they paused, Tom blinking for a moment as his eyes adjusted to the dimmed, sinister light, all the overstuffed men in overstuffed chairs.

Then he saw it: a big round table in the far corner, where there sat the same clutch of men his brother had introduced him to at the Joe Ryan Association dinner before the war: Subway Sam Rosoff, and Frank Hague, and Bob Moses, and the ramrod-stiff banker George V. McLaughlin, and even O'Malley, the gladhanding lawyer George the Fifth had put to work counting peanuts for the Dodgers.

"But Charlie, it's *exactly the same!*" he cried, almost in despair. "What was the point of it all?"

"They're what I need to run this town," his brother told him. "And I need you, too, to keep 'em honest — to keep *me* honest. That's what I'm tryin' to tell you."

"Jesus, Charlie, what happened to *us* being in charge?"

"Just see what they have to say, will ya?" Charlie insisted, grasping Tom's elbow in both hands and heaving him physically across the dining room. "We live in a city of giants, Tommy. Why not take advantage of that?"

"If they're such giants, why do they act like such little putzes?"

But it was too late. The men around the table had already begun to stand as they approached, half a dozen hands reaching out at them.

"Frank, you know the brother," Charlie said. "I hope you don't mind I brought him along to your table today."

Hague gave a shake of his dour, deacon's head. When Tom reluctantly held out his hand, Hague merely blanched and nodded, then turned back to the sepulchral conversation he was having with Sam Rosoff. Tom felt a touch and turned to see the smiling face of Bill McCormack right next to his.

"So Charlie finally got you here," he said, his crystal-blue eyes twinkling as merrily as a those of a wolf with a cornered rabbit. "Though I'm thinking he had to all but kidnap you."

"That's a fair guess," Tom said, looking McCormack over. He seemed as robust and cheerful as he always did, his hair nearly white but still full.

"Well, I hope we can make it worth your while."

"You know, I was just tellin' my brother, this is almost the same crowd from the Joe Ryan dinner," Tom said to him, letting his gaze run around the table. "There's just one person missing."

"Who's that?"

"Why, Joe Ryan, of course."

"Oh."

McCormack, looking unfazed, turned back to his plate of lemon sole.

"Where d'ya think he might be?" Tom asked.

McCormack shrugged. "How should I know?" he said as he expertly flaked apart the fish.

"Think maybe he's at Toots Shor's, where you have lunch with him almost every day? Or is he meeting you there later?"

"Joe's an old friend. I listen to his troubles, try to give him what advice I can. God, I hate to have the fish if it's not Friday," he said evenly. "What I wouldn't give for a good piece a red meat! But doctor's orders."

"No, General, you don't understand!" Their conversation was steamrolled by Bob Moses lecturing Charlie loudly from across the table, his voice making heads turn throughout the Palm Court. Calling Charlie "General," as he always did, turning it into a condescension, the way that only Bob Moses could. "You might as well clear out *all* of Coney Island, now that we've got a start on it!"

Moses half stood as he talked, reaching out absently to grab up the butter dish, the salt and the pepper, spraying condiments randomly across his plate. He was well into middle age and mostly bald now, but he looked nearly as powerful as McCormack, Tom thought. He had dark eyebrows still, and dark, deep-set eyes. With its outsized nose and ears and the turned-down mouth, his face was as imperious and intimidating as a stone idol's.

"Look, General, there's no use holding on to any sentimentality about it! We already cut out the Gut, now it's time to do the rest. A bunch of carny stands and rotten bathhouses sweating the vodka out of dirty old Russian men! You take them 'em all out *now*, start building the public housing you *need* for this city. The banks, the contractors, the trade unions — they'll all back you. The people who'll live there will love you for giving them 'em a beach vacation every summer!"

"How will they like it in the winter?" Charlie asked with a small smile.

"Who cares?" Moses thundered, waving a hand dismissively. "In the winter, they can hole up inside with their new television sets. They want a beach in February, they can move to Florida!"

"Our Moses has the way to the promised land all mapped out," McCormack said quietly by Tom's elbow as more covering laughter rang out. "The original couldn'ta been any more officious."

"You sure it isn't a little more than advice? What you say to King Joe, I mean?" Tom persisted.

"Now, why would that be so?" McCormack asked, finally putting down his knife and fork and looking Tom in the face. His voice remained low, the cheerful grin still in place, but his eyes looked focused and hard, Tom saw, poised for the fray. "Who d'ya think I am to order anybody about? I'm just the president of Aetna Sand-and-Gravel —"

"And Penn Stevedoring. An Jersey Contracting, and McCormack Oil and Gas, and probably a dozen other enterprises nobody even suspects you have a finger in," Tom said. "In fact, unless I miss my guess, you're the mystery man they're talkin' about in the papers. The Mr. Big who runs the Port of New York."

McCormack said nothing, only continued to scrutinize him, when they were interrupted again, this time by the waiter coming to take his order. Tom pointed to something on the menu without half knowing what it was. When he looked back, he saw that McCormack's grin had returned, though it was about as warm and reliable as black ice over a gutter puddle.

"Stop pullin' my leg," he said, in a voice like flint. "You know as well as I do that no one man could run the Port of New York. There's over seven hundred piers out there, an' half the shipping in the world goin' in and out every day. Plus only about sixty, seventy thousand of the toughest sons a bitches you've ever seen, God love 'em. Anybody who could run all that, every day—run it the way the papers say it's run, with an iron fist? Why, that man would have to be bigger than the chairman of General Motors and the president of the United States, rolled into one. And all without anyone knowin' his name!"

"Maybe," Tom allowed. "But then how is it you were the one my brother called in when the tugboat men went out on strike?"

"I'm a good mediator, I won't deny that. I've told you, I know what the men want, I came up the same way."

"Everything the City needs to survive—turned on and off like a spigot. Then you're called in, and lo and behold, the strike's over with none of the men's demands met. And you end up with the new harbor committee, chosen to decide the whole future of the port."

McCormack returned to his fish, chuckling perfunctorily. "Comic-book stuff, son," he said. "No one man can run the port alone, just as no one man can run this city—much as Bob Moses over there would like to try. Besides, I spend most of my time up in Greenwich these days, leaving as much ·a the business as I can to Bill Junior. Anything I might tell Joe Ryan, I'm just tryin' to help."

"What about Cockeye Dunn? You just tryin' to help him, too?"

"What're you talkin' about?"

Just then the waiter returned to slide an overstuffed club sandwich onto the table before Tom, complete with little tasseled swords skewered through each of its quarters. He was pleased to let McCormack dangle as he pulled out a wooden saber and bit into one of the quarters.

"Cockeye Dunn," he said, when he had finished chewing. "He's in the Tombs right now, for puttin' five bullets into Andy Hintz in his apartment hall-way. You remember Cockeye—you were on the Joe Ryan dinner committees together—"

"I know Johnny Dunn," McCormack said impatiently. "He's a nasty little squirt, with some outsized ambitions. Runs a few piers below Fourteenth Street, but thinks he should have his own shipping company! Believe me, he's just more of the old head lice, like what your brother combed outta the Brooklyn docks."

"Is that so?" Tom asked coolly. "That why Hogan's people are goin' down to see him every day?"

"Wastin' their time!" McCormack scoffed.

"Really? All it takes is one man can make a difference, if he knows enough. Just look at what we had with Abe Reles," Tom said, looking directly at McCormack, wanting to see how he responded.

He'd seen the change when he went down to take a look at the pistol locals himself, over on the West Side, not long after McCormack had made his great drama of stopping the tugboat strike. There was an air, a feeling that reminded him of his days back in Brooklyn. The men restless again, unwilling to take it any longer. The docks themselves falling apart, more dangerous than ever. There was a brooding, a violence in the air everywhere he went.

"What're you sayin' now?" McCormack asked, looking back at him just as steadily.

"Just that it seems a lot like old times again. The men standing up to King Joe again," Tom said, returning to his sandwich. "The feds pressuring him to keep the docks open for the Marshall Plan shipments. Mike Johnson ripping the lid off his operations every day on the front page of the *Sun*—"

"Oh, I see. It's the power a the press we all have to worry about now. You *do* see too many movies, son."

"Sometimes all it takes is that one man—that one loose thread—to undo a whole enterprise," Tom told him. "Maybe you're right. Maybe it is beyond any one man to run the port anymore. I saw where there was another hiring boss shot in the street, up in Inwood—killed in broad daylight. Then there were King Joe's goons beatin' up those Negro longshoremen who tried to hold a sit-down strike in his office last week. Bashing their heads in with lead pipes, before they threw 'em down the stairs—"

"Ah, that's right, I forgot that you're a great friend to the colored man," McCormack said calmly.

"Don't they get to work, too?"

"Of *course* they do," McCormack told him, losing his temper a little at last. "Don't take me for one of those idjits who believes that one man is any different from another. Don't forget, Darwin was an Englishman. It's no coincidence all that nonsense started over there."

"But—"

"But you can't expect any man to give up what he's made for himself without a fight. Nobody gave me a thing in this world I didn't take for meself. It's the same for those fellas down there now. Your coloreds will have to fight their way in, just like all the rest of us."

"You mean the men you have working for you now? Most of the boy-os on your payroll are ex-cons with rap sheets as long as your arm. It's like you're runnin' the Sing Sing auxiliary down there."

"I believe that men deserve a second chance," McCormack said primly.

"A *second* chance?"

"A third an' a fourth, then—whatever it takes. Who am *I* to judge them?"

"No, that's left for whoever presides over their trials for murder, an' manslaughter. Meanwhile, you go on assembling yourself an army."

"Ask anyone down the docks—I'm always good for a touch. I look out for the men."

"Your generosity is legendary. But what you've got is a war down on your docks. It's in the papers every day, an' you have no idea how to control it just yet. *Do* you?"

"Haven't you heard? It's a new age. No one can be bossed anymore," McCormack sneered, refusing to take the bait.

"Laugh all you want. You're bein' squeezed from all sides now, and you know it. All it would take is one man talking. The right man. One you can't get to *this* time—"

"Look all around you, at this table here, and what do you see?" McCormack shook his head violently, his voice low and angry but proud. "*Workingmen.* This is the first great city in the history of the world run by the people, *and here we are.* Any problems there are on the docks, anywhere else—*we'll* settle it."

"Yes, I know—*subsidiarity.*"

"We know what the men want, an' what they need. We came up the hard way, same as they did. Better us than some reform contrivance, like a *port authority.*" He spat the words out as though they were an obscenity.

"Yes, you'll grant anything in the world as a privilege. But nothing as a right."

"Why don't you find out? What would *you* like as a privilege?" McCormack asked him suddenly. "Maybe some help with those relief packages you're tryin' to send over to the poor Jews in Palestine?"

Tom tried to think of what to say, his mind reeling.

"C'mon, don't be so surprised. You just accused me a bein' Mr. Big," McCormack scoffed. "You think I don't know what goes on down on any pier in this port?"

Tom hesitated, still unable to say anything, the air in the Oak Room feeling suddenly close and stuffy despite the vaulted, cathedral ceilings. Across the table, Bob Moses was still beating his brother about the head and shoulders with the future.

"You have to go at it with a *meat* cleaver, General! What's the City gonna be in ten years, twenty years, with the population explosion? *Big towers, surrounded by highways!* That's what you have to have! How else is anyone gonna get around? Where else are you gonna fit all these *goddamned people?*"

"What're you filling that freighter with you got down there?" Bill McCormack was speaking softly by Tom's elbow, beneath the blare of Moses's tirade. "Old K rations? Army surplus blankets?"

"Medicine. Penicillin—maybe an ambulance, if we can get it," Tom admitted.

He wasn't sure what he *was* doing, exactly. All he knew was the inclination. He'd started when he saw the war refugees Charlie had gotten into the country. Mostly Jews from Italy, freed from the camps there. Not quite as wretched as the survivors from the camps in Poland he'd seen on the newsreels, but still men and women who jumped and twitched at sudden sounds, their faces always harried and lined with a fear unto death that would never go away. Gentle people, many of them—middle-aged professionals and artists, seamstresses and clerks, set upon by thugs.

He'd helped settle them into the refugee camp up in Oswego—and there they had remained for more than a year, thanks to the regular denunciations of some southern congressman who wanted them sent back to wherever they had come from.

"For once in your life, haven't you wanted not just to *know* the right side, but to really *do* something about it?" McCormack was asking him.

"How do you mean?"

"I mean, why fool around with sendin' over blankets, an' canned shit-on-a-shingle? You think that's gonna win a war? You want 'em to win, get 'em what they really need. Guns. Grenades, bazookas. Maybe even tanks an' planes."

"You could provide that?" Tom asked—shamed even as he said it by the man's exactitude, his hardness and determination.

"For cost." McCormack shrugged. "Tell you the truth, I like the fight in those sheenies, too. They might be men to work with, someday. Just get me expenses, I'll provide everything—even the crews an' the dock."

"You'd do all that? And in return for what, precisely?"

Bill McCormack put his head back and laughed. "Why, as a favor, of course."

"What kind of favor?"

"Oh, I'm sure I can come up with somethin'," he said, grinning—leaning in toward Tom and showing him his hand, balled up in a fist. "C'mon. Haven't you ever wanted not to think about the consequences of everything, but just for once to know what you want, and reach out and . . . *take it?*"

And when he said it, Tom knew that he did.

30

Acapulco, 1953

He awakened into darkness, in the hour just before dawn. Not sure of where he was, lying in a strange bed, in a strange room, and able to think only, *This must've been what it was like for Reles.* The case slipping into his consciousness as soon as he was awake.

He groped his way to the bathroom in the cavernous house and was heading back to bed when he heard the voice that must have woken him in the first place. It was her, calling his name, softly but urgently, over and over: *"Tom. Tom."*

He moved in the direction of that voice, running his hands along the walls until he got his bearings. He turned another blind corner and there she was, the vision emerging from the darkness again, this time in a white nightgown.

"Tom," she said again, her eyes large and expectant, her mouth open. "There you are."

She wrapped her arms around him, and he held her tight and kissed her on the mouth. She clung to him, almost frantic to kiss him back, on his neck and cheeks and his closed eyes. He kissed her again, long and slow, then rubbed her arms as she shivered against him.

"Hold me. Hold me—"

"I will."

Trying to think of Ellie, or of his brother, or anything else in that moment. Just not the touch and the feel, and the smell of her.

"Hold me," Slim was saying again. "Just hold me." And he was going to break away but instead he was kissing her again, her leg sliding up and down his as they stood together in the dark room. She took him by the hand and led him into the open living room, where he'd sat the day before with Charlie. Guiding him over to the big picture window, where she stood expectantly, her hands braced against the sill. He kissed her neck, and she shuddered and leaned back into him, her eyes closed. He ran his hands over her breasts, then kissed his way to the edge of her jaw, and then her ear, and she moaned and rubbed back into him, and he felt for the straps of the thin white gown that was all she was wearing. He slid them slowly off her smooth, round shoulders, and she leaned her head back against his and let the gown fall, let it pool at her feet, leaving her naked before him.

Out the windows they could see the sun just beginning to come up over the crescent bay. The first edges of the night wearing away, and the inky purple of the sea emerging, and the ghostly white beach. She pushed herself back against him, sighing. He reached down and ran his hand along the roundness of her bottom, he ran it down over the softness of her slender, tapered back, and then he couldn't delay any longer and put his hands on her hips. He moved into her as they both grunted, and sighed, and she cried out, their heads against each other, as they made love while they watched the sun come up. And after they did, all he could think about was that morning on the roof at the Half Moon Hotel, and how bright and cold it was, and how his brother turned and watched the gulls wheeling over the beach.

He woke up again on the floor, her limbs clutched around his, the early-morning sun very warm now on their bodies. She had half pulled the gown up over her, but mostly she was still naked—just as he remembered, her body as sleek and trim and smooth. One hand pulled up against her cheek as she slept with a frowning, childlike concentration. Ellie slept much the same way, he thought then — a dreadful feeling in his gut when he could, at last, think of her. Not one of shock, or guilt, or shame so much, because he had known that he was bound to do this since the moment he'd first seen Slim again, from the moment he stepped down off the plane. The feeling more of a long, wearying disgust with himself — something, he realized then, that he had been carrying around for years.

"I'm sorry," she murmured as she woke up, one hand so delicately, adorably pushing back a dirty-blond bang that he had to look away. "I'm sorry, I'm sorry, I know I messed everything up again."

"Stop it. You didn't."

"I'm sorry, I'm sorry," she groaned, falling over on her back, and despite himself he looked lovingly at the fall of her breasts, at her sex.

"Slim, *you* didn't mess anything up. I'm a grown man."

"Not so much," she said. "Not so much either you or your brother. You're really a couple of boys, still, going around the world having adventures."

More adventures.

He pulled himself up to a sitting position, and it was her turn to stare admiringly at his fit, athletic body. She snuggled in next to him, her head against his stomach.

"Oh, but give me a young man's body!" she said, and sighed.

"That's enough!" he said, moving away from her, angry now, and pulling his boxers back on after searching desperately for them along the floor for a few humiliating seconds.

"What, do you think that's some kind of betrayal of him? After what we just did? After what we did all those afternoons?"

"Why d'ya think he left like that?" Tom asked, ignoring her question.

"Why? Because he was hurt — just like a little boy," she said, lifting herself to her feet and sliding her negligee back on in a series of motions that excited him almost as much as when she'd pulled it off. "Because he understood that I'm never going back to him."

"We were the ones who did this to him. It was our fault — what happened to him."

"What *happened* to him?"

"What he became, how he got into this mess."

She gave a throaty laugh — one of the kind that used to drive him wild when they were alone together.

"Have you ever noticed that people are always doing things *to* Charlie?" she asked him. "Has it ever occurred to you that maybe — sometimes — he does them to himself?"

She pleaded with him to go down to the beach with her that morning. He didn't want to go, asking her how would it look if it got back in the papers in New York, investigating assistant DA out on the beach in Acapulco. But she only gave him one of her tight, brittle smiles — something else he remembered.

"What's next, Tom? You're going to tell me you're a high officer of the United States?"

"It could cost us everything, Slim. It could cost *him* everything, if what I'm doing here gets compromised."

Her face fell then, and she looked suddenly vulnerable and sad.

"Please, Tom. Just help me show the flag. You don't know what it's like, going out there every morning. Now that they all hate me."

"Then why don't you stay up here?" he asked, but he knew he was going to go.

He knew that he couldn't deny her anything, at least not for that morning. She made a phone call, and there was a car, and a chauffeur, and after he'd taken a shower he found that there was a big picnic basket, and a bucket holding a good white wine on ice. She looked as perfect as ever in a simple white one-piece Catalina suit that plunged daringly between her small, comely breasts. There was even a robe and a pair of silky blue trunks for him.

"Whose are those?" he asked, though he knew he didn't really want to hear the answer. "Melchior's? Or Princeton's?"

"I don't know," she said, looking at him coolly over her sunglasses before she turned to go out to the car. "Maybe they're your brother's."

They drove down out of the hills of Indian laurel and past the scythe of beach where all the building cranes were gathered. It was early yet, but he could see it already filling up with tourists — many of them of the El Ranchito variety, he noticed, middle-aged widows and divorcées from the States, noses smeared with sun cream, making their way down to stand in the water.

They kept going, through the Old Town and out onto a peninsula. Past La Quebrada, the rocky little mountain, where he could already see the famous cliff divers performing for the tourists. Flat-stomached, dark-haired young men, who crossed themselves, then spread their arms and dived like fishing birds into the rocky shoals 150 feet below. They turned away with the road, headed out toward a cove and a beach that was half empty and devoid of the cream-smeared Americans. Here there were cranes, too, but only one hotel of stacked white layers, the people scattered loosely across the sand.

"Look around. This is the Big Crowd's private preserve," she told him. "At least until the tourists find it."

She strode out on the sand like a princess, gazing straight ahead through her sunglasses, her pretty, slender shoulders flung back. They settled into a couple of lounge chairs under a matching striped umbrella right in the middle of the beach. It felt to him like a challenge — the glass and pastel mansions along the cliffs staring down like so many empty eyes.

"That white lump is John Wayne's. His wife is an actress down here," she said, ostentatiously pointing out the homes of the stars along the hills.

"John Wayne has a Mexican wife?"

"He has nothing but. The purple monstrosity out there on the Quebrada? Just past the divers? It belongs to Dolores del Rio, of course."

"How about that one?"

She sighed and gave him another faint, sad smile. "That's Merle Oberon's place, the bitch. I'm afraid I made a scandal of myself there, too."

"How?"

"Oh, she had this idiotic rule! No one could go barefoot on the stupid marble floors she had put in. So, I refused to go in, just walked all around the edge of her house. Well, I mean really! She expects us to accept that bare feet are going to ruin her new marble?"

He peered back to try to see the hard-bellied brown figures diving like birds off La Quebrada — devoutly wishing he could join them. Ahead of them lay a shallow bay and a verdant, hilly little island, wooden fishing boats plying their way around it. Somewhere behind them he could hear the steady gurgle and crank of construction machinery.

"In a few years this will all be gone, too," she said, without looking, her voice plaintive. "Just like the Centro back in Mexico City. Just like Manhattan, with all those horrid slab-and-glass buildings."

"If you hate it so, why d'ya stay?" he said, irritated with her now, angry with himself.

"I just need to show them," she said. Her voice much smaller, pleading—nothing like that of the defiant woman back in the dining room of the Del Prado. "Please, Tom. Just stay with me, so we can show them. That they can see I'm here with my husband's brother, and I'm not some abandoned woman."

"There's no one watching you, Slim," he said without much conviction. One look told him otherwise. All up and down the sands, the well-appointed necks of the other sunbathers swiveled away when he stared back at them, eyes turned as rigidly to the dark blue sea as Slim's were.

Most of them were women. But there was suddenly a steady relay of men needing to take a dip. Running slowly past them to the sea and back, their hairy chests tanned to a deep red-brown, gold medallions and bracelets glinting in the sun as they jogged by, sneaking in a quick glance and a smirk.

"Do you *see?*" she whispered.

Just then a sweet-looking little girl, no more than nine or ten, ran up to them, a shy grin on her face, hands held up to her mouth. She performed a little curtsy in the white beach shift she wore over her bathing suit, while Slim stood up to greet her.

"Why, hello, darling," she said, smiling radiantly at the child, touching her barely tanned cheek. "To what do we owe the pleasure?"

"I just wanted to know," she said in almost flawless English, "do you really fight bulls."

Slim swung her head up quickly, though her smile never faded. Spotting immediately, Tom knew, the grinning, leering faces all around them, especially the women who had put the child up to it. She still didn't lose her smile, looking back down at the girl, who had begun to giggle now, taking a step or two backward as if she knew she had done something naughty.

"Why, no, darling," Slim said in a loud voice, looking slowly all around her. "I don't really fight *bulls*. Just cows."

The child skittered away, looking perplexed. There was a laugh or two from along the beach, the leering faces turning cold and looking away.

"Satisfied?" he asked her.

"I know. It's silly. But that's what I'm left with," she said, turning to lie back in her beach chair, looking out toward the bay. "To hell with them. To hell with them all. That's the way it was with us, once. Remember, Tommy?"

"Yes. I remember," he said, his voice flat.

"We couldn't leave each other alone."

"No, we couldn't."

"Even though we knew it was wrong." She took off her dark glasses and smiled bitterly at him. "Imagine that. Being so gone for each other you do something even though you know it's wrong."

She was right — they hadn't been able to stop once they were both back in the City. He kept telling himself that what they had done was an anomaly, some crazy accident of their time together. A product of her confusion before the wedding, of their sojourn in another, unreal place. More *adventures,* foul and squalid and anonymous enough to last a lifetime — never to be repeated.

But they were. Two days after he had lunch with Charlie and his friends at the Plaza, he called her, when he knew she would be alone. After that, neither one of them tried to call it off, and he never remembered truly wanting to, no matter what they told each other afterward, between the sheets of borrowed beds. Each in turn breaking down and picking up the telephone. Their relationship only making it easier. Calling her one day when he thought his brother was out at a Board of Estimate meeting — only to hear his baritone in the background asking her who it was. He nearly panicked and hung up. Listening, instead, to her cool voice, as she told him: "Yes, it's your brother. Yes, he's right here. Do you mind if I say hello first?"

Murmuring, then, in the sexiest voice he could imagine, an address they had used before.

How she could lie. How they both could.

The logistics of adultery came easily enough to them, as he imagined it generally did. That was what made it such a desirable game. They usually met in mid-afternoon, the hour of choice for adulterers. She mostly took charge of it, arranging to meet where she was doing her shopping, or in a friend's apartment. But she left it to him just enough that he had to be an active participant, figuring out where to find rooms in what had been first-rate hotels, just fallen from grace. Sometimes they might go all the way out to the house in Bay Ridge, where they were sure to be alone and unquestioned, but he didn't like it there. Too many ghosts — of Claire, and Jimmy, but also the ghosts of himself, and even her, the people they had been just a few months before. The shades of them all together, such as they were, their makeshift little family around the summer Sunday dinner table, talking and laughing at once.

"How is it with him?" he asked her out there early one evening, just as the change from the day was coming on, the legions of men and women who worked by a clock just beginning to climb out of the hot, grimy subway. Listening to their footsteps and their voices on the sidewalk. The two of them still lounging on the bed, having made love for half an hour. *The way one could forget oneself in this city.*

"How *is* he? What kind of a question is that?" she said, with real scorn in her voice.

"I miss him. I worry about him," he told her. "I know he could use me, but we don't see eye to eye so much anymore, and I don't want to be a burden to him."

"No, this is much better," she said. "Jesus, do I look like your confessor?"

"I worry about the people he has around him. I want you to help me look out for him, that's all —"

"Oh, Christ!" She felt about for her bag by the side of the bed and the tossed-over bedclothes, until she finally managed to produce a cigarette and a small, cunning red and black lighter.

"I thought it would be glamorous — first lady of the City. But you don't have any idea what it's like to deal with those men as a woman," she told him, shuddering. "All those awful old pols, with their baggy suits, and their bad breath, and their body odor. They love nothing better than to push in close to you and put their hand on your knee. Every time we entertain, I want to sneak upstairs and take a shower."

After two or three flicks she got the cigarette to catch, took a deep draw, then tossed her long blond hair behind her and looked at him balefully.

"On Sundays, we take a promenade about the mansion grounds," she said, her voice brittle and sardonic. "He likes us to walk around and talk with anyone there in the park, on the other side of the fence. There's a very Old World feel to it all. All we need is a goddamned gazebo."

"Slim—"

"If I'm not around, if I manage to find *something else to do*," she said significantly, "he sits out there in his shirtsleeves anyway, and spends the whole afternoon talking with whoever will listen to him. Like he's a retired suit salesman in Pompano Beach."

"And how about you? Do you really arrange the flowers in your pearls? Answer the mail in a hat? And what *was* that report?"

"Go to hell."

Tom regretting the words even as he said them. He had come to enjoy her company by then—enjoying her as a person, as well as something he had to have. Her quick wit, the way she loved a joke in turn, and the layer of old sadness just beneath it all. Knowing it was going to hurt all the more to give her up, as he would have to give her up—and wanting to hurt her for it in kind.

"Just seems to me there's a whole lot of acting going on up there."

She fixed him with her all-business look. "And you want to play director, then?"

"Damnit, Slim, he's scared," he said, relenting.

"I know it, Tommy," she said, leaning over toward him, her voice sincere and urgent now. "And what do you think I am? I can see the way he tosses and turns in bed at night. He hits the Bromo Seltzer like it's scotch. But I don't know what to do about it."

"We need to get him some help."

"We need to get him to quit," she snapped. "I see the sort of help he has. He has too much of it already."

"I know what you mean."

He was too busy then, taking what he wanted. Letting Bill McCormack pile a dock full of munitions for him. Amazed at how easy it was to come by, and to conceal, in the shed on just one of the countless piers lined up one after another along the North River. Still not sure if he was doing it because he believed in the cause of a Jewish Palestine, or if he was, as McCormack knew, just tired of picket lines and protests and talks in dusty halls, and wanted for once to see something *done*.

The loading was to take place on a moonless spring night. He went down to the Chelsea docks with Natie Cohen and some ten or twelve large, taciturn men Natie had found to bring along. Dressed like movie seamen in high-collared sweaters and caps, their leaders introduced only as "a Mr. Samuels and a Mr. Weintraub." There were bulges on the belts under their sweaters, and Tom almost laughed.

"This isn't going to be a shoot-out," he said, "no matter what you may have heard."

"In case we are interfered with," the one called Mr. Weintraub said, shrugging, his face so serious that Tom, almost unable to believe this was even taking place, decided to let it pass.

The tramp freighter was already tied at the dock, just as McCormack promised it would be. Tom was appalled once again by how much the docks had physically deteriorated, the wharves cratered and crumbling, the machinery rusted and old—much of it a death trap, to the unlucky crew, he thought. *What is on going on here?*

But the cargo waiting, just as McCormack had promised. Long wooden boxes of rifles and crates of grenades, and ammunition. True to his word, he'd even procured an entire, disassembled tank, and the parts of five planes. There were three veteran crews of longshoremen on hand, who set to their task at once with furious, skillful energy. Natie Cohen's recruits left as extraneous as Tom always had been in the presence of such men, reduced to holding the flashlights as they supervised the loading. Tom wondering how many of them had worked a full shift already that day, and what time they'd have to be back for the shape-up.

At the head of the pier a dazzling burst of white light opened up, illuminating everything, and all but blinding them. Natie Cohen's men ducked into the pier shed, Mr. Samuels and Mr. Weintraub scrambling for the weapons under their sweaters. Some of the others cracking open a box of the rifles in desperation and swearing at the sight of them — encased in grease with the bolts removed.

Tom crouched and peered down toward the end of the dock, shielding his eyes with his hand. Cursing softly to himself — wondering if it would be best for his brother if he were to jump into the dangerous, dirty black water, thick with old hawsers and anchor chains, and the drifting iron hulls, and try to swim for it.

"Ahoy down there!" came a familiar voice.

Bill McCormack strolled up the dock, hands in his pockets, wearing a fedora and a fine alpaca coat against the night chill, an even wider grin than usual on his face. Behind him, Tom could just make out a gaggle of hard-looking men clustered around the trucks the klieg lights were set on. Strolling up the dock as well was a phalanx of uniformed cops, nightsticks in hand.

The whole scene reminding him of something: the night his brother raided the Camarda locals over in Brooklyn. The men and women roused out of their homes around the docks, staring vacantly into the cold white light, trusting none of it. Only now he was on the other end of the farce.

"Just wanted to see how you're gettin' on," McCormack called out, nodding to the men on the crews as magnanimously as a king acknowledging his gardeners.

They had halted when they saw him, faces wary behind their burdens, but now they went back to filling the hold. The cops leering at Tom and the others out of the darkness behind McCormack, tapping their clubs on the pier as if they'd have loved to wade on in and start breaking heads. Tom's mind racing as he tried to steel himself for whatever might come now.

"Fine night for loadin' a ship, i'n't it?" McCormack asked, halting a few feet from Tom and Natie. "Don't let us obstruct ya. Your brother just wanted to make sure you had some proper protection, that's all. I've heard it can get very dangerous of late, down on the waterfront."

"We're obliged to you," Natie said drily. "For everything."

"That you are. But it's all right. I'm always happy to see the furtherance of a good cause — no matter the legal technicalities."

"Just taking what we pleased," Tom said.

McCormack nodded but stayed where he was, content to keep his show of force before them. Tom looked again at the hard-faced men he'd brought with him. They didn't much resemble the well-dressed mob *shlammers* from back on the docks in Brooklyn. Instead they looked like real longshoremen, in their old checkered jackets and dungarees and caps and the thick, blocky shoes of the piers. More of McCormack's ex-cons, no doubt, paroled from upriver—a less controlled, more desperate bunch. If he gave the word, the cops would stand aside, or maybe join in with them. The loading crews would run for cover as soon as it started, he knew, leaving only him, and Natie, and Natie's Jewish navy.

"It's just the currency of exchange down here," McCormack said, still smiling, as he came forward and took Tom by the arm, and walked him a few more yards down the pier.

"What do you want?" Tom asked him directly, his jaw set hard in the darkness, hoping McCormack couldn't see the trepidation in his eyes. Berating himself for his terrible foolishness.

"Only a favor, like I said."

"What's that?" Tom braced himself.

"For you to go an' have a little talk with your old friends. Those meddlesome priests down at Saint Francis Xavier's—"

"About what?"

"I think you know *that*, son," McCormack said, his voice menacing and hard, as he had never heard it before. "About how we might come to an understanding concernin' the difficulties the port is now enduring. Perhaps the question of a donation to the labor school they're running there, or the widows' and orphans' fund—"

"Did I hear you right, Bill? You're tryin' to buy off the church?"

"Don't be an ass," McCormack snapped. "I'm just a Catholic businessman, trying to do what's right by everybody."

"God himself couldn't do any more."

"What's that now?"

"Never mind," Tom told him, looking at the mob of men waiting at the end of the pier, their faces feral and expectant. Making the decision he had to—tempted though he was, in one crazy moment, to call the man's bluff.

"I'll go talk to the priests. I'll tell them Mr. Big wants to make a deal."

"You do that, son," McCormack said, his voice softer, a spectral grin spreading briefly across his face. "You'll see—it'll be what's best for you, it'll be what's best for your brother."

"Thanks for the opportunity," Tom said, and meant it—though McCormack, already walking back down the pier, turned and looked at him over his shoulder, head cocked to pick up any note of sarcasm.

"I'll leave you the lights," he said instead as he walked off, the police and his goons falling in behind him. Tom knowing that he meant the offer as a further show of his strength. To let them see he could have a ship loaded with contraband weapons in light as bright as day, in the middle of New York Harbor, and no one would dare say a thing. "It'll help with the loading. I believe in safety first, as you know!"

He stopped once more before he got to the end of the pier, to go over to the loading crews and hand out ten-dollar bills to each of the men. Tom watched as they lined up to take them—their faces wary, suspicious, each of them nodding in acknowledgment before going back to his task.

Later that night, when at last he got back to his basement apartment in the Village, all he wanted to do was call her up. Knowing it was impossible, but just wanting to hear her voice on the other end of the line, sultry with sleep, knowing who it would be. Instead he poured himself a couple of fingers of Black Bush and lit the stove. Sitting before its open door, trying to get warm, and thinking over everything that had happened that night—the whole of it like a dream to him now in the growing warmth and the whiskey fumes of his kitchen.

Which was when his phone rang.

New York, 1949

He awakened just before dawn. Not sure exactly where he was at first, or who was with him. Hearing only the voice repeating his name over and over again, attached to a question: "Are you O'Kane? Are you the mayor? Are you O'Kane?"

The two questions together exasperating him. Causing him to shake his head while still in his sleep, wanting to call out in his confusion, *No, of course I'm not the mayor, I am O'Kane.* The fog clearing only after yet another and another repetition of the question: "Are you O'Kane? Are you the mayor?"

Coming fully awake to find himself to his immense surprise in his pajamas, in the mayor's bedroom at Gracie Mansion after all. Still wondering, *How the hell did I get here?*

There was a young man seated on the edge of his bed, looking down at him, and for another confused moment he thought it must be Tommy, though he looked nothing like his brother, was younger than he'd been even when he first came over. There was no sign of Slim anywhere, but for some reason he didn't quite understand himself, he wasn't surprised, worrying for the moment only about what the young man at his bedside might have done to poor Joe.

"Are you *Mayor O'Kane?*"

The pallid youth's question insistent, almost demanding now. He wore a pair of glasses, and a gray and black sweater with a zipper, and the dungarees that the teenagers had, and that even Slim liked to wear around the house sometimes. *A sexless, functional, utilitarian garment,* he thought, *like something they'd have in Red China . . .*

"No, I'm not O'Kane. But I'll take you to him," he said evenly to the boy, sneaking glances at him to see if he seemed psychotic, or was carrying any kind of weapon, while he got his robe on. Trying to think what might have happened to Slim as he calmly led the young man out of his bedroom and down the second-floor corridor. In the dark, he nearly tripped over some used rags and buckets of varnish and cleaner the workmen had left in the hall, the boy wrinkling up his face as they passed it.

"How do you sleep here with that *smell?*" the boy asked.

"An occupational hazard, I'm afraid. They always have to polish up the mayors, they get tarnished so easily," he said, looking up at the portraits of all his predecessors lining the walls. *La Guardia, the little punk,* shining the brightest of all, the rest of them fading slowly into nearly unfathomable darkness as they receded into colonial times.

It was another project of Slim's — part of her makeover of Gracie Mansion that the newspapers were so interested in. They passed a bigger painting, an elegant Claude Lorrain seascape that she'd persuaded the Met to send over — a view of an old harbor at dusk that he always found very restful. There was a pastoral of some cows munching grass by a pond, and a nice portrait of a middle-aged O'Connell by the head of the stairs, the Liberator looking strong and vibrant, and in command — everything he wished he himself still was.

He led the young man down through the living room, where he promptly bumped into the rearranged furniture, as he did most nights. Slim had insisted upon it, telling him — and the press — *Everyone wants to sit near the mayor.* It was true, his visitors always seemed pleased to find themselves so close. It was just he who couldn't stand it, as they closed in upon him.

They went into the staff kitchen, where Charlie gestured for the lad to sit in one of the Formica chairs around the small matching table and started to make some coffee. He pointed to one of the cabinets.

"Would ya get the milk an' sugar, please?"

"What about the mayor?" the boy asked, suspicious, sitting where he was.

"We can't very well wake 'im without taking his morning coffee to him, can we?" he asked, and the young man nodded, seeming to accept the logic of that, and got up to search through the cabinet.

When he turned his back, Charlie peered out the window at the guard booth. There he could see Joe Previtel, his special police adjutant, leaning back in his chair, his feet propped up and his head leaning back against the booth, mouth wide open.

Could be sleeping, could have his throat cut, he thought, trying to give Joe the benefit of the doubt. He pressed the button the size of a small doorbell just below the coffee percolator, and watched as Previtel bolted up, nearly cracking his spine. Charlie nodded grimly, his best guess confirmed, and went to sit down across from the boy while the coffee gurgled.

"Tell me, what did you want to talk to the mayor about, anyway?" he asked him.

"Juvenile delinquency," the young man answered forthrightly. "I want to discuss juvenile delinquency with him."

"Why? Are you afraid of juvenile delinquents?"

"No," the boy said, seeming to consider the question gravely. "But sometimes I wonder if I might *be* one."

"*You?* Banish the thought! Tell me, would a juvenile delinquent have the resourcefulness to break in to the mayor's mansion?"

The boy shrugged. "I just climbed the fence out there," he said, a little proudly.

"It's six feet high, an' made of pointed iron."

"It was easy enough. I've been here for hours already, wandering around the lawn, an' inside. I couldn't find the mayor's bedroom anywhere, though."

"Don't sell yourself short."

At that moment, a squad of cops led by Joe Previtel came barreling through the kitchen door, knocking it flat off its hinges. They paused for a moment, blinking at the two of them, then threw themselves on the boy, shoving him to the ground, beating him with their nightsticks in the ribs and along the side of his head, twisting his arms behind his back until he yowled in pain.

"Stop now!" Charlie snapped, yanking one of the cops off him. "You already put my door down for the count."

"Jesus, Your Honor, I thought he'd snuffed ya for sure," Previtel huffed, his broad face glowing red and his chest heaving.

"Funny, I feared the same for you. But fortunately, the both of us were only asleep."

He helped the boy back up to his chair. He was crying now and trying not to, sniffling and taking deep, frightened breaths of air. Closer up, Charlie could see that his face was blotched with pimples like small volcanoes. *Such an unpromising boy, in every way,* he thought regretfully. *How quickly our paths are set for us.*

"Take a breath, son," he said, not unkindly, going to fetch the coffee, which was ready now. He poured the boy some and got out more cups for the cops, who sat or leaned around the table and the cabinets.

"Press'll be here any minute. You know how Arthur is with that radio," Previtel warned.

"Yes, well, I'm afraid it'll be much less dramatic than his usual murders — at least now that we know you're alive, Joe," Charlie snapped. "Take a sip, boy — not too much at first, you don't want to burn your mouth. Thaaat's it."

The boy drank tentatively, seeming to feel better and better able to control himself. Charlie smiled at him.

Slim — where is she?

"Now, boy-o, tell me if you encountered anyone else on your rambles around this fine home and grounds?"

The boy blinked at him, shook his head, and took another sip of the coffee.

"You're sure now? Nobody at all? Not a very beautiful lady, say, one who looks like the faerie queen?"

He shook his head again. "No, sir." He looked closer at Charlie. "Say, are *you* the mayor?"

"Bright boy! Figured that out all on yer own, did ya?"

"Why'd ya lie to me?"

"Because that's what I do for a living, son."

Slim, where is Slim?

He looked up at Previtel and the rest of the cops.

"Joe, the rest of you, I want you to go through the whole place. Inside, outside, even check the basement and the attic. Make sure that Mrs. O'Kane isn't here."

"Yes, Boss!" Previtel said, looking slightly embarrassed.

"What is it, Joe? Did you see her come in last night? Speak up, there's no terrible scandal here. You know as well as I do she likes to break the dawn with her café society pals."

"Yes, sir," he said. "That is, no, I don't think she *did* come in last night . . ."

The sense of alarm heightened in Charlie again, threatening to blow the roof off his head.

"No? But then she would've had to enter through a dream, wouldn't she?"

"I . . . I really don't know, sir. She might've come in very late —"

"Never mind. All the more reason to search the house and grounds. Whattaya doin' with this one here?"

"Off to Bellevue, I think, for a little observation," one of the cops said, lifting the boy out of his seat by his belt. The young man looked as if he were about to start bawling again.

"You're takin' me to the *nuthouse? Where all the maniacs are?*" he asked in terror.

"Hush, hush now. It's nothing so bad. This is a separate ward for juveniles who aren't yet delinquents," Charlie said, trying to reassure him. "You'll be outta there in no time. Just give the nice policeman your phone number here, so he can call your poor mother."

Looking up to the big cop, already manhandling him to the door, Charlie made a cutting expression at his throat. "I don't want him bein' roughed up anymore, he's just a kid. You hear me? Joe can stand the embarrassment. He's earned it."

At that very moment a gnomish little man with a huge camera appeared at the door, like an apparition from a gory German fairy tale. He held a long cigar in the corner of his mouth, seemed to have nicotine inscribed deep in each and every fold of his aged skin, and wore a raincoat that looked as though it had just been caught in a scrimmage. He immediately snapped a blinding flash, catching perfectly the whole story of the terrified boy, the menacing cop, the mayor making his slashing motion.

"Good mornin' to you, too, Arthur," Charlie told him, motioning toward the table. "Would you like a coffee?"

"Big story here? Mayor catches major crime boss?" the photographer cracked without removing his cigar. He waddled over to the table and indiscriminately picked up the first used coffee cup he saw, drinking its contents down.

"A little light on the bourbon, Chief," he chastised Charlie.

"Sorry, Arthur. And I'm afraid there's not much of a scoop here — any chance we could keep the poor boy's picture out of the paper? Spare his parents, and his future prospects?" Charlie asked, but Arthur only looked at him as if it were he the police were carting off to Bellevue.

"Forgive me, I guess I'm not fully awake yet," he told the photographer, and walked out onto the lawn in his robe and his slippers, anxious to avoid any further questions from the little man. He walked over toward the fence and stood there, looking out across the river, while he tried to ignore the police rummaging through the house behind him, and searching the magnolia bushes for the most famous model in New York.

Where was his wife?

He turned back — and saw her coming across the lawn toward him like a furtive Cinderella slipping in from the ball. She was walking barefoot in the wet morning grass, holding her heels in one hand. She had on the same midnight-blue designer gown she had worn out the night before, one more glorious concoction of lace and sequins and ruffles. She had no makeup on anymore, and her blond hair fell loose around her shoulders, looking delectably tousled, but he didn't think she had ever looked quite so beautiful.

She looked up and spotted him. Smiling instantly and making her way toward him without breaking stride.

"What's with the Easter egg hunt?" she asked, looking around at the cops on their hands and knees in the shrubbery.

"We had an intruder," he told her casually, kissing the cheek and the neck she offered. Smelling her usual smell, her perfume, the delicious scent of her young skin. *But something else as well, maybe — something familiar but unplaceable.*

"My God!" she said, her mouth dropping open, putting her arm through his to draw him closer. "Are you all right?"

"With a crack police guard like mine?" he told her, smiling and looking into her eyes. "I was just worried when you weren't back."

"Oh, it was only the usual nonsense," she said in slightly too quick a rush of words, while trying to restrain a yawn. "The dinner went on forever, and then afterward Ann and Billy insisted we all go down to the Village and hear some Dixieland. I think they just wanted a better venue for their fight."

"Just as well, then," he said, unable to keep the sadness from creeping into his voice.

"Yes, just as well."

Still arm in arm, they turned back to the view of the river. It was just beginning to come alive, its long barges and scows pushing their way south against the current.

"Y'know, it's a shame Clairey never liked this place better," he said. "I think she would've enjoyed being the lady of the manor, if she'd been well."

He himself had loved so much to stand out on the back lawn in the evening and watch the end of day. Staring at the gleaming white Triborough, and Hell Gate bridge in the distance. Enjoying the way the ships' lights twinkled in the dusk, the red and blue streaks across the sky. Indulging the furtive fantasy that he had never shared with anyone else, not even with her. That he was the poor boy who had risen not to the people's mansion but to the manor house. She nuzzled closer to him, and he felt lightheaded.

"I'm sure she would have," she said in a low voice. "I know I do."

"Y'see that bay there?" he said, pointing to a strip of desolate, industrial waterfront. "That's Pot Cove, over in Astoria, where they used to smuggle the fugitive slaves to freedom."

"Why did they have to hide them? They were already in the North," she asked, indulging him, he knew, her head still on his shoulder.

"Because that was the big political compromise of that day. They passed the Fugitive Slave Act to keep the Union together. Because, you know, it was very important to keep together a country that still believed in dragging innocent men and women halfway across the world an' sellin' 'em into bondage."

She looked up at him oddly.

"Are you sure you're feeling all right? Your face looks awfully flushed," she said.

"I'm fine," he told her, turning away from the fence to face her. "How was the benefit?"

"Oh, it was the usual bore, put on for the unusually boring," she told him, though he knew she didn't mean a word of it, thrilled as she was for any chance to appear again before an audience.

"And did you sparkle, an' give them all a thrill, the way you always do? The way you did for me?"

"Stop it! You'll make me blush in front of the NYPD!" she protested, smiling. "How did he get in?"

"Why don't you tell me?"

"What?"

"Sorry—who?"

"The intruder, of course! Charlie?"

He realized that she'd had to repeat herself, his mind drifting somewhere.

"Sorry. Seems he jumped the fence. Wanted to talk with me about . . . juvenile . . . " He fumbled, the conversation receding all of a sudden in his mind, distracted by how it could be that someone had placed an enormous stone on his chest, forcing him down.

"We were lucky, then," she said, looking up at him sharply, her eyes wondering.

"Yes, very lucky," he said faintly as he collapsed, bringing her over with him as she tried to break his fall. Grateful for the softness of the well-tended lawn.

"We were so lucky," he said just before losing consciousness, feeling strangely happy to see her beautiful face hovering over him.

32

New York 1949

"Where am I?"

Another strange room. A grimy tube of light flickered in the ceiling above.

"Bellevue," Tom told him.

"That's ironic."

"Why?"

"Never mind. What're they sayin'?"

"First things first. How do you feel?"

"Like a juvenile delinquent. First things first: *What is it?*"

"They think it's a coronary heart condition," Tom told him reluctantly.

"What's that mean?"

"Second cousin to a heart attack," he said. "From overwork."

He tried to lift his head up but felt dizzy immediately and fell back onto the pillow. Looking to his side, he saw an old man's hand on the rail of the hospital bed — realizing only after a long moment that it was *his* hand, so old and gray did it appear, sprinkled with liver spots, a tube inserted into it. Suddenly, he felt like weeping.

"Where's Slim?" he asked instead.

"Out having a cigarette. She's been here beside you the whole time. I just told her I'd take a watch."

"Jesus, is it that bad?"

"No, Charlie, they think you'll be fine. But the work —"

"How're the papers playin' it?'"

"Very nice, very sympathetic. You even bumped the good cardinal from the front pages."

"Did I?"

"Yes, he finally accepted defeat, went up to Val-Kill to have tea with Mrs. Roosevelt."

"I'd like to have been a fly on the wall at *that* little encounter," he said, laughing faintly, despite how much it hurt his chest. Tom was alarmed to see how gray and listless his face looked, his eyes watering up freely.

"You've got to take it easy, Charlie. That's all there is to it," he said gently. "You have to get eight hours sleep every night, cut down the smoking, get some regular exercise —"

"They say lots of things, but *they* don't run the City of New York, do they?" he said, his fine blue eyes looking blurry and tearful and small in the middle of the big pillow. "I can't just lay it aside. The job is with me every minute, from when I wake up in the morning until my head hits the pillow. And when I fall asleep at night, I dream about it — dreams that're so real they leave me tired in the daytime."

"Surely, Charlie, there's some way you could —"

"No, Tom, there isn't," he said, cutting him off. "I must see to it that our laws are enforced and our streets kept clean. I must see that our health precautions are observed, and that our children get a good education, and that the old and the feeble get to eat. I must see that good homes are put up for the slum dweller, and that our hospitals are clean and well run for the sick —"

"All right, Charlie!" Tom tried to assuage him, alarmed at the rising hysteria in his voice.

"You were the one had that priest come an' talk about my duties at my swearing-in, Tommy," he said, grabbing at his brother's jacket and shirt. "I think about that still: all my duties and responsibilities, and God help me if I betray them —"

"You've never *betrayed* anything, Charlie!"

But his brother was rambling on, oblivious. "Talk about Eleanor Roosevelt, you know I saw the big man himself, not long before the end. I'd flown back in from Italy, and he came up to New York for a parade, a few days before the election. It rained all that day, but he had to take it. They drove him through four boroughs in an open car, wavin' an' wavin' to the crowds, just a hat and a rain slicker to protect him, but he took it.

"He had to show he could still do it. There were too many rumors he was sick; it was too obvious from the way he looked, all the weight he'd lost. They'd planned out a few way stations where they could stop an' at least change his clothes, get him dry an' warm for a few minutes. They had me wait in one a those, some little house in the Village. He wanted to talk to me about runnin' for mayor, maybe even governor, after the war was over, but I could barely concentrate on it, lookin' at him. The man was all wrung out, Tommy. The mind was still there, but his legs were sticks, his face a skull. His jaw falling open, he was so tired.

"But they toweled him off, an' put him in a fresh shirt, and out he went again. To ride on through the drivin' rain, grinning an' waving to all the idjits. That's me, don't ya see, Tommy? I can't rest an' relax any more than he could. It doesn't work that way! You can't let the job get ahead of ya, even for a moment. Clairey warned me—"

"Then why don't you quit?" came a soft voice from behind Tom.

Slim stood in the doorway, holding two cups of coffee. She handed one to Tom and went to sit on the edge of the bed just behind him, gently stroking Charlie's legs under the blankets with her spare hand. She'd had the servants bring over a change of clothing from the mansion, and now she looked as poised and cool as she always did, in a man's Brooks Brothers shirt and an appropriately demure gray skirt, her hair tied up in a ponytail. To look at her, no one would have known she'd been up all night, much less sitting beside a hospital bed for the past eight hours.

Charlie blinked at her, uncomprehending.

"I mean it. Why don't you quit, then?" she repeated, gazing into her husband's face, and in a flash Tom saw how brilliant the idea truly was.

"It's not that easy, Slim. Vinnie Impellitteri would become mayor, for cryin' out loud. Some mobbed-up court clerk! We only put him on the ticket because we couldn't find an Italian who wasn't a communist or a crook—"

"Then you could say you won't run again. It will give them plenty of time to pick a successor. That seems simple enough, doesn't it?"

Tom thought he saw a light go on in his brother's eyes, like a drowning man suddenly spotting a rope. Slim looked up at him as well—her face making a silent appeal, he thought: *a way out.*

"I dunno, Tommy," he said slowly—but Tom could pick up the note of hope in his voice. "I do have an obligation to the voters . . ."

"What do you owe them anymore, Charlie?" he said, making the case for him. "You've given forty years to this city, working your way up from cop, to DA, to mayor. Walkin' a beat, dispensing justice. Sending the worst killers this town's ever seen to the chair. Where does it say you have to serve as mayor till you're dead?"

"It would be good for us, Charlie. We could go away somewhere, see a little of the world until you get your health back," Slim pleaded, her voice sincere. Glancing at Tom as she said it. He picked up her meaning easily enough: it would be good for them, too. Give them the chance to get out of this whole dirty business they couldn't help themselves from—

"Maybe that would be the best thing," Charlie was saying, running a hand over his chin, his face imbued with a little more color already. "What good can I do anybody dead, or laid up like some invalid? Maybe I should quit while I'm ahead." He gave a small chuckle. "I could even endorse Frank Hogan to succeed me—*that* would shake 'em up, the whole lot! Have the prosecutor himself in the mayor's chair."

He face twisted suddenly in alarm.

"But what about the money? Forty thousand a year as mayor—where would I ever make that again?"

"There are plenty of people who would be glad to hire you, darling, with your experience," Slim cooed at him.

"Sure there are," Tom joined in. "Colleges, universities. Foundations. You could come back to the law firm with Natie and me, be our rainmaker. It's not like before the war, Charlie. They practically pave the sidewalks with gold now."

"That's just the new mica concrete, that sparkles like that," Charlie said, trying to jest—but the idea obviously intrigued him. "Maybe that would be the way. We could even go out to California, visit brother Mike for a spell an' see if there's any possibilities. You know, I always wanted to see the golden West—"

"That's it, Charlie," she said encouragingly. "Keep thinking that way, my darling. There are so many opportunities."

They left him soon after, when he drifted into what looked like a very peaceful sleep, still mumbling about the possibilities. On the sidewalk outside the hospital, she offered him her hand almost formally, and he was tempted to kiss the small white glove. But when he did touch her she squeezed his palm tightly in hers, speaking to him in a low, urgent voice.

"Tommy, it's —"

"I know."

"No, you don't. It's —"

"I do know," he said, hushing her. "It's the best way to stop it — for all of us. He's killing himself in that job. The two of you should go. To California, or wherever. And then —"

"Yes," she said. "I know."

She had shown up soon after her phone call in the early-morning hours — made from a booth in some downtown club, with the sound of a horn in the background, and a slow jazz guitar, and laughter that was a little too forced. Arriving by taxi, minutes later. Sweeping down to his basement apartment in yet another frilly cloud of a designer gown, a bottle of good champagne in her hand — glowing still from the adventure of her night out. Giggling to see him in his gun-smuggling clothes as he shushed her and pulled her inside. Holding her against the door, and kissing her over and over there — she was unable to get another foot inside before he had the gown off, and then everything else. They had the champagne only afterward, enjoying each other at their leisure on the couch. Telling each other about all the things they'd done that night, across the different worlds of the City. Staying up for the rest of the night they had, until it was time for her to get back into her gown, and her taxi, and head uptown.

"Until it was time for me to turn back into a pumpkin," she told him out on the sidewalk, smiling but with the sadness plain in her eyes.

"You? A pumpkin? It's the rest of us who shrink back to our quotidian existences when you're out of sight," he said as gracefully as he could, thinking how much he was going to miss her.

"My God, I thought he was dying, right out there on the lawn. I couldn't live with myself, if it was over worry for me —"

"I know. I feel the same way."

"Goodbye, Tommy."

"Goodbye, Slim," he told her, though they both knew they would see each other the next afternoon at the hospital again, and the day after that, and the day after that, and who knew for how long after that until Charlie — finally, maybe — made up his mind and moved them away to California.

Outside of the hospital they really did try to keep away from each other. No more phone calls in the middle of the afternoon that made his heart leap. No more rushing halfway across town to meet her for an hour. All the intricate wiring of an affair, gone dead for good.

Instead, he went down to the labor school that he knew Father Phil Carey was running at Saint Francis of Xavier's, on West Sixteenth Street. Following a stream of men in laborer's clothes into the basement, under the stone image of the saint waving a crucifix admonishingly over them. He was surprised to see how many more men there were already downstairs, the air thick with humidity and body odor, coffee and cigarettes. He could hear voices lecturing and chalk squeaking on a blackboard somewhere, while other men — all of them looking like they were fresh from the docks, or a construction crew — were hunting and pecking at a couple of typewriters, inking and cranking away at a mimeograph machine.

He found Father Carey easily enough in the next room. The little priest's light hair was lapped with gray now, and he no longer wore a sweater or spoke with his head down, but there was still the same Barry Sullivan smile about his lips and eyes. He recognized Tom at once, greeting him with a happy shout and a thump on the back, pressing a cup of stale, bitter coffee into his hand before he led him around a pillar and into a corner space that yielded as much privacy as the crowded rooms allowed anywhere.

"Looks like business is good, Father," Tom told him, almost shouting to be heard above the general rumble of the crowd.

"We have three hundred men down here now," Father Carey acknowledged, watching impishly as Tom took a sip of the rancid coffee and made a face. "But it's not just the numbers. You saw them out there. The men are doing it for *themselves* now. They're even running their own newspaper out of the basement here, *The Crusader*."

"Impressive," Tom admitted, amazed by the sight of so many big men working at office machines.

"There's no stopping them, Tom. Not after the war. It's not like before; now they want everything that's coming to them. Taxi Jack O'Donnell even threatened to burn us down."

"Did he!"

"He gave me a ride back from the docks last month, in his big chauffeured Chrysler. Made a point of telling me all about how, when the communists painted a hammer and sickle on the side of his church, he told the congregation from the pulpit where their headquarters were. The next week, sure enough, there was a big fire at commie central. Then he tells me, just as he drops me off here, 'And Father Carey, you see we know where your address is, too.' Can you believe that one?"

"He sounds like a storm trooper."

"Oh, storm trooper, hell! I wouldn't want to insult the poor storm troopers. No, O'Donnell's just a horse's ass. A nitwit . . . a *bum*. That's all he is. Threatening to burn down a church! Willing to let King Joe Ryan put him in his back pocket, just so he could keep his fancy cars and his fat parish bank account to show the cardinal!"

His enthusiastic rancor halted abruptly, eyes falling.

"It was purest nonsense," he said, "and I never felt the least afraid. But you know, just the act of getting into his chauffeured car like that — it reminded me of Peter Panto, all over again. These idiots still thinking they can kill free men like dogs, right out in public."

"They wouldn't dare."

"Not in the church, maybe. Not out in public. But these men . . ." He motioned all around him. "All we tell them is, you don't save your soul in church, or on your knees. You find salvation in this world through prayer and work with others. They do the rest. We've got them on the run now, Tom — King Joe and his whole crowd. We even have the cardinal behind us."

"Francis Spellman?" Tom asked, astonished.

"He had us up to the Powerhouse just last week, Father Corridan and myself, asked about the work on the docks. Heard us out, then said to keep him informed, let him know if there was anything we needed." Carey grinned. "I think it's because we've got Dorothy Day and *The Catholic Worker* with us. Do you know what he said, when Taxi Jack asked him to denounce her? 'That woman may be a saint!'"

"Ah, that's horseshit, Father, an' you know it!" a nicotine-soaked voice boomed at Tom's shoulder, and looking up Tom was surprised to see not a workman but a priest's collar. "The cardinal's just hedging his bets. He acts like he's with us, then he goes an' makes *Bill McCormack* a Knight of Malta, for God's sakes —"

"Here's another Jesuit for you, Tom — from Amsterdam Avenue, by way of Wall Street," Father Carey told him. "This is Father John Corridan, though we all call him Pete, for reasons that will shortly become obvious. Together, we're a regular Mutt an' Jeff act."

The priest was taller than anyone else in the room, over a head taller than Father Carey. He looked about to enter middle age, his pate mostly bald, but he possessed a broad, athletic build, with wide shoulders and big, wide hands that made Tom's knuckles pop when they shook. He moved quickly and decisively, and behind his dour, almost sneering expression, there was a ready anger in the man.

"Bill McCormack?" Tom asked. "He's a knight now, too?"

"Sure, an' why not? That goddamned Spellman! Who the hell does he think he is? He could put the docks in order in five minutes if he would ever read the riot act to those sons of bitches! Instead, he gives them the highest honors in the church, for Christ's — *Pete's* — sake!"

The words were all but spat out through the priest's thick lips, each one punctuated by the thrust of the burning cigarette he held between two fingers. His breath smelled heavily of smoke and cloves, and he seemed to Tom more like a shipyard boss, running a shape-up, than any priest he had ever known.

"He wanted me to deliver a message to you," Tom told him, remembering his purpose.

"Who?"

"Mr. Big himself. I fell into owing him a favor, so I told him I'd do it."

"Ah, that's the way the waterfront works — it's the way this whole city works!" Corridan said, his eyes gleaming. "They inveigle you into owing something. A loan, a bet, *something.* Then they own you. What does Mr. Mc-Cormack want for his favor?"

"He says he wants to talk. He wants you to name your price, whatever it is, and he says he's not an unreasonable man, an' you an' he an' Joe Ryan can reach an agreement, he's sure of it," Tom recited.

"That's what you agreed to tell us?" Father Carey asked, while Corridan glowered above them.

"That's it." Tom nodded. "I said I would do it. What I didn't say was that I would also advise you to tell him to go shove his price and his offer up his arse. Better yet, I wouldn't get within ten feet of the man. There, I said it."

"Well, you're a hell of an emissary," said Corridan, a slow, crooked smile spreading across his face. "Whattaya think he means by this?"

"I think he means that by sending me, his offer will look like it came through the mayor. Which I can assure you, *it did not.* I haven't even told Charlie about this. It has nothing to do with my brother."

"You may not be as right about that as you think, but God bless you anyway," Corridan told him cryptically, throwing a big arm around his shoulder and towing him across the room. "It's one more proof: we've got McCormack on the run at last."

"Is he?" Tom's voice skeptical.

"Sure. The feds are pressuring King Joe to keep the docks running at all costs, so they can get the Marshall Plan shipments out to Europe. No more of his finaglin' around, and they can't risk a wildcat strike by the men. Hogan's squeezing him from the other end, here in Manhattan, with the criminal investigations. And meanwhile, Mike Johnson's series in the *Sun* is putting everything together at last, ripping the veil off just who Mr. Big really is. It's like bringing the boogeyman out of the closet."

Father Corridan gestured to a bank of beige metal file cabinets that reached up to the basement ceiling.

"We've got all the rest. There's the whole sordid history," he told Tom fervently. "The *biblioteca apostolica* of Bill McCormack an' his waterfront empire. All the theft — did you know that last month they lifted an entire electrical generator, right off the docks? Millions, maybe *hundreds of millions* in goods stolen every year!

"Over here," he said, pointing to another stack of cabinets, "these are the rackets. The loan-sharking, the bookmaking. All the beatings, and the knifings, and the killings. It's all opening up. Everybody's talking since Cockeye Dunn and his boy-os got convicted of murder. Pretty soon we'll have a straight line—right up to King Joe, and then on to Mr. Big himself."

"It will take more than the facts to stop Bill McCormack," Tom said slowly. "We thought we had it all set up before. Thought we had enough to blow up the whole waterfront. But things tend to slip away."

"We've got it all now—enough for a thousand indictments on every pier! And all of it written up in triplicate, the copies held in safe locations. I don't think even McCormack would try to burn a church, but we're taking no chances."

"First you have to get Dunn to talk," Tom told him, looking over at his mountainous file cabinets. "Then you have to get people to believe him—a lowlife racketeer like that, feeding off the men for years. It won't be easy. But I agree with one thing—if McCormack wants to talk, he's not winning."

He looked up to see Father Corridan grinning wolfishly at him. The priest leaned over, slid open the bottom file cabinet—and pulled out a half-empty fifth of Dunphy's.

"I think this calls for a war conference, Mr. O'Kane. Care to join me?"

The rest of the afternoon and the evening wore away in a blur of drinks and of bars, across the width and breadth of the West Side. The priest, now in a dark coat and hat, like a huge crow, talking to him very intently. The last thing he remembered that night was walking arm in arm across the cathedral-sized waiting room of Pennsylvania Station, with Corridan and a much shorter man with a dramatic sweep of dark hair, whom Pete had introduced as a writer. The three of them singing some patriotic Irish song at the top of their lungs. Tom thinking, in his last smear of a thought, *Well, if anyone can send the devil back to hell, it's this one.*

33

Acapulco, 1953

He made his way back up the sands to the hotel as soon as he knew they would be in the office. Trudging past the Big Crowd in their lounge chairs, the men baking themselves a still deeper red-brown, the matrons remaining a pure white under their parasols and bandanas, commanding the Indian maids who crouched by their sides, digging into picnic baskets and buckets of rapidly melting ice for finger sandwiches and bottles of pink champagne. Tom sure he could feel their eyes following him, beneath sunglasses and umbrellas—wondering if he was becoming as paranoid as Slim.

In the hotel, he struggled with the change and the international operator in his meager Spanish, trying both to make himself understood and to keep from shouting his business across the echoing, tiled lobby. There was a long silence as he waited for Ellie to come on, picturing her in the hushed, carpeted office, the Seven Sisters grads gliding briskly through the halls.

"Tom! Where are you?"

He could hear her voice at last, as if down the other end of a wind tunnel—sounding, he thought, a little plaintive and confused.

"I told you! Acapulco!" he repeated, watching heads turn across the elegant lobby, trying desperately not to shout.

"Why are you *there?*"

"It's complicated! I came down with Charlie, to talk to him."

"How did that go?"

There was a sudden break in the constant blast of the winds when she spoke, and her voice came across abruptly close, and intimate. Filled with an immediate, tactful sympathy that made him feel even more like a louse.

"He went back to Mexico City. There was a ... disagreement," he said awkwardly, trying to explain as cryptically as possible for anyone who might be overhearing.

"With you?"

"No."

There was a pause on the line.

"With . . . *her?*"

"Yes."

There was another pause — one so long this time that he was afraid he might have lost the connection.

"So you're there . . . with her."

"Yes. Look, Ellie, he just stormed out. She's supposed to give me a ride back."

"Today?"

"Well . . . I don't know. Look, it's complicated —"

Her voice coming back to him, both wistful and ironic. "I bet."

The operator was back on the line by then, saying something in Spanish that he could barely fathom, but surely pertaining to money. He tried to talk over her: "I'll call you when I'm back —"

The operator kept talking, the windstorm on the line blowing back up again. He thought he could just make out the words Ellie was saying, though afterward he wasn't sure, they sounded so strange — the tone still angry, but anxious for him at the same time: "Tom, don't let him trap you down there . . ."

He walked back across the immaculate white sand, still contemplating what she'd said. *How would Charlie ever trap him?* It didn'tw make sense. His brother, whose name he would clear — who he wanted only to redeem.

Just as soon as he finished sleeping with his wife . . .

Slim was standing above their picnic basket when he reached her, the blanket over her shoulder, beach umbrella in her hand. He noticed the crease of muscle in her well-tanned arms.

Arms strong enough to kill a bull? he wondered idly. *At least an old and tired one?*

"What's up?" he asked, trying to tamp down the note of hope in his voice. "We're leaving already?"

"Everybody is. Didn't you notice?" she said, gesturing around. Looking around, he could see the Big Crowd all trudging together off the beach. All of them — the kerchiefed matrons and the bronzed playboys, the little children and young wives — headed north along the little peninsula, plodding along as dutifully as sea crabs responding to some tidal imperative, their maids and their valets scrambling to gather up their possessions and follow. In their wake, a darkness was spreading slowly across the Caleta, something he had failed altogether to notice coming back from the hotel, he had been so engrossed thinking about Ellie, and his brother.

"What is it? An eclipse?" he asked, uncomprehending.

"La Quebrada," she said, pointing to the mountain. "Every day the sun moves behind it at noon, and we all follow it over to La Caletilla."

He took the umbrella and the picnic basket from her, and they began to make their own track across the cooling sands. Tom and Slim were the very last, and by the time they reached the knot of trees the Caleta was the shade of a late afternoon before a thunderstorm. Even as the shadow moved over their beach, it seemed to recede from the one ahead of them, like a tarpaulin being removed from a ball field — leaving the white sands ahead as pristine and sunlit as what they had just left. Slim was a little ahead of him, and now it was her turn to smile back at him — trying to tease, lowering her sunglasses, her lips smiling but her eyes filled with trepidation.

"Slim," he said compulsively, and then he took hold of her elbow and guided her into the little grove of trees, away from where anyone could see.

She smiled wider and gave a little laugh, mistaking — or trying to mistake — his urgency for lust, her long, tanned legs moving against his. She closed her eyes and kissed him, and he could taste the sea salt on her tongue. He pulled her closer to him, but broke the kiss.

"Slim," he said, and she knew. Her face falling as he held her by her arms.

"Ah, hell," she said, pulling away from him and running a finger across his hair, pushing away a stray hair. "It's just such bad timing! It always was."

"I don't know about that," he said, still holding her — still wanting to kiss her, as he always did when she was this close. "It was the two of us taking what we wanted, regardless of anyone else."

"I know. And I liked it. I won't say that I didn't like it," she told him defiantly. "If I'd met you first —"

"If we'd met first, would it have still been what we wanted?" he asked softly.

She made no answer but huddled against him in the deepening shade of the deserted beach. His arms around her, holding her to him and warming them both.

"It was the best thing I ever had," she said, her face wet against his chest now. "I know we hurt him, I know we did, and I know it's impossible now, but I won't regret it. I won't say that it's wrong, or a sin, or some kind of delusion. If we betrayed him—"

"We *did* betray him."

"If we betrayed him, he sold himself out a long time ago, Tom. At least we did it out of love."

"Yes, love. That's the best excuse there is."

34

New York, 1949

Whenever he could stand it, he went to see Charlie in the hospital, sure that she would be there. But they seemed to have a negative attraction now, a sixth sense for avoiding each other that was at least as strong as the pull between them had been. Meanwhile, Charlie transferred himself up to Saint Luke's as the weather improved, where he could sit out on the screened porches, and look down into Morningside Park, and the lovely green canopy of trees above it.

He was clearly improving, the color coming back to his face. Already, though, Tom could see the job encroaching again. The messengers from City Hall walking the hospital corridors. Councilmen and deputy mayors and district leaders cooling their heels with the magazines in the waiting room—rumpled, bright-eyed men in cheap gray suits, who looked like waiting was what they did for a living, and something they could go on doing until the end of time.

He noticed Robert Moses there, too, the way he might notice a battleship among a fleet of paddle wheelers from Prospect Park. Not waiting for anyone, but always in motion, striding out of his brother's room with a briefcase, or a sheaf of signed papers. Walking pitched forward, his disdainful stone face leading him onward like the bow of a ship—two or three assistants, as energetic and contemptuous as he was, scrambling to heel. Acknowledging him as perfunctorily as possible, if he did at all: a quick, sharp nod or a purse of his lips, as if Tom, too, were some lingering municipal blight he would have to take care of sometime in the near future.

"You know he's quitting," he couldn't resist saying early one Saturday evening when Moses hurtled past him, alone for a change. "It's been in the papers an' everything. And I suspect Mr. Hogan won't be needin' your services."

Moses stopped and addressed him, much to his surprise. "Don't be silly, I'm not going anywhere." He stood rigidly across Tom's path, fists perched confidently on his hips. "You think it matters who the *mayor* is?" he scoffed. "Nobody could fire me if they wanted to — and believe me, they don't want to! I could tie this city's nuts in a bow. But that's not why I'll stick around."

"Why, then?"

He took a step forward, a bigger, taller man than Tom had quite realized before, his face as scornful as ever.

"Because I bring them *solutions,* that's why. All you and your liberal friends bring them is *problems.* Your coloreds and spics agitating to get into public housing. Your pinko priests on the waterfront — in twenty years there won't even *be* a waterfront! Soon as they put the jet engine in commercial production, it'll all move by air. Planes and cars, that's the future."

He bent in over Tom, his face still leering but imbued with real devotion. "Don't you see it? There's money again. Down in Washington, here in the City. With urban renewal, we can finally start to build again. We don't have to negotiate for every damned lot, we can just *take* it —"

"You mean throwing people out of their homes."

"Screw *people!* You can't let *people* get in the way, or you won't ever accomplish a thing!" he exclaimed, balling his hand up in a fist and making a pounding motion. "We can build six new expressways, *now!* Hook up the whole road system, keep the City from strangling itself with traffic. Put up enough public housing in the bargain to make all you little reform nellies happy."

"That all sounds very democratic," Tom said in a huff.

"Grow up!" Moses told him. "Democracy doesn't enter into it. Things are going to be changing *fast* now — too fast for a lot of people to keep up. This is the first chance we've ever had to do things *right,* develop the City on a logical basis. It may be the last one we ever have."

He strode across the room, pausing at the door to deliver one last sneer.

"And I wouldn't be surprised if the General decides to stick around after all," he said. "Trust me, son. Power is no easy thing to give up."

He stood out in the drizzle early the next morning, watching Father Corridan conduct Mass on a West Village pier. The tall, balding cleric looking incongruous in his priestly robes instead of the wrinkled black suit they were all so used to, bareheaded under the light rain without the black slouch hat that he wore like another appendage.

It was that time of day Tom had always liked best on the waterfront, when the harbor was still coming awake all around him. The North River dock as crowded with men as he had ever seen it for a morning shape-up. Pier 59, King Joe Ryan's home turf, right in the heart of the pistol locals. But this time, each and every one of the men in their worn work clothes stepped forward patiently, hat in hand, to take the body and the blood of Christ in his mouth and move back down the long concrete wharf, blessed and forgiven, his soul bleached pure as the lamb again.

When they were done, Father Pete finished off the sacred wine, then made the sign of the cross over all of them. He raised his arms to pray, and the men all dropped together, reminding Tom of how his whole platoon had gone to its knees when the chaplain blessed them back in Italy, right before they tried to take another goddamned hill. He found himself kneeling with them now, praying for the first time since the war.

"God grant that our just demands will be met, and that we may work in dignity, and honor," Corridan was intoning solemnly, his voice as deep and rough as the weather filtering in off the river. "May God protect each and every one of us this day."

He held out his hands, and the men rose again as one. Smiling and laughing now, swaggering off the dock. Behind them the black-hulled ships waited forlorn and abandoned, their cargoes untouched. Father Corridan and the men from the labor school at Saint Xavier's handed them mimeographed leaflets, headlined *The Longshoremen's Case,* as they left. The priest swearing genially as he pulled off his white and purple robes, crumpling them into a heap and molting back into his comfortable black clothes and hat.

"For Pete's sake, if we're going to keep going out this early, I'm going to have to stick to straight goddamned whiskey at night," he muttered to Tom, his eyes bloodshot but still merry. "No more chasing it with beer. Jesus, it was only the promise of that wine at the end that got me through."

"Are they going out?" Tom asked.

"See for yourself." Corridan pointed proudly at the men moving away from the docks, piling into the nearest diners and bars, or starting the long blocks east to the BMT. "It's the same all over the harbor. Men are walking off the job on every pier from here to Red Hook, and over to Hoboken. War — it's wonderful!"

Tom could see, too, the *shlammers* skulking back by the pier sheds. Dressed in their fine suits and coats, hands thrust deep in their pockets. Faces bristling with menace. But the men ignored them as they streamed back past them, or jeered or gave them the bird — a few even jostling them as they went by, looking back as if spoiling for a fight.

Tom followed them, walking away from the river to an overgrown, aged office building at Nineteenth and Eighth, the fake-marble exterior encrusted in grime. Inside there was a wide, utilitarian metal elevator that seemed to be in working order, with a few more well-dressed thugs lingering around it, trying out their scowls on one another. Tom dodged into the stairwell by the door, preferring to go up unannounced. There was a cry behind him as he did, but the heavy door with its wire-glass window slammed shut behind him, and he took the stairs two at a time. He heard the door below open briefly, but there was no sound of any pursuing footsteps as he climbed up and up the metal-tipped stairs. Only a sour reek of food scraps, and cigarette butts, and insecticide, plus here and there rust-colored splashes on the walls and the railings, and a few abandoned workmen's caps and hats.

"The Joe Ryan Memorial Stairs," he said to himself, panting, on his way up.

When he got to the top, he pushed his way back through the heavy fire door again and made straight for the office suite ahead of him, the only one on the floor. There was another *shlammer* in a good coat standing out by the elevators on this floor, too, but he never saw Tom until he was past him. The double suite doors were stained so as to look like something of heft and quality, like oak or mahogany, with the grand designation INTERNATIONAL LONG-SHOREMEN'S ASSOCIATION, JOSEPH P. RYAN, PRESIDENT-FOR-LIFE stenciled across them in beautiful gold letters. But in fact they felt almost as light as plywood, and opened easily to a quick pull.

Tom found himself in a spacious reception area, facing a high desk and a secretaries' anteroom, behind a low railing. There was a further façade of legitimacy here—a deep carpet on the floor, and a couple of couches, and framed photographs on the walls, most of them featuring King Joe Ryan shaking hands with politicians and bishops who looked faintly embarrassed. But the upholstery was fraying, and the carpeting held the damp waterfront smell of fabric that never quite dried, like someone's perpetually leaking basement.

This early, there was no receptionist behind the imposing front desk, no secretaries at work yet. He vaulted the low railing and headed straight for the office beyond, twisting open this unlocked door, as well. Across the room were two familiar figures, leaning against a windowsill and staring out in the direction of the piers, their heads swiveling around instantly at his unannounced intrusion.

"Gentlemen!"

King Joe Ryan's face looked as comically surprised as it always did, in all its ridiculous, oversized features—the large, heavily veined nose, ears as cauliflowered as an aging club pug's. His mouth hung open slackly, then seemed to slowly masticate whatever it was he wanted to say. Next to him stood Bill McCormack, his head tilted up like an alert schnauzer's, his twinkly eyes now two dark buttons glaring in Tom's direction.

"Don't worry, I took the stairs. The same ones you threw those Negro longshoremen down, when they got sick of picking the tarantulas out of the banana cargoes you gave 'em. Another great moment in the history of the International Longshoremen's Association."

"You promised to do a thing for me," McCormack said without any of his usual preliminaries, his voice jagged and hard as a saw. "That's the only excuse I see for why we shouldn't show you the same way out."

"You wanted me to deliver a message to the fathers down at Saint Xavier's," Tom said. "It's done."

"Is it? And what answer did they give you?"

"I told them," Tom said slowly, "that you wanted to know what it might take to settle things between you—"

McCormack looked mollified. "That's all I asked."

"I also told them that they'd be mad to strike any kind of a deal with a man like you. I told them that the only reason you'd want me to be your messenger was to imply that the mayor was behind your offer, and would serve as guarantor. I told them that wasn't true, that it never would be true — that my brother would never sell the workingmen of this city."

McCormack's eyes were narrowed to razor-thin slits.

"Is that so? I wouldn't be so sure of that, if I were you —"

"I didn't stop by to hear any slanders of my brother," Tom said, cutting him off. "Just to let you know that I kept my word."

"You little punk," McCormack said, putting out a hand to grasp King Joe Ryan's desk, as if to keep himself in check. "Funny, I heard you weren't such a jaunty lad before your brother was the mayor. I heard when you went up to Emil Camarda's office you were white as a sheet, and about ready to piss yourself."

"Is that a fact?" Tom said, trying to sound as offhanded as possible — wondering how much McCormack had heard about that day, and from whom. "You may be right. But fortunately, I was with Peter Panto that day. He was brave enough for the both of us, in the face of your killers."

"Such insolence. If my Harry were alive, he'd slit you chin to navel. Hell, I got half a notion to do it myself —"

"That doesn't sound much like subsidiarity to me," Tom said. "Take a close look out there, the two a ya. Your waterfront is slipping away from you."

"We'll see about that. Tougher men than your priests have tried an' failed," McCormack told him.

"Have they? And how d'ya think it's gonna go for you with Hogan himself in City Hall? I hear even now he's up in Sing Sing, hearing Cockeye Johnny Dunn's last will an' testament about just who he's been breakin' heads and slittin' throats for all these years."

"Cockeye Dunn! The man's a criminal, runs a couple piers down here, an' starts puttin' on airs. He'd never rat, and even if he does, no one will believe him," McCormack scoffed, but Tom was sure he detected a note of uncertainty, maybe even surprise, under the man's usual bravado. King Joe Ryan was still trying desperately to work his tongue and teeth around a word.

"Don't be so sure. Governor Dewey's stayed his execution, just to see if he'll gab. I suspect that being on Death Row has a way of concentrating a man's mind — and loosening his tongue."

"You think I made my way on the docks for forty years to be brought down by the testimony of some small-time hood like that?" McCormack answered, smiling at him malevolently. "As I recall, you tried that once before."

"It's a new day. Get used to it, Mr. Big," Tom told him, and turned to push past the *shlammer* out by the elevators, another short, broad man with a chest like a bull's, who reached into his coat for something.

"No!" McCormack said quickly, causing the man to hesitate. But Tom was already bringing his fist up, driving it into the *shlammer*'s chin, knocking him back into a display case of civic and church medals awarded to Joseph P. Ryan. The man rolled off to the floor, momentarily stunned, the blackjack he'd been pulling out flopping out onto the carpet like a hooked fish.

"One more cheap shot!" McCormack snarled.

"Subsidiarity forever!" Tom grinned back at him, trying to ignore the sharp ache in his hand.

"You ... you ..." King Joe Ryan sputtered apoplectically, the eyes of everyone else in the room, even the dropped goon, turning to him, waiting to see what he might possibly have to say.

"You tell that Dorothy Day that she's no lady!" he got out at last.

Tom laughed all the way back down the stairs.

"You gave it all away."

He stood on the screened porch at the hospital, next to his brother, staring at the document there with the heart falling out of him. All but unable to believe that what he was looking at was real, even with all of the official seals and watermarks of the City of New York attached to it. Worst of all was the name stenciled in so beautifully at the top: *Robert Moses*.

Tom picked up the sheaf of paper and read from it again, shaking his head. "'City construction coordinator.' Jesus, Charlie, you know what this means? The power you gave him?"

"Sure —"

"*Do* you, Charlie? It means he can condemn any building, anywhere, and have it ripped down. He doesn't even have to have a real reason."

"You know I had to give him the tools —"

"He *has* the tools. A bulldozer and a sledgehammer—that's all he uses anymore. Now you've added an atom bomb."

"Tommy—" his brother said wearily.

"It was bad enough you went an' put Bill McCormack in charge of that committee on the future of the harbor. Now you want to give the rest of the City away to Bob Moses. You really signed this?" he asked again, as if trying to convince himself.

"I had to, Tommy. Somebody has to run things."

"Why?"

"Whattaya mean, 'why'?" Charlie said, irritated.

"I mean *why* does somebody have to run things the way you're talkin' about? Why does there have to be one more boss, lording it over all the rest of us? And not even one we elected."

"Don't be naïve, Tommy."

His brother looked away, over the fine park below. He was sitting in a rattan-backed wooden wheelchair, wearing a robe and pajamas. It was late spring by now, and the damp, stifling heat of the City had already come on, but Charlie had a blanket draped over his legs like an old man.

"Somebody's got to be in charge, and who knows this city better than Robert Moses?" he asked plaintively. "He knows how to build."

"Maybe once. Now I think he just likes to tear down. Look at what he's doing out at Coney Island. Wiping out a whole neighborhood, and half the boardwalk with it. And the Bronx—"

"He's a modern man, Tommy. He has a vision; he can see what the City's becoming, and what it has to become. We've got to move forward, keep up with the new age."

"He's mad as a hatter, if you ask me."

"Do you see that park below?" his brother asked, gesturing at the lovely green sweep of the treetops. From somewhere below they could hear the screams and laughter of children playing, though most of them were blocked from view. There was the hiss of pool sprinklers, and every now and then the thunk of a bat against a ball. Mothers and nannies pushed baby carriages along the promenade, and old women sat on the park benches, clutching their pocketbooks with both hands.

"Nobody even thinks about it much, but it's a work of genius. A jewel. A park carved out of a cliff, both beautiful and eminently useful at the same time. Can you imagine anyone buildin' something like that today?"

"Yes, I can. Just not Robert Moses—"

"And just up the street is Columbia University, and a block over in the other direction is the Episcopalians' big bloody cathedral. The whole city on a hill, right here! We need people who can build like that now, Tommy."

"Wielding the pickaxe to tear into that cliff was likely an Italian or a Negro, an' no doubt there was a Paddy on the wheelbarrow, to cart it all away," Tom said fiercely, crouching down by his brother. "We *all* built this city, Charlie. You know that as well as I do. These men you think we can't live without, they *need* you to believe that. Can't you see?"

Charlie sighed but kept refusing to look at him, staring down into the lush green trees like he was a hundred years old.

"It's the things you do that you can never break free of," he said in a dry, ruminative voice. "That's what you don't realize when you're young. It's a chain you start, an' you think you can break it anytime. But you can't."

"What're you talkin' about, Charlie? What the hell're you talkin' about? Because by Christ I can't figure a thing you're on about anymore."

"I remember when I first began to glimpse this city, from the top of the Woolworth Building. The *real* City, in all its limitless strength and power. Its heights and its depths, and all the light an' shadows in between. How it worked and how it disported itself, in all its awful glory. And here we are."

"Charlie, are ya all right?" Tom asked sincerely, afraid that his brother was having a stroke. But Charlie simply shook his head and turned to look at him at last.

"Elections are all well an' good, Tommy. But I knew it a long time ago, ever since I climbed up that building with a load a bricks on my back: within the city that you see all around you—the one that lives by explicit laws and observances—there exists another city, just as real. One that lives by its own, *un-*written rules and commandments—but ones that are no less binding, just the same."

"You're leaving, but you're putting a permanent government in place before you go," Tom said bitterly, standing up again and looking away from his brother. "McCormack with his harbor, Moses with his highways. Who else are you leaving in charge, in your marvelous invisible city?"

"A city like New York, Tom, it's got to have great men — not good men — to run it."

"Run it for *what,* exactly, Charlie? Run it for *whom?* That time is gone, Charlie. You said so yourself. For better or worse, the people run it now."

"People today have no more moral sense than a pig, or a dog," Charlie snapped. "They think a park like that is just given to them by God, because they're good Americans. These are the days of the split atom, Tommy. We're held together against the chaos by the grip of a few strong men, that's all."

Tom started to open his mouth to reply, but then he realized that for once, he had nothing left to say to his brother, nothing at all.

"Goodbye, Charlie."

"Goodbye, Tom."

They shook hands, and Tom walked in off the breezy screen porch, sure that he was headed somewhere, but with no real idea where, or what for.

35

New York, 1953

"I thought we had him," Hogan said at the end of another long day spent going nowhere. Studying another adoring photograph of Bill McCormack on the front page of the *Daily News.* Hogan sitting back in his office chair as rumpled and informal as Tom had ever seen him, his hands behind his head. Tom and Ellie across the desk from him, both of them utterly exhausted after tracing and retracing their way fruitlessly through still more boxes of evidence.

"Yes?" Tom asked.

"That spring. What was it, four years ago?" he considered. Tom letting him act it out, knowing full well he knew what year it was. *The year you didn't become mayor* — "You remember? When we had Cockeye Dunn up in the Dance Hall, and I got the governor to give him a reprieve?"

"Yes," Tom said. "I remember."

* * *

It was as if there was a pall over downtown, Tom had thought at the time. Over all the clubs and the saloon back rooms. As if they were all waiting for a sick man to die. Or maybe a way of life.

By then the front-page pieces were coming out every day in the *Sun*, ripping open King Joe's rackets on the waterfront. Speculating openly over whether Bill McCormack was really "Mr. Big." A major gambling ring had been exposed in Brooklyn, cops being hauled up before special committees and grand juries all over town. It seemed as if there was a new scandal in the papers every day. The City writhing through one of its periodic fits of conscience, purging and expelling all the rottenness it could before it choked to death on its own filth. Men he had known for years were openly frightened, fixers and chiselers who had never considered they might not be above the law.

His brother was trying to close up his office by then. Tom coming around again despite their last break over making Robert Moses the king of everything, hoping to be of some help to Charlie as he wrapped things up. He had expected him to be all the more relieved, glad to be getting away from the whole hornet's nest that was now opening up, the corruptions within corruptions.

But to his surprise, Charlie seemed edgy and apprehensive, the serenity that had come over him when he first made his decision to quit now worn away. Tom would berate himself later: *I should have picked up on it then.*

"I don't know, should I really be leavin' now that everything's bein' ripped wide open?" Charlie asked him, visibly fretting. "Wouldn't this be the time to get somethin' done?"

"Too late for that," Tom said drily. "At least, now that you've signed the City over to Bob Moses."

"But how d'ya think they'll remember me if I quit now, after one term?"

"As an honorable man," Tom told him. "That's a rare enough thing for any pol, never mind in this town."

"Jesus, remember the things we were gonna do?" he said, running a hand along the back of his head. "How was it we didn't get to them?"

"I think they were things *I* wanted you to do, Charlie. Me and my big-mouthed priests," he said more gently. "I'm sorry for pushing all that on you. Like Mr. La Guardia said, it was you in the headache seat now, not me — *you* who had the responsibility. I should've understood that better."

"Don't blame yourself, Tommy," Charlie said, his voice less frantic but so sad that Tom wanted to go to his brother and hug him like a small child. "It's not your fault. It's just what Claire was always warnin' me against. I got ahead of meself at last, that was the whole trouble —"

"Never say that, Charlie! You did better than most, and no worse than any."

"Well, well," his brother said, looking down as he seemed to mull it all over. "At least, God knows, I'm leaving office a poor man. That should prove how honest I was. My poor wife!"

"There's plenty for you t'do, Charlie," Tom said, kneeling beside him now and patting his face. "First things first. You'll come back to hang up your shingle with me an' Natie. 'O'Kane, Cohen, O'Kane' — OCO, how's that?"

"All we'll need is to get a partner whose name starts with *L*, give him first billing."

"C'mon now, stop feeling sorry for yourself! You'll be a great rainmaker for the firm, an' you won't ever have to go into court. You could always teach, too, you know —"

"I was thinkin' it might be nice to be an ambassador," he told Tom, looking up now. "Maybe somewhere down in Latin America — Mexico, or Venezuela. I got to speak to Mr. Acheson about it at that Waldorf banquet the other night, and he said he was surprised — most people want Paris, or London."

"But not you."

"Caracas, Mexico City — places like that, they're gonna be the next battleground in the Cold War, you can count on it," he said, his eyes brightening as he warmed to the subject. "I can still speak some Spanish, you know. I want to be of some *use*, Tom."

"You will be, Charlie."

"An ambassador, Tommy, think of that!"

"Yes, think of it."

"And you know, Slim would make the perfect ambassador's wife. I think she'd love it, don't you?"

"Yes, she would," he'd said softly, thinking, *That would end it once and for all. Make sure it was ended and never resumed.* "She would at that, Charlie, she would at that."

New York, 1953
"It was the Dance Hall that almost broke it open," Hogan told them. "The Death House up at Sing Sing. We put Cockeye Dunn up there two months before his date of execution, then his own appeals kept pushing it back even further. Before he was through, he watched seven men go to the chair. But it still didn't break him."

"That sounds barbaric," Ellie said. Hogan gave her a look, but she didn't lower her eyes or look away, Tom saw.

"He was pretty barbaric himself, Cockeye Dunn," Hogan said after a long pause. "From what we knew, he was part of maybe thirty-five murders. And maybe we didn't know the half of it. He controlled all the trucking around the pistol locals by then, but he still liked to do the work himself. Beating men senseless with a lead pipe. Shooting them, if that didn't do the trick. He liked to keep his hand in."

"Just the next generation of *shlammers* and *shtarkers*," Tom interjected. "Moving up to take control—just like Albert Anastasia with his mob. In control now, with nothing to stop 'em."

"Sure, that's how the City has changed." Hogan sighed. "There were always men like that on the payroll. But they never called the shots. Until now."

He got up and to Tom's shock took out three glasses from a cabinet behind the desk, pouring each one of them a full two fingers of good scotch. He snuck a glance over at Ellie and saw her blushing with pride. The ultimate tribute.

"Here's to crime," Hogan said, gesturing toward their glasses before swallowing half a mouthful and falling back into his chair. "That was his undoing, though. Dunn took it upon himself to go shoot Andy Hintz over in the Village. Big fight over who would run Pier Fifty-One. One pier like that, it was walking-around money to Johnny Dunn. But he had to go and shoot Hintz—shot him five times in the belly, on the stairs of his own apartment house."

"And that should've been that."

"Right. But Hintz was tough, he stuck around for weeks. We hauled Dunn into the hospital, got a deathbed ID, just like they do in *Dick Tracy*. He was *cool*, Dunn. Even then, he didn't flinch—just asked Hintz, *'Are you sure you're rational, Andy?'* You know — waterfront talk for *'How'd you like us to come back an' kill the wife an' kids?'* But Hintz wouldn't budge."

Hogan leaned in toward them over the desk, his eyes glowing.

"And now, *now* we finally had a case! All those years on the waterfront, and we finally cracked one. We had Hintz's identification, and his wife wasn't scared, either. She'd come out on the stairs when she heard the commotion, found her husband lying there, holding in his guts. That's the trouble when you go kill a man in his own house."

"The dirty bums," Tom muttered. Thinking of the boardinghouse over on North Elliott Place. *Panto's fiancée, Alice, that lovely Italian girl.*

"It took the jury about ten minutes to convict," Hogan continued, leaning over his desk, hands balled into fists to support him. "And then we had him. Johnny Dunn was a miserable punk, but he knew everything, was connected to everybody — just like your Mr. Reles. He'd run King Joe Ryan's dinners with Bill McCormack, worked hand in hand with him for years. We had Dunn, and he could give us everything. If he was so inclined."

"So you put him up in the Dance Hall," Ellie said slowly.

"We did. We put him in the Dance Hall, and then we put it out through the papers: *'Talk or fry.'* We figured he'd get the message."

Tom remembering the Death House from his own trip up with Pep Strauss and Martin Goldstein, all those years before. It looked and smelled just like every other prison wing he'd ever seen, of piss and excrement, and sweat and men's fear. Maybe a little better than usual, even. But there was something different about it, something infinitely more oppressive — something that made it feel like living twenty-four hours a day on the ocean floor. The Dance Hall was quieter than any other prison he'd seen. More subdued, save for the raw, jangling bursts of false jollity or terror that came out of nowhere, like the sounds of a cat jumping on a piano keyboard in the middle of the night. The lights blinking and going out, then flashing back on again with each execution. He could see how a man could easily break, long before he'd sat through seven of those nights.

"By the time I got up there, he was beginning to crack. They'd already had to sedate him once," Hogan continued. "He was wearing the death uniform. You know — the white shirt and the black pants, with his head shaved. I'm sorry, Ellie, but I wanted death to be as visceral a thing as possible for him. I even had him taken off the sedatives, and given his last meal already.

"His wife was in the cell with him, making her last visit. She was worried because she'd spotted the prison priest coming down the corridor. He was going to visit another condemned man, a killer named Santo Bretagna, but she was afraid it was for Johnny's last rites. She asked him, 'What's he doing here?' and I'll never forget it, he said—you'll pardon the language, Miss Abramowitz—but he said, 'Don't worry, he's just fireproofin' the dago for tomorrow.'

"I should've known then I wasn't going to break him. When I came in, he told his wife he needed to take a break. Told her to go get herself a cup of coffee, and by the time she came back, he'd be off Death Row. She smiled, and kissed him, and did as he said. But once she was gone, he told the guard not to let her back in. 'We were smiling, and I want our goodbye to be that way,' he said.

"Then it was the same old game," Hogan went on, shaking his head, his voice filled with disgust. "He told me, 'I can make you governor. Hell, I can make you president!' He said, 'With what I have to tell you, you can turn the City inside out.'"

"That's exactly what they were all afraid of," Tom said. "All the big men. They were holding their breath, all over New York, afraid he'd give you the dope to do just that."

"He was a very convincing fellow, too, Johnny Dunn, when he wanted to be," Hogan said, nodding. "He'd look me right in the eyes and say these things. He had a face like an old rock, pitted and marked, with that one gotch eye of his protruding. Like a man with a beast inside him who couldn't wait to get out.

"He told me he wanted full immunity, just like the deal your brother gave Abe Reles," Hogan said, with a little nod of acknowledgment in Tom's direction. "He told me he wanted to walk once he finished testifying, it was the only way he'd stay alive. He said he'd give me it all—including Mr. Big."

"And what did you say?" Tom breathed.

"I told him I had to confirm the information first. I told him if he really could give me all he said he could, well then, I'd see to it he walked with time served. And he nodded, and we shook on it, and he started in."

"But then?" asked Ellie.

"Then he started in naming names, and they were the same dead men,"

Hogan said with a sigh. "Every killer he named was already dead, or had already beat that rap. The pols he named were the usual peanut chiselers. Two-bit councilmen from Queens who'd retired before the war. Minor ward heelers from the Bronx who were peeing their pants in some nursing home. It was all smoke and mirrors."

"And Mr. Big? Did he name McCormack?'"

"No." Hogan shook his head. "He just said no, it wouldn't do him any good even to walk free, with a man like that after him. I told him, 'You've wasted my time, Mr. Dunn. But worse than that, you've wasted your own, and you don't have much of it left.' And I went out and I told the warder, right in front of the cell where he could hear me, 'Don't let the wife back in. He doesn't want to see her again before he dies.'

"He still wouldn't talk. I even prevailed upon the governor to give him another stay—just to see if he'd crack. All he left me was a note. You know what it said? 'Thanks. I got another last meal.' Then they strapped him in, and pulled the switch, and there went the best case we ever had to break up the waterfront rackets.

"I went up there the presumptive mayor of New York," Hogan concluded, still sounding bitter and a little puzzled by it. "And I came back down another bum."

"They knew you didn't have the goods," Tom told him. "Once that was clear, you didn't have a hold on them anymore."

"But how would they know? I kept it as secret as possible, my little conversation with Mr. Dunn," Hogan told him, irked by it still. "Nobody knew outside this office—"

"It didn't matter. Dunn was dead," Tom explained. "That told them everything they needed to know. If you'd got something—something hard, something you could use on them—they knew he'd still be alive."

"I was double-crossed," Hogan said as matter-of-factly as he could, Tom knew—only the barest wisp of disappointment still evident in his voice.

"Yes. What else?"

New York, 1949
Tom remembered the day, too. A summer evening, less than a week after Cockeye Dunn's execution was on the front page of all the tabloids.

347

The cars coming and going in front of Gracie Mansion. The rumors flying so fast and furious that he caught wind of them at the county courthouse. Rushing uptown as soon as his trial let out, running up the little path to the mansion. His heart sinking as soon as he saw all the cars out front — the reporters and the photographers pouring over the place like ants on a lollipop. The big black limousines of the borough leaders already pulling away.

He spotted Slim walking up the driveway just ahead of him, moving swiftly despite the three-inch heels she was wearing. Dressed in another perfect designer outfit she'd obviously just been modeling at a gala.

"Where are you coming from?" he asked gently as he caught up to her, taking her arm.

The smell of her neck and hair, so close, still intoxicating to him.

"The Waldorf. It was a benefit for children's relief in Europe," she said, her voice sounding close to distraught.

"I was in court," he said.

"Isn't that interesting? How convenient for him!"

"Slim, you think —"

But by then they were both inside Gracie Mansion, amid the clots of reporters milling about, the photographers snapping pictures of anything and everything — all the old vases, and the Claude Lorrain seascape, and the portrait of the Liberator she'd borrowed from the Met.

"Tom O'Kane, what do you think of your brother's decision?" one of the reporters asked, recognizing him.

"What decision is that?" he asked testily.

"You haven't heard? Then I guess he didn't discuss it with you."

"I don't know what you're talking about," he insisted, though in fact he was sure he did, his heart sinking in apprehension nonetheless as he waited for the man to tell him.

"He's running again! He's resigning his resignation!"

"Oh, *that* decision."

"So, *nu*? Whattaya think?"

"It's a dark, dark day," he said, suddenly sick and tired of it all, not even trying to hide the anger in his voice.

"Tom —" Slim tried to restrain him.

"Mrs. O'Kane—what do *you* think? Surely he discussed his decision first with *you*, his wife?"

"We have nothing more to say for now!" Tom exclaimed, dropping Slim's elbow but putting a protective arm around her, pulling her away from the swarming newsmen and up the stairs. The photographers nevertheless flashing away shot after shot of Slim's grim, stunned, almost tearful face.

"So. You went back on it. Without saying a word," Tom told him.

Charlie was waiting for them in the cozy sitting room Slim had remade for him upstairs. He was bent back deep in an easy chair, a glass of scotch and soda balanced on one arm. His face red, and excited, and a little guilty, like a schoolboy who's been caught kissing the maid, Tom thought.

"It just sort of came together, all of a sudden," he tried to explain. "The boys all came up, and wanted a meeting—the borough leaders, some a the others. Next thing I know, I'm the nominee again."

"Just like that?"

"I *won't* take this, Charlie," Slim said savagely. "I'm not helping you campaign for reelection. I'll go to Europe. I'm not going to watch you drop dead making some goddamned stump speech!"

"I'm not going to die, Slim—"

"*I'm your goddamned wife, Charlie!*" she hissed at him, as loudly as she dared with the newsmen still downstairs. "Don't I count for *anything?* Don't I even get a say?"

"Of course you get a say, Slim—"

"But only after the *fact*. You can go to hell!" she said, storming out of the room. As she left, she wobbled on one of her heels and almost went down. Before they could move to help her, she had both shoes off, hurling them across the room just above Charlie's befuddled head.

"I think that went well," he tried to joke when she was gone. Tom only stared at him, pouring himself a stiff shot of scotch and plopping onto the ottoman next to him.

"What the hell, Charlie?" he asked, despairing. "What the goddamned hell?"

"I had to do it, Tommy," Charlie said, keeping his voice low. "They were gonna lower the boom. They said they made up their minds, and they wouldn't stand for Hogan."

"No?"

"No. They said they'd make him fight a primary. They said they'd get Impellitteri to run, with all the Lucchese money behind him. They even threatened to get the Genoveses to come in, get behind that little commie, Marcantonio. Vito Marcantonio — can you imagine?"

"No. I can't," Tom said stonily.

"Neither could I," Charlie said, mopping a handkerchief across his forehead. "But they said they didn't care. They said they'd elect who they liked, an' take the consequences afterward. Just no Hogan."

"And when did this whole change of heart come about?"

"I dunno. I think they've been planning it for some time," Charlie told him earnestly. "They never did like how I shoved Hogan down their throats in the first place. I think they were just afraid Dunn would talk, and when he fried instead —"

"Who else was here?"

"Hmm? Whattaya talkin' about?"

"I know I wasn't here. I know Slim wasn't here. But who *was* here? Besides those stooges, the borough leaders, I mean?"

"They have real power, Tommy. You can't just go against 'em —"

"That's not who we're talking about. Is it?" Tom interrupted. "Who else was here? Bob Moses? Sam the Subway Man? Mr. Big?"

"I *had* to do this, don't ya see, Tom? I *had* to agree to run again," he pleaded, ignoring the question. "It was this, or turn the City back to Tammany Hall."

"Yes, it's nice to be invaluable, isn't it, Charlie," he said sadly. He put down his drink and stood up. "And when they take you out of here on a stretcher, who's gonna hold back Tammany Hall then? Or Moses, or McCormack?"

"I don't know, Tom, I don't know." His brother shook his head fervently, exaggeratedly. "All I know is, I have to do this now, or the City is going to be run by a *bunch of gangsters!*"

That made Tom laugh out loud.

"Don't kid yourself," he told his brother, watching the evening shadows spread out like spilled wine across the East River. "It already is. They just have better suits."

36

"More cigarettes. How thoughtful."

He pushed the two cartons across the table to Neddy Moran, smiling despite himself at the man's tone.

"And handin' 'em over just like that. Without making me dance for 'em like the organ grinder's monkey," Moran said, raising his eyebrows.

The big man looked good, Tom thought. There was a mouse under one eye, and a red splotch on his forehead, but he was trimmer and his skin was a better color than Tom remembered. He sat up straight in his chair, and a sense of confidence seemed to radiate from him.

Or maybe, Tom thought, *it's just that he doesn't give a damn anymore.*

"What'dja do to your face?" Tom asked.

"Oh, that?" Ned Moran said, smiling as he touched the mark on his forehead. "That was due to a little run-in with a lathe in the machine shop."

"But you're all right now?"

"Sure," Moran said with a grin. "You should see the lathe."

He swept the cartons of cigarettes over to himself, with a big right hand that Tom saw was chafed and scabbed over, all along the knuckles.

"I gave up smoking," he said, as if he were reciting the rosary, "but these're as good as cash in here."

"They're yours, with my gratitude," Tom said across the bare, scarred little table in the visitors' room.

"Your gratitude? For what?" Moran scoffed.

"For the way you cared for Claire. The way you took care of her. And for my brother. I didn't understand that before."

Moran looked away, embarrassed, and gave a little nod of acknowledgment. "She was a wonderful lady," he said softly, then cleared his throat. "Your brother can look after himself."

"That's what I'm up here for."

"Really? An' the whole time I thought this was a familial visit."

The gears had started falling into place the same evening that Hogan told them about Cockeye Dunn in the Dance Hall, and how close he had come to breaking open the whole waterfront. Wondering again, when he remembered that day with Slim and his brother up at Gracie Mansion, about the mysterious visitors and just who they had been, telling his brother he absolutely had to run for mayor again. Shutting Hogan the prosecutor out of City Hall, once they were sure he had nothing he could make stick.

The borough leaders, his brother had said. Sure, Tom could see that. But who else? And whose bidding were they doing?

Thinking about Dunn in the Death House made him think of Sing Sing again, and Neddy Moran up there, and then it had all made sense. Or at least he thought it had. Moran, who had arranged that mysterious meeting of his own, during the war. *With "the borough leaders," of course. And who else?*

Upstate, the season had begun to turn, the gorgeous fall foliage fading and curling up on itself. The leaves were thin enough on the trees that he could see most of the prison clearly from the platform, including the low, gray wing that was the Dance Hall. Thinking again of the night they'd brought out Pep Strauss and Marty Goldstein, with their shaved heads, in their simple black pants and white shirts. Thinking of Neddy Moran, taking his brother to see Frank Costello, and what he remembered Hogan saying about it: *Costello is really more of a politician than a mob boss. A glorified gambler, someone who carries messages for his friends. And one of his friends is Albert Anastasia.*

"I wanted to ask you just one more thing," Tom said carefully. Trying to fight down the fear within himself.

"Oh, I doubt that very much," Moran said cheerfully, smirking back at him across their old table. "Prosecutors have a way of seeing that one thing leads to another, and then another, and another. Until the next thing y'know, they're putting a rope around your neck."

"No, no. It's simple enough," he said. "It's just this: you were lying to me about goin' up to Frank Costello's apartment that time during the war. *Weren't you?*"

"I told you I was there," Moran said, and sighed wearily. "I told Rudy Halley and the Kefauver boys the same thing, and I would tell them the same thing again today—"

"No—that's not what I mean."

Standing shivering on the southeast corner of Columbus Circle, stamping their feet to stay warm. Charlie dressed in his country's uniform. Walking into the dazzling, art deco lobby of the Century apartments. A life filled with splendor, and all for some thug . . .

"What I mean is, you lied to me about what happened once you went upstairs. You went into that room with him. Didn't you?"

Ned Moran looked away, tapped his fingers on the tabletop, and glanced longingly at the cartons of cigarettes.

"I dunno what you're talkin' about," he said perfunctorily. "I told you, your brother told me he was goin' back into the bedroom, to talk about corruption in the shirts contracts. I didn't go in—"

"Nuts!" Tom told him, bringing his palm down hard on the table in his frustration, the sound echoing through the room. Moran didn't flinch, of course, just sat looking at him inquisitively with his legs crossed.

Costello more of a politician. Carrying messages for his friends.

"That's a lie, and you know it," Tom went on, jabbing a finger at him. "You didn't take my brother up to see the Prime Minister of the Underworld because he wanted to clean up the great army shirts racket! And even Charlie would've known better than to discuss anything with a man like that without bringin' along at least one witness, one piece of protection, for himself."

When he was done, Ned Moran looked at him sideways for a long moment. Then his hands moved quickly across to one of the cigarette cartons, his big, powerful hands ripping it open, tearing the label off a pack and getting a smoke lit and in his mouth before Tom could even offer a match. He took a long drag, then sat back in his chair, still studying him.

"All right," he said at last. "All right, maybe I'm done coverin' for OK Charlie at last. Maybe there's one O'Kane, anyway, who wants to know the truth."

"I do," Tom told him fiercely, though inside he was dying.

"Mind you, I won't testify. It wouldn't do a damned thing for you in court if I did anyway, save to win me another perjury conviction."

"I know that. All I want is the truth, and I can take it from there."

What did Costello want?

"Oh, is that all? Just the truth?" Ned Moran laughed — much in the same rueful manner that Hogan had, Tom reflected, when that topic had arisen. "I don't know the truth, son. I just know what I saw that night."

"And that is?"

Moran let out a long breath of smoke, then nodded.

"I went into the room with him."

"I *knew* it. Who else was there?" Afraid the fear would make his knees tremble.

"There was Costello, of course — the Prime Minister himself. A couple of his boys. That silly peacock, Joey Adonis, who ran his Jersey gamblin' joints for him. Those mutts, Carmine De Sapio, and his little brother from Hoboken. 'Three-Finger Brown' — you know, Lucchese?" he listed carefully, then paused before looking Tom straight in the face.

"And?" Tom said.

"And every one of the Democratic Party borough leaders. Save for Ed Flynn of the Bronx, who was off doin' something for Roosevelt at the time. But all the rest."

"What did they want?"

"It's not what they wanted," Moran said, keeping his eyes on Tom as he stubbed out his cigarette. "It's what your brother wanted from them."

"Did he get it?" Tom asked drily, making sure to get the words out one at a time.

"Yeah. They said he could be mayor of New York," Moran told him, still searching his face for some reaction.

"He didn't *need* that," Tom said fiercely. "He was going to be that anyway! He didn't need those sons of bitches!"

He could picture it all too readily, to his shame. His brother — dressed in his army general's uniform — sitting in a straight-backed chair before all those cheap pols and mobsters sprawling over the couch and bed, and the easy chairs in Frank Costello's bedroom suite. Having to please them. Already half in the bag, on their way to a prizefight or a whorehouse. Judging whether his brother was fit to be mayor...

"That's not what he seemed to think," Moran said gently. "He told me that day, 'I've got to go see the boys at Frankie Costello's if I'm gonna be mayor.' And I told him I didn't think he should go anywhere near Frankie Costello's, but he said the boys wanted it, so there he would go."

"I suppose he thought he needed the money," Tom said haltingly. "But that was all?"

"What else would there be?" Moran asked him speculatively, blowing up a cloud of smoke in front of his face.

"Was . . . was anything said about . . . Anastasia? Anything at all? About a favor—"

Moran cut him off, laughing bitterly. "Jesus, but you really believed what those idjits with Kefauver were putting out there!" he scoffed. His face open and frank as he waved away the smoke, looking Tom in the eye. "No, nothing got said about Mr. Albert Anastasia. If there had been, I would've dragged our boy out by the collar myself, believe you me."

"Costello was just setting himself up. Making sure he could run his gambling operations again, once the war was over and La Guardia was gone," Tom said, piecing it together. A backwash of relief starting to seep in around the shame. *Oh, Charlie, you are a fool. But no worse . . .*

"There wasn't a whole lot to it," Moran said, nodding. "We weren't there more than ten, fifteen minutes. We went in the back bedroom, an' they sat us down, an' someone offered your brother a highball, but he said no thanks. Then he told 'em he was running for mayor, and he would like to have their support."

"He told that . . . that *gangster* he wanted that?"

"He said . . . he said he would make sure New York was a town they could do business in again," Moran said, stumbling over the words, looking a little sick to his stomach. "That's all he said, an' then they nodded, an' Frankie Costello said if that was the case, then he had their support."

Tom felt ill himself. "Their support? What did that mean?"

"He said whatever it took. They'd do whatever it took."

"And then?" Tom asked.

"And then that was the end of it," Moran said, flicking out the words like a man trying to get a loose piece of tobacco off his tongue. "Then they all shook hands with him, and they went off to their show, or their fight, or their whores, and we went home to Brooklyn and our families, an' that was that."

"He didn't discuss it with you anymore on the way back? Nothing ever came up about Anastasia?"

"No, and no," Moran said firmly. "I drove and he sat in the back, as usual, and I don't know that either of us said a damned thing until I dropped him off. The next day he was off to Washington, and his war, and I don't know that we ever discussed that night again."

"I see."

The two men sat facing each other across the little table, the fallen idol between them. Tom shook his head in disgust, though he felt like laughing at the same time.

"Walking right into it! Not even understanding that the meeting itself was a setup. That they'd have everything they needed over him, just getting him up there to Costello's."

"I know."

"He never gave a damn about gambling, the numbers, any of that," Tom went on. "He didn't want his cops bustin' up the corner dice game, or raidin' bookies. You remember how he was, always trying to get it legalized?"

"That I do," Neddy affirmed.

"Ah, Charlie! Jesus, Jesus. He didn't think it was a crime, so he must've figured where's the harm, some of that money might as well go to his campaign—"

"Now you're askin' me for the truth again," Moran warned. "I can't say that we ever talked about his reasons. But you know your brother. He can be as clever as a snake, and as innocent as a newborn babe. Sometimes all in the same afternoon."

"Clairey was right. He finally got ahead of himself."

Moran crossed himself at the mention of her name, then leaned back and lit up another cigarette.

"So who did have Reles thrown out that window?" Tom asked himself out loud.

"That I can't tell you. Only about the great cabal in Frankie Costello's penthouse," Moran said.

"And that was all?" Tom asked one more time. "That was the whole conversation? Nothing else? No one else was there?"

Neddy put his head back and blew a long funnel of smoke toward the ceiling while he thought about it. He looked around at Tom, started to shake his head — then caught himself.

"Oh, there was one other fellow. That grinnin' prick with his chest always puffed out. Like Lord Cock Robin —"

"Who?"

"He's been doin' a lot of testifyin' of his own, lately. Before Dewey's committee on the waterfront. You'd be surprised, the time you have to read the papers around here. You know the man — the one they're always callin' 'Mr. Big.'"

37

Mexico, 1953

They left for Mexico City that same afternoon, in a cream-colored Bentley from Señor Perusquia's garage. Slim behind the wheel, driving like a fury. She pushed it close to a hundred once they got up to the skinny, two-lane strips of blacktop that cut across the plateaus. Barely slowing even for the hairpin turns on the winding roads up and down the interminable mountains. He was going to tell her to slow down, aware that one pothole, one crumbling shoulder would leave them flattened like the glistening silver wrecks of armadillos scattered along the asphalt. But when he had to ask himself why it was the two of them shouldn't end up with such a fate, he couldn't think of a single reason.

He made her slow down only when they approached Cuernavaca. Aware by then they couldn't make Mexico City before dark. Less afraid of dying than of breaking an axle, or running out of gas in the middle of nowhere, and having to spend whole days out on the road with only each other.

"All right, but I won't go stay in Shangri-La with that fucking Henry Fink," Slim said, not looking at him, her face half hidden by the pastel Chanel scarf she had wrapped around her head and the sunglasses she was still wearing even though it was nearly dusk. "It's Friday night, and they'll all be there. All his Big Crowd, and the old vampires. I couldn't stand the sight of them."

"You won't have to," Tom told her as they drove down into the valley, already smelling the sweet, heavy scent of the rose fields, and the waxy, white tuberoses from Chiconcuac.

They stopped along the cobbled road into the town, to speak to the same procession of mestizo women headed back into town at the end of the day. Between Slim's Spanish and Tom's money they were able to get a room in the small, pink house of an elderly woman, high up on the hillside. The house was neat and airy, and well swept — much cleaner than the bungalows of the Shangri-La. The old woman served them a roast chicken and a couple of glasses of beer out on the tiny patio, then left them to each other.

As it happened, the house was a block or so up the hill from the nightclub, and angled enough to allow them to look right into its shabby bar and courtyard. Eating in silence as they watched the staff prepare for the evening's festivities.

There was a small bleating noise, and they both looked down to see the band walking up the hill from the zocalo in the gathering dusk. They were dressed already in their mariachi costumes, tuning their instruments as they came, a few more notes from a horn or a guitar floating up to them.

"This should be good," Tom said, but Slim only blew some more smoke out through her nose.

"It's about as authentic as Henry is," she said. "Half the time, they end up playing 'Shine On, Harvest Moon,' or 'Stormy Weather' for the expats."

An ice truck pulled up, then the Coca-Cola truck, and after that the Cadillacs began to arrive from Mexico City, big and black, or white, growling powerfully along the driveway. Disgorging first the Big Crowd, dressed in impeccable evening clothes, none of them sitting yet, but looking around at one another in seeming expectation. The American expats came later — older and imperious, most of them dressed in rumpled and even stained jackets, or tired dresses. Their appearance brought Henry Fink dancing out across the terrace, and everyone felt released to sit down. The band broke into a mariachi number, then the love ballad that he remembered Charlie singing in the car.

Lisboa Antigua reposa
lena de encanto y belleza —

"Don't you hate them," Slim breathed. "Don't you just hate them?"

"Who?"

"The Americans. Look at how they're dressed — it's a calculated insult, right there. And the Big Crowd, too — for taking it."

"You used to like it."

She looked at him, her gaze level and unsmiling. "I loved it. When we first got down here, it seemed like such a goddamned relief. At least from what was going on in the City. And Charlie was almost like his old self again. Before everything went wrong."

"I'm sorry," he said, and meant it. "I should have tried to see you again, to get down here and check in on him. Maybe —"

"Maybe nothing," she said, cutting him off. "There wasn't anymore *us* by then. As we just discovered. And Charlie was very happy to be down here. He was even happy with me. At least, until the Kefauver hearings. It was a good thing for him to leave the City. He just should have done it earlier. And never gone back."

"Maybe that's so," Tom said softly into the Cuernavaca night.

New York, 1950

He had gone to see Charlie when he was readmitted to the hospital. Lying on his back, his face on the hospital pillow shrunken and sallow. Opening his eyes just as Tom sat down next to his bed, looking as fearful and disoriented as a child.

"Which one?" he asked.

"Which one what?"

"Which hospital am I in this time?"

"Ah. Doctors Hospital."

"Well, that's good. Best to have a hospital with doctors." He winked at Tom. "How d'ya like my inspection tour of the City's medical facilities?"

"Lovely. You can stop anytime now."

"Hey, how'd you get in here unannounced?" he said, propping himself up on one elbow and looking around. "What happened to Joe Boyle?"

"Your cop? I think he went to get something to eat."

Charlie sighed. "I have some bad luck with bodyguards, all right. Just yesterday, a little old lady got by him. Said I had promised to make her nephew Elmer a magistrate."

"What'd you say?"

"I asked, 'Can't young Elmer wait?' You know what she did?"

"No."

"She looked me up an' down, then she said, 'I don't know, Charlie, the way you look, anything can happen.'"

When they stopped laughing, Tom could see that his brother's eyes were filled with tears, but there was a look of relief there, as well.

"So you're really going?"

"I am at last," he confirmed. "Mr. Secretary Acheson's got me Mexico, just like he promised. The paperwork's all done an' submitted. All that's left is to announce it to the press."

"And then Vinnie Impellitteri will be mayor of the greatest city in the world."

"Then Impy will be mayor," Charlie confirmed — and added in a voice like a remorseful boy's: "Are ye mad at me, Tom?"

"No, Charlie," he said, and smiled sadly at his brother. "I didn't want you to run again in the first place, if you'll remember, and I don't want you killin' yourself at your job. The City'll get by. We've survived worse than Vincent R. Impellitteri in the past, an' we will again. You just go down to Mexico an' get well again."

"Thank you, Tommy," he said, clutching his hand. "God bless you, boy. God bless."

Cuernavaca, 1953

"So we went down to Mexico," she said. "Seemed like a good idea at the time."

"Yes."

"Did you know, he wanted to have a ticker-tape parade when we left?" she asked him.

"No. I did not."

"'A big sendoff with all the trimmings,' was how he put it. He kept bringing it up before Neddy Moran. Finally I put my foot down. I told him I was not taking part in any parade, and that if he threw one for himself, I would stay behind."

"Thank God," Tom said, and sighed.

They sat silently for a few more minutes, looking down the hill at the club terrace. A few couples were dancing now—almost all of them from the Big Crowd, most of the expats sitting about and watching. The band playing a very credible rendition of "If I Didn't Care."

"But you know," she said slowly, turning her head to look at him, "why shouldn't he have had a parade?"

"What?"

"I mean, besides the fact that it would be pompous, and self-aggrandizing, and a great waste of money," she added. "If he wanted to have a parade for himself, well, why not? Isn't that one more part of the great boys' adventure of the O'Kanes?"

"Well . . ." He fumbled for the words, and she nodded triumphantly, whatever she was thinking confirmed.

"You know it as well as I do," she said. "Because there *was* something wrong. Because there was something not right about it all along—"

"About *what?*"

"About all of it. About *him.* He knew it, too, as much as he ever admits anything to himself. He didn't fight me on the parade. Instead, we just had the official car take us down the driveway at Gracie Mansion. I remember the cop there jumping to a salute. Charlie had us go around town, to say thanks to some of the doctors and nurses at all his hospitals. But that was as much of a parade as he pulled. I remember it was a very quiet day in the late summer, barely a soul on the street."

She leaned over toward him now, speaking quietly.

"We crept out of town like a couple of thieves in the night. And why was that, Tommy O'Kane? What was it you've dug up? What was it we all knew was wrong all along?"

"I'm still not sure," Tom told her, rubbing his chin. Wondering if he really wasn't, or if this was the last lie he would tell her.

Slim laughed unexpectedly, the sound tinny and grating against the music floating up the hill.

"You're not sure? My God, have three people ever been so able to keep a secret? Even from themselves?"

"I'm not sure — not yet."

She sat watching him, curious, waiting for him to continue. Then she understood.

"So you're going to ask him it — whatever it is — straight out."

"I am."

He sat rubbing the folded-up strip of paper in his pocket. The one from the medical examiner's report on Abe Reles: *Withhold information by order of DA.* Wondering if he should show it to her, try to explain.

"My God. And you really think he's going to tell you? *Now?* When all he's *got* is what you think of him?"

"That's what I'm worryin' about."

"But ..."

"But I think it's only going to work if I start with a confession."

"A confession. *From* you." He nodded his head, and she looked at him for a beat. "And you want to know if I want to go first."

"That's right."

She laughed again, even more unpleasantly than the last time. "And they say chivalry is dead. No, please, be my guest. He's already sure he knows what I am."

That night they slept together for the last time, under the pink bedspread in the neat, pink house of the nice old lady. Neither of them saying anything, spooned up together because they had to be in the narrow bed. Tom held his arms around her, and she was stiff and unmoving against him at first, but eventually she reached up a hand, then another, to hold his wrists. Her body started to shake, and he realized she was crying, and all he could think to do was hold her tighter, and nuzzle his face along her hair. Wondering, as he did, what the hell he could ever tell Ellie.

38

The Bronx, 1953

He spent the day before he left for Mexico with Ellie's family up in East Tremont, a long-delayed dinner to meet the parents. It was a Sunday afternoon, but even so he could hear the booming the moment he started to walk down the stairs from the Third Avenue el. It was coming from the east, like the sound of rock being smashed by something harder than rock, over and over again. Punctuated every few minutes by a high, ominous whining sound, followed by a gabble of excited shouts and then an explosion. As he walked south on Marmion Avenue, away from the sound, a thin, silicate-gray cloud drifted slowly over him, making him cough and swear before he was able to cover his face with a handkerchief. The few women and children on the street hurrying past stared at him wordlessly, holding their own handkerchiefs or the lapels of their coats or the sleeves of their dresses up over their mouths.

Ellie's parents lived on the third floor of a five-story walk-up, indistinguishable from the other five- and six-story walk-ups that filled both sides of East 176th Street. It was a large, high-ceilinged, scrupulously clean apartment, humid and steeped in the rich smell of cooking meat when he entered. Her parents greeted him in the apartment's L-shaped foyer. Her mother, Judith, small and birdlike and effusive, wrapping an arm around his neck and giving him a loud kiss on the cheek. Her father, Nat, a tall, stooped, somber man with kindly eyes behind his black-framed glasses and the steely arm muscles of the presser he had been for most of his life. He shook Tom's hand enthusiastically, until Ellie made him stop before it turned to jelly.

"Let him go now, Daddy," she said, beaming, from farther back in the long foyer, trying to look amused but more pleased than she could readily hide. "He gets worn out enough chasing the bad guys all week."

"It's like a war zone out there," Tom said, before Ellie came to take his coat and kiss his cheek, and quietly hush him.

"Don't — or we'll never talk about anything else!"

They ate in the dining room, decorous and genteel, and more carefully preserved than any crime scene he'd ever been at. The shiny wooden table was covered with a lace tablecloth that anyone in County Mayo would have envied. A curtained glass cabinet held ceremonial candlesticks and silver serving dishes, and a bottle of Slivovitz and one of kosher wine from Schapiro's, with its distinctive trademark on the label: "the wine you can almost 'cut with a knife.'"

Ellie had made sure he'd brought a good bottle of burgundy from Manhattan, and she insisted on opening that. The four of them laughing and talking easily together, with Ellie's mother alternately regretting that her other daughter was away at college and bombarding him with questions about the office, and what it was he did for Mr. Hogan. They ate a lamb shank cooked so tenderly, the meat nearly fell off the bone, and broccoli steamed until it was as limp as a dishrag, and some sort of potato dish that was delicious but seemed to possess the density of industrial concrete. The whole time the booming continued, the sound pounding relentlessly through the windows open against the unseasonable fall heat outside.

"Do you hear that? It's the road — Mr. Moses's great big road, coming to get us!" Ellie's mother told him when they had finished. Sitting in their sunken living room, with its matching couches and chairs around a proud new coffee table. Eating slices of the seven-layer cake Ellie had baked for dessert, and sipping the Slivovitz from tiny, ornate, white-smoked brandy glasses.

"Ma, I thought we were going to have a night off from the road for once," Ellie gently chided her, putting a hand on her leg.

"Who can ignore it?" her mother protested. "It's shameful. To clean and clean all day for company, and look what it still brings in!"

She pointed at one of the broad, white windowsills, where Tom could see, even from a distance, a mound of fine black powder, growing steadily even as he watched.

"All day long! It's like living in Appalachia!"

"You can't fight City Hall," Nat said dolefully from across the coffee table, holding the brandy glass as delicately as an eggshell in his immense, flattened hands.

"I remember the day I first heard it. It was the summer after the war," she told them. "There was this boom, way off in the distance. Just one big noise, just like that. Like it was some sort of signal. I was afraid it was a gas main. But no, that was just the starting gun! Then there was another, and another, and you're thinking it's got to stop soon. But it never did. It just kept coming closer and closer, all these years."

She gave a little shiver.

"Mr. O'Kane—"

"Tom, ma'am."

"Mr. O'Kane, I just want to say how much I admired the work that yourself and your brother have done on behalf of the colored people and the Puerto Ricans," Ellie's mother told him, sitting stiffly at attention, as if to pay proper homage to the seriousness of the subject. "It's right that someone should help them. We've had many more of them moving up from Morrisania in recent years, and I can tell you, they're perfectly lovely."

"Ma—"

Ellie was blushing now, and rolling her eyes, but her mother remonstrated with her.

"What did I say? It's true! We even have a mixed couple in this building. The Smiths, up on the fifth floor. He's colored, she's Jewish—nicest people you can imagine! We got no problems, everybody gets along. But just because there are some colored now, they try to make out this is a slum! I'm not joking, that's what they're calling it—*slum clearance!*"

"It's what they have to call it, Mrs. Abramowitz, to get the money from Washington," Tom told her.

"They call these buildings tenements. *Tenements!*" she exclaimed, pushing forward to the edge of her couch. "My husband and me, we *know* from tenements! That's what we came here to get away from."

She shook her head in frustration.

"We raised our girls here, gave them the life we wanted for ourselves. And now they want to say we live in tenements and slums, and they get to pave a highway over us!"

"An . . . an *expressway!*" Nat stuttered in disgust. "Like a fancy new word makes it all right!"

"All these years, we could see it coming, but we did nothing," Ellie's mother said softly now, as if she were talking about some dreadful secret. "Mrs. Edelstein, in the building here, she tried to get people together to do something, but they would rather not think about it. Who can concentrate on trouble so far away? Then, almost a year ago, just in time for the holiday season, we get an *eviction* notice!"

She bit off the word with contempt, having to stand up and walk around the sunken living room in her indignation.

"Everybody did, all up and down the street. *Eviction* notices! Like we were drunken bums who can't afford the rent! Like we were *drug addicts!* But not from the landlord, even. From the City of New York! All written up on official stationery, and envelopes: 'Hello, you have ninety days to get out!' Like something out of Russia! We lived here twenty years, now we got three months to get out!"

"It's what Mr. Moses likes to call 'em — 'shake 'em up and get 'em moving' notices," Tom told them grimly. "There's no force of law behind the deadline. He's just trying to intimidate you —"

"*That's* what we said!" Mrs. Abramowitz told him triumphantly, retaking her seat. "Thousands of people, ordered out of their homes, so they could build a . . . a, a *big road!*"

"For what?" Nat asked, his eyes brimming with anger between the thick black glasses. "So people can get to New Jersey fifteen minutes faster?"

"We knew our rights. Mrs. Edelstein, she was a marvel, organizing everything. Me, I did what I could —"

"You were *great*, Ma," Ellie put in, the pride in her voice piercing Tom to his core.

"Ach, you can't fight City Hall," Nat said again, shaking his head.

"But we *did*. We got lawyers to help us, and an engineer, and traffic planners. They drew up a whole map, showed how this big road, they could run it down along Corona Park North. Take it two blocks south, all you have to knock down is five apartment houses. Not throw fifteen hundred families out of their homes, the way they have it now."

"They mapped it all out," Mr. Abramowitz said. "You'd get to Hackensack just as fast."

"Then we went over there and took a look at what's coming," Judith said with a small shudder. "They kept telling us, 'Don't worry about the eviction, the City Real Estate Bureau will find you a new place to live.' So we went over to see where the road was already."

She looked around at them all before continuing, an expression of real horror on her face.

"What we saw, I can't even tell you. They turned the City into a giant dump. We went into some of the buildings over there, the ones that were still standing? Garbage all over the place. Garbage — and worse! — filling the lobbies. *Animals* living in there. *Bums* living there, pulling out all the copper plumbing. Broken glass everywhere, the stairs broken."

She leaned forward, to speak even more confidentially of the things she had seen. "Worse yet, there were people still *living* there! Whole families, living out of their suitcases like *gypsies!* They told us, the ones who would talk to us, the City moved them there once they tore down their old buildings. Every night, they could hear the bums outside in the hall, scratching at the locks, trying to get in. And guess what? The City charges them *rent* to live like this! Worse — every time they move them someplace ahead of that highway, they charge them *more* rent!"

Real tears of frustration, of bewilderment welled up in her eyes now.

"Not that we gave in," she said. "That only made people more determined to fight, because we had no place to run. Finally, last spring, we got a big meeting down at City Hall, with the Board of Estimate.

"Half the neighborhood went down. We had to rent school buses to take us, there were so many people. Mostly the women, because it was in the daytime, the men couldn't miss work, but there were hundreds of us. It was such a good turnout, we thought they'd have to give in! The mayor was there, the city council. James J. Lyons, the borough president, he said he was with us . . ." Her voice trailed off, mouth twisting cynically.

"It didn't matter," she resumed. "None of it mattered. We got down there, and we brought out all our charts and diagrams. We brought our lawyer, and our traffic engineers, and our city planners. Then, halfway through, *Moses* comes strolling in. Walking right down the aisle like the big *I am*. Nobody was listening anymore to anything we had to say. That excuse for a mayor, Impellitteri? He was scrambling around to get him a chair. I thought he was going to bring him some water next.

"Right away, you could see that Moses was the boss. He went over and talked to each one of the borough presidents, laughing and whispering with them. They weren't paying attention to a word we said anymore. They didn't even have the courtesy to pretend to be interested. Like we were *nothing* to them.

"After that, it was all over. I knew it, even if I didn't know it yet. They weren't even listening anymore; they just waited until we made our presentation and sat down. Then Mr. James J. Lyons stood up and said he had changed his mind, and they had to run the expressway where Moses wanted it.

"Mrs. Edelstein, she jumped right up and said to his face, 'Mr. Lyons, you've double-crossed the people.' Lyons, *he* started yelling, 'Demagogue!' at the top of his voice. Impellitteri started yelling for her to apologize. But she wouldn't do it. She just looked at Lyons, and at the mayor, and she said, 'You're both a couple of rotters. You double-crossed the people.'"

"What will you do?" Tom asked quietly.

"Thank God, Nat took the training course on how to x-ray plane parts. It's a good job. He starts out at the defense plant in New Jersey next week. He's going that way anyway, we might as well move. I suppose we'll have to get a car, find a place somewhere."

"We're both taking the driver's ed course now," Nat said brightly, his voice again full of the optimism of a man who had always made his own living. "You wouldn't believe how cheap houses are out there, how much room you can get. We'll be all right—"

"But it won't be like *this*," his wife said, dejected. "The whole neighborhood gone, and everything it was, and everything it could be. What kind of a city is it, that lets a wonderful neighborhood, a neighborhood full of good people, get ploughed under for a *road?*"

"I don't know, ma'am," Tom said sadly, looking over at Ellie, who was rubbing her mother's back, her own eyes sparkling with tears.

"I'll say one thing," Judith told him, a kindly smile forcing its way through to her face. "This never would've happened with a great mayor like your brother, God bless him."

* * *

After dinner, he walked out with Ellie in the dying light. Ellie held tight to his elbow with both arms, head nestled neatly into the curve of his neck.

"They like you a lot," she told him quietly.

"Did they? That's nice," he said.

"So do I," she said softly, looking up at him with her wry smile.

"That's even better."

He leaned down and kissed her on the mouth, and afterward her smile was wider, and not wry at all.

"I like them, too. No, that's not the right words for how I feel about them," he told her. "They seem like the best people on earth."

"They are. How perceptive of you."

"I'm very keen that way. Although, I must say, I think I swallowed a bowling ball somewhere along the way."

"Yes, Ma goes a little overboard on the kugel," she said, and chuckled.

"Either that, or it was the cake," he said, and she slapped him with her pocketbook.

"Well, don't worry. You'll only have a few thousand more opportunities to get it right," he told her, trying to make his voice sound jocular, although he knew it didn't.

"Is that right?" She laughed. "I'll be at home, perfecting my baking? While you're out, chasing down the criminals."

"Something like that."

"And what if I don't want that?" she asked, her eyes teasing but her voice serious.

"I don't know if Mr. Hogan will put up with it, a married couple working for him."

"So you'll have to stay home with the baking."

He held her hands in his and smiled down at her. The evening had begun to grow cool. The wind from the east whipping up again, blowing the fine, stinging dust through their hair. He stood looking at her, just because he wanted to, her sweet face and her deep brown eyes looking steadily back at him.

"I'm serious," he told her. "I can't imagine spending the years with anyone else."

"It's not, you know, that sometimes I don't think I would like to have exactly what they have," she said slowly, tilting her head down. "A home, a family of my own — of *our* own. Jesus, what am I saying? We're already talking about children! But other times, I think I would just go crazy, sitting around with the girls at their mahjongg game."

"Don't worry. We'll work it out, one way or t'other," he told her. "After I get back from Mexico, I'll have a proper proposal for ya, and a proper ring, and a plan."

"After you get back from Mexico. And him, and *her*," she said. "Then we'll see."

"That's all in the past, I told you —"

She stopped him with a look. "All right. We'll see."

"We will," he said — and almost told her right then and there about the note he'd found on the medical examiner's report. *Withhold information by order of DA.* About all that Neddy Moran had told him about who had been in the room with his brother, and what they'd said, and everything else that he'd begun to fear and suspect. But he didn't.

"I'm going to stop in Atlanta first," he told her instead. "On the way."

"Why?"

"Mr. Tick-Tock Tannenbaum —"

"One of the rats!" Ellie exclaimed.

"I got a lead on him from the feds. That's where he's holed up these days."

"What do you think he's going to tell you?" she asked, already trying to figure out what it could be.

"Just what went on in the Rats Suite that night. Or, more important, just *who* was there that night."

"And assuming that he tells you anything, how good do you think it's going to be?"

"I don't know. I don't know if I can trust anything he'll say, a murdering bum like that. But whatever happened, I need to know everything I possibly can before I go down to Mexico."

He stopped and turned to face her again on the sidewalk.

"I don't know what I'm going to find out down there. And I don't know what I'm going to do when I find it."

Ellie only nodded, as if she already understood everything he was thinking. "I know you'll do what's right, whatever you find."

They kissed again, and she put her hand in his as they started walking toward the construction works.

They didn't have far to go. The building of the road was less than ten blocks from her parents' home by now, and a scene of devastation unlike anything he'd ever seen before, even in Italy during the war. All of a sudden, the cityscape melted into a pile of pure, mindless wreckage, for as far as they could see. Uprooted trees tossed atop heaps of clothing, and piles of bricks and smashed-up wood, and sinks and toilets, and loose doors and busted-up furniture. Littered all over the top of it were heaps of real garbage: coffee rinds and eggshells, and empty fifth bottles, and fish heads and old newspapers, and open sewage — whatever else the bums and the winos and the retreating, desperate people Ellie's mother had seen had thrown on top of it all, in their shame and their despair.

"Jesus," Ellie breathed, as they watched it all. "Jesus Christ."

Over the nightmarish landscape scuttled teams of indomitable workmen in yellow vests and hardhats. Men possessed of the same confident, wiry strength Ellie's father had. Grinning and shouting despite the lateness of the hour, and the grime that covered their faces and their work clothes.

As they watched, a crane operator maneuvered a wrecking ball against the wall of another walk-up, as carefully as a man tapping a soft-boiled egg for his breakfast. He tapped it once, twice, then all of a sudden the whole wall gave in, a shower of bricks cascading down into the ditch and a great cloud of dust speeding rapidly toward them.

Ellie and Tom turned simultaneously and tried to hurry back, but it was too late. The dust overtaking them even as Tom put his arm around her shoulder and guided her quickly back through the gathering darkness. The streets deserted now, save for a stray knife sharpener, gray-bearded, in his thick, dark clothes and black hat. Hurrying his pushcart past them, his eyes wide, as if he had been caught up in this hellish place by mistake, far from home.

39

Atlanta, 1953

He took the Pennsy down to Washington, then changed at Union Station for the Silver Comet, on the Seaboard Air Line road. The train was a shiny new streamliner, with a sleek stainless steel engine and all-room sleepers, painted on the outside with flamboyant streaks of green and orange and yellow.

Everything was very modern and splendid. There was a high-topped observation car with air-conditioning, and a glass roof, and carpeting and pretty new turquoise cushions on all the chairs. There was a dining car with real inlaid china, and a club car with a shower-bath and a barber on duty at all times, and even a library car. And as soon as they pulled out of Union Station in the nation's capital, the conductors gathered up all the Negro passengers and marched them swiftly back into the colored car.

They were the best-dressed people on the train, Tom thought, in their new suits and dresses and hats for the folks back home. Some of them were ministers with their collars on; others wearing Phi Beta Kappa keys, or were hunched or white-haired with age. They walked back through the train with stiff-legged dignity, and the expressions on their faces were worse than anything he'd ever seen, even on the mobs of refugees that used to flounder past their tank columns during the war.

He looked away, telling himself that he was on a job. Thinking uncomfortably about how many men he'd heard testify, using the same expression: *It was a job.* Traveling down on the very same line, to some of the very same places. Blending in with the drummers, and the regional managers, carrying their own little kits, like Pep Strauss had.

The wolf held at bay. Playing pinochle in the club car, nursing a drink, and reading The Saturday Evening Post. *Playing at being a real person with a real life. The ice pick or the garrote tucked discreetly away in the overnight bag. Another job in another town . . .*

* * *

The train pulled into Terminal Station less than nineteen hours after leaving New York, just as advertised. It was still twenty of eight in the morning, but Tom had already been up for two hours, showered and dressed and breakfasted in the elegant new dining car, where a colored waiter served him coffee and bacon and eggs made by the colored cooks in the kitchen. He checked his bags in the Italianate villa of a train station with its twin cupolas, then killed another couple hours in the coffee shop, trying to chew his way through a copy of the morning *Constitution*. When the terminal clock struck ten, he threw a dollar onto the counter and caught a cab to the address he had from his friend with the feds.

The place turned out to be a light-fixture store, on a relatively quiet block of Peachtree Street, a mile or so north of downtown. It was in a low, long building, with the name ZACKS inscribed apologetically over the door, a dark-green awning pulled down against the heat, and a variety of Tiffany glass and little pagoda lampshades residing dustily in the front windows. It was a block where you could fall asleep just trying to walk down it, he thought.

He had the cab let him out around the corner, then walked quickly back past the window and in the door with his fedora angled down over one side of his face, not wanting to give someone the chance to see him coming. But just the alacrity with which he entered the store gave him away, the salesman looking up immediately at such an unaccustomed purpose of movement. One hand slipping inside his buttoned jacket, until he saw Tom's face and he stopped — a sickly smile creasing his visage, the hand dropping guiltily back out at his side like a schoolboy caught raiding the cookie jar.

Even in the muted light of the store's interior, Tom recognized him at once. *Tick-Tock Tannenbaum.* He'd sprouted the first, gradual curve of a paunch, in the twelve years since Tom had seen him last, and the close-cut, carefully barbered hair had receded past the crest of his forehead and was flecked with gray. The face had grown a little jowly, but there was still the same long, drooping nose, the heavy, almost Asiatic eyes, the sleek, batlike ears that he would know anywhere.

"How may I help you today, sir?" he asked in a loud voice. Fixing Tom with his eyes, then letting them go flat, and cold, and dead. The usual cheap gangster's trick, until Tom told him, "Knock it off, Tick-Tock," and the impish, boy's smile that he remembered replaced it, his eyes gleaming.

"Let me show you some of our newest line of lampshades just over here," he said, still booming, taking Tom by the elbow and leading him toward a far corner of the store, by the window and the moribund Tiffany.

Tom peered back deliberately into the interior of the store, in the direction Tannenbaum was steering him away from. Behind the counter he could make out a sharp-eyed man with a tie a little too gaudy, and a suit cut a little too sharp for the proprietor of a sleepy southern lamp store. He also seemed decidedly interested in what they were saying.

"Go easy with the boss here, huh," Tick-Tock pleaded quietly once they were out of earshot, gesturing lavishly toward a row of brownish lampshades that looked to have last been cleaned sometime before Pearl Harbor. "Whattaya you guys want from me anyhow? Ya had me testify against Dandy Parisi three years ago, ya see how that turned out —"

"Shut up for once in your life," Tom told him, smiling pleasantly. "I don't want you to testify. Not now, anyway, and probably not ever."

"Who is it, then? LA? Look, the only guy I ever knew about there was Benny, an' he's long gone —"

"Shut up, I said," Tom told him, pretending to admire a red pagoda desk lamp. "What I want is information — background. That's all."

Tannenbaum chuckled for real. "Ohhh, I see, and I should give that to you why, because you fucks wrecked my life?" he said, waving a hand around the room. "Lookit this. All these fucking lampshades. Drivin' me nuts bein' around 'em all day. Ya know, Eva Braun used to make lampshades outta the skins of dead Jews. Sometimes I think she musta made one out outta mine, end up here —"

"You're a disgusting piece of filth. And shut. The. Fuck. Up," Tom told him again.

"But I don't get it, I really don't. Ya come in here askin' for somethin', ya must have somethin' to gimme. Maybe cash?" Tick-Tock went on, looking suddenly hopeful as the thought occurred to him. "No? No money? Then why the hell should I help you?"

"You talked once before without money," Tom said easily. "You talked, and talked, and talked. All over the country."

"That's because I was facin' seven years up at that black hole in Dannemora," Tannenbaum told him, "And because of your brother."

"My brother?"

"Sure. He took me for a little ride upstate one afternoon. Over a hundred miles outta the City. God, that felt good after being cooped up in that cell for so long. Nice fall day, the leaves turnin' already."

"Where'd ya go?" Tom asked, trying to make his voice sound as if he knew the answer and was just testing him for some reason. Allie gave him his impish, boy's grin again.

"Up home, of course. Dear old Loch Sheldrake, 'the most affordable, most companionable, most delectable resort in the Catskills.' Just so I could watch 'em dig up Hyman Yuran."

"Poor old Hyman Yuran."

The shmatte foreman. Lepke's front, yet another one fingered because it was supposed he might talk. Sweating and lumbering around the hotel pool, with all the damned screaming and splashing kids who wouldn't let him sleep. Thinking the hard blonde in the car might really be interested in him. Carefully knotting his best tie, and slapping on his cologne in the dreary, humid little room . . .

"That was pretty funny," Tom said slowly. "Dumpin' the body in your parents' swimming pool excavation."

The boy's grin spreading slowly from ear to ear. "Yeah, well, that was nothin' compared to watchin' 'em dig it up. That whole brand-new pool. Sammy, my old man, runnin' around shoutin' about who was gonna pay for it—"

"What didja have against 'em, anyway, Tick-Tock?" Tom asked him. "What did they ever do to you, besides take you off Orchard Street, raise you out in the country in a nice hotel?"

"Don't that speak for itself?"

He held out his hands, the grin souring his face.

"I was twenty-five years old, my old man still had me waitin' tables, goin' around settin' up beach chairs. Layin' out the shuffleboard court like I was one more cabana boy," he told Tom.

"The only difference was, you got to own the joint one day."

Tannenbaum shrugged. "When was that gonna be? Next year in Jerusalem? You don't know my old man. He wouldn't pay me till the end a the season. Not one dime. I didn't even get to keep the tips. There I was, walkin' around all summer with nothin', no money to go out with girls. I couldn't even go to the picture show in town."

"So because you were cinematically deprived, you decided you might as well get a start bumpin' people off."

"Hey, I needed to do *some*thin'—"

"There was always college."

"Eh, I tried a couple semesters. College wasn't for me. After that, my old man got me a job as a tailor's apprentice, at the College Shop up on a Hundred and Thirteenth Street. But that wasn't for me, either. Spend my whole life measurin' those Ivy League fucks for their tweed jackets and their nice suits? Crawlin' around on my hands an' knees to check how their nuts fall?"

"So killing strangers was all that remained."

"I'd see all those guys around the hotel in the summer." He shrugged again. "Lepke, and the Gurrah. Shimmy Salles and Curly Holtz. They always had money, they always had girls, no matter how fat an' ugly they were. They did what they wanted, didn't take no shit from nobody. They liked me, too. They were always tellin' me I should come work for 'em, I could go far—"

"Ah, isn't that special!"

"So, one day I run into Big Harry Schacter, down in the City. He worked for Lepke, asked me if I wanted a job. I told him sure, if it paid. They started me off at thirty-five a week. Just doin' little jobs at first, you know? Some *shlamming,* throwing stink bombs in stores that wouldn't pay off. Sluggin' a couple fellas. Nothin' like killin'."

He was speaking freely now, living up to his nickname. His words soft and rhythmic and unending, just like the sound of a ticking clock.

"They moved me up from there. Maybe help take care of a body or two, like with Hyman. Drivin' the cars, deliverin' packages, that kinda thing. They were payin' me a hundred twenty-five a week by then; it was a living. And I made it on my own, without my old man takin' every goddamned nickel some yenta tipped me."

He paused for a moment, as if trying to remember what the point was.

"But I never killed nobody." He lit up again. "I never admitted to *that.*"

"How was it again they pinched you, anyway?" Tom asked.

"Ah, it was over Charlie Workman's apartment, out in Brighton Beach.

You remember, Charlie the Bug? Who went over to Newark an' shot Dutch Schultz in the crapper?"

"I read about it. What were you doin' there?"

"Just tryin' to stay out of the way. Lepke was still on the lam an' goin' nuts that anybody who used to work for him might rat him out."

"So you came back when he got arrested."

"Sure. But then Reles, that piece a garbage, he gives himself up an' starts talkin' a mile a minute. I went back up to New York, went over to Charlie's place in Brooklyn —"

"Why would you do that?" Tom interrupted.

"Why would I do what?" Tick-Tock asked, his weighted, Oriental eyes blinking slowly.

"You know you're in trouble because one of your old partners is in stir, sin-gin' his heart out. So you go over to see a man who pulled the most famous job what ever was? Somebody like Charlie the Bug, who was more wanted than anyone ever was wanted or ever would be?"

The endless flow of words ceased for a moment, the clock halted.

"Why?" Tick-Tock repeated. "Because I figured, you know, maybe he could fix me up, get me a little money to get away on —"

"Why would Charlie the Bug have any money? He could barely show his face. You saw how he lived."

Allie Tannenbaum was silent again, face fixed in a tight, close-mouthed smile.

"You tell me then," he said thickly.

"You went there because somebody told you to go there. Didn't they?"

Tannenbaum shrugged once more, and slowly wound down. "Well, ya know, maybe somebody might've *suggested* Charlie could help me out . . ."

"No, they didn't. They told you to go there because they knew Charlie Workman was about to be pinched. Didn't they?" Tom said. "They told you to go there because they wanted you to be in jail just then, and that was the best way to do it and make sure it looked right."

"That mighta happened," Tick-Tock Tannenbaum said slowly. "So what if it did?"

"Who told you to go get yourself arrested, Tick-Tock?"

"I dunno, if I ever did know," he said tightly. "I put those sorts a things outta my head."

"We'll get back to that. Maybe you'll remember. Maybe it was somebody who had word of when the cops were coming for Charlie the Bug and wanted to make sure you were there, too. Didn't you ever wonder about that, Allie? Or did you have certain assurances?"

Tannenbaum gave a small, wry laugh. Over his shoulder, Tom noticed that the head of the man back behind the counter went up, like a Doberman's ears lifting at the sound of an intruder.

"I never knew from assurances. I went where they told me."

"A little out of your depth, weren't you, Allie?" Tom said, taunting him. "The rich boy's son, operating with Murder, Inc. You'd give 'em your best movie-gangster stare, but that didn't work on *them,* did it? You were scared to death a those fellas. Weren't you?"

"They were very scary guys," Tannenbaum said offhandedly. "Especially if you didn't do what you were told."

"And you were told to get yourself arrested. By *whom?*"

He noticed that the man behind the counter was looking up again, his face all attention, almost *visibly* listening. Tom moved suddenly around Tick-Tock and strode across the store toward the man, whipping his assistant DA credential with its police-style badge out of his jacket and holding it up.

"Excuse me, sir, can I have a word with you —"

Before he was halfway across the room, the man turned on his heel and walked quickly out the back of the store without uttering a word. Seconds later, Tom could hear a car engine starting up, then receding rapidly down the street.

"Ah, whatcha have to go an' do that for?" Allie moaned when he turned back to him. "Now I'm gonna get the heave-ho —"

"There are many opportunities today for a trained radio technician," Tom told him, lighting a cigarette. "Also, there are marvelous opportunities in dry cleaning and carpet-stain removal."

"Funny."

"Just answer the goddamned question. Who told you to go over to Charlie the Bug's and see that you got yourself arrested?"

"Well . . ." Tannenbaum hemmed, "I'm not gonna testify to it. But I couldn't swear it wasn't the Prime Minister."

"Frank Costello?"

Tick-Tock just looked at him.

"All right. Now we're getting somewhere. So then you went for a nice ride in the country with my brother, and decided to talk."

"Sure, why not?" Tannenbaum grinned. "He was a very persuasive guy. After all, they elected him mayor twice—"

He could picture the long ride upstate. Neddy Moran at the wheel, maybe a detective with him up front. Charlie in the back seat with Tannenbaum, speaking kindly to him in that expansive, fatherly way he had. *The way he had used on Tom himself.* Asking Tick-Tock how he'd gone wrong, telling him it wasn't too late to turn his life around. *Unless maybe it wasn't so hard to put this particular witness at ease.*

"But that isn't why you talked, Allie. *Is* it?"

The heavy eyes blinked slowly again. Tom wondering how he ever lasted so long in gangland with such an obvious tell. *Because he was a useful idiot. For jobs like this one.*

"Whattaya mean? Why not? I cut a deal for myself. When Reles started singin', it didn't make any sense not to—"

"But that wasn't why you did it. Somebody *told* you to sing, too, just like they told you to get arrested. Didn't they? And was that same person good old Francis Scott Key Costello?"

"It mighta been." He shrugged defensively this time. "Look, I was tellin' the God's honest truth about all those jobs—"

"Sure, why not?" Tom told him. "They wanted those cases to stand. They wanted those boy-os off the street by then, they'd gotten a little too loud and a little too famous. And they wanted to make sure you could get very close to somebody else."

"I can't read people's minds—"

"No, I guess you can't," Tom conceded, chuckling. "But you can tell me exactly what happened in the Rats Suite the night Abe Reles went out the window."

"Reles! That piece of filth?" Tannenbaum scoffed. "Reles and his goddamned glass of blood snot? The man was a goddamned walking contagion, it's a wonder we didn't all catch TB—"

"I don't give a good goddamn about his personal hygiene, Tick-Tock."

"They ever tell you what he an' his pals did to that poor girl back in Brownsville? The one who wanted to be the singer? When she wouldn't give 'em a tumble they just *took* her—raped her an' beat her all night long in some lot, then dumped her back at her old lady's with a few bills. Told her they'd finish the job if she went to the cops?"

"He was scum. So what? You're gettin' religion awful late in life."

"Yeah? Well, let's just say I don't give a damn about him. Why should I tell you anything about it?"

Tom sighed and flicked a hand out suddenly, grabbing ahold of the sleeve of Tick-Tock's fine sharkskin jacket.

"Some nice work here, Tick-Tock. A beautiful piece of cloth," he said, rubbing it between his thumb and a finger. "That silk tie must've cost you a penny, too. Much more than your average lampshade salesman can afford—"

"Look, I don't know what you want—" Tick-Tock protested, pulling his sleeve away.

"You're going to help me because otherwise I'm going to go straight from here to the closest police station and tell them all about whatever shenanigans you and your bashful boyfriend are runnin' out of the back of this store," Tom told him, grabbing his wrist again and squeezing hard.

"Yeah? You might be surprised." Tick-Tock tried to leer at him. "I'm friends with the cops down here—"

"Then I'll go to the detective squad. And if you've iced them, too, I'll go straight to the state troopers, and then to the feds. You really want to bet there isn't *one* cracker sheriff in this state just dyin' to run some wise-ass New York sheenie into the penitentiary? You ever seen the chain gangs they have down here, Allie?"

"It wouldn't do any good," he protested more feebly now. "It's like I said before. I can't testify about anything I was an accessory to. You know the law—"

"And I told *you*," Tom said, yanking him closer by his wrist, until he was right up to his face. "I'm not interested in testimony. You tell me what I want, I'll turn around and walk right out of here, and you can go back to running the great Zacks Department Store and Hominy Grits Crime Ring. You'll never hear from me again. But you better tell me all of it, every single thing. And you better tell me now."

He let him go then, and Tick-Tock stepped quickly back, pouting at him reproachfully. He bit his lip, looking once again like a schoolboy, even as a middle-aged man. Tom wondered idly if that was all they were at heart, all these killers—just malicious schoolboys stuck in the casual sadism of the sixth grade.

"All right, then," Tick-Tock said finally, his voice nervous and petulant. "All right, but you might not like what you hear. Don't say you didn't ask for it."

"Just give it to me straight," Tom told him, as hard and impatiently as he could, trying to hide just how right he had guessed his fears. "What happened?"

Mexico City, 1953
They left the pretty hillside town, with its beautiful old churches and its small, well-scrubbed houses, at first light. Tom behind the wheel of the Bentley now. The air already fragrant and springlike, the lost green world of the Borda Gardens inviting and romantic behind its crumbling walls.

"You have to ask yourself," Tom said, shaking his head. "Why would anyone ever leave such a place?"

"A better question is, why would anyone come in the first place?" Slim said from the passenger seat.

She sat with her head back against the top of the seat and her lips painted a bright red and not quite closed, as if she were just waiting for someone to kiss her, though he suspected that in fact she was merely hungover. He assumed she was sleeping when she didn't move her head to look at all the gorgeous scenery. But then she spoke, without opening her eyes or moving her head.

"So. When are you going to have this little talk with your brother?"

"I don't know," he said, and shrugged. "Soon as I can, I guess."

"I see." She pulled off the dark glasses, blinking in the morning sunlight, her eyes looking sad and the skin around them strangely pale and smooth. "He'll hate me forever, you know. You, too, but mostly me."

"I don't know about that."

"Sure you don't."

She put the glasses back on her face, and her head back on the seat.

"That's because you're a man. But if you were a woman, you'd know. Men always find a way to forgive each other. It's the woman they blame, when it's all said and done."

"Charlie would take you back in a second."

"No, he won't. Not after this."

There was a short silence between them, punctuated only by the rhythmic rubber *whoomp* of the tires over the edges of the concrete sections that made up the highway. They were moving back onto one of the roads named for the fugitive president. The pavement flat and white in the sun, laid out across the fissures in the wide green valley not unlike like the flat, obscene tongue of highway he had seen emerging from the blasted neighborhoods of the Bronx.

"What will you do, d'ya think?" he asked, suddenly solicitous of her. She picked her head up again, looking at him for a long moment over the top of the sunglasses, as if she were going to say something but thought better of it.

"I don't know," she said flatly, staring straight ahead through the windshield. "Stay down here for a while, maybe. I don't know that there's too much for me back in the States, save for a great many people I don't want to see, and who don't want to see me."

She leaned slowly back again.

"Then again, there's nothing for me here, either. That makes it even."

"Seriously," he said, glancing over at her from the blinding gleam of the highway, broken only by the occasional metal grillwork propelling itself at him at a crazy speed. Another bus packed to the rafters, with its radio blaring, and its chickens, and the little shrine of girlie photos and saints' cards in front of the wheel. Always going full blast as they passed, the brown-faced children with bad teeth and the faces of angels leaning out the window, leering and laughing, waving and sticking out their tongues.

"Seriously," he said. "What do you think you'll do?"

"There are people who might do something for me —"

"Melchior? *Princeton?*" he said, suddenly, irrationally jealous again.

"— but there's always a price to be paid for that," she finished, pushing up her sunglasses and looking at him balefully. "Goddamnit, Tom. I know I've had the morals of an alley cat. You don't have anything to say on that score, even if you are planning to confess."

"Sorry."

"There were some people, back in Acapulco, from this British airline. They thought maybe I could do some customer-relations work, something like that. Can't you just picture me in a little blue airline uniform? All the *mamacitas* will be so pleased."

"It doesn't have to be like that, Slim."

"Ah, but it does," she told him. "It does until my name clears, or my looks go, whichever comes first. Until nobody cares, or nobody cares to remember. Unless —"

"Unless what?"

"Unless you want to give it another go. It's not too late, you know."

She was looking at him seriously, he knew from the tone of her voice, without looking back at her.

"But it is," he said, his voice a croak after an hour of driving. Hoping she didn't mistake the dust for emotion. "It was too late — it was *wrong* — from the moment it started."

"That's why the big confession? Call me a moral idiot, but I still don't see why it was wrong. Two people, wanting each other —"

"Because it was just a desire," he said almost viciously, looking back at her again. "Because that's all it was. Because it's no different from anything the Big Crowd here, or the Big Crowd back in New York get up to. They do what they want, they take what they want, and they wreck the rest, but it's only a desire. An impulse. Something they need at that moment. For the money, or the ego, or the prestige, or maybe just to stop the buzzing in their heads. They like to wrap it up in the name of progress, or the future, or the way of the world. But it's still just what *they* want, and they don't care even if it means the death of a good man."

"Or a bad one," Slim said, looking back steadily at him.

"Or a bad one, then. It's still not right, and I won't pretend it is. I won't pretend what I want is good, just because I want it," he said, adding, almost apologetically: "Not even for you."

To his surprise she said nothing, only put her dark glasses back in place and looked out through the bug-freckled windshield.

They marked their course by the twin volcanoes, Popocatépetl and Iztac-cíhuatl, the Raging Man and the Sleeping Woman, as seen from the other side now, their white peaks growing closer and closer. By midday they were approaching Cortés's pass, and he dutifully asked Slim if she wanted to stop for some lunch, but she just shook her head. Tom steering the car up and over and down toward the city, thinking to himself that these were probably the last few minutes they would ever spend alone together, and neither one of them had a damned thing left to say.

Then they were back in the city, his concentration thankfully absorbed by the need to maneuver amidst all the careening trucks and the rickety buses, the little taxicabs still revving and screeching, still honking around him as loudly and impatiently as a swarm of bees. By the time he was able to pull up in front of the Hotel Prince and toss the keys of the Bentley to the doorman, the underarms and the back of his shirt were soaked through with sweat, but he knew it wasn't due to the traffic.

They walked in together and took the little cage elevator up to his floor. She tried to laugh as they got in it, asking him, "Why am I nervous? Why should *we* be nervous—" but that was all she could get out. The broad back of the elevator operator, the same man who had helped him wrestle Charlie back up to his little penthouse adobe, hunching ever so slightly at each of their words.

She walked down the hall with him toward his room, her heels echoing loudly along the festive new linoleum. Pulling off her sunglasses in the cool near darkness and rubbing them nervously with a handkerchief.

"Goddamnit, Tom, can't we just talk for a minute about what I'm going to say to him?"

"Say anything you want," he told her as they paused outside his door, Tom rummaging in his pants pocket for the key. "But if you want to talk to him first, you'd better do it now."

"Damnit, Tom, don't you see that it should be us *together?*" she pleaded as he fiddled with the lock, frowning at it, since he was sure he had locked the top bolt before he left but found that it was open now. "It's still there, what we had. You saw it for yourself the other night, or wasn't that you with me?"

"That's over—"

He swung open the door at last, the words dying in his throat. Ellie was sitting on the brightly colored, imitation-Mexican blanket that was his hotel bedspread. She was wearing an adorable blue traveling suit, with a little matching hat. The black metal table fan at his bedside table was gently blowing at the edge of her hair, and it occurred to him that he had never seen her look any lovelier. It occurred to him, too, that this might be the last time he would ever see her.

"Ellie!"

"So," Slim said, holding her dark glasses defensively out in front of her — for once at a loss for words. Her face twisted as if she had just spilled a platter full of drinks on the floor.

"So," Ellie said to her, standing up and straightening her blouse and the little matching jacket. "I hear you're a real actress. Maybe you can manage an exit."

"I'll go up to El Ranchito, say goodbye to Charlie," Slim said hurriedly, backing out the door, her eyes darting back and forth between the two of them. "I won't stay long."

"There you go," Ellie told her.

Slim shut the door, the sound of her heels receding rapidly down the hall, while Tom tried to think of something to say.

"Ellie—" he started, then shook his head and sat down on the bed, next to where she had been. "Ellie, I've been a goddamned fool."

"I knew that before I came down here," she said drily, though he could hear the deeper hurt and anger in her voice. "So did Hogan. Why do you think he sent me?"

"I'm not talking about the case," he said, looking up at her. Wanting to put his arms around her hips, to hold her to him. Wanting to say something that would make it right, though there was nothing he could say now and no holding that would do any of that. *And the worst is yet to come,* he thought.

"The last thing I ever wanted to do was to hurt you. And I'm sorry that I did, and it was damned stupid, and anyway it's all over, done with for good," he said, the words running on without him, like some bad movie melodrama, or even worse, something on TV. "And I know there's nothing I can say to make you believe that, so I'm sorry, I'm so goddamned sorry, and all I want to do is make it up to you. That means more to me than the case, or my brother, or the whole rotten mess I've made of it."

She looked at him from across the room, her face stolid, then impatient, then starting to crack with anger.

"Ah, goddamnit!" she said, putting a hand to her face. "Ah, goddamn, this is so damned *predictable!* All of your words, everything you did — the whole thing. I should've known it."

She turned away from him, and her shoulders gave a small heave. He got up and went to her then, but she was already moving away from him, wiping at her face with her hand, the sob choked back. She shook his hands off her, turning to look at him dry-eyed.

"No, no. I'll be damned if I'll cry in your arms now!" she told him. "You came down here on a criminal investigation, or at least that was the official excuse. Is there anything left of it? Are you ready to pack it up and get out of here now?"

"No," he told her, straightening up and meeting her gaze. His sadness and his shame still flicking through him like little steel slivers. "No — and yes. I think I know how to close it up now. Give me another couple of hours with my brother, and that should do it."

"You're really that close?" she said, her voice doubtful but intrigued, too, despite herself. He could hear it in her voice. "This isn't just some desperate move to cover for yourself?"

"I think I know everything I need to know. I just need to hear something from him."

"Yes? How are you going to get that?"

"By confessing," he said, starting for the door, thinking again how lovely she looked as he passed her. Wondering if she would still be there when he got back, but not wanting to insult her by asking.

"It seems to be my day for it," he said instead.

41

"Were the cops asleep?" he started. Wanting to square away every detail he could, once and for all. Pacing himself, trying not to let Tick-Tock see through the dim light of the store how heavy his breath was coming.

Tannenbaum snickered. "Sure. When weren't they asleep? Every night, they'd go right into their rooms an' start snorin' like your old pop-pop."

"So asleep they wouldn't have heard a thing?"

"Nah. Reles kept the radio on all the time. He'd play it all damned night. We hated it at first, but you got used to it."

"What did he have it on?"

Tannenbaum shrugged and put his hands out. "How should I know? That goat-glands channel. *Make Believe Ballroom*—he liked that *schmaltzy* dance music. He'd listen to anything. He had it on twenty-four hours a day."

He could see it. The cops snoring in their rooms. The gentle strains of an orchestra in a far-away hotel ballroom on the radio, drifting out through the hotel wing. The doors closed, a light on under one of them.

"Not a creature was stirring, all over the house," Tom said softly. "Just the rats."

"Yeah. If you wanna call it that," Tick-Tock said, an edge in his voice.

"Four-thirty in the morning. But you were awake. You knew someone was coming."

"Nah, how would we know—" Tannenbaum tried to object, but Tom cut him off.

"Don't kid me. I know you had plenty of ways to get word in and out."

"All right, then," Tannenbaum admitted. "Sure, we knew it."

"All of the rats knew."

"Sure. Mickey Sycoff was in the room with me. Sholem Bernstein was across the hall. We was ready an' waiting. Just like we been told."

Lights under all the doors, the men dressed already, sitting up. Smoking nervously, listening to the beautiful dance music. Maybe a crooner's voice: "If I didn't care . . . "

"Somebody came in," Tom said. "Didn't they."

"Uh-huh."

"Who?" Tom managed to get out.

"Your cop friend," Tick-Tock said, terse for once in his life. "You know — the one everybody called the Old Man."

Tom blew out a long stream of smoke, trying to hide from Tannenbaum how relieved he was that the man he named was not his brother.

"Jack McGrath?"

"Uh-huh."

"You're sure? It was just him, nobody else?"

"That was enough. You didn't fool around with a guy like that."

Of course, it would be McGrath, he thought. It would have had to be someone with authority — real authority, not just on paper. Enough to make sure the job got done, and everybody kept their mouth shut about it later, no matter what happened. Somebody with his own key to open the great iron door on the Rats Suite . . .

Treading silently down the hall on his rubber cop-shoe heels the way he'd learned all those years before, walking a beat between the water and the dead. Giving a little tap with the key on the doors of the other squealers. Walking them down to Reles's room, with the beautiful music still seeping out from under the door: "If I didn't care / Would it be the same . . . "

"He had us wear our best suits. The clothes we wore in court," Tick-Tock told him. "He made sure a that."

"Of course. He thought of everything."

"The funny thing was, Reles was dressed up, too."

"Was he, now?"

"Sure, you saw him. That gray suit with the blue sweater? That's what he always wore, at least when it was cold."

"He was up, too? Dressed already, just like the rest a ya?"

"He was dressed, all right. It looked like he'd fallen back asleep, though. McGrath had to knock a couple times before he opened the door."

The little man staring blearily out at them. Half asleep, a waltz going through his head. It was the time of night when his guard, when anyone's guard would be down. The Old Man would know that, too ...

"That cop, the Old Man? He was done up, too. Full dress uniform —"

"Of course. Complete with gloves?"

"Sure, I guess so. Reles let him right in. The rest of us after 'im —"

The four killers seated around the little table. Bernstein slender and intense, Sycoff moon-faced and staring. Tannenbaum grinning his larkish boy's smile. And Reles — and the Old Man. Five men in a room, waiting for something to happen.

"Reles was confused at first; he didn't know what everybody was doin' there. But then he started grinnin' like the cat that licked up the cream. He started sayin' how he was gonna be glad to see the last of us suckers."

"That's why his wife was so upset the night before," Tom reasoned, mostly to himself. "McGrath told him he was graduating. He thought he was goin' away, and he was never comin' back."

"The Old Man told us we were goin' down to Washington to talk, on a federal case. He said when we gave our testimony there, we'd be free men. The government would take us anyplace we'd like, give us a new identity, some money to get set up. He said we should start thinkin' about where we'd like to go — that Abie already had his deal worked out."

"I'll bet he did."

"He kept grinnin' at the rest of us," Tannenbaum said, smirking, fiddling with a little night-table lamp made out of a figure in a jockey outfit, leaping a fence on his horse, while a fox that was missing a leg stared back at him. "He was in pretty bad shape by then. He'd lost some hair, he'd lost weight, and he was coughin' all the time by then, fillin' up his goddamned glass of blood. But he still thought he'd put it over on us. I don't know what the Old Man told him, but I bet he thought he had a better deal. I bet he thought he was gonna go down to Havana, or Rio, and have everything he wanted, just the way he always talked about."

"Sure he would. He always thought he had the inside handle on everything, and the real dope on the future."

"So then McGrath stands in front of us all and makes like he's giving out with a little speech. Seeing as how this was the last time we'd be together, he wanted to thank us on behalf of the State of New York for our service, blah-blah-blah, and how he hoped we would now be peaceable and law-abiding citizens. Oh, I'll never forget that!" Tick-Tock grinned. "Sounded like somethin' right out of a parole officer's handbook!"

"Yeah, he would've thought of that, too."

The hard cop, reading out what sounded like a perfunctory spiel in his dress uniform. Citations filling his uniform chest, perfect white gloves on his hands.

"Then he takes off his hat an' he says, 'Thank God that's over,' an' he tells Reles, 'How's about we all have a drink in honor of the occasion?' And Reles, of course, bein' the cheap bastard he is, gives us all his big eyes an' says, 'Where would I get a drink?' Tryin' to hold out on us, tryin' to fool us, right to the end.

"But the Old Man didn't go for it. He told Abie, 'Don't fuck with me, boy-o, I know you have a goddamned bottle of Chivas in your underwear drawer. Now go an' get it and a glass for everyone, an' *not* one a those you spat up a piece of your lung in.' And Reles just grinned at that, like he was a bad little boy, and went an' did as he was told."

Tannenbaum gave Tom a sneaky smile and shook his head.

"The whole time Reles is gettin' his bottle an' roundin' up the glasses, the Old Man is movin' around the room, workin' on somethin'."

"The escape rope."

"You're quick."

"Not quick enough."

McGrath stripping the sheets off the dirty, unmade bed. Pulling a piece of the improvised wire antenna off the back of the radio. Winding the sheets around it with startling, practiced speed.

"Whattaya doin' with that?" the little man asking him as he noticed, pausing in the midst of putting the glasses out.

"Just a little experiment with the radio reception," McGrath telling him, wrapping one end of the wire and sheets around the foot of the radiator. He tugged the shade that was always down at night, then pushed up the window. Gazing out at the still-invisible ocean there before him. Sniffing the pungent, dirty tide, listening to the sullen shuffle of it up and down the sand. Looking down then at the kitchen roof extension six flights below, the sound of a fan laboring somewhere in the darkness.

The salt air and the cold, bracing in the open room. The little man blinking and shaking his head. Realizing something's wrong with the shade up, but he can't figure out what.

"But I ain't coming back?" he asks.

"No. You're not."

"He made him pour out a healthy shot for us — bigger than Reles wanted, you could see that. He was startin' to groan about that, too, the cheap son of a bitch, but the Old Man told him to shut it. He said he wanted to make a toast. He held up his glass an' made us all stand, then."

"I'll bet he did."

"Yeah, he planned it pretty good for a cop," Tick-Tock said, snickering again, and shook his head. "He put himself right beside Abie, with the rest of us between him an' the door. Then he lifted up his glass an' said, 'Here's to the rats of the Half Moon Hotel; may we meet again when we're all in hell! Down the hatch!' He threw it down in one gulp, an' we did the same."

"That's how he had the booze," Tom said. "And then —"

"Then it all happened real fast —"

He could see it almost before Tannenbaum described it. Reles choking and coughing on the big shot of scotch. The Old Man grabbing him up by the elbow, steering him toward the window . . .

"Let's get you some air, lad!"

Giving the rest of them a look, just in that moment, that was enough to serve as a command. Reles still coughing, the Old Man pounding him on his back, whispering encouragingly, "Easy now! Easy! Let it go down!" Even as half a dozen more hands latched onto his arms, his legs. Propelling him toward the open window, the hand still pounding his back, keeping him coughing, keeping him from making any comprehensible protest at all even as he felt himself suddenly flying out into the cool, lovely, early-morning air of the seashore. The blackness of the sea, and the distant, twinkling lights along the shore rushing past him. Turning upside down, as he fell, unable to scream, or cry, or talk at all. Barely even able to comprehend what was happening to him, the fall expertly timed for that, too. Just enough to kill him, but not enough to let him recover beyond the one, stray thought, maybe, that he was headed for the pitch-black hell he always pictured his victims tumbling into . . .

Before he hit.

"He had it all down," Tick-Tock said, almost admiringly. "Soon as Reles goes out the window, he tears off the sheet rope he'd made, throws it down after him. He told me to take the bottle, an' Mickey and Sholem to grab the glasses. Threw 'em all right down the incinerator, just like that. It was perfect. Then we looked out an' saw that Abie wasn't dead yet."

"What?"

"Nah, the little son of a bitch was down there on the kitchen roof, crawlin' along like he was gonna get to the edge an' jump down."

The three squealers looking at one another silently, wondering what was going to happen next. McGrath peering down like a madman through the early-morning gloom. Watching the little man crawling along the kitchen roof in his suit, wondering when he was going to cry out, or even get up. Then he stopped, rolled over, legs pulled up like a dying animal.

"That was it. Then we went back to our rooms, an' waited for it to be light."

"And the Old Man never said a word to you?" Tom asked. "When he was haulin' him to the window, I mean?"

"Nah. He gave us a look. That was good enough for us."

Tom nodded, absently putting out his cigarette in the ashtray of the jockey figurine jumping the fence.

"That's leadership," he said.

Mexico City, 1953

He walked out on the roof, heading for his brother's tiny adobe penthouse. Nothing had changed much in the past three days, he noticed — but then he doubted if anything up on El Ranchito had changed much in the past three years. The cushioned deck chairs were neatly arranged around the bright-striped umbrellas, and middle-aged American women were lying in two of them. Their hair was freshly done, and the bottoms of their two-piece suits were pulled up high over their belly buttons, and their legs and arms and torsos were already baked to a deep brown. As he walked past he could see them sneaking looks at him over their red and blue drinks, and their copies of *Look* and *Collier's*. They appeared new to the roof, and Tom could only wonder if they had seen his brother yet, and if he had seen them.

"Have you eaten anything yet? Pishta's just settin' up for lunch."

His brother greeted him at the door, wearing the same blue shirt, gray slacks, and loafers without socks he'd been wearing that first afternoon. His face was ashen, and he looked almost stricken, Tom thought, grasping the doorjamb like he was trying to hang on after a physical blow.

"I'm fine, Charlie," he said. "All I want is a word with you."

"You know she's gone, Tommy," he said, staring off into the middle distance. The words came tumbling out of his mouth like broken teeth, and Tom listened although he had no patience for it anymore. "She was just here. She told me that's it, she's leavin' me for good."

"I'm sorry, Charlie."

"She told me she doesn't love me anymore, and it's all over. She's going to Reno and file for a divorce. Nevada! Why—when she's already in goddamned Mexico? Jesus, the papers will have a field day with it, Tommy! I thought for sure she'd come back, sooner or later, Tommy, I surely did. But now that's all done, she doesn't love me after all—"

"I know, Charlie."

"I asked her if there was somebody else, and she said it was none of my damned business anymore! Can you get over that one? D'ya know who it is, Tommy? Is it that goddamned bullfighting ponce, that *Chu Chu?* One of her big Acapulco friends? That Princeton fella—"

"Yes, Charlie. I know who it is."

They walked up to Chapultepec, through all the familiar, cheerful chaos of the streets. The calliope wheeze of the roasted-corn stands, and the men selling balloons and sweet potatoes and sections of honeycomb. The boys scrambling after them to sell them lottery tickets, and copies of *La Prensa* and *El Universal,* or carting along their shoeshine boxes, or simply begging with their hands out, running beside them saying over and over again, "*Por favor,* mister, *por favor.*" The fashionable young people streaming out of their offices to the cafés for lunch, and the construction workers whistling and calling out merrily to women from the many holes they were tearing in the ground, and the streams of the gawking white-clad peasants that never seemed to stop coming, and he could see very well now how his brother might consider it all an acceptable substitute for New York City.

They walked and walked, neither of them daring to say a thing. Striding swiftly down the broad, leafy sidewalks of the Paseo de la Reforma, until it began to rise. Following it more slowly then, up a steep hill toward what looked like a medieval hodgepodge of a castle at the peak. Tom feeling the wonderful, clear air turn thin in his lungs as they climbed, a sense of something almost like exuberance radiating through him, that he knew enough by now to put it down to the lack of oxygen to his brain.

You have to be careful up here.

They were passing through a huge, rambling park. All around them were streams and manmade ponds, gracious walkways and little benches. Clumps of well-dressed families and less well-dressed tourists moved by them, veering off at signs for a zoo, or the presidential palace, the different museums.

"Lovely, isn't it?" Charlie said beside him, huffing, turning to look back down at the city. Red-faced now, but still talking, always talking, but not saying a thing. "It's a sacred spot. They were building Toltec temples up here more than seven hundred years ago—"

"Were they now."

"It's been a fortress, a military academy, a palace for kings and presidents—"

They walked on a little while more and came to a shockingly stark, modern memorial—six white pillars with black eagles nailed to them, surrounding a contemporary pietà. A fierce-looking woman holding a dying boy in her lap. Her head was turned away, toward another boy who stood staunchly by her side, as if demanding to know why he wasn't dead, too.

"The monument to *Los Niños Héroes*," Charlie told him, mopping at his ruddy face with a handkerchief. "The Boy Heroes. They were cadets here, when it was a military academy. Just kids. When General Scott's marines stormed the hill, one of 'em struck the flag and wrapped himself in it, then jumped off the cliffside. The other five jumped with him. Heroes forever, dead for God and country, and that goddamned fool, Santa Anna."

They sat on a bench by the monument, facing down into the genial whirlpool of the city, Charlie gesturing vaguely again. Tom knowing it was time but still letting him talk. Wanting his brother to talk on forever.

"And meanwhile, down there somewhere," he said between huffs, gesturing vaguely with one hand, "down there were the San Patricios, the Saint Patrick's Brigade. Waitin' on their scaffolds for the flag to rise."

"So you've said."

"They worked those guns like the devil, knowing they'd all be hung if they ever got caught. Shot any Mexican troops who tried to surrender, but they still got took. Can you imagine it? Thirty men, standin' there in those carts, hands tied behind their backs, nooses around their necks."

He wiped some sweat off the back of his neck with his handkerchief and shook his head.

"And why did they cheer, Tommy? That's what I'd like to know. Why did they cheer when they saw the Stars 'n' Stripes go up, and they knew they were going to die?"

"I can't say, Charlie."

"Was it relief just to finally get out of the sun that morning an' be done with it? Was it the heroism of their former comrades, their *former* fellow Americans, storming the fortress? Or was it just a big fuck-you?"

"Charlie, I have something to tell you—" he tried to begin, but Charlie interrupted him.

"Loyalty is a complicated business, a very complicated business, Tom—"

"Charlie, it was me who was with Slim," Tom told him straight out. "It was me who slept with her, before she even was your wife. I don't know about anything she's done down here in Mexico. But we were together, in Florida and up in New York, and I'm deeply ashamed of it. I wish it had never happened, but that don't mean that it didn't."

He told it to him, forcing the words out, and sat and watched his brother's face as it changed from incredulity to shock, to anger and then bewilderment. Charlie opening and shutting his mouth two or three times, before he finally stood and walked off behind the monument, staring down the steep cliff into the trees below, where once the Boy Heroes had gone over the side. Tom walking right behind him, pursuing him closely but saying nothing, the silence between them drifting into unbearably long minutes.

"Was that everything you wanted to tell me?" Charlie asked him at last, in a small, ominous voice.

"No, Charlie, it wasn't."

"Fire away, then."

He turned to face Tom, the city at his back. His hands were shoved deep into the pockets of his slacks, and there was a look on his face not quite like anything Tom had ever seen on him before — bitter, and hurt, and grieving, but spiteful as well. *The face that was exactly what he wanted.*

"I know it was Jack McGrath in the Rats Suite that night," he said. "And I know it was you who put him there."

"What? What's that?" Charlie asked, shaking his head like a fighter who had just been jabbed a few too many times in a row.

"The night Abe Reles went out the window. McGrath was the one who went in an' did it. And it was you who sent him there."

"This is a nice one-two, Tommy, I tell you that," Charlie said bitterly, half turning from him, jingling some change in his pocket. "This one of your prosecutor's tricks? Something your Mr. Hogan taught you? You tell your brother you put the horns on him, then hit 'im with the accusation —"

"It's not an accusation. It's the truth."

"Who told you that? Not McGrath —"

"Allie Tannenbaum, for starters —"

"That little punk?" Charlie said contemptuously. "He'd put an ice pick in his mother's neck, if it meant he could go to the movies that afternoon."

"He's got no reason to lie. And he was there, as an accessory. They all threw him out together."

"How can you buy a story like that? It could've been anyone. All the cops up there —"

"The cops were asleep. It was McGrath who went in, put the whole thing together. It could *only* be somebody like the Old Man. Somebody with his authority. Somebody who could make the rats do it — and make sure they kept their mouths shut."

"How d'ya know it wasn't just them, on their own initiative?" Charlie continued to bluster, although his heart was obviously not in it, the words as dispassionate as if he were asking directions to the zoo from one of the passing tourists. "You know what a piece of filth Reles was. I ever tell you what he did to this girl? How you can let them libel a man like Jack McGrath—"

"He's gone now, Charlie."

"*What?* The Old Man?" Charlie's mouth hung open, wobbling a little from side to side. "Never the Old Man! We were just talkin' about him the other day—"

"He's dead. It happened just before I came down."

Trying to talk to him one more time, the morning he started down to Atlanta to see Tick-Tock Tannenbaum in his lampshade store. It was just before they took him into surgery, an oxygen mask clamped down over his face. The Old Man grinning back at his desperate questions as they literally wheeled his gurney down the hall. Unsure if the smile really was from the drugs, as the interns assured him. As unsure as he was about the final words McGrath did croak out, when he pulled the mask off just before they pushed him through the swinging doors: "Always another . . ." he rasped. "There's always . . . another . . . one . . ."

"I got the wire in Atlanta, right after I saw Tannenbaum. He never made it off the operating table."

"I see. So you're willin' to besmirch the name of a dead man, a man who can't defend himself—" Charlie started in.

"Nobody's besmirching anyone. It's not the Old Man I'm concerned about."

"So why—"

"Because he was in there for *you,* Charlie," Tom told him. "It took me a good long time to figure that one out, Mrs. O'Kane's idiot son. But God help me, I did it. He'd do anything for you, he *had done* anything for you, ever since you walked a beat together out in Red Hook.

"That's why he was there that morning, too," Tom continued, standing face-to-face with his brother now, his voice low and intense, against the occasional passing tourist. "That's why he was there before we were. In his best dress uniform, making sure everybody got their stories straight, and no reporter and no outside doctor got a good look at the body before he was ready."

"He was the straightest cop there ever was—"

"That's right. He never took a dime for himself, and he drove all the child

397

molesters out of Brooklyn just like Saint Patrick drove the snakes out of Ireland, and he never owed anything to anyone in this world."

Tom paused for breath in the thin air, and to let his words sink in.

"But he loved *you* like a son, Charlie. He'da done anything for *you.*"

"Ah, this is just nonsense!" his brother said scornfully, waving a hand in the air and turning his back on Tom, then walking away in a little circle before he came back. A few of the tourists turning their heads before they returned to their camera sites. Snapping the pietà, snapping the black eagles on the white pillars, and the flapping flag, and everything else there was to snap.

"Pure speculation, and the word of a killer! It's a whole lotta nothin'!"

"This isn't," Tom said, pulling out the photocopy he had made, of the little piece of paper from the medical examiner's report. The scribbled line in the margin. Reading: *Withhold information by order of DA.*

"It's from Dr. Robillard's report."

Charlie snatched the paper up when Tom handed it to him, glaring at it angrily, then crumpled it up and stuck it deep in his pocket before he turned away again.

"That's evidence, Charlie—the original, I mean. Safe back in Frank Hogan's office," he said softly.

His brother said nothing, only continued to stare down into the chaos of the city.

"I know what you were doing in Frank Costello's apartment, Charlie," he went on. "Neddy Moran told me about it. He told me about everyone who was there—including Bill McCormack. He told me what they wanted, and what you said."

"Another felon's testimony," Charlie said weakly.

"Ah, Charlie, you couldn't deny Neddy Moran if you wanted to, not now," Tom told him, disappointed by this answer, too—even though he had thought it would not be possible to be any further disappointed by Charlie O'Kane. "You're joined to him as surely as Peter was to Christ, and it won't do you any more good to foreswear him."

"That was ten years ago I went up to Costello's place, Tom," Charlie told him, his voice tense. "I couldn't tell you myself what exactly I said in that room—"

"But I imagine you'd remember the gist of it." Tom sighed.

"I imagine I would that," Charlie admitted, pacing away and back again, hands in his pockets.

"It all fits together — save for one thing," Tom recited. Starting back on that morning, at the Half Moon Hotel.

"The man Reles was going to send up next was Albert Anastasia, the enforcer the Camardas used to police their docks. King Joe Ryan's docks — *Bill McCormack's docks*. That couldn't be allowed to happen, it would've threatened everything — ripped the whole town open.

"So — you send Jack McGrath in to see the little man gets thrown out the window. You even had the other rats in there already, to help him do it. Tell me, were they planted for that very purpose in the first place? Or did McCormack just get to them once they were already inside — bribe them, threaten them?"

"This is ridiculous," Charlie protested.

"Not that it much matters," Tom continued. "The other rats — Bernstein, Mickey Sycoff, Tick-Tock — they provided the muscle to get Reles out that window. They did what was needed. A few months later, you have Neddy Moran pull Anastasia's card from the police wanted files. What did that matter, either? You had no case against him."

"There wasn't, goddamnit!"

"No — not with your lead witness murdered," Tom said, unflinching. "It's a done deal. And in return, Bill McCormack and his friends meet you in Costello's apartment, and say they'll make you mayor."

"Sure," Charlie said bitterly. "You've fit it together all very neatly, with me as the monster in the middle. Do ya really think I'm a monster, Tommy?"

"No, I don't, Charlie. That's why we're havin' this conversation —"

"Really? I thought it had to do with you sleeping with my wife. I seem to recall it started out like that."

"What I want to know is *why*," Tom said, as calmly as he could. "Why did you do it? Was it because you wanted to be mayor so much? You didn't need those bums — they needed *you*. So *why*, Charlie? Because you're *not* a monster. Why did you do it? Did you think you really needed McCormack? Did you think you really needed those fools to run the city —"

"They're not fools!" Charlie barked. "And of course I needed them. They're smart men —"

Tom snorted. "They're half smart, Charlie. You know that. Somewhere, God help ya, I'm sure you know that. They're all very clever, your Big Crowd, but they haven't a vision in their heads that extends beyond a monument to themselves and the smell of a dollar."

"What the hell did it matter? What the hell does any of it matter?" Charlie said, looking back at Tom from the edge of the cliff a few feet away. "And all over Abe Reles! That human turd! What did it matter if he went out the window, instead of on the hot seat—"

"It mattered. And you know it mattered," Tom said, cutting him off again. "So *why*, Charlie? You could've got yourself elected mayor anyway. *Why* would you let yourself be used like that? God help me, it's the one thing I can't figure out—"

"You want to know why?" Charlie said, turning suddenly and walking back to him, talking fast and loose now, a crooked grin on that raw face.

"I put in with them because I *had* to," Charlie told him. "I wasn't free to go off and play working-class hero, like you and your communist priests—"

"They had somethin' on you," Tom said, suddenly comprehending, a stray current of sympathy swelling up in him, along with the shock. "Of course. Oh, Charlie. They had something on you all along. But what—"

"It was your friend, you know," Charlie said, grinning his awful, sickly grin in Tom's face, the bright, clear, Mexican day all around them feeling increasingly surreal. "You remember: Peter Panto?"

"*Panto?* What about him?"

"Who do you think gave him his guarantee? Huh? Why d'ya think he got in that car that night?"

Tom felt numb and cold, standing out in the sunlight.

"It was you," he repeated dumbly. "You told him it was safe. You got him in that car that night."

"Sure," Charlie said, his voice quick and lucid now—quicker and sharper than Tom had heard it since he'd been in Mexico, he realized. "A guarantee from the next district attorney of the borough. A sitting judge, a hero cop— who better? *The brother of the man who believed in him like no other. I* told him it would it'd be safe, and he believed me, and got in the car. And then he was dead."

Tom could see the staircase again, out at that miserable Jersey farmhouse. All of it so carefully arranged to leave him paralyzed with terror at the end. The car speeding off into the darkness, leaving him alone there. Panto walking up those stairs, the lamb to the slaughter. Knowing even as he did that it was a trap. Knowing but still going up there. Holding on to the promise Charlie had given him, from his own mouth . . .

"Someone that fine. You let that happen to him, someone that fine."

"Aye, I did, Tommy. That's the monster I am."

"So it's all been so much obfuscation. *All* of it, since the moment I got down here. All the poetry, and playin' the tour guide, an' mourning after the good old days, an' Daniel Boone. All the self-pity, and the booze, an' the tears over the wife who left you. When in fact you never gave a tinker's dam what happens to any of us."

"Ah, it's not like that, Tommy!"

He felt as though he needed to sit down now. The fight, the strange rawness seemed to go out of his brother at the same time. Charlie looking away again, speaking softly and dispiritedly now.

"I didn't mean to, Tommy," he all but pleaded. "He played me perfectly —"

"*Who* did?"

"McCormack, of course. Remember how I told you, maybe that I just wasn't that smart? Well, I wasn't joking."

The remains of him, the band of that silly hat. Leaking out of the soft, gelatinous earth, with the smell of chicken shit everywhere . . .

"How?"

"McCormack told me he wanted to make the peace. He told me he was losing money every day on his docks, he just wanted it all settled, he didn't care which way. He came to me, Tommy, and asked me to arrange it."

"Arrange *what,* exactly?" Tom asked, trying to concentrate.

"A parley. A truce, a sit-down. He said he was afraid that things were getting out of hand on the piers. He said he was afraid something would happen to Panto, to that priest. To you —"

"*Don't* tell me this was you trying to save your little brother!" Tom snapped.

"I'm just tellin' ya you what he said," Charlie continued sadly. "He said he just wanted everything to run smoothly. He wanted to set up a meeting. Panto, the Camardas, Anastasia. King Joe Ryan. With me there to preside over the whole thing, and make it kosher."

"And you went for it," Tom said, covering his face with his hand.

"Aye, I did, Tommy. God help me, I fell for it. Oh, I thought you'd be so pleased!"

"Jesus, Charlie, how could you?"

"That poor boy came to see me, and I gave him my word of honor, face-to-face, that it would be all right. How was he not to trust that, Tommy?"

Charlie next to him, pleading with him, his hands out. His eyes welling with tears.

"The next DA, tellin' him everything's all right," he went on. "His men were gettin' desperate by then, you said that yourself. They needed a deal, and he came to me in my chambers at the courthouse and asked, 'Is it okay? Can I trust it?' And I looked at 'im, that poor boy, so much like you. With his beautiful girl, and all his courage and his honesty. Like a saint he was – like somethin' outta history. And I told him, 'Yes, yes, it's all right. Trust me, it'll be fine.' I told him not to tell anyone else, either, we wanted it all to be secret. That's how well McCormack set it up. Not the press. Not even you, Tommy – not even you."

"Not that it would've made any difference," Tom said slowly. "For I would have told him he could trust you, Charlie."

"I thought it was for real, Tommy," Charlie said urgently, sitting down next to him again. "You've got to believe me on that, at least. I thought the deal was on the up-an'-up, I swear to God!"

"Did ya, Charlie? Did ya really?" There was a taste like rusted iron in his mouth.

"On my life, Tommy. On Claire's immortal soul. McCormack, I waited with him all that night. He rented a suite up in the Roosevelt Hotel – oh, he thought of everything! A whole suite, up on the ninth floor, with enough chairs for ten men. A room in the back. So no one would see, he said, because publicity is the death of negotiations. There was a bar set up, and nice white linens on the table, and everything ready!

"And there I sat, and waited like an idjit. And waited and waited, while Bill McCormack ordered himself up a nice, bloody steak, and ate it right in front of me. He ate up every bite, then soaked his bread in the blood, and licked his fingers. And then he looked at me an' said, 'I don't believe those boys are coming,' as easy as that!"

He could see it, too: Charlie pacing about the dim, shabby room while Mc-Cormack finished his meal. Doing his best not to catch the man's eye—to spy the glint of knowledge there.

"I could barely believe what I was hearing. But there was a phone call," his brother was saying, "and he picked up the phone, and said a few words, then he turned to me as calm as ever, an' said, 'There's a problem, Charlie.' And then I knew that he'd played me all along an' that poor boy was dead."

"Why, Charlie? Why didn't you stop it then?"

"Because how could I, Tom?" Charlie said, his voice shaking. "How could I go out of that room, and tell everybody I was the biggest fool in the world? How could I tell them that I killed that boy?"

"Because you had to, Charlie—"

"And he was smart, Tommy! Oh, he was smart as the devil! He never threw it in my face, never admitted he planned it all. He just went right on, playing the game—making out they'd set him up, too. He told me, 'You see, we can't stop now, Charlie. You see what these boys are like? Completely lawless! That's why we've got to get you elected DA,' he told me. He said, 'You've got to clean up this city, and I swear to God, I'll help ya do it.' He said, 'You can't quit now, Charlie, you've got to make sure that poor boy didn't die in vain.' Invoking his name even then, with his corpse not cold in the ground!"

"And you went for it?" Tom asked him.

"I had to, Tommy. He was right: If I didn't, then what was it all about? What did that boy die for? And he was true to his word, McCormack—at least at first. All of a sudden, there were witnesses comin' forward all over the borough. All those years, nobody had put together a capital case on a mob hit. But *we* sent seven men up to the Dance Hall. We broke the back of Murder, Inc.—"

"Didn't ya see he was still playin' you?" Tom said, interrupting him. "Didn't you see that, even then? Sure, you got to clean up a few loose operators. Men makin' too big a noise, men not under anyone's control. That just consolidated his own power, made sure you got some headlines at the same time. But they were nothing."

"They were notorious murderers, Tommy!"

"Men are murdered every day down at the docks, Charlie, quick and slow. You got to send a few killers up to the hot seat. But McCormack got *you* to raid the Camarda locals, instead of Lehman's man. Didn't he, Charlie? Thanks to you, he made sure those books were never found."

"What choice did I have by then—"

"It all ran like clockwork, Charlie, didn't it? All those witnesses comin' in, testifying against this or that gunman. You saw to it that they all got put in with Reles. We were goin' crazy, searchin' the roofs around Coney Island for snipers, when he had his men inside the whole time. By the time Reles went to finger his man, Anastasia, Bill McCormack already had his hand around his throat. Thanks to you, again."

"It was already too late by then, Tommy," his brother said, slumping forward on the bench beside him, looking down at the ground. "I couldn't go back on him, or he'd see to it the Panto story came out. And what did it matter, Tommy? What was Abe Reles anyway?"

"You mean," Tom said, turning slowly to look at him, "what was Peter Panto compared to you?"

His brother was quiet for a moment, before continuing in a thick, flat voice that sounded as if he were still trying to convince himself of something. "Mc-Cormack told me if he couldn't run the docks, it would be chaos. He said they'd throw out King Joe. Harry Bridges and his reds would come in from the coast, tie up the whole port, and it would all be my fault—"

"Oh, yes. King Joe Ryan: the indispensable man."

"Reles had to go, Tommy. I had no choice. I told the Old Man, and he said he'd take care of it. He always looked out for his boys—"

"I'll bet he did," Tom said, balling his hands into fists and running them over his thighs. Shutting his eyes for a moment, in the vain hope that it would all go away. "So you sent the best cop in New York in there to see that Reles died, and a vicious killer walked free, and peace reigned once more on the New York waterfront."

"It was just the way of it, Tom!" Charlie cried out in frustration. "It's the things powerful men do that binds them together. It's blood on the hands that builds trust—"

Tom cut him off. "It was just melodrama, Charlie, didn't you get it? Star witnesses coming forward, dramatic trials. And the whole time, you playin' the perfect part of the district attorney. It was *all* something outta the movies, a bunch of shadow play."

"That isn't so, Tommy. I made choices—"

"The choice you could've made was to walk away, once the war came. You could've gone off and done any damned thing you wanted, and been free of it. Let them find another patsy—if they could. But *you* couldn't by then. Could you? You couldn't leave it alone. You loved what you saw up on the big screen, and in the newspapers. *You* thought you could be the hero mayor, too."

"I thought I could do some *good*, Tom. They were all workin' on me to be mayor by then—Spellman, McCormack, Moses, Tammany. Even the Roosevelts—"

"Don't forget Frank Costello."

"There was nobody else possible. McCormack told me they wouldn't accept Hogan. If I didn't run, some mob stooge would be mayor—"

"Like Vinnie Impellitteri?"

"It's easy enough for you to say, isn't it? Well, no man ever ran a great city with his hands clean—"

"No, I understand it now," Tom told him. "You would become one of them. Another indispensable man, just like all the others. Another superman the City couldn't do without."

"You can mock it, Tom. But that's the way the world works. You would never accept that, Tommy—"

"The way of the world, Charlie, is that a good man gets a quicklime grave in a chicken farm in New Jersey. While the Bill McCormacks order a living human being thrown out of a window, then go to Mass each day for the photographers," Tom told him, standing up. "How fortunate for us all that's the way of the world. Otherwise we have to consider the possibility that we had somethin' to do with it."

Charlie stood up with him, pulling himself to his full height, as regally as possible. He was still a little taller, Tom saw, but now he couldn't stand all the way up, his back hunched, in the manner of old men.

"I guess you're just a *little* monster, then, Tommy? Sleeping with your brother's wife—not such a great crime. Is that how you justify it?"

"I don't," Tom told him. "It was the worst thing I ever did, and the way things turned out, I'm probably going to pay for it the rest of my life. But I never told myself it was *the way of things*. I never told myself it was anything but what I wanted, and that it was wrong."

"So what becomes of *me*?" Charlie asked him. His voice was sardonic, but Tom could see, to his dismay, the real anxiety still in his eyes. "Are you gonna haul me back to New York in irons after all? It's up to you, Tommy. If you really think I should, I'll go back and face the music. I'll go back and tell the truth, the whole truth."

"That's hard to do," Tom told him, "when you've already told so many lies."

"What the hell do ya mean by that?" Charlie said, but Tom was already beginning to walk away, down from the monument to the Boy Heroes, and all the flags.

"Don't worry, I'll find my own way back," he called over his shoulder. Charlie took a step after him, then stayed where he was, balling and unballing his fists.

"Hey, Tom, how d'ya like me now?" he called after him, the passing tourists staring blankly and moving away. "How d'ya like your big brother now?"

He took his time walking back to the hotel, and when he got there he didn't go in right away but lingered in the Alameda, the leafy park across the street, where he bought some peanuts from another small, shoeless brown boy, and fed the pigeons while he sat and tried to think. At last when it started to get dark he went up to his room, hoping against hope that he would open the door and find her there.

But as he expected, the room was empty save for his luggage — a couple of small travel bags, and the typewriter case that smelled of ink and old felt. He opened the case, unlatched the sleek, green Smith Corona portable, and placed it on the little desk.

It was then that he saw the note there. No room number, no telephone. Not even signed, but clearly in her hand. It read simply: "When you finish your report, leave it at the front desk."

He read it over twice, simple as it was, then nodded and sat down at the desk. He slipped a piece of the Hotel Prince's stationery from the shallow desk drawer, beside the Bible, and rolled it into the typewriter. Then he began to write, pecking with two fingers at the elegant, light-green letters stamped on the thick, dark-green keys.

43

Mexico City, 1953

He got out to Balbuena early the next morning, wondering which of the three cars he was likely to see pull up by the airport terminal: the Bentley, or the big black town car from the Pasquale brothers, or a car from the hotel. Or maybe none of them, considering how people felt about him these days. He had just checked his luggage and was heading out toward the field when he saw the town car lumbering up, the conscientious face of Beneficio behind the wheel. *Charlie.*

His brother came ambling slowly across the terminal, with his big, important walk, saying hello to the many people who recognized him and called him Mr. Ambassador. He was dressed more formally now, in a seersucker suit and a silk tie with a clasp and cuff links, until he looked almost like a man of importance. He nodded somberly as he came up to him and Tom nodded back just as seriously, while he wondered what the hell there was left to say between the two of them.

"Tom," he said, pressing his hand tightly in both of his and casting his eyes down. "Tom, I'm sorry about some of what got said yesterday. That is —"

"I finished my report to Hogan," Tom said, cutting him off, sparing them both. "You can rest easy. I'm not going to recommend a deportation proceeding."

"That is good news," he breathed, and to his dismay Tom could see that he was truly relieved.

"The case wouldn't be worth it," he continued.

"No? None of it?" Charlie said nervously.

"When it came to Panto, you were just the dupe — like you said," he said, carefully casting each word into a dagger. "The only possible witnesses left would be gangsters, and accessories to the fact, who have already lied under oath. Same thing with Reles. The rest of it — conspiring to hide the Camardas' books, colluding with leading figures in organized crime — all of it would be impossible to prove. You and Moran and Costello all lied your heads off so much at the Kefauver hearings, it would be hard to get any jury to believe anything you said anymore."

"God, Tom, no reason to be bitter about it," Charlie told him, looking hurt. All the rawness he'd finally penetrated down to the day before, covered up again. The usual, bluff veneer of the politician safely back in place.

"I've forgiven *you*, ya know —"

"Slim was right, then."

"What?"

"Never mind. I thank you for your forgiveness. I truly do, Charlie."

Charlie gave a long sigh. "You know, sometimes I wish we could just go back."

"Back to before you started associating with the worst criminals in America?" Tom asked, but he knew Charlie was barely listening to him.

"I mean all the way back. To one of those other lives we talked about. The road not taken —"

"Which road was that, Charlie? It's hard to keep 'em straight anymore."

"—where maybe I was still the best fireman on the Hudson River. With a fat country wife up in Haverstraw, and you come up to see the grandkiddies, and tell me stories of all the goings-on down in the big, dirty, wonderful old City —"

"There's not much call for firemen on the Hudson these days," Tom said politely.

"You know, I'm glad it all fell apart," Charlie told him, his face suddenly off-kilter.

"Which part do you mean?"

"The marriage, bein' the mayor. All of it. Toward the end there, I think it was killin' me. It felt like I wasn't even me anymore — like I was just fading away —"

"It's tough being a movie image," Tom agreed.

"What's that? You're speakin' in riddles today, Tommy," he said, cocking his head a little angrily.

"Never mind," Tom said, suddenly feeling tired beyond all measure. He looked over his brother's shoulder toward the parking lot, hoping to see a car from the hotel—dreading the thought that he might see the cream-colored Bentley.

"Damned if I didn't wish I was travelin' with ya, Tom," Charlie said brightly. "You know, for all the traveling the both of us have done, it's funny we've never gone anywhere together, isn't it?"

"Yes, it is."

"What I wouldn't give to get back for one more look at that big, bawdy old town!" he said, grinning, and for a moment Tom feared he might actually break into one of Henry Fink's soft-shoe numbers. "Y'know, if this deal works out with those Pasquale brothers, they're talkin' about sending me on a 'round-the-world plane trip. Wouldn't that be fun! Sixty days of it, and you know, maybe we could stop off in the City, just to have a look at the place—"

"Don't come back to New York, Charlie," Tom told him directly, his voice even but serious. "Don't ever come back, or at least not for a long, long time. I'm telling you this not as your brother, but as a lawyer."

Charlie flushed deeply, unable to come up with anything to say for once.

"Well, at least it's good to hear you still describe yourself as my brother," he said, and moved in to give Tom a hug, slapping him gently on the back. "That's what I'll always be, Tom, and try to remember it, an' forgive me if you can."

"I'll try, Charlie. I'll try damned hard."

The first boarding call came over the intercom, in Spanish and then in English and French, and started a small pigeon's flurry of activity around the terminal.

"All right, then, Tom," Charlie said, fading away from him, a cockeyed grin still on his face. "I'll go wave goodbye to ya."

"You do that, Charlie. I'll look for you," he said, picking up his briefcase and heading for the plane. He wasn't surprised when he heard his brother call his name again, turning reluctantly to look at him one more time.

"Tom! Tom, you know she was right." He shrugged helplessly, smiling as sadly as he could, in the middle of the terminal. "You know, I finally got ahead of myself!"

Tom tried to smile but couldn't, so he gave half a wave, and boarded the plane with the rest of the passengers. Scanning the parking lot from the top of the steps, spotting no sign of her before he ducked into the cabin. He settled into his window seat, unlocked his briefcase, and tried not to look out at the parking lot again, at the figure he knew was still standing there, and the one he knew was not.

He busied himself going over his notes, rustling through the pads of yellow legal paper. His thoughts shifting here and there, like the hands of a three-card monte dealer, moving his jacks and queens. Straying inevitably back to Ellie, then to his talk with his brother the day before.

Picturing him there in the empty hotel room, waiting for Peter Panto. Watching Bill McCormack finish his steak . . .

He had last seen McCormack a couple of weeks before he left for Mexico, just by accident. Up at Keen's Chophouse, the old actor's watering hole off Herald Square, with all the rows of white clay pipes hung along the ceiling and the famous naked odalisque propped up against a lion, behind the bar. He was just going to use the upstairs men's room, when he heard a collective shout, and a rush of familiar voices coming from the Bull Moose Room, one of the private dining rooms there.

Looking in, he could see there was an old-fashioned beefsteak in progress, beneath the dusty mounted moose heads and the pictures of Teddy Roosevelt in his pith helmet and his San Juan Hill togs. A room full of men devouring buttered slabs of beefsteak and bread with nothing but their fingers, and drinking schooners of beer. They sat facing one another at a table that ran the length of the room, with long white butchers' aprons covering their suits, on which they wiped their blood and grease-laden hands, laughing and braying at one another across the platters of meat.

They were, he saw, many of the same faces from the Joe Ryan dinner in the Commodore ballroom, and his brother's lunch at the Plaza. Taxi Jack O'Donnell in his monsignor's hat. Bob Moses at the far end of the table, grinning contemptuously at everyone else. Francis Cardinal Spellman, the butcher's apron carefully covering his splendid red cardinal's robes, his cherubic face beaming happily.

A large man with a great slab of a face danced merrily up and down the table, distributing tickets to all of the diners. Tom recognized him for O'Malley,

George the Fifth's boy, who had graduated from counting the peanuts to running the Dodgers now.

"One for you, and one for you!" he said gleefully as he passed out the brightly colored ducats for the Garden. "Bill says it'll be a helluva fight tonight. Two Puerto Ricans!"

"Great, they'll *both* have knives!" someone called out, and the room exploded in laughter again, the waiters pushing past him to distribute still more hunks of meat, and beer.

It was a celebration, he realized. The afternoon had brought Bill McCormack's last appearance before the governor's waterfront crime commission. It was at the county courthouse, just down Centre Street from the office, in a hearing room with vivid WPA murals on the walls, featuring the Brooklyn Bridge, and the laying of the subway, and the first Dutch settlers with their blunderbusses, walking out to euchre the Indians. He had gone over near the end, slipping into one of the wooden pews near the back.

McCormack had sat facing the spectators, up at the witness table. He sat very erect, as always, with his chin tilted up and his chest thrust out, though there was a cane with a silver jackal's head hanging ostentatiously from the arm of his chair. A twitchy, well-dressed lawyer sat next to him, but McCormack never consulted him, answering everything calmly on his own, permitting himself only a hard, cryptic smile when he thought a question cut too close to the bone.

"For the last time, will you answer the gentleman? Is it true you're the Mr. Big in the papers, and on the TV news?" the lawyer from the commission said, trying to browbeat him.

McCormack shook his head once, tightly, before the question was out of the man's mouth, brushing his own lawyer back with a hand when he tried to whisper in his ear.

"That's a lot of rubbish," he said evenly. "I have heard myself called 'the Little Man's Port Authority.' With all due modesty, I would be proud to accept that characterization."

"Mr. McCormack, you've been described as one of the richest men in New York," the commission counsel said with a harrumph. "You have a penthouse apartment on Fifth Avenue, a summer estate on Round Island, off Greenwich, Connecticut, and a yacht. Does any of that sound like a 'little man' to you?"

"I have worked for many years on the waterfront, and I have tried to invest my money wisely, I won't deny that. But I've been largely retired from the day-to-day operations of business for almost a year now."

"Mayor O'Kane made you chairman of the Committee on the Future of the Harbor for the express purpose of correcting the port's downward spiral," the commission lawyer said, thrusting a finger at him. "Yet your final report had almost nothing about pilferage, or loan-sharking, or the shape-up. All you called for was 'one or two purposeful, practical men to straighten the whole mess out—'"

"Isn't that always the way of things? *Shouldn't* it be?" McCormack asked benevolently. "Gentlemen, let us not be deluded by those who seek to attack the port's problems merely by seeking wings of purity. We cannot blame them on a few shylocks, or thieves, or two-dollar horse players. All these so-called experts, who think a forklift is an Emily Post device for correct eating! They dream up Captain Kidd lurking in the shadows of our piers, plundering the port and leaving a trail of blood in his frantic getaway."

"Mr. McCormack—"

"You'll have to excuse me, Mr. Chairman!" McCormack shot back, rising now to his full, proud height, and slowly, conspicuously collecting his hat and his jackal-headed cane. "I'm finished for today. I'm a retired businessman, with only a nominal interest in public activities. If you have anything to ask me beyond the morbid fantasies to which you treated me this afternoon, you may contact my lawyer."

He started to turn away, then stopped, lifting his chin defiantly in the direction of the open-mouthed crime commission.

"You may even subpoena me."

He walked down the center of the room, limping and leaning heavily on his cane, and as he passed, the spectators spontaneously began to rise. Just a few of them at first, but then more and more, until they were all of them standing and gawking, and craning their necks to watch the man pass by and disappear through the oaken double doors of the courtroom.

Then Tom was face-to-face with him again, in the restaurant. He turned away from the beefsteak to the bathroom—only to nearly run into McCormack. He was standing in the still-open toilet door, his suit freshly brushed, his face recently splashed with cologne and the smell of a mint on his breath. As tall and imposing and bull-chested as ever—infinitely harder and more lethal than he had shown himself in the courtroom.

"Well, if it isn't the King of the Jews," he said breezily, looking down at Tom.

"Mr. McCormack," Tom said, and nodded. "What's happened to your cane?"

McCormack grinned at him with his teeth alone, his eyes filming over with rage. It was the sort of smile he imagined a barracuda would make.

"You know, sometimes I regret my public reputation," he said softly. "It would be a pleasure to break you in half."

"Don't let that stop you," Tom told him, feeling his breath coming short and swift. "Do your best. Whatever happens, I won't kick."

McCormack gave him another, more wintry smile. *The wolf back on its leash.*

"I won't give Mr. Hogan the excuse," he said. "Now that his old boss the governor's commission has run out of steam."

He started to push past him, but Tom stopped him with a hand on that broad chest. It wasn't a hard push, but he saw the man's eyes flare again, and he wondered for one crazy moment if they really were going to fight.

"I won't keep you from your friends," Tom said quickly. "But there's one thing I really would like to know."

"What's that?" McCormack asked thickly.

"How d'you expect it all to end?"

"End? It all ended today. Your pals lost. Again."

"I mean what do you expect to happen with the waterfront now? They showed your old friend King Joe to the door—how did Kempton put it? 'Like an old hound gone in the teeth'?"

"Joe Ryan is a good friend, and a good man," McCormack said tersely. "After laboring so long in the vineyards, he'll get to enjoy the retirement he deserves."

"But I don't understand the rest of it. How long do you think you can go on like this?" Tom persisted. "The docks are falling apart. You know it as well as I do. The theft's out of hand. Every year, there's more lines going to Baltimore, or Philadelphia, or New Orleans. Down in Washington Market, your truck line's shaving so much off the shops and the restaurants, they go all the way over to Jersey for their produce—"

"That's where you and me see things differently, laddie," McCormack told him, a glint of triumph in his eyes. "You see a vast iniquity perpetrated on the poor restaurant owners. I see a place where my old man was cast aside like a horse to the knacker's yard after a lifetime of hard work—and where his son now makes the rules."

"But how do you expect it to *last?* You know the shipping lines are already experimenting with automation. Put everything in big metal crates, haul it out by crane. They could move the whole port over to Newark or Elizabeth tomorrow, leave you high and dry—"

"And when have you ever known a businessman to resist progress if it saves him so much as a dime?" McCormack said, a knowing smile on his face now. "They'll go if it makes them money, no matter how nice the docks are. But you want that we should go and invest the public's money, fixin' crumbling piers and rotting wharves that'll all be lying empty in a few years anyway."

"But what about the City, then?" Tom said, stunned by his casual cynicism. "This is a port town. Why, it's half the economy—"

"No! Nothing like that. Maybe a tenth." McCormack chuckled. "And less and less every day. You noticed, maybe, those big airplanes in the sky, comin' in to land at the airport your brother was farsighted enough to open? The trucks rollin' across Mr. Moses's bridges? The port's done here—there's no sense cryin' over it."

"And what about *you,* then? That's *your* business!"

"You'd be surprised who owns the land under much of the waterfront now, or maybe you wouldn't," McCormack said, and almost chuckled. "Once the docks are gone, who d'ya think's gonna want to live out on the water? Only the richest people in the world. It's a brand-new day, Tommy. The City's changing, just like it always does."

"But that'll take years—"

McCormack shrugged, and smiled wider. "So? We have to provide for future generations, don't we, now?"

"So this is all about your son?" Tom asked—realizing suddenly something was missing. "Where is he tonight, anyway? I didn't see him in the Bull Moose Room. He wasn't down at the courthouse —"

A cloud passed suddenly across McCormack's visage, the smile fading quick as a sucker punch. There was another roar from the beefsteak, and Tom was suddenly very conscious of the urine stink wafting out of the men's room. But he kept his eyes riveted on the face of Mr. Big.

"He's no longer working for me," McCormack said, his voice sounding like an old man's for the first time since Tom had known him. "You'll hear about it soon enough. He . . . he's had a late vocation —"

"The *priesthood?*"

McCormack could only nod.

"He threw it all back in your face. *Didn't* he?" Tom wondered aloud. "All that dirty money —"

"We brought him up to be a true son of the church, his mother and I," McCormack said feebly. "Any Catholic parent would be proud —"

"But *you're* not. You did it all for him. You built the great empire of McCormack, and you broke anyone who got in the way. The competition. The unions. King Joe Ryan, *my brother.* Peter Panto, all the men who made you so much money. You broke them any way you could, anyone who got in your path, even for a moment, and you told yourself you did it all for the many future McCormacks. And now your only son's gone and walked away from it all."

"You should go about your business," McCormack told him in a voice like chipping flint. "You should shut your mouth and go about whatever you were doin'."

"But it's you who's going," Tom told him, wanting to laugh. "Maybe the waterfront will become the next Fifth Avenue, and maybe it won't, but either way it won't be the great kingdom of McCormack. In a few years, you'll be gone, and your own son will sing your Mass at Saint Patrick's. But the one thing he won't give you is another little McCormack."

"Get out!" McCormack growled, and pushed roughly past him, back to the room full of his drunken, howling companions. He hesitated for a moment in the doorway, Tom saw, and all the red-faced, blood-smeared men inside raised their schooners of beer to him, before an exiting waiter closed the door and left them to one another.

* * *

415

"You were right."

There was her voice, just above him, and then she was sliding into the seat beside him. Dressed in a neat gray traveling suit with hat this time, a perfect copy of the blue suit she had worn the day before, and one that made his heart ache.

"Ellie—"

"There isn't a case here," she said, fastening her seat belt and flinging the report he'd typed the night before into his lap. "I didn't want to believe it, but you're right. We'd never get a conviction, not for Charlie and not for Mr. Big. Everybody's already lied so much, there's no making the truth stand up."

"I'm glad you came. I hope—" he started to say, but then the takeoff announcements came over the loudspeakers in Spanish, and English, and French, and there was so much noise from the propellers that no one could hear a thing. So instead he simply looked at her.

"Let me ask you one thing," she said, when they began to taxi into position for takeoff and they could talk again. "That's what the confession was about. Wasn't it?"

"I'm not followin' you," he said.

"Yes you are. You went and confessed to your brother about you—and Slim," she said, grimacing. "You told him because you knew it would bring him down, didn't you? You knew once you did that, he'd want to hurt you right back. Even if the only way he could do that was tearing down the image that *you* had of him, once and for all. Even if it meant destroying himself."

He shook his head, grinning ruefully. "That's too much psychology for me. I can't say I ever thought it out like that."

"Not consciously, maybe. But you did."

"I was just trying to do what I thought was right, and get to the truth of the matter."

"Like taking up with Madame Matador again?" She raised an eyebrow at him. "I'd almost believe you did that on purpose, too. Just so you'd have the excuse to confess."

"It's not that intricate," he told her, grimacing. "I just lost myself for a time. I'm a fool, Ellie."

"So you say. With a mind like that, you might have a career in politics after all."

"I don't want one. At least not now. I just want to go on working for an honest man. And I want to spend a lifetime making this up to you."

"A lifetime?" She tisked, her voice weary. "I don't know about any of that just yet. I don't know if I want to go on prosecuting people, and I don't know if I can stand to sit around the house all day with a bunch of kiddies."

She looked at him frankly, her eyes grave and searching, as their plane moved into position and began to pick up speed, racing toward the end of the runway.

"I think we should take it all day by day for now," she said, tears welling in her eyes. "You hurt me, Tom. You really hurt me."

"I know I did," he said, but when he took her hand in his she did not pull it away. He gave her fingers a gentle squeeze. "I know I did, and I'm more sorry about it than anything I ever did in my life. I'm serious. Whatever you want, I'm for you."

She looked back at him and smiled a little, sniffed back a tear, squeezing his hand in return.

"We'll see," she said. "We'll just see."

The plane reached the end of its alarmingly short runway and thrust upward, rising off the ground in a slow, tight circle before shooting for the space between the white volcano peaks, the Raging Man and the Sleeping Woman.

Still holding her hand, Tom looked down through the window for the figure he knew would be there. He spotted him easily enough: his brother, standing with his legs thrust apart, over by the parking lot, waving his hat at the plane in a grand, sweeping, politician's gesture. As they rose, he grew smaller and smaller beneath them.

NOTES ON SOURCES
AND ACKNOWLEDGMENTS

This is a work of fiction. Real historical characters appear in it, including Peter Panto, Frank Hogan, Fathers Philip A. Carey and John M. "Pete" Corridan, Burton Turkus, Toots Shor, Henry Fink, William McCormack, Robert Moses, Cardinal Francis Spellman, Generoso Pope, Frank Costello, "Sam the Subway Man" Rosoff, "King" Joe Ryan, Monsignor "Taxi Jack" O'Donnell, Frank Hague, Cockeye Dunn, the occupants of the Rats Suite, the remaining members of Murder, Inc., and assorted other hoodlums and racketeers, both in and out of high office.

There are other characters who will no doubt bear a resemblance to real individuals. They are, however, fictional. In order not to cast aspersions on the innocent, I have invented names and backgrounds, and even altered slightly the dates of some actual events.

My goal was to depict New York City in all the gaudy glory of its postwar heyday, and to sift to the bottom of what remain to this day some of its worst and most mysterious public scandals. These have been largely forgotten, but once they held both the nation and the world's greatest city spellbound. They provided the gist of a Pulitzer Prize–winning series of newspaper articles, investigations that would make the careers of some of the most renowned prosecutors of our time, and America's first major, televised congressional investigations, the Kefauver hearings.

Did I get to the heart of one of the greatest locked-door mysteries of all time? I can only compare my conclusions to the conjectures of Burton Turkus, "Mr. Poison," the assistant district attorney who sent the killers of Murder, Inc., up the river.

In his book *Murder, Inc.,* written in 1951 with Sid Feder, Turkus speculated about the presence in the Rats Suite of a "guard who did not sleep [and] opened the door for an outsider that morning—a stranger never mentioned, either then or in all the recurring revivals of the Reles scandal in the past ten years. Such an outsider would have had to be someone with considerable authority—authority enough to gain admittance and to keep his presence quiet afterward. If one of the witnesses, say, had awakened and spied him, he would have needed such authority that he could have sealed the witnesses' lips by a threat of a prison term, perhaps, or a murder prosecution, or death. And finally, his authority would have had to be such that Reles would have accepted his entry into the bedroom."

As such, one part or another of this story has been told before, in iconic dramas such as *A View from the Bridge, On the Waterfront, The Godfather: Part II,* and countless other books, movies, and plays.

Fortunately for me, there has been a wealth of outstanding nonfiction and investigative journalism regarding the period my book covers. When it comes to depicting the people and events that defined the murky, lethal world of New York's vanished waterfront—and especially the tragic murder of Peter Panto—I am endlessly indebted to my old (well, not *so* old) friend Nathan Ward and his wonderful book *Dark Harbor: The War for the New York Waterfront.* For a Red Sox fan, he sure knows his Brooklyn.

James T. Fisher's brilliant history *On the Irish Waterfront: The Crusader, the Movie, and the Soul of the Port of New York* was indispensable in steering me through not only the harbor, but the theological disputations of the Catholic Church at what was the height of the "Catholic moment" in both New York and the United States. So too was John Cooney's outstanding biography *The American Pope: The Life and Times of Francis Cardinal Spellman,* which included some terrific anecdotes.

The definitive work on Abe Reles and the incarceration of the other squealers in the Rats Suite is the late Edmund Elmaleh's *The Canary Sang but Couldn't Fly.* Eddie had researched Murder, Inc., for almost a decade, and died, suddenly and inexplicably, almost on the eve of the book's publication—an especially cruel fate for a first-time author. He leaves behind an invaluable and riveting study, and his literary legacy has been well protected by the very generous Kathi Kapell. Eddie and I spoke a couple of times when we were working on our respective books. I don't believe I told him anything he didn't already know, but he was a tremendous help to me.

Very useful as well was Turkus and Feder's inside story of fighting the mob, *Murder, Inc.: The Story of the Syndicate,* and Leonard Katz's *Uncle Frank: The Biography of Frank Costello.* And as always, the bible on gangland, Virgil W. Peterson's *The Mob: 200 Years of Organized Crime in New York* came in very handy.

Yet no source on the whole career of Murder, Inc., particularly in the context of Brownsville and the Jewish-American experience, proved more helpful than my friend Rich Cohen's vivid, bold, and uncompromising *Tough Jews.* Rich knows where all the bodies are buried, figuratively and literally.

When it came to crime and its intersection with the governance of New York, I relied on George Walsh's superb account, *Public Enemies: The Mayor, the Mob, and the Crime That Was.* Very helpful too, in tracing the rise of New York's first postwar mayor from penniless immigrant to Gracie Mansion, was William O'Dwyer's unfinished memoir, *Beyond the Golden Door,* closely edited and supplemented by his brother, the last fighting liberal, Paul O'Dwyer. And my friend Peter Quinn's *Looking for Jimmy: A Search for Irish America* was also a great aid, right down to its Woolworth Building cover.

Barry Cunningham's *Mr. District Attorney* is a fine biography of the legendary Manhattan DA Frank Hogan. And the greatest American book ever written about urban politics, Robert Caro's *The Power Broker: Robert Moses and the Fall of New York,* proved as valuable as ever, particularly when it came to describing the wanton destruction of the old Bronx. Jan Morris's *New York '45,* meanwhile, is as scintillating and effervescent as the time and the place it describes, a small but hugely pleasurable treasure.

To lead me through the vanished Mexico City of over sixty years ago — then a bustling, colorful capital of fewer than three million souls, just at the beginning of the runaway growth that would transform it — I turned first to Carlos Fuentes's seminal novel *Up Where the Air Is Clear.*

Pete Hamill's classic memoir *A Drinking Life* provided not only an invaluable take on Mexico City through the eyes of a transplanted American, but also served as a terrific guide to Mexico in general and particularly Acapulco — also transformed now beyond recognition. Quite helpful too were the collections *The Mexico City Reader*, edited by Ruben Gallo, and *Mexico City Through History and Culture*, edited by Linda A. Newson and John I. King.

Just as useful to me as all these outstanding books were the many newspapers and magazines that New Yorkers once took for granted. I begin, of course, with Malcolm "Mike" Johnson's series of waterfront exposés in what was the glorious penumbra of the *New York Sun*. There has really been nothing else like it in the history of American journalism: fifty front-page pieces over the course of two years. The series won Johnson a well-deserved Pulitzer — though it was not enough to prevent the setting of the *Sun*, the closing of which marked the beginning of the end of the golden age of New York newspapers.

I owe much of my descriptions of Mayor William O'Dwyer's Mexican exile to Lester Velie's shrewd and meticulously reported articles in the August 7 and August 21, 1953, editions of *Collier's* magazine. Just as well executed and even more daring were Velie's pieces for *Collier's* on Bill McCormack and the battle for the waterfront: "Big Boss of the Big Port," February 9, 1952, and "A Waterfront Priest Battles the Big Port's Big Boss," February 16, 1952.

Time magazine's cover story on O'Dwyer — "New York's Mayor O'Dwyer: A Hell of a Town" — ran in its June 7, 1948, issue; while *Life*'s cover story on the second Mrs. O'Dwyer, Sloane Simpson — "New York's First Lady Entertains U.S. Mayors" — appeared on May 29, 1950. Both were valuable, although much more so was Mimi Swartz's poignant study "Sloane, Alone," in the June 1997 edition of *Texas Monthly*.

For my depiction of both El Ranchito and Henry Fink's Shangri-La in Cuernavaca, I am indebted to Philip Hamburger's superbly rendered "That Great Big New York Up There," a "Reporter at Large" piece that appeared in the September 28, 1957, issue of *The New Yorker*. I am sorry to report that the subject of Mr. Fink also provided an object lesson in the fleeting nature of the new journalism. I had the good fortune to run across the Internet memoir of an American expatriate, a young married woman with children and some sort of show business background, who went to live in Cuernavaca in the 1950s and wrote very well of both the city and Fink, whom she knew and liked. I was able to use some of her descriptions, but when I went back to properly credit her, I found her site had been taken down from the web, and it has since disappeared entirely. She has my apologies for not being able to offer her the kudos she deserves.

In general the Internet proved to be as simultaneously helpful and exasperating as it always does. Other media also were of use. My description of Toots Shor's came in good part from watching Kristi Jacobson's terrific documentary about her grandfather's remarkable watering hole. Nothing else was really necessary.

In writing this book, I have been blessed, as always, with having so many wonderful friends, relations, and colleagues to rely on.

Professionally, I must thank as always my friend and agent, Henry Dunow, and all of the wonderful, friendly, and efficient people at Dunow, Carlson, and Lerner, especially the ever-patient, efficient, and helpful Yishai Seidman.

Henry did me yet another great service by finding a home for this book at Houghton Mifflin Harcourt. This is my first outing with Houghton, and they have proven to be an excellent choice in every possible way. My publisher, Andrea Schulz, was immensely patient, helpful, and friendly. My editor, Nicole Angeloro, improved *The Big Crowd* immeasurably, with her insights and gentle but firm insistence on keeping what is a very complex story as clear and as concise as possible. Margaret Wimberger, with her meticulous copyediting, fact checking, and cheerful encouragement also made an invaluable contribution to the finished manuscript. I found all three of these individuals to be good company as well as consummate professionals. Any mistakes or problems that remain after their work was done are strictly my own fault.

I would also like to extend my thanks to two people who first believed in this book and brought it to Houghton Mifflin Harcourt. They are Eamon Dolan and Jane Rosenman, who was to be my editor but was never able to serve as such. I regret not having had the chance to work with her, but it is at least a consolation to run into her regularly on the streets of the Upper West Side.

The contributions made by friends and family are too many to mention here, I'm embarrassed and very grateful to say. I have acknowledged some of them in the dedication: my sister Pam Baker and her husband, Mark Kapsch, who have been so good about putting me up on my New England sojourns and so supportive in many other ways. My wife, Ellen Abrams, has been a wonderful helpmate as always, not only in promoting this book, providing me with a tutorial in women's fashions from the postwar world, and tracking down any number of 1950s tourist pamphlets on the Prince Hotel and Mexico City, but also in always believing in this story and encouraging me to write it.

Finally, I would like to thank three people who were very much friends in need: Nancy Sheppard and (two of) my (other) amazing brother(s)- and sister(s)-in-law, Matt Brinckerhoff and Sharon Abrams. You were lifesavers.